DEVIL'S GOLD

A Novel

DEVIL'S GOLD

A Novel

Barry Raut

MILL CITY PRESS | *Minneapolis*

Mill City Press, Inc.
212 3rd Avenue North, Suite 290
Minneapolis, MN 55401
612.455.2294
www.millcitypublishing.com

ISBN - 978-1-936400-13-3
ISBN - 1-936400-13-8
LCCN - 2010931302

Cover image: From "Hermann Goering admiring Hans Makart's painting, 'The Falconer' given to him by Adolph Hitler for his birthday." Library of Congress.

Cover Design by Dan Bittman, Design Team One
Typeset by Kristeen Wegner

Printed in the United States of America

For Shirley

CHAPTER ONE

Pieter Maxfield, chief conservator of the Mendelssohn Museum of Art, lingered in the Dutch gallery. His eyes scanned
each of its sensuous seventeenth-century paintings like a circling
hawk in search of a breakfast morsel. His reward would be a
trace of discoloration, a fresh hairline crack, evidence of worms
in a frame, even the slightest plea for his considerable restorative
powers.

His attention this day was both professional and personal. Pieter roamed the galleries devoutly, hovering over his charges
like a mother hen. His mission was to make sure they all stayed
healthy and that their every need, no matter how small, was attended to. But this gallery was special to him. He loved the Flemish Baroque and its theatrical flair, its stark contrasts of light and
shadow, the flicker of candlelight on golden skin, the deep void
behind brooding figures.

As the *maestro di maestri,* Caravaggio set Pieter spinning.
The painter's monumental *Adunanza di la Santi,* Gathering of the
Saints, dominated the adjoining Italian Baroque gallery. He was
the one who inspired the others with his heaven-sent canvases so
contrary to his unholy carryings-on. Peter Paul Rubens, the Flemish master, had much the same impact on the conservator, as did
the gifted portrait painters Frans Hals and Anthony van Dyck.
And there was Velásquez, two rooms down. The Spaniard's figures, he was sure, would yield a heartbeat under a stethoscope.
Although a proper parent can show no favorites, Pieter would
readily admit that these were his.

His attachment to Flemish painting was also swayed by

his own given name, Pieter, spelled the Dutch way, after Pieter Brueghel the Elder, maybe the greatest Netherlandish painter of the sixteenth century. Stuart Maxfield, Pieter's grandfather, himself a prominent New England landscape artist, had offered the name, thinking that it might someday inspire the child to seek a career in art. The grandson showed talent with the brush, yet his patience and obsession with detail, plus his high tolerance for solitude, led him to the life of a conservator.

Pieter stood an imposing six-five. He had a power-lifter's strength in his muscular frame, an attribute well concealed by the result of his fondness for good restaurants, and of his own culinary flair; remnants of four years in the University of Maine weight room were showcased daily as he hoisted, without effort, heavy stone sculptures and massive frames on and off the worktables and easels in his beloved lab.

On this visit to his favorite gallery Pieter indulged himself. He stood for a long time before a painting by the Dutch artist, Judith Leyster. The picture was simply titled *Dutch Mother and Child, c. 1634.* The woman was dressed in brownish black, one of the thousand or more blacks in the palette of a true master. Her gown bled off into deep space, and she wore the close-fitting Dutch lace cap and white ruff collar of the period.

The child appeared to be wriggling on her mother's lap, the "aren't we done yet" expression on her face captured brilliantly by the artist. She wore a dress of brocade rendered with meticulous detail in copper and gold and brown. Her sturdy Dutch shoulders were draped with a wide band of fairy lace so real to the eye that it appeared to have been laid directly on the picture plane. Yellow curls dangled impishly from her tiny, matching lace cap.

What struck the chief conservator were the faces. And the

spectacular hands. The faces of the two sitters beamed with life. Their cerulean eyes locked on his, insisting that he return their gaze. Posed smiles seemed about to break into laughter. Flushed cheeks warmed the entire painting, and the softness of the hands created a tactile sensation that could only have been rendered by genius.

As he stared at the figures, a bizarre tingle surged through Pieter Maxfield, and the hairs on his neck lifted. A feeling he could not explain rattled the man who could not be rattled. He rushed back to his lab bewildered.

He went straight to the phone.

"Angela Desjardin," she growled softly. Her voice was like rare brandy, ever so lightly infused with Italian and a dash of French.

"Angela? This is Pieter. I . . ."

"Pieter, I'm in a meeting."

"I don't care if you are. You've got to duck out of it and meet me in the Dutch gallery. A strange thing just happened to me up there, and we've got to talk," he blurted into the phone.

"Strange thing, you say?" she half-whispered through her teeth. "I've got a lot of strange things happening to me. I've got six strange people in here with six strange opinions, none of which happens to coincide with mine. I'm up to my hoo-hah with the Matisse, I have no idea where my trailers are, and we're going to be here every night through Sunday, guaranteed, if they even come at all," Angela Desjardin snapped from her end. "Can't this strange thing of yours keep till later?"

The Mendelssohn's young curator of European painting was beginning her second year on the job. She had been swamped by a spate of important temporary exhibitions from day one, most of which had been negotiated by her predecessor, Nicholas

Castle—poor, brilliant, rock-headed Nick Castle, who had been unceremoniously dumped following a fatal encounter with the director, one he should have known was unwinnable. The last of these traveling sideshows was the enormous Henri Matisse retrospective. The Fauve master's stunning collection of paintings, collages and sculptures was in transit from Charleston in four semis and, by an ironic twist, delayed five disastrous days by Hurricane Pablo. Leave it to the irascible Picasso to rain on the parade of his nemesis from beyond the grave, an irony not lost on Angela's nimble mind.

Angela was saddled also by a key piece of a major museum expansion program that was way off schedule, mostly her fault, according to the director. For reasons unknown, he had given her the thorny task of reconciling the adamant demands of the remaining curatorial staff for permanent space in the new plan. The odds were heavily stacked against her—the way she liked it, as they rendered the battle infinitely more interesting.

"No, it won't keep till later." His tone softened. "C'mon, Angie . . ."

"Don't call me that. Don't call me *Angie!* You know how I hate that."

He continued, unmoved. "Give yourself a break, *Angela.*" He stressed the name. "You need one, sounds like—and maybe your hostages could use one from you, aye?" Pieter said, *"aye"* a tell-tale vestige of his Maine breeding a stone's throw from the Canadian border. "Fifteen minutes, I promise," Pieter pleaded.

Silence.

And then, "Oh, why not—I need to come up for air anyway," Angela said impulsively. "Before I do or say something I may regret later. I'll be there in ten. But you owe me."

"Okay, I owe you. In ten," Pieter said. He slapped the

receiver down before she could change her mind, rose from his work table and hurried toward the door.

Pieter Maxfield's sanctum sanctorum was an enormous white room smelling of solvents, varnishes and pigments. It was strewn with the exotic tools of the museum necromancer's craft, the means to resurrect lifeless works and summon their long-stifled spirits. Easels holding canvases in various states of healing stood like obedient retainers on the paint-and-chemical-spattered floor. Large, flexible hoses hung like giant pythons over each workstation to inhale and expel airborne contaminants, fumes and the other unpleasant residue of restoration. The entire work area was lighted by rows of suspended fluorescent fixtures and the fading afternoon sun which streamed through the skylights and the large windows overlooking the loading dock.

Pieter stepped from his workroom through a hidden opening into the remains of a soaring Nabataean temple. Significant pieces of the massive sandstone edifice unearthed by a renowned local archaeologist in the '30s had been rejoined within the museum's long, three-story glass atrium extending from the great rotunda to the main entrance of the building. The archeologist, Dr. Stanley Peterson, gave his spoils, pillar, portal and pediment, to the Mendelssohn long before cultural property laws would have kept such treasures at home. Home, in this case, would have been Jordan. The temple ruins had since formed the core of the building's main floor nave and created permanent exhibit space for loosely-related artifacts from the ancient world. Pieter snaked through the urns, idols and mummy cases to the rotunda and took the broad, marble steps two at a time to the second-floor galleries.

Pieter Maxfield and Angela Desjardin were exact opposites on the color wheel: he was the primary blue whose passions ran fathoms beneath his surface calm, and his sturdy roots sunk deep in the unforgiving coast of Maine anchored an unflagging sense of right and wrong; she was the complementary orange, fiery and unpredictable, a taker of risks whose intensity lit up a room. She drove her colleagues to distraction with her gunslinger style, but she was also warm and funny and brainy and profane—blessed with a gift for totally disarming even her harshest critics, when it suited her.

Angela was late as usual. Pieter twiddled before the Leyster, his celebrated patience once again stressed by the woman who could at once infuriate and delight him. He had turned to leave when she whipped through the tiny oval still life gallery connecting the Spanish rooms and the long, richly-paneled Dutch gallery, hair askew, nearly thumping into him as she rounded the corner. Angela had her mother's hair, long and black and shiny, which was forever in disarray from her nervous habit of running her fingers through it endlessly and twisting a few strands in moments of anxiety or total focus. Today it showed the signs of another meeting run amok.

"Sorry. I couldn't end it. So what is it, aye?" she said, mimicking Pieter's quirky patois. Angela missed nothing.

"I thought you weren't coming," he said, annoyed.

"Well, here I am," she said as she took a deep breath and forced herself to downshift.

"Like I said, what's this about?" she repeated.

"What it's about is this," Pieter said, nodding toward *Dutch Mother and Child, c. 1634.*

"This? The Leyster? Is this why you dragged me up here?" She glanced at the sumptuous work. "What about it?"

"What do you know about it?"

"Why do you care?" Angela enjoyed the little game they

had played since the day they met, she tormenting him with faux brusqueness or good-natured needling, Pieter countering with a well-chosen zinger or ignoring the bait altogether, the retort that riled her the most. It was a game that only reinforced their fondness for each other and their mutual trust and respect.

"Stop playing me, Angela. I hate it when you do that. There's something not right about this picture. You know what it is. And it has to be big and ugly, too, or I wouldn't have freaked like I did. Give it up, Angela."

"What? The great sphinx freaked? Over this? I thought you knew."

"Knew? Knew what? Would the World's Foremost Authority enlighten me, please?"

"You really don't know?" she said, studying his guileless face. "No, I guess you don't."

After a sticky pause, she warned, "Let it ride, Pieter. Please, just let it ride. Who knows what a bag of snakes you could be opening here."

"And just what snakes might those be?" Pieter fired back.

She knew that it was useless to duck the question; he'd never let up until she spilled what she knew, so she continued.

"Okay, here's what I know, and this is all I know. Registration's a blank. They have nothing. Most pieces loaned to the Mendelssohn have no file, sad to say, except for the paperwork on the loan itself and the staff sigs for hanging it up here," she said. "We have zip on this one. No provenance, no record that Leyster ever painted a mother and child, not a word, which is very unusual.

"The best clue is what you don't see. There's no signature, aye?" she said, pointing to the lower right corner.

"So what? Lots of painters don't sign their work, at least

some of the time."

"True. It's just that Leyster used a monogram," Angela said. "Always she used a monogram. There's no mistaking it—a '*JL*' with a little star, for 'lode star,' which is what her name means. Do you see it anywhere?"

"No, but . . ."

"Pieter, if you paint this well, and if you're knocking heads with the likes of Rembrandt and Hals who work right down the street, you'd want people to know whose picture it is, wouldn't you? You'd sign it, believe me. Every Leyster I've ever seen is signed.

"But for whoever wants us to think this piece is a Leyster, it would be smarter just not to mess with a mark and hope that it slips under the radar, rather than try to fudge it. I mean, how long would it take you to spot a signature laid down 300 years after the piece had been painted? Maybe thirty seconds, on a bad day?"

"You know a lot about Leyster," he said, moving on.

"I did a paper on her at Cambridge," she said. "Back during my libber days when no one paid attention to women artists.Yet one cannot have studied Frans Hals and not know Judith Leyster, can one?" Angela gibed, gently mocking Pieter's art history training which she knew was not all that shabby.

Pieter let it drop. "So, what do you think about it then? You're the expert."

"That's easy. I think it's a sensational painting–one of the best pieces in the museum, no question. It's no secret that Judith Leyster was a gifted painter," Angela declared. "She even *worked* for Hals in his studio at one time. It's no surprise that some of her portraits were once thought to be his, like her *Lute Player* in Amsterdam, which I'm sure you've seen?"

"I have," Peter said stuffily, recalling the picture at the

Rijksmuseum.

"Look, I've seen Leysters all over the world, and believe me, although she had some very good days, she was no Frans Hals," Angela pronounced.

She took a deep breath and exhaled slowly, mentally ticking off what had made the great Dutch master one of the three or four most remarkable portraitists ever. Then she looked deep into the painting, more for pleasure than reinforcement, and said in a dismissive tone, "If I may be so bold, this is no Judith Leyster. Case closed."

Pieter looked stunned. "Case closed? How can you say 'case closed?'" he said. "Did you just come up with that?" he asked incredulously, reading her intense concentration as having evoked some kind of divine revelation.

"Not exactly. I've thought about it."

"You've thought about it? So why haven't you said something? Why case closed?"

"Figure it out. First of all, I can barely deal with what I've got on my plate right now. Number two, this is a loaned piece, and I have no curatorial responsibility for it. Finally, can't you just imagine me popping into the man's office and saying, 'This is no Leyster, Herr Wolff, this is a Hals'? Think about it, *mein leibchen*," she said in a perfect Munich accent, mimicking the director's Teutonic inflections. "Look, I'll leave this place someday, but I'd like to do it on my own terms, thank you very much."

"So you think it's a Hals, then?"

She ignored his question. "Oh, and one other small detail. I assume you've read the label. 'Loaned by Dr. Erich Wolff, 1986.' He put it here himself a long time ago," she said, referring to the Mendelssohn's seventy-something director-dictator. "It's his *piece*, for God's sake. Do you want to run to the Wolfster with, 'Why would you, omniscient leader, loan and exhibit to the public this incredibly beautiful painting which some fool had so woefully misattributed—misattributed downward, no less!" Her voice rose, and her speech shifted back into high gear as she considered the implications. "I have problems aplenty. One more I don't need. And you, Pieter, obviously don't have nearly enough of them," she said with finality.

"A Franz Hals?" he repeated.

Angela knew that Pieter was unmoved by her histrionics, and that he was not about to turn her loose until she gave him the straight skinny. She'd been there many times before, and he'd always won, just through that annoying way of his that she simply could not abide. So almost in relief, she said softly, "Okay. Look at those eyes. Look at the skin and those hands. This painting's so alive, it scares me." She paused and then concluded, "Nobody paints like this but Franz Hals. Trust me."

They stood without speaking. Pieter finally broke the hush of the empty gallery. "I do trust you, Angela. But you know we can't just walk away from this."

"Yes, we can."

"No, we can't."

The curator flashed him a weak smile of resignation. "Well, if you won't let it go, then you'll need to deal with the rest of them, too," Angela said as she raked her long, tan fingers once again through her midnight hair.

Pieter flinched. "The rest of them?"

"You heard me. There are three more you could touch almost from where you're standing that would freak you out all over again. And they're all from Dr. Wolff's secret garden of mysterious masterpieces. I can't believe even *you* haven't stumbled over them by now."

She glanced at her watch. "Well, that's your fifteen minutes. Gotta go." She gave him a quick peck on the cheek, a token apology for being Angela, a chronic condition for which she rarely atoned, and blew out of the gallery leaving Pieter in her back-draft.

He stood motionless long after she had gone, his gaze fixed on *Dutch Mother and Child, c. 1634*. As his eyes withdrew at last from the painting, a second pair of eyes followed him from the room. They had watched and recorded it all, unnoticed, unblinking from the half-light of the adjacent Italian gallery.

CHAPTER TWO

Angela hurried back through the empty second floor galleries, half-fearing that, even in her brief absence, her office would already have been reduced to rubble by the contentious pack of curators left to their own devices. Most days she would inhale the treasures which lined her path, if only for a moment, and they would remind her of why she had chosen this work. This day she glared straight ahead, hugely frosted at Pieter Maxfield.

Angela had had a bad feeling about that gallery. She figured months ago that any nosing about would come to no good. *Just walk on by,* she told herself, and she had. Now comes Pieter, tripping over those pictures in his typical fashion, and they're back in her life. Merda!

She paused at the top of the twisting staircase and looked down into the Greco-style rotunda. A tiny burst of enlightenment erupted in her consciousness. These little flares no longer surprised her; she had come to expect them and rely on them for guidance when she was confused or ambivalent. She knew that she'd have to deal with the paintings—lay them to rest before she would get any rest of her own—and that it would get very nasty. This she felt deep in her Sicilian bones, like a rising storm stiffens the marrow and seizes the joints.

While Angela pondered the grief ahead, she drew strength from the smooth marble balustrade as she ran her fingers along the railing, and images of Don Carlo Vittoria's sprawling villa elbowed their way into her mindspace. They came refreshingly unannounced, as if to save her from this totally crappy day. It wasn't the first time in recent months that her *dolce nonno,* her sweet grandfather, had commandeered her thoughts. It was the grand rotunda which had conjured up the majestic Grecian ruins silhouetted against the sunset; how often she had contemplated these sacred stones from his veranda high above the island's southern coast until cool twilight settled on her.

The experience was spellbinding. A warm, sure hand seemed to lead her away from the ominous paintings in the Dutch gallery into dolce nonno's shimmering olive groves on the seaward slope, among the rows of her grandfather's treasured yellow roses which he manicured lovingly on sleepy Sicilian afternoons, and then to the mainhouse and the rich canvases which graced its gardenia-hued, rough stucco inner walls. It was these paintings, which Angela later recognized as the progeny of the iconic European masters, which had stirred her passion for great art and brought her, ultimately, to this place. Unconsciously, she touched her hand to her breast where years ago, in one of her typical Angela moments, she had had tattooed a delicate yellow rose as her own personal genuflection to this dear, sweet man.

Angela Desjardin was destined for no ordinary life. Her mother, Maria Vittoria Desjardin, was Sicilian through and through, reared in the protective custody of Don Carlo Vittoria. The bastard child of a peasant girl barely in her teens and a father beaten to a lifeless pulp by the girl's offended siblings, Don Carlo was adopted by his village, nestled in the hills beneath the not-much-larger town of Vittoria.

Taking the name of the town, Don Carlo Vittoria became prosperous and powerful. He controlled from his tiny village most of the wine, olive oil and citrus traffic from the eastern port of Catania to the ancient Greek sanctuary of Agrigento, and he was much loved in this place of his untidy birth.

He was hated as well, as most powerful people are, which

accounted for his small army of protective family retainers and several close *guardie* who hovered over Maria, and later, *Angelina*, little Angela, like hulking bears over their cubs.

Maria's protectors did little to contain her spirit as she scurried over the surrounding ruins. She led them on sweaty chases that challenged their stamina and their eyesight; her chameleon-like talent for hiding among sandstone columns and fallen drum sections and entablatures, plus the blinding white sun, made her outings unnerving for them. Returning her to Don Carlo without incident, when she grew tired of tormenting them, was a relief. Maria was proud of the nickname they gave her, *La Lucertola*, the lizard, and she exploited it at every chance. These halcyon days among the ghosts of the ancients led her to the only life she could possibly imagine.

Don Carlo reluctantly released her to Cambridge to study the stones. Here Maria met Guy-Alain Desjardin, only son of the famous French archeologist team, Jacques and Camille Desjardin. The free-spirited chameleon, dark from the Mediterranean sun, and Guy-Alain, the fair-skinned, blue-eyed romantic from Paris, took their degrees and pledged their love beneath the spires of the great university beside the rippling River Cam.

A full Sicilian wedding followed, commencing in Vittoria's eighteenth-century Church of Santa Maria delle Grazie on the Piazza del Popolo, Cardinal Carboni officiating, and culminating with a spectacular reception at the villa, attended by more than a thousand guests. The festivities lasted three days, and it became legend in the village, forever to be known as *Il Matrimonio di La Lucertole*.

Angela's birth was greeted with a second epic celebration. The infant's triumphal entry from Paris was met with a dizzying round of parties and a stream of townspeople bearing gifts.

From that moment she was sanctified by the villagers. Angelina was adopted by them, as had been Maria and her precious dolce nonno before her. Her now-and-then visits brought them happiness, and they would shower her with treats.

As she continued down the marble staircase and her thoughts returned to the troublesome Dutch gallery, Angela heard Don Carlo's gruff, gravelly voice: *When you decide to do something, Angelina, do it. Don't piss around.*

As expected, she found the weekly meeting of the curatorial expansion team in shambles. Agreement among the Mendelssohn's stewards of the collection on even the least significant issues was not going to happen on this day.

"Let's end it for now, shall we?" Angela said, barely masking her irritation. "Give it a rest for a couple of days and we'll try again, say Thursday, same time?" The others nodded in unison, the afternoon's first and only sign of consensus. They rose as one and left without speaking. The gulf between them seemed insurmountable given the monstrous egos involved, and the museum director knew this. Wolff was only yanking her chain, getting them all worked up so he could swoop in at the last minute, chew their contentious patoots and do whatever he was planning to do all along.

Angela sighed, tipped back in her rickety swivel chair and focused on the irregular brown water splotch on the ceiling attributed to "the great frog strangler of '95," as the locals referred to an epic rainstorm some years back. Lack of budget and a barebones maintenance staff had bequeathed in perpetuity this Frankenthaler stain to her and those to follow. *Miro. Arp. No, Matisse— definitely Matisse,* she speculated as the amorphous shape above her head conjured up comparisons undeserved.

Damn! Matisse! she suddenly remembered.

"Jerry, where are my trucks!" Angela shrieked.

Angela's intern was used to her outbursts. They amused him, and he took no offense. He answered her quietly and calmly from his worktable just outside her office door, "They're somewhere in the mountains of West Virginia, due in here by noon tomorrow if the creek don't rise, literally. I just hung up with Mid-States. Best they could do, they said."

"Check again one more time before you leave, will you please. And buzz the guys downstairs. We've got tons of prep before the semis roll in. They know what to do, just tell them to get off their sweet arses and do it, okay?"

"Your wish is my command," Jerry answered. "But if you don't mind my saying so, Angela, your language is getting more colorful by the day. It's not becoming."

"And you're *becoming* a giant pain in the *behind*. How's that?" she fired back. Her sharp volley aside, Angela liked Jerry Mason, and he adored her. Simply said, he got the job done. The more work she dumped on him, the more he ate it up. And, for a man-child who had barely begun to shave, he was as crafty as a cardinal in the fine art of palace intrigue, a dubious gift that would serve him well as a career museum pro. *Some have it, some don't,* Angela thought. Jerry was her secret weapon.

He shook his head in mock disapproval. "Okay, but you've gotta work on it, Angela. It won't enhance your career."

It was long past seven, and Angela was starved. The café was closed, and she would have to raid her Snicker's stash for sustenance—if Jerry hadn't cleaned her out on one of his stealthy midnight requisitions. She still had a night's work ahead, but try as she might, she could not exorcise the encounter with Pieter in the gallery or the foolish commitment she'd made to herself at the balustrade. Sticking her proud Sicilian nose into those paintings could be one hell of a ride: *How often do you run across four major-league masterpieces posing as minor-league wannabes,* she thought, *hiding in plain sight for years? And how many people who should have known better had walked right past them hundreds of times?* Angela knew that intruding into Erich Wolff's business could be disastrous, yet her terminal hubris led her to wonder for whom. She had sensed a shootout in the cards from their first exchange. She didn't know where or when, or that it would take such a bizarre twist, but a fight to the finish was as clear to her as high noon in Dodge.

They disliked each other from her first and only interview. The director had greeted her stiffly as she entered his dreary domain. Angela forced a tight smile as she gripped his icy hand firmly and responded in kind. He motioned for her to take one of the crudely hewn, leather-cushioned chairs which she judged to be from the early Teutonic period, whenever that might have been. Erich Wolff settled in a high-backed swivel version behind his equally graceless desk. Heavy drapes hung on either side of a single window, and only a rather ordinary medieval tapestry and a few dark landscapes, badly in need of a good scrubbing, hung on the walls. They were an odd choice, given that he might have had his pick of thousands of uplifting masterpieces from the Mendelssohn's considerable inventory, in which ninety percent of the collection remained in storage at any one time.

Wolff looked every year of seventy. He was tall and sinewy, with silver hair and blue-steel eyes. Round, titanium-rimmed lenses straddled his beaklike nose. A perfectly knotted blood red tie of expensive silk set off his finely tailored, slate gray Giorgio Armani suit. The shirt was white, plain but pricey, with French cuffs flashing gold links which might have been buttons from a fancy-dress military uniform. His natty attire and his imperial cachet signaled that he was not your garden-variety midwestern museum director. Angela had heard stories about him, most of which she had passed off as more legend than truth; yet whoever Erich Wolff is, *bring him on,* she thought as she girded for the worst.

"Well, you come well-papered, Miss Desjardin," Wolff sniffed as he glanced at her curriculum vitae, invoking tired academic mumbo jumbo for her sterling record at Cambridge, the Sorbonne, Princeton, and the Vatican museum by special papal appointment. It made him look silly, and Angela was not impressed.

"I tried to prepare myself," she said.

"*Try* to prepare yourself, my dear. We all continue to try. Learning is a journey, don't you agree? Not a destination."

"I could not agree more, Dr. Wolff," she answered abruptly, barely disguising her annoyance with his patronizing "my dear" and pompous tone, not to mention his belittling use of "Miss." *That would be* Dr. *Desjardin,* she thought. His narrowing eyes suggested that her brittle inflection did not go unnoticed, and just as abruptly he shifted into full-blown inquisition mode.

Wolff's probing grew increasingly confrontational over the next hour. Angela parried skillfully, vexing him more, and once it was clear to her that her goose was cooked she actually began to enjoy the contest. But just when it seemed that the sparks between them had reached the flash point, to her astonishment he suddenly rose from his chair and said, "I think you will do, Angela.

"Please see my assistant, Herr Bergdorf, to work out the details. Friedrich prefers 'Herr' to 'Mister,' incidentally. It is one of his many endearing quirks. I am in charge, of course. I will want to know what you are doing at all times, and I personally will approve all decisions on your handling of the collection. Herr Berg-dorf will explain the protocol. I am frequently away, and when I am gone he will act for me.

"You may call me Herr Wolff—an endearing quirk of mine as well." He seemed to enjoy his little joke as he managed a tiny, twisted grin, bringing an end to it. Angela rose, took his cold hand once again and said, "Thank you, Herr Wolff." She offered, in return, something less than her usual high-beam smile, and that was that. The battle lines had been drawn.

He was a shrewd cookie, which made her wonder why he had hired her; he must have known she'd be trouble down the road. *Maybe he's just bored and needs a little juice in his life,* she speculated. She was just as baffled by why she had accepted—most applicants, at least those with any brains at all, would have bolted from such a testy encounter and never looked back. But truth be known, it was Wolff's creepiness that drew her to him and to this place like a moth to flame—that her morbid curiosity, a childhood trait she had never quite outgrown, was the culprit in such a cockamamie career choice. From the start, there was for her the distinct odor of evil in the walls of the prim and proper Mendelssohn; she could smell it like ripe mold in a damp basement. She would pay the price for messing in his business. Angela lifted the receiver to call Pieter.

"Maxfield."

"You're still here. Good," she said.

"Of course I'm still here. I never leave. I sleep in one of the mummy cases outside the lab, the big one, second from the left, if you ever want to reach me after sundown. Just knock on the lid. I have no other life. I . . ."

"Oh, for God's sake, Pieter, put a sock in it," she snapped. Angela wasn't in a game-playing mood, but then she was no longer annoyed with him, which was something. "Pieter, why don't you meet me up in the gallery first thing in the morning? Nine okay?"

"Nine okay," he answered. Then, in a conciliatory tone, he said, "Dinner tonight? I'm cooking."

Yes! The surefire way to a hungry Sicilian girl's heart, she thought. "Oh, you're cooking, alright. Sure," Angela said. "Come by for me. I'll be here. I'm always here. I have no other . . ."

Pieter hung up the phone.

CHAPTER THREE

Pieter was in the Dutch gallery at eight-thirty sharp, hoping for a few minutes alone before Angela swooped in at nine. It was the calm before the storm, the quiet time before the hoards of children tumbled from their big yellow buses and swarmed through the Mendelssohn's hushed halls, squealing and squirming and pinching and poking as cheerful docents chirped their well-rehearsed litany of "dos," "don'ts" and "don't even think about its."

Pieter wanted to believe that the children took away something of value—images of Chaim Soutine's bloody canvas of a splayed animal carcass perhaps, to share, eyes rolling, at the family supper table, or their guide's grizzly description of the slimy organs inside the Egyptian canopic jars, for sure. He knew they thought the mummy cases were cool, because he could hear them through the laboratory door. *Is there a real mummy in there? Yes. Can he get out? No, he's dead. That don't mean anything. He can get out, I'm tellin' ya. He can? Sure he can. At night. Not now? No, not now. He's asleep. I thought you said he was dead. Please move on, children.* Pieter could write the script from memory.

But, for now, it was just Pieter and the work. He stood uneasily in front of the Leyster-Hals. Ground zero. Three more, she'd said. He scanned the walls, doing his best to avoid eye contact with the enigmatic mother and daughter who once delighted him but now taunted him. They know. They were there. They had felt every brushstroke of their creator as he gave them life. But they simply smiled cryptically, like the ethereal sitter in da Vinci's masterpiece.

His eyes settled on the Petrus Christus, two frames down. It was a small painting, ten-and-one-quarter inches by seven-and-one-half, the label said: *Man in a Blue Smock, 1449. Oil on panel.* The painter had rendered the face in detail as if by a brush with a single hair. The result was a landscape in high relief as much as a face, with every pockmark, every wart, every wrinkle in its place. It was a remarkable portrait.

"Petrus Christus, *Man in a Blue Smock.* Bingo!" Angela had slipped up beside him in his trance. "I couldn't sleep," she said, apologetically.

"You're early," Pieter said, miffed, yet pleased all the same, as he always was in Angela's presence.

"But isn't this better?" she said in her best Lucy imitation, in a frame of mind decidedly more upbeat than the evening before. "I'm here to help you, Charlie Brown." Despite her pedigree, Angela had acquired a taste for the profundity of Charles Schultz, whose characters would, now and then, insinuate themselves into her own eccentric persona.

Angela had gotten very little sleep the night before, which was not like her. In spite of an engine that raced during her hours awake, she usually crashed at day's end. The excess adrenalin which still pumped from yesterday's unexpected disinterment of old and deeply buried bones, plus three cups of very black Starbucks, had launched her straight into her morning orbit.

"You're here to help, like the government," Pieter said dryly.

"Yes! Like the government! So where shall we start? Do you want them all at once, or shall we do them one at a time and savor them separately, like the old bull in a pasture of alluring cows?" she teased.

"I think I feel more like the old bull this morning. Let's do them one at a time. I don't think I could handle them all at once. So I was right about senór Christus here, aye?" he said.

Pieter knew that identifying the remaining suspects was a done deed. Although he wasn't sure which ones Angela was going to pull out of the line-up, he knew she'd be on the money. He just wanted to get them under the hot lights of his lab *tout de suite* to exact a full confession.

His mind had already leap-frogged "who painted what" as he wrestled with what Wolff was up to. Pieter had to assume that the works were his to hang; putting them up here would be his call. Still, where he got them was another matter, particularly seven- or eight-figure pieces, which they seemed to be. And why he had passed them all off as the work of second- or third-tier painters, painters who even on their best, or luckiest, days could barely hold a palette to Hals or any of the others they're pretending to be?

Erich Wolff knew better. Pieter was sure that the man could peg any of the masters almost from a single brushstroke or a particular hue. Wolff had forgotten more about European art than most of the current crop of museum heads ever knew. So what are they doing up here? It's like he's daring us to find them. Like the cerebral killer in a police procedural, he's playing us, and he has for thirty years.

Angela's voice jarred him out of his reverie. "Senór Christus it is," she said. Pieter's attention resurfaced, and he tried to focus on the painting in front of him. Fretful thoughts scurried like cockroaches into the crevices of his brain and lurked there. They would not leave his head until he found some answers.

"There's no sin in hanging a Petrus Christus," Angela said. "He was an okay Flemish Renaissance painter and he was a fixture around the neighborhood. He painted on wood. They all painted on wood back then. . ."

"I know that. Go on," Pieter interrupted, showing un-characteristic impatience. "Who's to say this one isn't a Christus?"

"*I'm* to say," she continued, enjoying enlightening Pieter with her own erudition, "Like the Hals, there's no signature, see? Don't expect one. Fifteenth-century panel painters signed the frame, not the painting, and most of the frames from that period are long gone."

"So?"

"If there were a signature, we'd know it was a fake right off, would we not? A clever touch, not adding one. A pro would know that.

"I see you agitating, Pieter, so I'll move it along. Why, you ask, is this not a Christus?" She answered her own question. "Be-cause Petrus Christus wasn't good enough to paint this piece. If this isn't a van Eyck, I'll buy you the biggest bottle of Dom Péri-gnon in town."

Pieter was hooked. The cockroaches slept. "Van Eyck. Okay. Say more."

"He was magic with the brush. Jan Van Eyck could paint rings around the rest of them back then, Petrus included. But he had all these other little tricks. He diddled with things, like Rem-brandt, and what came out was so unbelievable that some experts were sure for years that he was the one who actually *invented* oil painting. His foxy little secret was that he painted in layers of transparent oil, which produced phenomenal detail. And he used these tiny little brushstrokes that you can't even see unless you put your nose right up to the panel or use a glass. Go ahead, take a look. Can you see them?"

Pieter stood as close to the painting as his eyes would fo-cus. "Yeh, I see them, barely. You're right. Unbelievable.

"So if this is a van Eyck, we're looking at a very rare piece," Pieter said. "There are even fewer of these around than there are Vermeers. Maybe twenty we know about. Is this one on the list?"

"Well, you do know your history. I take back everything I've ever said," Angela said with a laugh. "No, I don't know if it's on the list of his known works or not, or even if one's missing. I don't need to know, because I don't *care*. The point is, my astute friend, we may be getting into some *merda profondo* here. Are you sure you want to step in it?"

"Can't stop now," Pieter said. He glanced at his watch. "Whoa. Maybe we'd better. In about twenty minutes we'll be trampled by munchkins."

"Okay, pick the easy one, and then we'll come back later. Anyhow, my semis are due, and I've got to be there on the dock when they open the doors," Angela said.

"The easy one? That would be Adam Pynacker here," Pieter said, gesturing toward a darkish painting about eighteen inches square with half a dozen or so rosy-cheeked people drinking and dancing and playing fiddles and passing out on a tavern floor. "You're going to tell me that *The Anniversary Party* is really a Jan Steen, right?"

"Pretty obvious, huh?" Angela said. "Why is that?"

"Well, this one's a no-brainer. Like you said about Leyster and Hals, Pynacker was no Jan Steen. He was barely Pynacker. And he never made a pub painting in his life that I know of. All he did were landscapes, and rather ordinary ones at that," Pieter said.

"I've always liked Steen," he continued. "With all his imitators, none of them could nail their characters in such awesome sleaziness and still make a picture look like a Sunday school picnic. Like this one. When you're not laughing, it makes your skin crawl, doesn't it?" he added. "Look at the husband and the barmaid . . ."

"Enough! Say no more. I surrender—it's a Steen!" Angela said. "Let's move on, please."

Just after ten—before the museum officially opened at eleven—what had begun as a gentle buzz in their ears crescendoed like an approaching swarm of giant insects as small clusters of fourth-graders, held loosely in tow by a cadre of nervous chaperones, moved amoeba-like through the galleries, headed their way.

Hands flailed for recognition as the children spotted the milk cow in the picture, or opined as to whether another painting was rendered at sunrise or sunset, or debated why the painter might have colored the grass purple instead of emerald green like everybody knows grass is supposed to be. Then they would vanish as suddenly as they had come, only to be followed by another swarm, and then another.

The spell was broken.

"Three down, one to go," Pieter said. "Why do I have the feeling that this last one is the bomb—not that the others haven't been."

"The bomb?" Angela laughed. "Pieter, if your suit of armor is back from the cleaners, I suggest you wear it. Let's come back about four, okay?"

"Four's good."

They left as the first wave of kids in scruffy jeans and beat-up Nikes swept past them. Like all the rest, the young scholars failed to take notice of the missing masterpieces hiding in plain view among the frost-breathing skaters, jolly balladeers, and tables brimming with half-peeled citrus, partially eaten pastries,

28

smoking candlewicks and other *memento mori,* subtle reminders of the capriciousness of death.

Pieter returned to the lab, where several of his patients waited stoically on their assigned easels for his gentle touch. The doctor forced himself to minister to their needs, deftly swabbing the upper right corner of a magnificent Corot whose silvery shimmer had darkened like tarnished sterling from years of neglect. But even the promise of a masterfully restored Barbizon landscape could not quiet his agitation as his brain scavenged fitfully for any scrap of insight as to what in holy hell was going on in that Dutch gallery.

CHAPTER FOUR

The gallery was empty when Angela and Pieter returned, except for the ancient security guard, who perched owl-like on his high stool. Ignoring him, the two meandered to the far end of the room, stopping briefly at a few inconsequential paintings, and then she nodded toward a small Baroque panel several canvases down from the bawdy Pynecker-Steen.

"I'd feel a lot better if there were a few people around. We wouldn't look quite so devious," Angela said softly when she knew she was past the earshot of the guard. "So look casual, and keep it down. I don't trust that little weasel." Since their morning reconnaissance, she seemed to have misplaced her trademark flippancy. She appeared tense and subdued. This was an Angela Pieter had never seen, and it effectively tempered the jolt of high adventure he'd felt only a few hours before.

"Doesn't this look just a little familiar to you," Angela said. They stood before a modest-sized vertical panel with all the classic earmarks of nonpareil Baroque painting—dazzling color, dramatic posturing, severe contrasts of light and dark, an intensely theatrical arrangement of subjects. The label read *The Flemish School, Followers at the Tomb of Jesus*, 1612.

"Now that you mention it, it's *very* familiar," Pieter said. "It's obviously part of something else. All the figures are looking to the left, but there's no tomb—and no Jesus. And it's too perfect to be so anonymous."

"Could you see it as the right wing of an altarpiece, a triptych where the tomb itself would be in the center?"

"Rubens! It looks like part of a Rubens altarpiece. Maybe

the Abbey of St. Margaret near Antwerp. I saw it years ago on my first backpack tour of Europe. It's the sketch!"

"Your memory's pretty good, Pieter. It's Rubens—the original modello for the right panel of *The Tomb of Jesus*. And it wouldn't stand alone, naturally, because on this altarpiece he connected the three panels in a single tableau like he did with *The Raising of the Cross* in Antwerp. Why he would've done a sketch for just one of the panels apart from the others is another question. It's very, *very* rare."

"And The Flemish School—that's absurd," Pieter said. "Even if you wanted to stretch the point and give the piece to Rubens's *assistants*, that still won't fly. Rubens did all his own sketches, except for Snyders, who did his animals. His grunts worked mostly on the final canvases."

"Grunts like Anthony van Dyck?" Angela said.

Pieter smiled sheepishly. "But I was right about the blockbuster," he said. "Do you have any idea what we have here?"

"Of course I do," she murmured, now totally subdued. "I have for a long time."

Just then, the guard slipped down off his stool, stretched himself, and wandered casually toward Angela and Pieter's end of the room. "I'm not comfortable here," she said under her breath, glancing sideways at the doddering sentry as he moved past them. His badge read *Alfred Nichter, Security*. "Let's go."

Pieter persisted. "Angela, there's a whole lot we obviously don't know about this, and I'm not thrilled about hitting up the Wolfman about it, at least not yet. I want to look at one or two of these puppies up close. Put them under the light," Pieter said, referring to the various infrared and ultraviolet devices in his hi-tech arsenal of conservational weaponry. "Maybe we can pull up a few clues as to what the hell's going on here."

"Pieter, go. Now," Angie tugged on his sleeve.

Pieter and Angela sipped on frosty mugs of Killian's in the back booth at Limerick's, the hot spot for the arts crowd amidst a tight cluster of mini-theaters, cinemas, galleries and other watering holes within spitting distance of the Mendelssohn. Named for the central town in County Limerick, Ireland, from whence the boisterous, red-faced proprietor Danny O'Dell hailed, the pub was best known for its long cork wall to which had been tacked maybe a thousand or more limericks tendered by patrons over the years. Most of the little five-line stanzas were outrageously foul and equally hilarious, and many immortalized the worldly proclivities of one artist, writer, composer or another, as would befit Danny's cerebral clientele.

They hastily agreed that in light of Angela's paranoia, which was by now beginning to rub off on Pieter, hanging at the museum would not lend itself to clear thinking. Anyhow, Pieter had done some of his best work over a steaming plate of Danny's shepherd's pie and a brew or two, and Angela was a familiar denizen of the cozy, dark-paneled pub. They felt safe there, and they were alone in the pub, having entered well before the happy hour crowd would descend and fill the place with smoke in spite of the city's ban on lighting up.

"Your trucks came in, I see," Pieter said. "I watched them out the window of the lab. You looked like one of those Bermudian traffic cops, pointing and waving your arms and shouting. All you needed were the white gloves and the little white pot on your head. Any problems?"

"None so far, knock on wood. It all checked out. We got all four trailer-loads in and up to the galleries. We'll pull the crates in the morning and see if everything's okay. It's going to be an unbelievable show, Pieter. Matisse drives me crazy."

They talked about the installation and Angela's struggles with the dueling curators. They talked about comings and goings in other museums. They talked about Danny's menu that hadn't changed in twenty years.

Finally, Pieter said, "I want to look at those paintings, Angela."

"What do you think you'll find? The labels are fake, we know that. But we'll never know why, unless Wolff tells us why. And what are the chances of that? Most likely, he'd tell us to pack our bags. I mean, Pieter, what's the point?"

"Maybe if we take a look . . ." he persisted.

Angela stared into her Irish Red, which by this time had lost its foam, as if she expected to extract divine guidance from the rust-colored lager remaining. Then she looked up. "Okay, *okay*—if it'll make you feel any better, let's slip one out for a few hours in the morning. Wolff's somewhere in Europe, I think, and if we're lucky, Herr Bergdorf won't be on the prowl. I think it would draw less attention if your people pulled it down. You're always removing things anyway," she said. "Just get in and get out. If anybody asks you about it, you'd best have a good answer."

"You're really stressed about this."

"Well, yes, I'm stressed about this. My gut tells me that we're into something really ugly, and neither of us will be quite the same when it's done with. But let's find out what it is and move on. We won't get any rest until we do."

"So which one do you want?"

"The Hals," he answered without hesitation.

"Then call me when you have it down. I want to see it," Angela said, sealing their fate. *Let the games begin*, Pieter thought as he glanced up at the muted TV screen over the bar where the

Indians were about to rip the Reds in another meaningless inter-league "Battle of Ohio." He hoped for a better outcome for him-self and the complex woman across from him.

Suddenly famished, they each ordered the stew and an-other Killian's as the first wave of happy hour regulars bumbled through the antique, leaded-glass entryway and settled into their familiar hives.

CHAPTER FIVE

Pieter Maxfield would normally have found the act unthinkable. Yet it was the best he could do on short notice. Later, on reflection, he was stunned by its sheer brilliance. His guilt, however, yielded to the convenient principle of the greater good as he elected to do the despicable deed. He could apologize later if necessary.

Well before ten, he went alone to the empty Dutch gallery and approached the objects of his growing fixation, *Dutch Mother and Child, c. 1634,* whose laughing eyes continued to torment him. Nichter, the guard, who seemed always to be parked nearby like an insomnolent Doberman, was nowhere to be seen, probably quaffing the last of his tepid vending machine coffee in the staff canteen before assuming his first shift of the day.

Pieter's attention turned from the painting to the frame. It was a masterpiece in its own right: a heavy, gilded creation with countless twisting scrolls, florets and other embellishments carved in deep relief. He chose a particularly vulnerable protrusion, took one last look around, and then with a sharp twist he snapped it off, leaving a dime-sized patch of bone-dry wood grain glaring conspicuously from the lower portion of the frame. Pieter slipped the broken piece into the pocket of his jacket and left the gallery quickly. As he returned to the lab, Poe's classic, *The Telltale Heart,* occupied his thoughts as he pondered, only partly in jest, if his offense would haunt him with phantom throbbing from the dismembered appendage, or whether sap would seep from the stub and pool at his feet.

Pieter watched through the cracked door of the lab,

which he had purposely left ajar, as the first wave of sixth-graders devoured the mummies, made puking sounds as the docent described the putrefied contents of the stone jars, wove their way through medieval weapons and armor without casualty, and stomped to the second floor. He followed from a distance, pretending, with white-gloved hands, to examine individual works along the way in his predictable morning routine.

He paused as they clumped in the Dutch room and finally passed on through to the next gallery. Alfred Nichter was ensconced on his sturdy oak stool at the near end of the room, arms folded, monitoring the inevitable few stragglers as they meandered through the passageway and rejoined their group.

After a short interval, Pieter entered the vacated gallery, spoke cheerfully to the humorless figure standing watch and strode purposefully past the long row of paintings toward the opposite egress. Seemingly about to enter the next room, he stopped suddenly, glanced down into the corner furthest from Nichter and stooped with his back to the curious sentry. With the deftness of a street magician he reached down, unpalmed the severed nub, held it conspicuously between his gloved fingers and turned it slowly, pretending to study every contour of the gilded protuberance. Then he stood, feigned as bewildered an expression as his modest thespian skills allowed, briefly scoped the gallery and walked back toward Alfred Nichter, who had noted every nuance of his charade.

"Alfred, I found this on the floor," Pieter said, holding the piece up for the guard to see. "It looks like it came from a frame. Did you notice if any of the kids who just went though here might have snapped this piece off one of the frames, or maybe bumped against it by accident?"

"No, Dr. Maxfield, I saw nothing," Nichter said, visibly

miffed by the inference that he had lapsed in his sacred duty as the vigilant watchdog of the collection.

"It had to have come from one of the frames in here," Pieter said, looking along the line of paintings that circled the room. "Do you think you could help me find it, Alfred?"

With a reluctant grunt, Nichter slid down from his roost.

"Here, you take the piece and see if you can find a match," Pieter said as he defied the universal "gloves always" rule and thrust the fragment into Nichter's hand. "You take this side," Pieter suggested offhandedly, assigning the guard to the longest wall where the Hals hung, "and I'll take the other side and the end walls." Pieter wanted Nichter to find where the missing nub belonged. "Look low on the frames, or at least up to where a kid might be able to reach or bump against."

Pieter moved slowly along the opposite wall, studiously examining each frame. Suddenly Nichter broke the quietude with an uncharacteristic eruption of glee. "Ha! Over here. I think I have found it," he said. The guard glowed with the thrill of discovery and partial redemption for his possible oversight as he stood proudly in front of *Dutch Mother and Child, c. 1634* and pointed at the frame's open wound. No sap dripped to the floor.

Pieter joined the guard quickly, took the piece from Alfred's outstretched hand and fitted it ceremoniously to the frame to confirm Nichter's find. "Bravo, Alfred! What eyes you have! I would never have found it."

Alfred Nichter beamed.

"Whoa," Pieter half-whispered, glancing up at the label next to the frame. "This is one of Herr Wolff's pieces. I think I had better take care of this right away before either of us takes any heat, don't you think?" he said in a hushed, conspiratorial tone.

Alfred nodded in hearty agreement, motivated by the implication that he might somehow share in the blame. It was his job to keep these things from happening, and he had no stomach for a scolding from the quick-tempered director.

"Alfred, I'm going to send a couple of my people up here to bring the painting down to the lab. With a little luck, I think I can fix it myself and have it back up here by the end of the day, or maybe first thing in the morning. Our little secret?"

"Ja, our little secret," Nichter said with a wink.

"Alfred, I can't thank you enough," Pieter said as he turned and left the gallery.

Shortly before noon, Ian Gabriel and Patty Whittredge, Pieter's two interns, rolled the Hals gingerly into the lab, taking extreme care not to bump against any surface or otherwise jar the masterpiece, as there was no way of knowing what damage even the slightest vibration might cause to its delicate, centuries-old substructure. Under Pieter's critical eye, they lifted the master-piece from the cushioned dolly and placed it image side up on the lab's large work table.

"Jeez Louise, that's one heavy piece," Ian said, as sweat beaded on his forehead. The intern spoke the truth. It was no small painting to start with—the canvas alone was more than three feet across and nearly four feet top to bottom. But the dense mahogany frame would add another nine inches all around and weigh as much as a small boy. It could be handled by one person, but not easily. Pieter would have no further need for his interns—any future heavy lifting would be done by him alone.

"It's here," Pieter spoke into the phone after his assistants had taken their lunches from the lab's mini-fridge and headed for the garden. The Arthur Mendelssohn Sculpture Garden, named for the boorish great-grandson of the museum's original benefac-tor, also the institution's self-appointed board chair for life, was a priceless gem in the museum's courtyard, surrounded by gallery wings on four sides and open to the sky. Its manicured green was home to two Henry Moore bronzes, a smallish red and black Sandy Calder stabile, a brushed stainless David Smith creation after his signature Cubi series, and an elegant George Rickey mobile, so finely balanced as to move constantly even in the natural stillness of the space. The world-class sculptures, all gifts of the chairman, were tastefully scaled to the intimacy of the garden. Although awkwardly mismatched, they were individually powerful, and popular if only for their superstar creators. The garden was a favorite spot for museum brown-baggers in the spring and early fall when the days were mild and the sun warm.

"You're looking at it?" Angela spoke into her cell from the bare-walled temporary exhibits gallery where she was meticulously examining each and every Matisse for possible damage from their harrowing journey over the mountains.

"I'm looking at it."

"How did you pull it off? How did you get it past that spooky guard?"

"Pull it off? That's a good one," Pieter laughed. "I'll tell you why, and how, when you come down."

"I can't come now. I've got a couple more hours here, at least."

"Now's not good anyway. I don't want anything to seem out of the ordinary. Besides, I have a little work to do on the frame—part of the story—and that'll take me until the end of the day. Come down a little after five, and we'll do some serious sleuthing together."

"Have you looked at it? Can you tell anything?"

"No. I don't want to mess with it until the kids leave for the day. They think it's down here just for the fix, and that's all they need to know. Gotta go."

"Fix? Fix what?"

"Later."

Pieter replaced the receiver and turned his attention to the small fragment of gilded mahogany. He cleaned the opposing surfaces of the severed nub and the frame with a short burst of compressed air from one of several hanging hoses and reached for the pot of special quick-drying glue which he had mixed himself for such emergencies. With a tiny brush he coated the exposed wood, blew on the two surfaces for a few seconds, firmly pressed them together and secured the joint with a tiny C-clamp. In the morning he would remove the clamp, fill and re-gilt the hairline crack that remained and return the painting to the gallery, with none the wiser.

Angela showed up at precisely fifteen minutes past five. Nodding toward the table, she said, "Is that it?"

"That's it. Look for yourself," Pieter said. "I've already been over it with a glass, and I can't find anything beyond what we saw upstairs, which was nothing. From other Hals pieces I've worked on up close and what I know about his brushwork, the strokes are dead on. The craquelure seems to fit with the likely age of the painting," he said, referring to the delicate patina of hairline cracks in the varnish which are common to old works. "I know that can be faked, but I don't think that's happening here. I know most of the tricks. So far, it's looking pretty good."

Angela stood over the painting and stared long and hard at the canvas. Then she brought her eyes as close to it as they would focus, appearing to commit to memory every square centimeter of the work as she crisscrossed slowly over the picture plane. Minutes passed.

"Give me the glass," she said, rejecting the lighted visor

for Pieter's long-handled magnifying glass, a treasured memento he had found years ago in a dusty little shop on Baker Street only a few yards from the famous 221b. More silence as she examined maybe three dozen random places on the canvas, all subtly different in color, texture and stroke. Then she broke the tension with a pronouncement of incontrovertible certainty: "Well, if it's not the greatest fake ever produced by humankind, it's a Hals. No doubt in my mind. You don't have to pull it out of the frame to satisfy me.

"But why would Wolff try to pass this off as a Leyster?" she said. "What's the point?"

"We could ask him."

"Not a chance. Not yet," Angela said. "Don't you want to look at the others?"

"Not really. For now, I'd assume that the others are what we think they are," Pieter said, "and I'm not hot for taking them down just now. Doing this one was tricky enough."

"Tricky? Just what did you have to do? And what needed fixing?"

"Well, it's kind of a long story, best told over a brew. Let's just say that we now have a co-conspirator up in the galleries."

"Co-conspirator? Are you referring to that snarky old guard?"

Pieter laughed. "Snarky? How can you say that? He's a very sweet guy, when he isn't being a thorough pain in the arse, as you're so fond of saying. Forget him. I think the issue here is no longer whether these pieces are the real thing. I'd bet a month's salary they are. There are a hundred things we could do to prove it for sure, if we had to. But that would take days, maybe weeks, and we still might be wrong. Authenticity was never the main issue anyway. The big question, as you so succinctly put it, is 'why?'

43

"Look, we don't have much time. We've got to remove the canvas while we can. We'll never get another chance. Help me flip it over—we'll pull the stretcher and give it the third degree."

"Got nothing else to do," Angela quipped, knowing that she was hopelessly hooked; even Pieter's lasagna couldn't draw her away now. But before she could get a grip on the frame, Pieter had already lifted the heavy painting easily and placed it face-down on the thick, quilted pad which he'd laid out at the opposite end of the table. "I can't believe you did that yourself—I could have helped," Angela said.

"You're the brains of this outfit, and I'm the brawn, re-member? That's why we're so good together," Pieter retorted, tossing off her reference to his strength, yet secretly preening at this modest compliment to his manhood. They stared at the back of the painting for several minutes, absorbing the gritty substruc-ture behind the facade that others rarely see and that only a pro could love. Many times the hidden parts would tell more than the image itself; Pieter hoped that this was one of them.

After eyeballing the reverse side of the aged canvas under the overhead fluorescent, then examining the back of the frame and the integrity of the ancient wood stretcher holding the can-vas, he said, "Well, let's get to it."

Ever so delicately he pried loose the rusty nails securing the stretcher in the frame and set them aside in order, clockwise. Slipping on a pair of thin, white work gloves and tossing an extra pair to Angela, he separated the mounted canvas slowly from the frame and held it to the light, studying the tacking edges all round to satisfy himself that the raw, unpainted fabric seemed as old as it ought to be. Angela watched wide-eyed, her heart thumping audibly in the tomblike silence.

"I don't see any red flags," Pieter said. "What say we escort the girls over to the darkroom, run a little UV over them."

"Do you mind if I take a quick look first?"

"No, go ahead," Pieter said and stepped away from the table, out of the light. Angela bent over the reverse, swept her eyes across it slowly in a grid pattern, across and back, top to bottom while Pieter looked on.

"Hell-o. What's this?" she said softly, almost to herself.

"What's what?"

"This," she said, making a small circle with her gloved finger in the lower right portion of the canvas an inch or so inside the stretcher joint.

Pieter focused intently on where she pointed. "What? I don't see anything," he said.

"You can't see that spot? Here. Right here," she said, accidentally touching the canvas. "It's about so big." Angela closed her thumb and middle finger in the shape of the letter "O." "Something spilled on the canvas, or bleached out, maybe."

Pieter squinted again into the corner. "Lord, how can you see that? Yeh, I see it now. Maybe ultraviolet light will bring something up, if it's anything. C'mon, let's take a look."

He lifted the canvas with all the care due a priceless masterpiece and carried it to the darkroom. Pieter's darkroom was a small enclosed area in the corner of the lab filled with all the bells and whistles needed to penetrate the darkest secrets, or diagnose the countless ailments, of the museum's collection. The equipment was essential also to protect the museum from clever fakery or hidden damage as it considered new acquisitions. More than once Pieter had rescued the Mendelssohn from major egg-on-face, not to mention serious financial loss, through the adept use of his high-tech toys.

Pieter placed the painting on a heavily cushioned easel,

image side against the soft, protective padding. He reached for a small device which held two miniature fluorescent tubes and a pair of ultraviolet bulbs, each the size of a slim cigar. Angela watched breathless as he switched on the UV lamp.

"Close the door," Pieter said.

Angela pulled the door shut, and only the unearthly ultraviolet glow pierced the blackness. Allowing a minute or two for their eyes to adjust, Pieter directed the beam toward the suspect corner of the canvas which Angela had discovered.

"Ah! There it is. Look at it," Pieter said. Under the eerie purple cast, a soft-edged area the size of a silver dollar levitated from the canvas like mist in the moonlight. Angela stared at the apparition, but with absolutely no clue to its meaning.

"Do you know what's going on here?" Pieter said.

"Tell me."

"It would be my pleasure. The UV rays pick up any surface aberrations—any superficial variations from place to place either in the chemical make-up of the fabric itself or whatever compounds may have been applied to it. My best guess is that the sizing Hals used to seal the canvas bled through the fabric— which it almost always does—and was somehow lifted from the back of the canvas right. . .here." He directed a beam from a pocket-pointer at the canvas, which registered a hot red dot no bigger than a pencil point on the lighter area.

"The sizing was removed, probably by accident, with some kind of chemical, maybe bleach, like you said," he continued. "Looks like somebody tried to eradicate something from the surface. He did a pretty good job, whatever he used, but if he wanted to hide what he did, he overlooked the sizing problem. *Capisce?*"

"Okay, I've got it," Angela said. "But what was it he removed? And, for that matter, why *he*? Couldn't *he* have been a *she*?"

"No, he wouldn't have been a she. Sloppy work. A woman would have tidied up a spot like this, right? You know how men are—you've seen my place. As for what he removed, if anything, UV light won't tell us that."

"Oh, great. So now what?"

"A little patience, please. All is not lost," Pieter said as he flipped on the overhead light.

"Infrared?"

Pieter feigned chagrin. "Ah, you're way ahead of me, as usual. Observe this cool little vidicon," Pieter said, reaching into the corner of the darkroom for what resembled a small video camera with a longish telephoto-like lens on one end, mounted on a sturdy black tripod. "If there's even a trace left of whatever was bleached out of that area, infrared will pick it up most of the time."

From the shelf behind him Pieter took a tiny portable monitor with a hooded screen no larger than the palm of his hand. He adjusted the tripod to the height of the lower edge of the canvas, aimed the vidicon at the target area, connected the monitor to the camera and replaced it at eye level on the shelf. Then he switched on the device.

Pieter and Angela's eyes were glued to the monitor as he slowly rotated the lens. The blur on the dull gray screen receded as Pieter manipulated the camera, and the image on the canvas became increasingly defined. Evidence of carbon residue, possibly lampblack from India ink, began to cluster in broken lines as the image took form. Suddenly it seemed that the last breath of fresh air had been sucked from the room.

"My God," Angela gasped.

Pieter froze, unable to speak.

In the center of the ashen screen, rising out of the ether, glowering at them like a phantasmal skull from the depths of bloody hell, hovered the universal icon of pure evil.

It was the chilling mark of the Third Reich.

CHAPTER SIX

The director sank into the buttery leather of aisle seat 2-B in the first class cabin of Lufthansa LH430, Frankfurt to Chicago. Its scent summoned up the long-forgotten essence of his father, Otto's, black leather long coat. He remembered it keenly from that December day spent with the elder Wolff at the Berghof more than six decades ago. Two episodes from his *kindheit* had remained chiseled in his memory; stimulated by this sensory serendipity, he allowed one of these occasions to wash over him as the ancient Boeing 747 lifted toward 45,000 feet.

He recalled standing tall in the warm winter uniform of the Hitler Youth, looking east from the terrace of the Fuehrer's Alpine retreat over the Untersberg between Salzburg and Berchtesgaden. The snow on its slopes was blinding in the afternoon sun as Otto Wolff looked on. The Great Man himself knelt on one knee, his hand resting firmly on the nine-year-old's shoulder. He murmured praise for the boy's loyalty to the Fuehrer and the Fatherland and admonished him to lead a life of total dedication to the Third Reich.

Hitler's menacing face semisoftened into a tight smile. Yellowed teeth exposed themselves beneath his trademark moustache. The boy caught a hint of his sulfur breath, and his eyes seared into Erich's soul as he sighed, *"Du sind mein Liebling."* You are my favorite. My darling. Then the Supreme Leader rose, took the spellbound child's hand, and led him back through the tall French doors.

His face a studied mask of detachment, Otto Wolff froze as the two disappeared behind the majestic panorama of the mountain range mirrored in the glass. Then he diverted his eyes to the twisting ski trails and the antlike specks that crept down the steep grade. A gust of icy wind slashed through his body in the defining moment which would haunt his days. Erich glanced once through the window at his father, who had turned away toward the mountain. Then he squeezed the Fuehrer's clammy hand as they wound their way deep into the labyrinth, the back of Otto's black leather coat forever etched in his subconscious.

The Fuehrer considered Erich's grandfather, Kurt, a hero of the Reich for his massive provision of weaponry to the war effort; the sprawling Wolff conglomerate produced the gamut of death-dealing devices for Hitler's killing machine, from fuses for bombs to Panzer tanks and most of the accompanying lethal essentials. As patronage to the patriarch, the Fuehrer had appointed his son, Otto, to the benign post of personal aide to Reichsmarschall Hermann Goering.

Otto's duties included assisting the Reich's Number Two in usurping from the collections of French Jews and the museums and galleries of France and other "liberated" neighboring countries important objets d'art. These would be placed under the beneficent wing of the Fatherland for "safekeeping" till war's end—works which met the Fuehrer's often bizarre standards of suitability for the Reich. Other so-called decadent pieces were consigned to the bonfire or sold for pfennigs on the mark to boost Hitler's war chest.

The appointment spared Otto from near certain death on the Eastern Front. His lowly rank of lieutenant, personally requested by his father, was intended to assure anonymity, yet his status with the Fuehrer was well known among the inner circle and required no conventional validation. Otto, in fact, proved barely a blip in the chronicle of Nazi history. His obscurity would later save his skin on Judgment Day, his propaganda value hardly market-worthy to the victors when compared with the rich pelts of the High Command.

Otto Wolff was a familiar face at the Berghof and at Supreme Headquarters in East Prussia. Hitler valued his counsel on his own personal obsession, a grandiose plan for an art palace unsurpassed by any of the great icons of the museum world. This he intended to construct in Linz, the Austrian town of his boyhood on the Danube. Wolff had been trained at the prestigious Munich Academy and, even as a young man, had been recognized as an art scholar of some note in the Fatherland. This impressed Hitler very much, particularly because of his own humiliating rejection by the Academy in Vienna when he was still in his teens. Wolff had embarked on an academic career before giving in to family pressure to join his father's empire. There, as a junior *Buchhalter*, he discovered his gift for numbers and the massaging thereof. There would be time enough for him to surface from bookkeeper to heir successor when the war was won.

Hitler also sought Wolff's insider views on the current status of war materiel production because of Otto's entrenchment in the family business and his links with Nazi Germany's maze of like purveyors. The Fuehrer found reports from his generals invariably skewed to please him; only Otto Wolff would tell him the truth, a quality, ironically, that he despised in his High Command as the war turned against him.

The boy, Erich, would often accompany Wolff, always at the request of the Fuehrer. He fancied Erich's innocence and his wide-eyed awe of him. During these visits Hitler showed a growing passion for the child, which only heightened Erich's worship of him in return, even as it exacerbated Otto's shame. While the boy's instincts told him that the Fuehrer's advances were less than avuncular, the same intuition prevented him from confiding them to Otto; even at nine he sensed that any revelation would not have served his father well. Soon Erich Wolff learned to exercise his gift for manipulation as the child became the predator, the Fuehrer in time succumbing to the boy's every whim.

Erich Wolff had been on the continent several weeks. First Paris; then Zurich for Arthur Mendelssohn's Matisse; Geneva, to see his banker, Rudolph Grüber, the cookie-cutter son of Andre Grüber who had handled his father's business; then Berlin for the Chagall; and Moscow, every bit as tiresome as he knew the Russians would be with their predictable but futile attempts at negotiation. Down to Rome, across to Catania and that miserable little rat-hole of Vittoria, back to his blessed Munich where the Reich found its roots, and finally west, and home—although even after thirty years, he could never think of the American city where he lived as "home." Because of Friedrich Bergdorf's frantic call to Don Carlo's villa, he had bypassed a nostalgic stayover in his true home of Bremen, opting instead to head straight back to his *Schloss auf der Rhein*, simply to ease his old retainer's mind.

Still, he was admittedly drained and glad to make an end to it, as his junkets were growing increasingly tedious as the years wore on.

Most of his circle remained intact and still hungry to do business. This had not changed since Otto Wolff long ago established *Das Rheingold*, The Rhine Gold, his father's sobriquet for the global network of shadowy art traffickers and patrons who fueled his nefarious trade in wartime spoils. The ring of conspirators which the senior Wolff had forged after the Defeat and controlled until his death was now the son's alone.

Erich Wolff prized the name, Das Rheingold. His father had applied it aptly to his enterprise, judging each golden masterpiece seized by the Reich during the Fuehrer's crusade the rightful property of the Fatherland in perpetuity. He had put his own spin on the adage, "To the victor go the spoils." To Otto, who won or who lost was immaterial. Only possession after the fact mattered. The victor would just have to come and get it, but first he would have to find it.

Otto Wolff appointed himself exclusive guardian of *Das Rheingold* and its assets for life, being, to the best of his knowledge, the sole survivor of the righteous Nazi crusaders who heroically liberated such treasures from their former unworthy owners; the rest had met their ends by the rope or by their own hand. Custody would pass to his only son when he had gone to his reward. Peacefully, and in his own bed, he hoped, unlike the others.

Erich Wolff also identified with the name, Das Rheingold, as it was the first of the Fuehrer's beloved *Der Ring des Nibelungen*, the epic quartet of operas penned by the larger-than-life nineteenth century hater of Jews, Richard Wagner. Erich knew by heart every note of Wagner's bombastic scores, and he could recite by memory the inflammatory librettos tracing the treacherous odyssey of a ring crafted from the sacred gold of the Rhine, the mythical band that destroyed all who possessed it.

Wolff was pleased with his acquisitions for Arthur Mendelssohn. It was in the director's supreme interest to keep the museum's board chairman happy. The reality was the two were entangled in a Mexican standoff. Should their business relationship ever surface, both would perish in disgrace, if not in the slammer. Mendelssohn was aware of Wolff's "other life" and was not shy about participating in it to the glory of his own stunning, if grossly tainted, collection.

Mendelssohn was also prone to moments of arrogance and indiscretion. The *Schweinehund*, as Wolff thought of him, could not be trusted, but their Faustian relationship was key to the director's hammerlock on the board and his total domination of the museum. The only debate might have been which was Faust and which the Devil, and if the question were ever raised between them, violent disagreement would surely have ensued.

Arthur Mendelssohn was the last of a dynasty whose legendary patriarch, with barely the shirt on his back, immigrated to America from Bavaria in the mid-1800s, entered through the port of New Orleans and worked his way up the Mississippi on the steamboats toward St. Louis. Gerhardt Mendelssohn hung a right at Cairo and continued east on the Ohio against the current, finally settling in what he sensed to be the most promising young river town of the ones he'd seen.

Through shrewdness, bold risk-taking, and hard work, he became extraordinarily wealthy as a merchant and landowner. He was generous with his fortune: in 1890, he gave the present-day equivalent of $50,000,000 for the construction of an art museum and donated hundreds of his own works to prime the pump for further acquisitions. The new museum was named in his honor.

Arthur, managing partner of the powerful Mendelssohn law firm, and kingmaker from statehouse to White House, took coarse pleasure in announcing to anyone who would listen that he had logged more nights in the Lincoln Bedroom than the Great Emancipator himself. He was also fond of visiting pain on those who did not please him, and he did not hesitate to inflict it. The greatest discomfort he reserved for political and professional enemies, but he relished also the occasional tweak among the city's social elite, a perversity enabled by his access to the darkest secrets of the horsy set. The wife-beaters, closet gays, cokeheads, corporate embezzlers, insider traders, cheating wives and skirt-chasing husbands he had all carefully catalogued for later use, if and when. While most of these offenses were generally known within the circle, public disclosure could ruin any of them and their families as well. Powerful stuff in the wrong hands, and Arthur Mendelssohn's hands were the last place one would choose for the safekeeping of private untidiness.

Unlike his dauntless forefather, Arthur Mendelssohn had no taste for swimming upstream. While he worked to hide the truth from himself through practiced self-aggrandizement and bullying tactics, wielding his easy wealth and influence like a blunt instrument, his cowardice haunted him in his lay-awake hours. Gerhardt Mendelssohn's traits of compassion, honesty, and sense of fairness were somehow displaced by moral turpitude and mean spirit in Arthur's genetic makeup.

As one could expect from such a pathologically petty soul, Arthur Mendelssohn reveled in sharing the juiciest tidbits with Wolff, whom he regarded as a partner-in-crime. Because a controlling number of the museum's board members had wandered unsuspectingly into Mendelssohn's cross-hairs over time, the director found the chairman's disclosures invaluable, and he, like Mendelssohn, would pull the trigger. If and when. All reason enough for the director to keep the *Schweinehund* happy.

As the jumbo jet settled over the water, Wolff sipped schnapps, the perfect cap to Lufthansa's first class fare of wienerschnitzel, spätzle, an unexpectedly good Rhine wine and Viennese *Schwarzkaffee*, his favorite. Thus numbed and sated, the director played over in his head the conversation of several months ago with Arthur Mendelssohn following the museum's monthly board meeting which led to this latest foray.

After a brief postmortem on some knottier portions of the meeting, the chairman had moved on to more self-serving matters. "Herr Wolff," he said in an affected accent, clumsily gutturalizing the *H* and pronouncing the *W* with an exaggerated *V* sound, *"Herrr Volff . . .*I have decided to follow your sage counsel on filling a glaring gap or two in my otherwise seamless collection. I've developed a considerable yearning for the pieces you've described, and I'd like for you to proceed."

Wolff ignored the chairman's slur. He had long become immune to Mendelssohn's insolence, although each occasion sharpened the director's taste for revenge. "I assume you mean the Zurich Matisse, the Chagall I sniffed out in Berlin, and, of course, the Kirchner nude I stumbled on through my colleagues in Paris. You really must have the Kirchner. That will be the hard one, you realize, squirreling it out of Moscow. Yet I never cease to be amazed at the power of the almighty American dollar over the Russians if you stack up enough of them on the table, which I will be obliged to do, no doubt.

"And the Picasso?" Wolff asked.

"No, not the Picasso. Just the three. The Picasso's too rich for my blood. I'm not made of almighty American dollars, you know. I mean, a million here, a million there . . ."

"And it could run into real money," Wolff offered dryly. "I know, I know. It could take a while, assuming the pictures are still available. They may be gone by now—you should have told me sooner." The director scratched a few figures on a pad and said, "The price for the three, including all the necessary gratuities, will be this," he said, pushing the pad across the glass desktop to Mendelssohn.

"Eight point three? Gimme a break, for God's sake! Your first number was *seven* point three. You know that. *Was ist* with you Nazis?" Mendelssohn bellowed.

"These are inflationary times, Arthur. Prices rise. *Das ist was ist,*" Wolff said coolly. "And remember, my friend, were you to acquire these lovely pieces at auction—which you could never do, of course—you'd part with at least twice this amount, maybe three times," he lied. "Such are the unique benefits of access to my cozy little brotherhood. So stop sniveling and show some gratitude, Arthur."

"Damn it, Erich . . ." the chairman whimpered. After an appropriate silence to allow his indignation to sink in, he said, "Okay. Do it. But don't screw it up. I want those pictures."

The director nodded, closing the deal. The extra million over his first figure was for Arthur's insult.

Mendelssohn took perverse pleasure in mocking the director's heritage. As a Jew, the chairman convinced himself that God had charged him personally with bedeviling the director for his past, for the sins of his ancestors, and for his carelessly concealed anti-Semitism. Mendelssohn fulfilled Yahweh's directive in basic schoolyard fashion, lacking the wit to mount a more biting and thus more entertaining assault.

Wolff hated this supercilious ass, and he tolerated him only as the means to his own end. His solace lay in knowing that he would bring down the overbearing swine in total disgrace at the moment of his choosing.

The director finally pushed back in the sweetness of the leather, seventeen million gross in paintings safely beneath him in the belly of the jet, eight point five of which would be his take, including Arthur Mendelssohn's self-inflicted bonus. Beyond the chairman's three pieces, several others for more civilized clients in Miami and Las Vegas rounded out the lot. It had been a good trip. He could sleep.

CHAPTER SEVEN

"*Fertig!*" Done. The gnomish man in the wire-framed spectacles lifted the rubber stamp with a grand gesture from the back of the canvas. It left in the lower right corner a small ring of India ink surrounding the unmistakable symbol of the Reich.

The frail academic held the stamp up for the uniformed Nazi officer standing over him to see. "Did you know that this mark came from the Sanskrit symbol for luck, Otto?" He stared silently at the raised rubber swastika for a moment, and then he continued in a wry tone, "And it will be good luck indeed if these pictures ever make it past the border. But, it's done nonetheless, Herr Lieutenant. Every blessed piece has been listed in the journal and stamped on the back—Property of the Third Reich, ja? These lovely pictures are ready now to be gift-wrapped for the Fuehrer and shipped off to the great Kunstmuseum in his demented brain."

"Be careful what you say, Ernst. You never know who might be listening, including me," Otto Wolff warned as he turned away to light a cigarette, explicitly forbidden in the tinderbox setting.

"You would never turn me in. I know too much. And be careful with that cigarette," Schmidt countered. "We don't want these lovely pieces to go up in flames before the Americans can steal them back, do we?"

They were in the main gallery of the Jeu de Paume, the little jewel of Paris museums used by the Nazis to store the overflow from the Louvre where stolen works were being warehoused in huge numbers. The art historian, Ernst Schmidt, had just completed cataloging the famed Gruenwald collection. Only in the final weeks of the Occupation had the family's elusive treasures been sniffed out by Goering's hounds and hustled off to the museum for expediting to the Fatherland, just steps ahead of the Allied forces driving from the west.

Long before, David and Anna Gruenwald had spirited away some five-hundred priceless paintings, sculptures and pieces of jewelry from their Paris apartment at 51 rue de La Boétie and their chateau on the edge of the Fontainebleau forest and secured them, or so they thought, in the cellars of Gruenwald's cousin Paul's winery in the south. The damp caves were not the best of hiding places for priceless masterpieces, but the best they could come up with on short notice. The old man and his wife were scooped up by the Nazis as they tried to board a vessel at Le Havre bound for Southhampton, and they paid for their tight lips over the collection's whereabouts in the ovens of their captors. A word from the mouth of a perfidious family servant to Otto Wolff's ear led to the discovery among the oak barrels and dusty bottles and to the capture of the elderly couple. Wolff himself had led the baying pack.

"Herr Schmidt, do I detect a note of cynicism?" Wolff said. "Surely you have not lost the faith? I myself am confident that the Reich's destiny is assured, thanks to the invincibility of our omnipotent Wehrmacht and the certainty that God is on our side," he continued, a wry smile on his face.

"Good grief, Otto, it's over! Why must we continue with this ridiculous charade?" the waspish professor snapped, failing to find the irony in Wolff's acid response. "We must be the last Germans in Paris." On orders from Berlin, Germany's preeminent art historian had stayed behind with Wolff to complete their mutual exercise in futility. As they worked feverishly, most of their comrades had already fled to the east, leaving a decimated Occupation force under the command of the new kommandant, General Dietrich von Choltitz.

"I look at this magnificent Hals," Schmidt continued, "and I grieve over what could happen to it. This painting will never see a single sunrise in Linz, of course, or any of the others. I want to take this poor mother and child home with me. They need love, Otto."

"If you're serious, Ernst, you know you can't do that, even now. Not this one, not any of them. Nor can I, tempting as it may be. Now turn these saucy wenches over to the packers. There's a truck coming tonight to take the last of the crates to the railyard.

"When are you leaving, Ernst? Are you going to Berlin, or will you be going back to Munich?"

"I'm leaving tonight, if I can find a train still running. I'll go to Munich, or whatever will be left of it. My mother is still there, and still alive, God willing. And I have a sister who lives with her. There is nothing for me to do until the Linz project gets underway." Ernst reddened as he realized the absurdness of his statement. Then he said with a smirk, "The Fuehrer has promised me a curator position there."

"Well, then, *Wiedersehen, guter Freund. Danke,*" Wolff said, taking Schmidt's hand in both of his own. Wolff's affection for his former teacher at the Academy was genuine and prompted the Nazi officer to insist on a first-name relationship between the two, a rare gesture in the culture of the Reich. His sentiment was also way out of character for a human being whose persona seldom warmed above freezing and whose conduct was uncompromisingly ruthless. He respected the scholar's knowledge and his passion for the great works; their bond was far stronger than his with Goering, whose passion for the Masters lay mostly in the acquiring of their fruits. Wolff also could feel Schmidt's pain over the uncertain fate of these delicious specimens, unaccustomed as he was to empathy. He wanted to assure his old mentor that they would be in secure hands.

He couldn't.

"Wiedersehen," Schmidt said, suddenly pulling his jacket around him as if he had gotten a chill, although July sizzled in the streets and made this stifling room in which they worked nearly unbearable. He left Wolff alone among the crates and canvases to be packed before nightfall. The Nazi officer silently reprimanded himself for his softness toward Schmidt, knowing that if his plan failed he would be obliged to implicate the gentle historian in the dastardly act, and it would not go well for him.

The black, unmarked Mercedes lorry crept into the Aubervilliers yard and rolled toward the arc-lighted area where a handful of khaki-clad soldiers, uniforms soaked with sweat, sat on empty freight wagons or leaned against loading equipment, smoking and talking. Aside from the insects that swarmed about the lights, all unnecessary motion had been suspended in the oppressive heat. The silhouettes of huge natural gas storage tanks loomed ominously behind the railcars, threatening total immolation of the entire trainload of priceless art in the event of an explosion.

An officer stepped from behind the idle work crew and approached the lorry which had come to a stop beside the last open car. Steam hissed from the locomotive up the track, indicating pressure enough to drag the last of Hitler's booty east once the rusty steel door slammed shut.

Otto Wolff stepped down from the cab and walked toward the black uniform. Maurice Gernand, the Parisian gallery owner, struggled down from the driver's side, unaccustomed to his teamster's role, and joined Wolff.

"Heil Hitler! the officer barked, saluting Wolff in the customary manner. "Lieutenant Wolff?"

"I am Wolff," he said, his return salute conspicuous by its absence. It was too late in the game and much too hot for Nazi bullshit, and he still had a very long night ahead. He made no effort to introduce Gernand, who earlier had stretched the baggy, gray coveralls of one of his gallery grunts over his corpulent frame in an attempt at disguise. "I presume you're ready to load? I still have much to do this evening and would like to get on with it," Wolff said.

"Ja, we have only your crates, and we can then seal the car," the officer said. "As you can see, the train is ready to move out. I am Captain Lesser." Wolff nodded imperceptibly. Although Lesser outranked Wolff, the lieutenant's relationship with Goering and with the Fuehrer was widely known and always met with deference, rank aside. Lesser's only desire at that point was to get this business over with as fast as possible and get the hell out of that yard and out of Paris—not coincidentally, Wolff's sentiment as well. He would overlook Wolff's insubordination.

"Captain, let us begin. You and I will check each crate against the bill of lading as they are placed in the car. There are twenty-five. When your men are finished, you and I will sign the bill and you will return one copy to your superior officer. I will keep the others," Wolff said. He walked to the back of the lorry, unbolted the doors and swung them open. He and Gernand stood aside as the soldiers trudged to the truck, none too pleased to be moving even their own bodies, let alone the heavy crates in the van. Wolff took his position with Lesser next to the open railcar, and together they checked off the crates one by one, noting the large stenciled marking on the sides, as the testy recruits, most of them in their teens, lifted them onto the bed. Gernand stayed with the truck, directing Lesser's crew on the handling of the crates and the order of offloading.

Otto Wolff had met with Gernand hours earlier at the dock of the Jeu de Paume when they had engaged in a similar task of transferring the twenty-five crates onto the dealer's lorry. Wolff instructed the museum's maintenance staff meticulously on the precise placement of the wooden boxes in the darkened vehicle, guiding them only by the light of a dim torch-lamp. "Last to first," he shouted—"Crates L-20 to L-25 furthest back, by the canvas. I'll tell you where. *Macht schnell!* Get to it!"

"*Bon Dieu,* it's hot in here, and I can hardly see! Why so picky with these crates?" one of the workers groused. "They're only going up to the east yard, is what I heard. Who the hell cares what order they're in."

"Who knows why these *Arschlöcher* do what they do," another answered. They had all picked up bits and pieces of the Occupational vernacular, most of it vulgar, including the oft-used word for one's bodily egress. "Just keep your mouth shut and do it, ja?"

"You know where these crates are headed, don't you? Berlin, what'll be left of it. To Petain's pal, Hitler. These are *our* pictures, you know. I've seen them stacked inside, thousands of them. He's taking them for 'safekeeping,' so they say. Safekeeping, would you believe!" another overalled Frenchman said under his breath, out of earshot of the Nazi officer.

Finally the last box was skidded into place, and Gernand slammed the rear doors and bolted them shut. He and Wolff climbed into the cab and the dealer steered the lorry slowly out of the dark access drive behind the once pristine Jeu de Paume, now little more than a discount brothel offering up forbidden master-pieces cheap to Nazi big shots with a lust for art.

Gernand turned onto Rue de Rivoli, then zigzagged seven or eight blocks north into the fashionable 8th arrondissement and entered the narrow alley behind rue de La Boétie. They came to a stop at the rear entrance of number 31, the address of the Gernand Gallery and, coincidentally, only a few doors from the recently vacated apartment of David and Anna Gruenwald, who had recently and quite strangely gone missing. It was where Gernand's staff always parked the lorry when they were not using it, and where any activity on their part would not draw a second glance from the neighbors or a cruising gendarme.

The two left the cab, opened the lorry again and climbed up inside, Gernand sweating like a ditch-digger, Wolff cool as an iced-down bottle of Mosel reisling. Torches in hand, they squeezed forward through a tight space between the crates that Wolff had prearranged in loading—no easy task for Gernand, whose thirty years of gourmandizing on the gustatory pleasures of Paris had left him only a few kilos short of sumo class—to an angular mass of tarp-covered cargo separate from the rest, nearly invisible in the dim light. They stripped away the canvas, exposing six wooden crates identical to the last detail with those that faced them. By torchlight Wolff and Gernand jockeyed the concealed containers forward, slid those from the Jeu de Paume behind, and covered the museum crates with the tarp. Switch made, they returned to the cab and drove north to the nearly deserted railyard.

Wolff watched with hawk's eyes as the six crates were hoisted into the railcar. These were units L-20 through L-25, all carefully packed earlier by Maurice Gernand with pictures from his gallery, all works of debatable quality by largely anonymous painters and wholly unworthy of sharing a lift to Alt Aussee with those in the other crates. On the other hand, even the true masterpieces already onboard paled next to the ones under the canvas in the back of Gernand's lorry. These were the cream of the Gruenwald collection: forty-seven paintings of inestimable worth by masters known to every French schoolchild—paintings which would begin their separate journey east as soon as the railcar door clanged shut.

The gallery owner stood sentinel by the lorry as Wolff and the Nazi captain signed the papers and two of Lesser's crew pushed the big door closed. It would next be opened at the entrance to the labyrinthine Alt Aussee salt mines near Salzburg, Hitler's temporary repository for works of greatest value; here the paintings would stay until the Reich stood victorious.

Wolff himself swung the iron hasp over the u-shaped staple and slipped the heavy padlock through it. The snap of the lock echoed in the fat man's ear like the cocking of a revolver pressed against his temple, although he would hear only the clack of gold coins emptied onto the Italian marble countertop of his private bank in the Marais.

Maurice Gernand had distinguished himself for his dexterity in maintaining respectability as a prominent Paris art dealer in the sixteenth- and seventeenth-century masters while achieving like status as art procurer for the Nazi elite, a high wire act worthy of the great Karl Wallenda. His transactions with Hitler, Goering, Goebbels and other lesser lights of the Party had made him an art world legend—and a famously wealthy man. For most, the mere thought of screwing Goering and the Fuehrer would have struck terror in the innards. In some societies, filching from the master would have earned a severed hand, or maybe two; in the Reich, the penalty would be worse. But to the greedy Gernand, Wolff's proposition was irresistible and well worth the risk.

The trusted aide to the Reichsmarchall had convinced him to co-purloin a king's ransom in paintings which had been earmarked for the future Fuehrermuseum in Linz, Adolph Hitler's dream of dreams. Otto Wolff's premise had been that the Nazis were only days or, at most, weeks from defeat, and that should his and Gernand's betrayal be discovered it would be forever shrouded in the ensuing chaos. Hitler and the others would have more to deal with than a few old paintings. And with the tens of thousands of works which had been swiped by the Reich—not to mention the Fuehrer's Final Solution which will most surely create the Final Distraction—their forty-seven pictures will be mere flyshit in the pepper. In sum, the downside was miniscule, far outweighed by the potential reward.

Once the smoke had cleared, Wolff ordained, the two of them would simply sell off the pieces one by one for an astronomical return, although, he cautioned the dealer, that could take time. It all made perfect sense.

Gernand's flesh tingled with the click of the padlock. The fat was in the fire. Whose fat was open for debate.

It was past midnight when they left the railyard and headed the lorry southeast. Gernand drove as fast as he dared through the total blackness of the Fontainebleau, refreshed by the pine-scented breeze of the forest, and cautiously negotiated the narrow, twisting route toward Dijon. Gernand and Wolff traded off in two-hour shifts, each stealing fitful sleep between their turns at the wheel. Hardly a word was exchanged, as one or the other was asleep for almost the entire time. Fortunately the road was theirs alone; the fuel shortage and the threat of German roadblocks reduced most late-night traffic to the occasional local weaving home after an evening of excess. By sun-up, they had crossed the Saône and were pointed toward the Jura Mountains and Switzerland.

Wolff's uniform and papers, plus the letter from Hermann Goering, granting him the full access of the Reichsmarchall himself, insured little more than a grunt at the Swiss border. By ten Sunday morning they were rolling through the deserted streets of Geneva, the well-scrubbed city on that western tip of Switzerland which nudged rudely into France's midsection.

Two security guards awaited them at the rear entrance to the Geneva branch of the Bank of Zurich. Wolff presented his credentials as a long-standing customer of the institution, as was his father, Kurt Wolff, and the munitions empire he pledged to the service of the Reich. The massive steel door rolled up, and Gernand inched the black lorry inside.

Almost before Wolff and Gernand had pulled their weary bodies from the cab, workers appeared with loading equipment. With the gentle touch of ones who had performed this procedure countless times, they removed each crate from the lorry bed and staged them for placement in certain of the bank's oversized vaults designed precisely for such treasures.

"Guten Morgen, Herr Wolff," came a soft voice from behind the Nazi officer and the overalled fat man as they stood beside the lorry.

"Herr Grüber," Wolff answered without turning.

"And how was your journey?" André Grüber said, stepping around and extending his hand to greet them.

"Very long," Wolff said. "This is my colleague, Monsieur Gernand. This is Herr Grüber."

Wolff and Gernand each took Grüber's soft, banker's hand in turn. "I see you have entrusted precious cargo to my 'safekeeping'—isn't that how you say it, Herr Wolff?" the tall, graying managing director of the Geneva branch said with a crooked grin.

"Safekeeping, yes," Wolff said. "And it's fortunate indeed

that there are benevolent enterprises such as your own, and people with the wisdom of the Swiss, who are eager to protect such possessions from falling into unappreciative hands—for a modest fee, of course," he fired back.

"Well taken," Grüber said, acknowledging that their little duel of words had ended in a draw. "You must be hungry. Come inside—breakfast has been set in my suite." Gernand stripped off his grungy overalls and tossed them inside the cab of the lorry as they followed the banker to his posh domain.

Following a sumptuous Swiss repast of cheeses, meats, fresh-baked croissants with preserves of Alpine strawberries, and steaming coffee, Wolff and Gernand were once again ensconced in the cab of the empty lorry, headed west out of Geneva. In spite of the heat, the dealer had once again donned the dirty overalls to avoid recognition, he said, as if anyone might know him, or care. Gernand settled into the first shift of driving, relieved to be done with the last risky portion of their caper. Now, with an empty lorry, he could relax.

Wolff's right hand absentmindedly caressed the smooth leather holster at his side. His thoughts turned to the day the Fuehrer had presented him with the sleek black Luger snapped inside. It had been on the terrace of the Berghof, and he had just advised Hitler of a significant cache of German drawings and etchings which he and Goering had uncovered in a recent mission in the south of France.

Hitler was aglow from his intimate chat with Erich, who had come to Berchtesgaden with Wolff, once again at the Fuehrer's request. Wolff was both pleased and sickened by the leader's interest in his son. At monstrous cost, it could only advance his own stature in the Reich; objecting, he knew, could exact the ultimate price at the Eastern Front. It was a price he was loath to pay.

This, too, would pass, he told himself.

Hitler was overjoyed with Wolff's acquisitions. It was in this euphoric state that, with great flourish, he handed to Wolff this masterpiece of weaponry nestled in a red velvet-lined case of hand-rubbed walnut. The pistol's handle was carved from ivory, deeply incised with the Nazi swastika. The barrel was elaborately filigreed, bearing the inscription, *To Otto Wolff, loyal servant of the Third Reich, with my deepest gratitude, Adolph Hitler.*

Wolff had never carried a weapon, although he was an expert marksman in his youth. He had always believed that in his line of work, constantly at the Reichsmarschall's side and surrounded by bodyguards, he had little use for one. He also disliked the bulkiness at his waist and considered the pistol an uncomfortable nuisance.

The Fuehrer had drawn his own famous revolver from its holster. "This is my unfailing companion. It never leaves my side. It is the one friend I can rely on implicitly to do my bidding whenever called upon. You see I am surrounded by protectors, but are they really my protectors? *This* is my protector," Hitler declared, as in a rare gesture of trust he handed the tiny weapon to Otto, and then to the boy, to hold. Wolff remembered the ecstatic expression on his young son's face when his "Uncle Adolph" placed it in his palm.

From that moment, Otto Wolff was never without his so-called 'protector,' although the need for it had yet to present itself. In time, its bulk grew comfortable and, as with Hitler, gave him a profound sense of well-being.

Wolff and Gernand had driven one hundred kilometers or so northwest, retracing the path of the night before. They were still a distance from Dijon and had yet to break out of the mountains, but the driving would soon be easier. The plan was to enter

Paris after nightfall, park the lorry behind the gallery, and go their separate ways. Gernand slowed the lorry and pulled off to the side. It was nearing the end of his shift, and he had an urgent need to pass his considerable intake of breakfast coffee, which had kept him awake yet now severely tested his aging bladder.

The two stepped down from the cab, stretched, and looked out over the chasm beneath them. Gernand pulled off his borrowed overalls and stood imperiously in his tailored, if slightly wrinkled, cream-colored suit, Master of the Universe. As Wolff watched from behind, Gernand stepped forward to the precipice and unbuttoned his trousers.

"Magnificent view, Otto," he said as he waited patiently for the first resistant trickle.

"Indeed it is, Maurice," Wolff said. The sound of Gernand's increasing flow on the roadside gravel masked the soft snap as Wolff unfastened his holster, lifted the leather flap, slid the elegant Luger into his hand, and flipped off the safety. The deeply etched swastika felt good in his palm as his index finger closed over the trigger. Wolff stood less than a meter behind the fat man, whose hands were fully engaged beneath his protruding belly and whose mind was completely focused on his blessed relief. Had he seen the shadow beside him on the gravel, arm raised, his labored heart might have achieved on its own what was to come.

The crack of the pistol echoed across the chasm as a small black hole opened at the base of Gernand's skull. For reasons unknown, he continued to stand, motionless, like a tree in the forest which momentarily refuses to fall after being severed at its base. Miraculously he dribbled to the end and then toppled forward into space, his business complete.

Wolff calmly replaced the Luger in its holster, stood on the brink and relieved himself as well, respectfully directing the stream away from the path of Gernand's plunge. He could see the back of the dealer's vanilla jacket through the scrub pine thirty meters below and the bright red stain slowly spreading on the collar. As an afterthought, he slipped over his officer's uniform the overalls which Gernand had pitched on the passenger seat. He would not wish to be spotted in full regalia behind the gallery in the false dawn. Then he climbed up behind the wheel and started the engine.

It was his turn to drive.

CHAPTER EIGHT

Early next morning Otto Wolff called SS headquarters in Berchtesgaden from his small suite in the Grand Hotel. Although Goering stayed at the Ritz while in Paris, Le Grand was Wolff's favorite. He was seduced by its opulence, the splendid Café de la Paix on the ground floor which once catered to the likes of Maupassant and Zola, and the Opera across the street, still treating those who could pay to the delights of Mozart and Verdi in spite of the Occupation. He asked for Hermann Goering and was put through immediately.

"Herr Reichsmarschall, this is Wolff."

"Ja, Wolff. Is it done?"

"It is done, Herr Reichsmarschall. All pieces have been taken to the train at the Aubervilliers yard. I supervised the loading of the crates myself late last night and personally padlocked the railcar. I have the key."

"*Sehr gut*, Wolff. Is the train moving?"

"*Nein*, but it should be headed east by noon. I watched it pull out of the depot, but it's still sitting in the marshaling yard with about a dozen others waiting to be sent off—some French bullshit about not working Sundays, even though they know it's your private train, Herr Reichsmarschall. I can't find anyone to complain to. That is what I've been doing most of night," he lied.

"I'll be at the mine myself to oversee the unloading," Wolff said. "I've ordered that the railcar not be touched, and as the key is in my pocket, I don't expect a problem."

"You did your best," Goering said. "Now come to Berchtesgaden immediately, Wolff. The Fuehrer would like a full account of the tasty delicacies you'll be bringing him. God knows he could use some cheering up. You can go on to Salzburg from here." Wolff detected a caustic tone in his superior's voice; he knew that those "tasty delicacies" would stick in Goering's throat. The Reichsmarschall had made it clear when they came upon the Gruenwald paintings that he coveted them for himself, and had hinted that he would make it worthwhile to Wolff should he find a way to secretly whisk them off to his Carinhall estate. "What the Fuehrer doesn't know won't hurt him, ja?" he said, with a wink. And then, as quickly as he had uttered the remark, he retracted his proposition with an awkward laugh as he recalled Wolff's tightness with his boss, and as visions of a firing squad cleared his greed-clouded brain.

"Ja, Herr Reichsmarschall. I will leave for Munich now. But travel to the east has become difficult, as you know. The trains are jammed to the rafters with our loyal countrymen desperate to holiday in the bosom of the Fatherland, or anywhere but Paris for that matter. Please tell the beloved Fuehrer that I will be there as soon as I can."

"The beloved Fuehrer wishes you here *tomorrow*," Goering said. "Show the authorities my letter—you'll be given a first class compartment to yourself, or they will answer to me. I will send a car for you in Munich. Auf Wiedersehen, Wolff. *Gute Riese!*"

"Auf Wiedersehen, Herr Reichmarschall."

Otto Wolf replaced the receiver on the cradle. He had left out the most interesting part of his weekend. *Let that be a surprise,* he thought.

The City of Light was in short circuit mode. Paris was crackling like downed wires, a human current alternating between terror and euphoria. Broken messages received via the

Underground informed them that Liberation could be only days away. Still Parisians were near panic over what pain the Nazis might inflict as their parting gesture. Hitler was not a gracious loser. His episodes of blind rage were legend, this they knew from their German occupiers, and no horror he might visit on their city would be unexpected.

Privately the Fuehrer confessed that to see Paris had been "the dream of his life." Yet, during his only visit to the city he confided to an alarmed Albert Speer, his chief architect, that he had often thought of destroying Paris, but changed his mind after seeing it for himself; "There would be no need," he said, because next to his *new Berlin*, "Paris will be only a shadow." Still the question haunted jittery Parisians: Would he spare their city or crush it like Warsaw? Which would it be? Thumbs up, or thumbs down?

The resentment of the puppet government, chagrin that the Vichy leader Petain had been so eagerly embraced, disgust with collaborators who kissed Nazi asses to save their own, and the collective shame of an acquiescent people all told was an explosive mix in search of a spark. Liberation, plus the inevitable Christlike entry of Charles le Grand into the Holy City, would touch it off. Wolff wondered if the arrogant bastard would ride side-saddle through the ancient gate on the back of an ass, and if palm fronds would be waved.

Paris was no longer Paris. Wolff was glad to leave. The Germans had been trampling each other to get out, struggling with heavy trunks and suitcases, hailing in vain for taxis to Gare de l'Est to hop trains before the threatened strike, although the French were always striking or threatening to strike about one thing or another. They'd become a surly lot, and les résistants lurked around every corner itching for a clean shot at any unsuspecting uniform that might happen by. Goodbye, and good riddance.

Wolff surprised himself with how easily he had disposed of Gernand. But in a world of narrowing choices, he had none other; the fat man had to go before he could announce their scheme to the world at large. Gernand's excesses of the body were matched only by his chronic boasting. And if stealing from the Fuehrer were the subject, he and Gernand both would have been guaranteed a prolonged and painful end at the first whiff of their perfidy.

To his credit, the good lieutenant was not one to disavow his own greed; even had the vainglorious dealer been deaf, dumb and blind, Wolff had no intention of sharing a pfennig's worth of this heist with anyone if, or when, the paintings might safely be dribbled out of the vault. It could take years, a timeframe which would have far exceeded the limit of Gernand's patience. Even if their larcenous relationship had gone full-term, the offensive *Schweinhund* would only have wasted his share, Wolff rationalized. He had served his purpose.

Otto Wolff was, in fact, very good at rationalization. He had honed his talent for justifying every act that served to enhance his own wealth or position. He easily accepted the premise that every work plundered was the legitimate property of the Reich, and he had no qualms about his role. It was simply part of war: *To the victor* . . . He had no quarrel with the Jews; before the war, he had many friends who were Jews, and he would have more when this was behind him. They just happened to be in the wrong place at the wrong time. He did not agree with what was being done to them, but that was not his business.

Likewise, Otto Wolff held that the few paintings he took for himself were owed him, small payment for his invaluable service to the Reich. Fortunate for him that his father's loyalty to Hitler and to the Reich was never passed down; it would only have gotten in the way.

He played the event on the precipice over and over in his mind as the train huffed its way across the Champagne countryside toward Strasbourg and the Rhine. Maybe someday guilt would surface, but none pricked his conscience on this day. Kurt Wolff would have done it in the blink of an eye, he thought. Probably did in the old days. They all did. Like father, like son.

He wondered what would come of his father. With the defeat, he would be accused of monstrous acts which were, for the most part, true. His father could hang, or would spend the rest of his life in prison, what little of his flickering existence remained. They would strip him of every factory, every house, every possession, except for his accounts in the Bank of Zurich which the Allies could never trace, nor would the Swiss ever cough up.

Face facts: Kurt Wolff was a confirmed Hitler henchman. While he did not dispense death directly, he had done quite enough to be well up the "A" list for serious retribution. The great Wolff Works almost single-handedly stoked the fiery belly of the Ruhr, churning out tanks, artillery, small arms, ammunition and grenades for the Reich by the megaton. The production of gas Wolff left to others—for humanitarian reasons, he moralized.

Kurt Wolff's compassion did not extend to the humankind in his own industrial empire. The prodigious output of the Wolff Works throughout the war could be credited almost entirely to slaves by the hundreds of thousands. There were Russians and Poles commandeered from POW camps in the east, Jewish women from Auschwitz and Buchenwald, and the captive French, Italians and Slavs from Wolff's grizzly work camps near his factories, all driven till they died from disease, starvation, or a merciful bullet in the brain. If the Nazi industrialist hanged, it would be more for his role as slavemaster than for his death-dealing tools of war.

Otto Wolff concluded that the Allies, and history, would not be kind to Father.

He slept through most of the lush vineyards and gentle slopes of Lorraine. He was comatose as the train clattered over the Marne and the Moselle, and didn't stir when the train lurched to a stop in Nancy. Only as it approached the Old City of Strasbourg did he surface from the exhaustion of his long night of mischief.

Finally, as the train screeched out of the place called "the crossroads of Europe" on a line halfway between Paris and Prague and plunged into the cool, dark *Schwarzwald* on the friendly side of the Rhine, Wolff felt up to sorting out his own future. The mysterious Black Forest blurred past the window of his empty compartment, a fit metaphor for his state of mind as he considered his options.

The war would be done in six months' time; Paris would fall, the Allies would free the French and surge into Germany under full steam, and the Russians would annihilate Berlin from the east. It had already begun.

He would be captured, and they may try to tar him with the same brush as Goering, no common thug; he was larger than life in the dark world of the Third Reich, even more reprehensible to the Allies than Bormann, Himmler, Goebbels and any of their sadistic deputies, Mengele, for example. The Angel of Death. *My God, they'll go crazy over Josef Mengele.* The outrageous Goering would hang; himself, probably not. But he was not likely to get off scot-free either.

What Wolff figured he had going for him, with all respect to the good German Albert Einstein, was his own personal Theory of Relativity. As Wolff saw it, everything was relative, crime especially. If one didn't count Gernand—*you can't count what you can't find*—protecting art treasures from the ravages of war and from falling into the wrong hands, misguided as it might be perceived, could hardly compare with the horrors which will be laid at the feet of the Madman's inner circle. Surely his captors will see that.

But there was the Euripides Factor: The gods visit the sins of the fathers upon the children, or something like that. It was conceivable to Otto that the "gods," in his case, could choose to assign guilt simply by familial association with the notorious Kurt Wolff. Again fortunate for him, his connection with the Wolff Works was practically nil; he was, coincidentally, "the son," and his great passion was the meek and mundane world of art, not world conquest. Although he had worked for his father as a minion accountant before the war, he could never be held accountable for the massive role the Wolff industrial behemoth played in the Reich, he reasoned, or for the labor camps which fed the factories of the Wolff empire.

In the Grand Guignol of the Third Reich, Otto Wolff was merely a bit player, he concluded. And because he played his minor part mostly from the wings, he hoped that he would hardly be noticed. Yet he would surrender. That would give him some control, a principle he learned at Kurt Wolff's knee and during his fireside chats with the other "Wolf" at Berchtesgaden.

Lastly, he would drop his trump card—he'd played enough Skat in his life to know when he held the winning hand. In his diary, Otto Wolff had noted painstakingly his and Goering's every acquisition as well as the final destination of nearly every stolen painting, drawing, sculpture, antique, rare book and piece of jewelry that passed through their hands. This information would be priceless to the ones tracking down the spoils, and what was one obscure Nazi lieutenant in exchange? His captors would be ecstatic.

Only transactions with "certain dealers" he had failed to

note, expecting that they could someday be useful to him.

Conspicuous by their physical absence from his scrupulous accounting would also be forty-seven paintings from the missing Gruenwald collection. These images, titles and their creators he had committed to memory and could be traced only by a ten-digit number assigned by the Bank of Zurich, a number known only to Wolff and locked securely in his brain. No paper trail existed to the indulgent Swiss city on the lake or to the subterranean gnomes who shared his secret.

Otto Wolff was on a roll. He had settled on a viable strategy to save his own humble arsch, or at least most of it, maybe, and he was still a good hour-and-a-half out of Munich. This left time to rough out a plan for afterward.

He couldn't fathom a sentence of more than five years. That would put him at forty-one, with plenty of good years ahead. He allowed that there would be no Wolff Works to return to—that the factories would be managed by new "denazified" Germans who would have conveniently distanced themselves from the "evil Kurt Wolff." Most important, with the business stolen from his father in retribution, which he fully expected to happen, most of his inheritance would vaporize with it. In a rare moment of honesty, he admitted that this would simply be poetic justice, but no less devastating to himself. *C'est la vie. C'est comme ça,* he thought impulsively, deferring more to the philosophy of the French than to the language, although he privately preferred French to his own guttural native tongue. Such is life. That's the way it is.

Otto Wolff moved on. What would be left after the dust settled was not much. With his father's assets in Germany wiped out, they would have roughly twenty million Swiss between them in Zurich. And as Kurt Wolff would have little use for the money, rotting away in the keep, the entire stash would be his. But it would be hardly enough to keep him in the style to which he had become accustomed.

He would have to work. Or steal. Honest effort in the post-war world would never give him what he needed. Here his train of thought lost steam. Then, as if by divine intervention, his mind momentarily idle, fragments of *Das Rheingold* wormed their way into his head: *Lugt, Schwestern! Die Wekerin lacht in den Grund,* the opening strains of Richard Wagner's steamroller of a first opera in his monumental Ring Cycle—traces of the last performance he attended at Napoleon III's magnificent opera house across from Le Grand before all the messy business at the Jeu de Paume began. Rhine maidens surfaced in his mind like Neptune's naiads in a Rubens mural and gratuitously filled in the spaces of the opening libretto: *They greeted the Gold nestled in a rocky reef, glittering beneath the surface of the water, and in a moment of foolishness they shared its secret with the evil dwarf, Alberich—that it will give unbridled power to the one who will make a Ring from the shining metal.*

Thus Otto Wolff's Das Rheingold, *The Rhine Gold,* was conceived: The handful of influential art dealers he had spared in his incriminating diary suddenly materialized as his own glittering Ring of Gold. Like connect-the-dots they formed a circuit on his mental map. Berlin. Munich. Dusseldorf. Bremen. Vienna. Zurich. Geneva. Paris. Amsterdam. Brussels. Rome. New York. None could risk exposure of their Nazi ties, yet none could resist a steady diet of forbidden fruit. Buyers would salivate over the private possession of plundered masterworks, and they would pay huge sums for just a taste.

The bad news was that Wolff's 24-carat dealers became, at the moment of the Ring's conception, forever hostage to its power, hopelessly pinched between the jaws of blackmail and greed, and there would be no escape—all in all, a flawless scenario for Otto Wolff's ambitious scheme.

Wolff's share would be astronomical. The hazard of masterminding such a brazen undertaking would demand exorbitant commissions which his collaborators would gladly pay, no questions asked. Because thousands of works would remain beyond the reach of restitution, most of their locations known only to him, he could be assured of a lifetime supply. Otto Wolff was overcome with joy. His future was secure.

Now only the business of Erich remained.

Defeat would destroy him. The boy had inhaled every wisp of Reich propaganda, and he was outraged that others his age in the Hitler Youth were sacrificing themselves on the Eastern Front and that he was not among them. The Fuehrer himself had intervened to spare him, but his adolescent mind had failed to grasp the gesture. The misguided teen idolized the insane man with the Chaplin moustache—Wolff knew this from that day in Berchtesgaden when the nine-year-old had first cradled in his small, trembling palm Hitler's deadly little revolver. At fifteen, Erich was no less mesmerized by him. Unfortunately, Wolff had little chance to influence his son in the years when one's personal gods materialize, and the stepmother Klara, as fanatical as the boy, only fanned his obsession.

Now it was too late.

Still, he would go to Bremen when he had finished in Salzburg and try to explain to his young zealot what was going to happen, that his blessed Reich would be crushed, and that Hitler would soon be dead. He will not accept it, of course; in fact, Wolff questioned whether he would accept it even after the fact. But he would try to prepare the boy.

Wolff decided that when it was over, Erich would remain

with Klara in Bremen until he was ready for university. Then he would go to America to be educated, as most of Europe would still be rubble, Germany the worst of all. It would be no place for a bitter and disillusioned youth to begin his life as a man. While sanctuary with the enemy would have seemed far-fetched to most Germans, it made perfect sense to Otto Wolff. The Americans are a strange lot, he reasoned, and they would embrace his son as a victim, maybe even a celebrity, once the war was over. They're a naïve bunch; how quickly they forgive.

The familiar black Mercedes was parked at the curb as Wolff emerged from Munich station. Nazi flags fluttered from the front fenders, designating a person, or persons, of high rank within, and the young Wehrmacht driver stood ramrod-stiff at the rear passenger door. His crisp gray uniform reflected in the mirror finish of Goering's personal vehicle, the door emblazoned with a meticulous rendering of the Luftwaffe's Grand Cross. The insignia was identical to that on the hefty medal which hung round the neck of the Reichsmarschall during his every waking moment, and sometimes even as he slept, attested to by the loose-lipped ladies who shared his bed and occasionally bore its painful imprint on their flesh.

"Gunnar, it's nice to see you," Wolff said, recognizing his superior's apple-cheeked aide.

"Herr Wolff," the driver answered with clicking heels, opening the door as the lieutenant handed him his valise, slid into the rear compartment and settled into the soft leather luxury of Nazi royalty. Soon he would be sipping Pilsbier from a monogrammed glass with the Fuehrer and the corpulent Goering. And he would delight them—delight the Fuehrer, at least— with elaborate descriptions of masterpieces which neither of them would ever see.

As they twisted through the emerald Bavarian terrain and upwards toward the Berghof, Otto Wolff caught a glimpse of his own eyes in the driver's mirror. He did not recognize them.

CHAPTER NINE

Precisely at nine, Otto Wolff strode through the Great Room and approached Hitler's study. White stucco walls stretched between elaborately carved wainscoting and a high ceiling supported by massive oak beams. Rustic chandeliers hung from the rough-hewn crossbraces like wagon wheels. The cavernous marble fireplace at the rear of the room was offset by a huge, multi-paned picture window overlooking the mountains at the north end.

Gobelin tapestries on the east and west walls, which Hitler's chief architect and interior decorator, Albert Speer opined added "an air of nobility," completed the intimidating effect—not that a room full of priceless masterpieces required any further embellishment. Hitler had had the chalet completely done over in the mid-'30s, transforming the once-crude hunting lodge into an elegant backdrop for some of the finest objets d'art on the continent.

As often as he had been a guest here, Wolff was still awed by the breathtaking array of paintings the Fuehrer had assembled in this room and others in the Berghof. Hitler had surrounded himself with more than five hundred works which he selected personally *to lighten the enormous burden of world conquest,* Wolff assumed wryly. He paused before his favorite, Vermeer's *The Art of Painting,* and indulged his passion as he had so often before.

Wolff knew that Hitler had bought the painting legitimately for 1.65 million Reichsmarks from Jaromin Czernin, brother-in-law of the Austrian prime minister. But he also knew that the aristocratic Czernin family of Vienna had not wished to part with their precious masterpiece at any price, and that a special envoy had convinced them that it would not be in their best interests to deny the Supreme Commander. They later professed pride that Hitler was so taken with their most prized possession.

Muffled conversation broke his thoughts and he continued on toward its source. As Wolff neared the study, he felt oddly ill at ease without the now-familiar heft of the Luger on his hip; the cold steel of the Fuehrer's gift had become warmer in his hand as the war turned sour. Hitler's goons, as a precaution against a repeat of the recent attempt on his life in Rastenburg, had relieved him of it on arrival. *Just as well,* he thought; *there was no point in inviting temptation.*

He could see through the partly open door a fire blazing in the fireplace. Although it was early in August and very hot at the foot of the mountain, there was always an evening chill high up, and the warmth was welcome. Wolff knocked quietly, and a familiar voice invited him to enter.

His boots clicked on the highly waxed parquet as he pushed the door open further and stepped inside. The Fuehrer and Hermann Goering were seated in two of the three large wingback chairs near the fire. The third was for him. A richly woven Persian rug covered the wood floor in front of the fireplace. The room, like all the others in the lavish retreat, was a jewelbox of masterpieces, smaller but no less stunning, which adorned the walls between the high bookcases. An Albrecht Altdorfer landscape of Hitler's beloved Danube River valley hung over the fireplace, coincidentally a gift from the elder Wolff in appreciation for the Fuehrer's many "kindnesses."

"Wolff!" Hitler said cheerfully, rising to greet him. He was a strange man, Hitler, ever deferring to intellect and breeding—a manifestation, quite possibly, of some deep-seated feelings of inferiority in spite of his capacity for terrifying the living hell out of those around him. Goering nodded but did not rise, in deference to his own bulk.

"Mein Fuehrer," Wolff responded with a crisp salute. "Herr Reichsmarschall."

Hitler motioned for Wolff to take the third chair by the fire. As they both settled in, the Fuehrer said, "You will join us in a Pilsbier? You must be ready after your exhausting journey for some refreshment."

"Ja, mein Fuehrer, a Pils would be good. Danke," the lieutenant said. Hitler pressed a buzzer near his chair to summon an aide.

"So things are not going well in Paris?" Hitler said. "Please give me the bad news first. I promise not to execute the messenger," Hitler said with a thin laugh. The Fuehrer's tinny, high-pitched voice so prone to fury and arousal still chilled Wolff, even after many occasions in his presence which had never been especially threatening or unpleasant. Wolff smiled cautiously at the Nazi warlord's awkward attempt at gallows humor and then spoke.

"You know how I dislike giving you unhappy news, mein Fuehrer, but Paris is not good. I will be brief: The French have become difficult where they used to be accommodating, and, frankly, the city has become rather ugly for Germans there—those who are left, that is. Les résistants are plinking at us from rooftops and windows, and there doesn't seem to be much we can do to stop them.

"Petain's people tell me the enemy is pounding us hard in the west, and that they'll be in Paris soon," Wolff continued. "The constant stream of our own wounded from the front seems to bear this out. The Parisians expect to be 'liberated,' as they say, any day now, which seems to be firing them up. And who could have been kinder to them than we Germans, ja? The worst is that our own people are scurrying home like rats; my train to München was packed belly to back. No, things are pas très bien in Paris, I regret to say. I'd hope that your generals are telling you this, mein Fueh- rer." Goering let pass Wolff's brash inference about the truthful- ness of his subordinates, opting for a low profile in the face of the eruption sure to come.

Hitler sniffed at Wolff's casual use of the French and glared at him as his account unfolded. While he remained silent, he flushed noticeably and his predictable twitch signaled immi- nent rage as the lieutenant concluded his brief report on the sorry state of Hitler's once-admired Paris. And then the Fuehrer blew.

"My generals? My gutless generals? My cowardly, lily- livered generals? How could this happen? They tell me nothing! I will execute them myself with my own pistol, every last one of them! Where is von Choltitz, Wolff! Have you seen von Choltitz?" Hitler screeched, referring to the neophyte kommandant of Great- er Paris. "Where is his garrison? Are they hiding in the cellars like sniveling women, afraid to shoot a few drunken French? Or are they drunk themselves? Where is von Stülpnagel?" he screeched like a crazed eagle defending her nest, and his face turned the hue of fresh beets. Hitler hurled his half-empty Pilsner glass at the fireplace. Shards ricocheted off the stone lintel onto the rug and the amber brew hissed on the hot hearth. The panicked Wolff ached for his Luger with which to defend himself, having never witnessed one of Hitler's patented tantrums; he was certain that the Fuehrer's promise not to execute the messenger had been an empty one.

Just then the aide appeared at the door with three full Pil- sner glasses balanced on a tray. He entered without comment or alarm, placed the tray on the small table between Hitler and the

Reichsmarschall, and quickly exited the room. His interruption stilled the raving Hitler as he sat, arms folded tightly across his chest, his face fixed in a dark pout.

Goering broke the silence. "The illustrious general Stülpnagel has been detained, mein Fuehrer. You will remember his deplorable role at Rastenburg, along with former kommandant von Boineburg-Lengsfeld who is also our guest at SS headquarters. Stülpnagel has been replaced with General Kitzinger." Not without pleasure, which with some difficulty he kept from his face but not his tone, Goering reminded Hitler of the traitorous acts of his rivals in the failed attempt on his life on 20 July and, by inference, his own undying loyalty to the Fuehrer.

"Well, then, where is Kitzinger? Wolff, where is Kitzinger!" Hitler said, now only slightly subdued.

"General Kitzinger left Paris three days ago, mein Fuehrer, along with most of the permanent garrison. They followed a group of wounded returning home from the west. They are most likely here in the Fatherland by now. Only von Choltitz and a handful of men stayed to defend the city."

Hitler slumped in his chair. Wet wood whistled and popped in the fire as the three of them sat motionless in the hushed study. "I ordered von Choltitz to burn the city, you know. Speidel, too. I want every bridge brought down, every monument in ruins," Hitler finally said, his yellowed teeth clinched. "I ordered them."

Wolff was stunned. *What's the point,* he thought. *Why do this? Would von Choltitz have the balls to tell the Fuehrer to screw himself? Would Speidel? Spiedel would. Probably they would just not do it. Who would be there to make them do it? Both would be behind barbed wire, anyway, before the SS would catch up to them.*

None of them spoke as Hitler stared into the fireplace

for a very long time. Then, without warning, a tiny smile crossed the Fuehrer's lips and his eyes glowed hot like the coals which had dropped onto the hearth beneath the flaming ash wood. As if by some miracle the black squall passed, and the Fuehrer said, almost childlike, "Wolff, tell me about what you're bringing me from Paris. What have you chosen for our glorious new Fuehrer-museum?"

Goering sat unfazed as he sipped nonchalantly on the chilled, amber brew, its foam leaving a small, bubbly moustache on his colorless upper lip. Few over the years had tasted the Fuehrer's bizarre behavior more, or had better weathered the storms; but this mercurial shift dazed Otto Wolff, one of the many grotesque proclivities of the Fuehrer he had heard about but never sampled firsthand. Somehow he managed to recover well enough to recite the litany of masterworks that had come by way of the heralded Gruenwald collection, the last and maybe the best of the Reich's "liberation" of Jewish-owned works from France.

Hitler savored every word. His lips formed a lupine smile as Wolff lavishly described each painting nearly to the brush-stroke. Then, suddenly caught up in his own bewitchery, Wolff launched into a sanguine recital of the forty-seven paintings in crates L-20 through L-25, the selfsame works which now rested safely in the vaults of the Bank of Zurich.

He waxed eloquent on the several fine Hals paintings, the two Rembrandts, the Jan van Eyck, and particularly the Peter Paul Rubens which he explained was, being a modello, painted entirely by the master, untouched by his apprentices. He then expounded at length on the Cranach panels, the Hans Memling triptych, the magnificent Caravaggio, and finally, the seven transcendent Dürer drawings.

When Wolff was barely half through, panic surged

through him for his foolishness but he continued like a runaway train to the end, inspired by the rapturous transformation of the Fuehrer. Goering flushed with envy as Wolff named paintings for which he had once lusted but declined to pursue in deference to the Fuehrer, whom he knew would have craved the works for Linz.

"No Vermeers?" Hitler said playfully, almost in a girlish giggle, obviously overcome with his extreme good fortune.

"No Vermeers, mein Fuehrer," Wolff said. "But you already have three of his finest—*The Geographer, The Astronomer* and *The Art of Painting*, which I couldn't help but admire as I passed through the Great Room this evening." Hitler's pleasure calmed Wolff, and he realized that his imprudent disclosure was irrelevant; long before his daring heist should be discovered, if at all, Hitler would be ashes and the Reich would be rubble.

"You've done well, Wolff," Hitler said. "When will the pictures be in Salzburg?"

"The train should be moving east now, mein Fuehrer. The cars were loaded and sealed before I left Paris, and the train was waiting to be sent off by the yard dispatcher. I will telephone in the morning to verify its location," Wolff said. "When it arrives at Alt Aussee, I will personally supervise their transfer into the mines. They will be safe there until we have won the war and the Fuehrermuseum is ready to receive them."

"When can I see them?" Hitler said.

"They are very securely packed, mein Fuehrer. To remove them now from their crates could damage them severely. I would prefer that you see them first when they're installed at Linz. You will have much to look forward to!" Wolff said, as if the Supreme Commander were a six-year-old.

"Yes, you're right, Wolff, as usual," Hitler said. And then

he turned to Goering, aware that his pompous Number Two despised being upstaged and would require stroking. "You have done well, also, Reichsmarschall, and remain my loyal friend," he continued, acknowledging the bloated hedonist's role in the pursuit of the choice works and his mentoring of Wolff. "Loyalty is rare these days in the Reich, don't you agree, Herr Goering?" Otto flinched at Hitler's proclamation, and he prayed that neither man noticed.

"Ja, I agree, mein Fuehrer," Goering said. He saw no need to twist the dagger further into the corpses of Stauffenberg, Rommel and the rest. He had prevailed, they had failed and they paid in full.

"However, Reichsmarschall, I want you to look into Paris immediately. Find General Kitzinger and bring that spineless sewer rat to me. I will deal with him myself. Telephone von Choltitz and assess his situation, and remind him that Paris is to burn if worse comes to worst. To the ground! Mach schnell, Herr Goering!" Hitler snapped as he returned to intimidation mode.

Goering nodded. Hitler rose, the sign that the evening was over. Wolff saluted and left the room hastily, his Pilsbier and, thankfully, his skin, untouched.

"I'm very sorry, Herr Wolff. The train has not yet left the yard. There's the strike, you know, which began soon after your train left for Munich. And there seems to be a problem with the engine. The mechanics have worked all night. A part is needed and . . ."

"I don't want to hear it. That train must move out. I don't care about strikes, I don't care about parts—just get it done!" Wolff shouted into the phone at the Vichy dispatcher. "If the railworkers won't work, use the Wehrmacht. This is the Fuehrer's train, do I need to remind you of that?"

"No, Herr Wolff, but . . ."

"No buts—do it, and then telephone me the instant it leaves the yard. Do you know where I am? I am with the Fuehrer, in Berchtesgaden. Comprenez-vous?"

"Je comprends, Herr Wolff," the dispatcher said weakly.

Without closure, Wolff slammed down the receiver, expecting that Hitler's "house spy" who had been nosing about his room had heard the exchange and would report it to his paranoid superior as he did all conversations within earshot. *Güt!* Wolff thought. *If the train never makes it out of the yard it will be too soon. It will probably be captured before it moves an inch. Ah, the French! The train might as well be welded to the tracks.* He felt safer now. Schmidt's words rang in his ears: *"It's over, Otto."*

CHAPTER TEN

Otto Wolff hung about the Berghof with Goering for most of two weeks, haranguing the railyard in Paris and aiding Hermann Voss, the designated director of the imaginary Fuehrermuseum, arranging and rearranging phantom galleries on fantasy floor plans cobbled up by Hitler and Speer. As Voss was enscounced in the Linz project headquarters in Dresden, where it had been since the death of the original director, Hans Posse, in 1942, the task was virtually impossible. It was a mindless board game with no end and which nobody would win, and it was driving him insane.

Wolff had begun to feel like a hostage in a real-life *Alice in Wonderland,* with Hitler playing the Queen of Hearts. As the Allies drove on Paris, sending the Wehrmacht into frantic and humiliating retreat, Hitler raged into full-blown paranoia with a constant salvo of shrill attacks on any and all within screaming distance. As best he could, Wolff set himself well out of range. Combat was not in his job description, thus he saw no future in standing deliberately in the line of fire.

Yet he was close enough to the Fuehrer to see the wasting of the man. Hitler's walk had become unsteady and hunched, his hands shook constantly, his twitch became acute, and his delusional schemes for reversing the tide and the ordering about of imaginary battalions stupefied a High Command which had long been resigned to defeat. He was fast becoming the White Queen, believing, and insisting others believe, the impossible: *"Why sometimes I've believed as many as six impossible things before breakfast,"* she *said to Alice.* It was tragic misfortune that his generals had botched their chance to put him down at Rastenburg.

Wolff was not with Hitler when Paris fell. He had been released by Goering to visit with Klara, Erich and his father, whom he had not seen in more than a year; the Fuehrer had returned to his *Oberkommando der Wehrmacht* in a gloomy forest in East Prussia, by now restored from the shambles rendered by the deadly attaché case that had nearly blown him to kingdom come a month before. Wolff was relieved not to have been there in the *Wolfsshanze,* the Wolf's Lair, when Jacques LeClerc's Armored Division waltzed into the City of Light on 25 August, overcoming only token resistance from von Choltitz and a few defenders— a diaphanous show of opposition staged mostly for an audience of one at supreme headquarters. History would not miss Wolff's absence from the Rastenburg bunker when an hysterical Hitler howled the deathless words, *"Brennt Paris?"* Is Paris burning?

Paris was not burning. When LeClerc reclaimed the city, not one bridge or monument had been destroyed except the Grand Palais which had been blown up by the Germans two days earlier. While most of the important structures had been mined in anticipation of the order, the explosives were never touched off. The defiance of the Fuehrer's spiteful directive by the compassionate von Choltitz was responsible for saving the great city for the ages. Wolff's beloved Opera House had been spared, and his luxurious suite at Le Grand remained intact.

No one from headquarters contacted him about Paris. What little he learned came from Hamburg radio. In a predictable understatement the announcer dismissed the so-called Liberation as premature and assured listeners that a dramatic military reversal was already in play. What Wolff knew was that Paris was a rout, the Wehrmacht was in shreds, and the Allied Forces would soon be blasting their way through to the Fatherland like *scheise* through a goose.

He spent time with his father who, in spite of his age and failing health, continued to rule the family business with an iron fist. Since Greta, Otto's mother, died, Kurt Wolff had obsessed over the output of his factories and spent almost every waking hour behind his desk or patrolling the facilities like a Doberman off the leash.

Otto joined the fragile chairman on his reconnaissance of the Panzer factory, where work had seriously slowed from earlier days despite the threats being barked nonstop by supervisors up and down the line. Thousands of walking corpses from the camps struggled to keep up, and many dropped at their workstations. They were dragged out to God-knows-where and "treated," Wolff presumed. The father, always cold and unapproachable, had grown even more distant. His eyes were sad, and bitterness dripped from every word. Otto knew that his father would last only a short time in prison if, in fact, he slipped the rope.

Seeing Klara was no joy for Wolff. But then he had not expected passion at his homecoming. She was possessed by the war and blind to the facts. The Fuehrer was the Almighty in her myopic eyes; she refused to accept any outcome but glorious victory and was certain that the tide would soon turn. Klara's sole criticism of Adolph Hitler was for sparing her hated stepson the horror of the Eastern Front. All the other boys were going. *It was his duty to die for the Fatherland.*

She reveled also in ridiculing Otto's *fancy* job *following Goering around with a broom and shovel,* as she put it, and made no effort to hide her disdain that he was not commanding a tank division or otherwise putting himself in harm's way.

Klara was not his reason for returning to Bremen.

Several days had passed since Hamburg radio had

broadcast its two terse sentences on the fall of Paris. As they'd
announced nothing about the condition of the city, he had reason
to hope that Hitler's ranting about wanton destruction had not
filtered through to von Choltitz, or that the novice kommandant
had flown in the face of the Fuehrer. If the latter were true, he fancied that when the smoke cleared the Parisians would dedicate a
boulevard, at least, to this unlikely hero of the French.

All but one of the lines between Bremen and Paris had
been cut, and Wolff had no idea of the fate of the train bearing
the final shipment from the Jeu de Paume to Alt Ausse. When last
he called, the disabled locomotive and its load was still hung up
in the Aubervilliers yard for lack of the elusive part, *probably a
six-franc bolt which could be bought from any local quincaillerie*, he
thought. He was considering still another attempt to reach the pathetic little toad in charge when the telephone rang.

"This is Wolff."

"Herr Wolff, this is Renaud at the Aubervilliers yard."

"Yes, Renaud, I was about to call. Where is my train?" he
pushed.

"Herr Wolff, I have very bad news for you, I'm afraid."

"Well, what is it? Give it to me, please."

"I'm sorry to tell you that the French forces have captured
your train, Herr Wolff. It was only a small number who came, but
there was no one here to defend it. They have broken open all the
cars and are now removing your crates. Some they have already
opened. I can see them from my tower. I don't know where they
are taking them or I would tell you. I'm afraid there was nothing
I could do, Herr Wolff."

"Nothing? You could do nothing to safeguard the property of the Fuehrer? He will be outraged, Renaud! You *should* be
afraid. I would watch my back if I were you. Maybe you should

make yourself scarce for a time, ja?" Wolff said. He couldn't resist twisting it a bit. He despised the collaborators as much as les résistants hated them; better to die fighting than live with the shame. But this rodent would have no shame. They never do.

"Mais, oui, Herr Wolff. I will make myself scarce, as you say. I am sorry, Herr Wolff." The line went dead. He would be calling his wife to begin packing their valises.

Herr Wolff wasn't sorry. He was ecstatic. The biggest risk had been the heist itself—the momentum of the war would favor him now. With the train in French hands, his darkest fears vanished; as the saying goes, the Fuehrer "will never know what he's missing."

Because the chances were slim to none that what he and Gernand had done would ever be discovered in the coming chaos, Otto Wolff was in the clear. Now only a few telephone calls stood between him and his destiny.

"Philippe, this is Wolff. You are well?"

"Otto! How good to hear your voice! Yes, I am well, merci."

Phillipe Moulin, Zurich's most prominent art dealer, knew Wolff's voice as well as any in his own family. The two had a long and lucrative relationship dealing mostly in the modern works which the Reich had declared "degenerate" but sold willingly or traded for those on the Fuehrer's "approved" list. He continued, "I hope you are safely out of Paris. I'm sure you know . . ."

"Yes, I know. It's very sad. I'm in Bremen with my family. But I may be called back at any time to Berlin, or Berchtesgaden, or Rastenburg, or wherever the Reichsmarschall might need me."

"I'm pleased that you are safe, Otto. To what might I attribute the honor of your call? How may I help you?"

"Philippe, what I'm about to say to you must be held in

strictest confidence. If you were to tell anyone, both of us could be in grave danger. Are you alone?" Wolff said.

"Yes, I am alone. And of course, Otto, anything you tell me I would never disclose. Not even to my own wife. But it sounds very serious. And why would I be in danger?" Alarm bells clanged in his head and he struggled to stay calm.

"Relax, Phillipe. It will only be serious and dangerous if what I tell you falls into the wrong hands. Otherwise, it can be an opportunity like you could never imagine. Can I trust you, my good friend?"

"Otto, you should not have to ask that question."

"Then listen carefully, Philippe. It's no secret except maybe to the Fuehrer and to my misguided son and Klara that this whole mess will be soon done with. My guess is sometime in the spring. With Paris gone, the Allies should make short work of us in the west, and the Russians coming the other way will sleep soundly in Berlin before the Fuehrer's next birthday."

"I can't dispute that, Otto. You would know better than I," Moulin said.

"While I've tried to remain above the fray," Wolff continued, "I don't expect that I'll be free to come and go for a while. Maybe only for a few years. But at the end of that time, here's what I intend to do."

"Bravo, Otto! A plan! I love a good plan. Tell me more," the dealer said, the alarm fading.

"I know we've done a great deal of business together, Philippe. In fact, looking at the records I've kept, I . . ."

"Records?" Moulin said.

"Of course, records, Philippe. I have detailed records of every transaction, a tedious habit I picked up from my father. Every painting, every drawing, every sculpture. Everything. That's not important to you, only to my plan. Let me continue," Otto said.

But it was important to Philippe Moulin. Panic shot through him, his intestines roiled, and he thought for a moment that he might soil himself, but he said nothing.

"When I'm free, whenever that may be, I want us to continue to work together. This time we work for ourselves, ja? Because of my excellent *records*—he emphasized the word for maximum effect—I know where there are thousands of wonderful pieces that can be dealt. And in spite of the, ah, sensitive, provenances of most of them, there are many people in Europe and in the United States who would pay huge sums to add one or two of these verboten bonbons to their sweets jar. Do you understand?"

"I understand, Otto. And now I see how this could be dangerous, for both of us," Moulin said.

"Dangerous only if our little venture should become public, Philippe. We wouldn't want that to happen, now would we, mon ami?"

"Most certainly not, Otto. It would never come from me, I can assure you!"

"Gut. Now," Wolff continued, "I believe I can extract favorable treatment from the Allies if I disclose the locations of pieces that my colleagues so unkindly appropriated from the unfortunate French. But if you and I have sealed the arrangement I've proposed, our past transactions—and transgressions," he chuckled softly— "would remain our little secret.

"There you have it. Naturally, there are other exemplary houses such as your own—in Berlin, Vienna, Paris, New York and so on—whom I'm certain will join our little circle, and we can all become famously rich together, don't you think? May I count on you, Philippe?"

Philippe Moulin was stunned. Wolff wanted an answer

now, and if it were not an affirmative one, his business, his life, was essentially over. The devil had come calling and made him an offer of Faustian proportions. *But at least Faust had a choice,* he thought. He had none.

And having none, he quickly concluded, he donned his most ingratiating gallery persona, even smiling into the telephone receiver. "Otto, I am deeply honored that you have selected me for your venture. You may count on me to be your most enthusiastic participant. Please keep me advised as to when we can expect to activate your most exciting plan."

Philippe Moulin was elated once the idea sank in. The risk quickly paled next to a quick calculation of his serendipitous new wealth. Had he not accepted Wolff's proposition, or if he had not been called at all, poor Moulin might one day have been sharing a cell with his caller.

This was Philippe Moulin's lucky day.

"I am pleased, Philippe. Yes, I will stay in touch. Incidentally, I'm calling our new enterprise Das Rheingold, the gold of the Rhine. Isn't that a good name? I expect there will be plenty of gold to share, ja? Auf wiedersehen, Philippe."

"A good name, yes. Das Rheingold," he repeated. "Au revoir, Otto." As he replaced the receiver, Philippe Moulin broke out in a cold sweat.

In the span of two days, Otto Wolff had corralled some of the most unscrupulous art profiteers in Europe and America for his clandestine "golden ring." Das Rheingold would open for business with a star-studded stable of dealers and auction houses revered by the bourgeoisie for their virtue and erudition, known among the cognoscenti as rogues of the highest order, and later fingered as major beneficiaries of Hitler's great art sweep of WWII. Within forty-eight hours, Wolff could count within his fold an even dozen of such larcenous luminaries in Amsterdam, Paris, Nice, Brussels, Berlin, Hamburg, Düsseldorf, Vienna, Zurich, Geneva, New York City and, ironically, Washington, D.C. *If the Americans can bivouac in the town square of Bremen, I shall occupy the Rose Garden of the White House,* he smiled to himself.

This left the final task of his return to Bremen, and the toughest.

It was Erich he had come to see. He would try to convince him of the futility of this war. And he would have to brace the boy for Hitler's demise, probably by his own hand. Wolff feared that the truth would only fan the flames and leave his young son forever branded with the evil mark of the Reich. Wolff had to smile at the irony: that he, who, without conscience, had put a deadly round in another man's brain only days before and wrested priceless treasures from defenseless Jews should be concerned for the morality of his own offspring was absurd. Yet, as men do, he yearned for a son free of sin, as different from himself as humanly possible.

Deep down, he knew that Erich was lost. At fifteen, his code would be cast in stone, and there would be little Wolff could do to change that. He blamed himself for not shaping the twig when it was supple and green, knowing that Klara only twisted it grotesquely when he was not there, which was most of the time. Now the odds against his having any currency with his son were astronomical given the boy's closeness to the Fuehrer, his grandfather's unseemly role in the war, and his stepmother's strident yammering about the Glory of the Reich.

Klara von Koch had been a huge mistake. His father had forced him to marry her after Erich's birth to Hilda Meyer. "To give the boy a proper mother," he said. The callow Otto Wolff had worked up a passion for the family's young housemaid, barely sixteen and dazzled by the dashing scion of the Wolff dynasty, and in a single, lustful moment they had conceived a child. This infuriated Kurt Wolff, and he banished the girl from his house once the child, whom they named Erich, was born.

Although Otto and Hilda had strong feelings for each other, the elder Wolff could not abide her low station in any role other than servant. And she was a Jew. This he could suffer in an otherwise able domestic, but it was the worst kind of poison in the mother of his own flesh and blood. It was bad enough that his first and only grandson innocently shared her detestable genes; her emergence as a bona fide in-law would shatter his status with the Fuehrer and the Party and leave him humiliated.

The Baron Friedrich von Koch claimed royalty through some convoluted pedigree which he could never quite diagram to Otto's satisfaction. His father-in-law's title, Wolff was sure, had been purchased, a practice not uncommon among the rich. But that mattered little—what did matter was his controlling interest in Koch Chemical works.

As chief scientist, he led the team that cooked up Omega Z, a cyanide crystalline compound which if not handled "responsibly" would deal instant death to any living creature that ingested its toxic fumes. As chairman he oversaw its manufacture and delivery to the camps of one Rudolph Hess "for the purpose of fumigating and disinfecting only," the Baron later insisted at trial.

Von Koch and Kurt Wolff had been close since 1916 when, as young German officers, they had fought side by side in the disastrous Battle of the Somme. Their battalion was crushed under the treads of Britain's new weapon, the tank, a grisly nightmare which drove Wolff's later obsession with the production of the devastating Panzer in his flagship factory in Bremen.

Klara, von Koch's only daughter, shared her father's hatred of all non-Aryans and his devotion to the Fuehrer. Humorless, unattractive and domineering, she was, in a word, unmarriageable. Not in a hundred years would Otto Wolff of his own free will have chosen this woman as a life partner. Only the intimidation of his father, plus the social embarrassment of fathering a child out of wedlock, had led to his meek surrender—a tragic display of weakness which he regretted from their loveless, and lifeless, wedding night. While Klara's acid rhetoric only drove them further apart, her vile influence over her hated, half-breed stepchild was insurmountable.

Wolff knew that if he expected to neutralize the venom which coursed through the boy's veins, he might as well have stayed in Berchtesgaden. If he could simply soften the blow of what was to come, and pave the way for any kind of bond between them, he would call the effort wildly successful.

In a rare moment together away from Klara, he and Erich stood in the formal garden behind the family's Weser Renaissance-style townhouse which fronted on the historic Böttcherstrasse, a block from the Marktplatz. Otto, Klara and the boy had settled into the early seventeenth-century structure when Kurt took a smaller place closer to the company's headquarters after Otto's mother died. Otto was the fifth generation of Wolffs to occupy the grand old mansion and Erich the sixth.

The gardener, Heinz, busied himself watering the old-fashioned roses which clung to a trellis near the back of the garden's high, moss-covered brick wall. Heinz had been a family retainer for more than thirty years, first for his father and now for Otto; the garden was his life. The old man struggled this summer against the blistering heat and lack of rain. Weeds had gained the upper hand, and the usually lush explosion of color had fizzled since spring. The withered garden showed the signs of impending defeat, *like the Reich*, Otto thought.

He could hear Klara shrieking from the kitchen as she turned up the heat under the cook. It was in this unsettling ambience, hotter than hell, with the devil's own mistress howling in the background, that Otto Wolff spoke.

"I know you're angry about not being at the front, but you're just a boy, Erich."

"I'm old enough to fight, father. I've been trained to fight! And all my friends are there!"

"You're fifteen years old, for God's sake. You're a boy."

But when Otto looked at him, he could see that Erich was no longer a boy. He stood nearly as tall as Otto himself, and his body was thick and hard with the sinew of his training. His Nordic blond hair and ice blue eyes labeled him as pure Aryan like himself, traits which would have been clear to the Fuehrer even as a small boy standing ramrod straight on the veranda of the Berghof.

"It doesn't matter how old I am. I can fight."

"Why do you think the Fuehrer kept you back?"

"Because he believes I'm not fit to fight. That should be obvious!"

"No, he kept you back because he knew you'd be killed. They're all being killed on the Russian front. Your friends are being slaughtered like lambs in a butcher shop. They're coming home in pieces, at least the pieces they can find. The Fuehrer cares about you, that's why you're not there. And I'm grateful to him for that."

"Mother wants me to go. She cares about the Fatherland. And she's ashamed that you're not fighting. Why don't you have a command, father? Won't the Fuehrer give you a command?"

"I go where the Fuehrer sends me. I'm not trained for the military. I'm trained to do what I'm doing."

"You mean stealing art for Goering? How will that win the war?"

It was a fair question. Otto Wolff fell silent, allowing the sting to pass, fighting the urge to defend himself, knowing there was no defense.

Only the wrangling of Klara and the cook penetrated the serenity of the garden. Wolff remained calm, and continued, ignoring the brutal question for which he had no answer.

"Erich, there's something that I must tell you."

"What?" Erich barked, his voice belligerent and his face crimson with anger, startlingly reminiscent of the Fuehrer's recent rages, Otto thought.

"Erich, the war is over. We have lost. You know that Paris is no longer ours, and the Allies are blazing through us like wildfire through dry brush. They'll be in this garden soon."

"That's not true! The Fuehrer is driving them back. We will soon be back in Paris, and in Stalingrad, too. He said so on the radio, and mother says that our victory is just a matter of time. And I could help, if only I could go to the front!"

"Erich, I know what's coming. I'm there, remember? I'm with the High Command every day. Not one general believes we have a prayer of surviving. Even the great Rommel was part of the plot to assassinate the Fuehrer, to stop the killing! Only Hitler thinks we have any chance. *Only Hitler.* In six months the Russians will be in Berlin, and that will be that."

"You're lying! I know you're lying!"

Otto restrained himself from striking the boy. Instead, he said in a soft voice, "No, Erich, I'm telling you the truth. And I will also tell you that the Fuehrer talks constantly about his own death—to me, to Goering, to Himmler, to anyone who will listen. He is planning to kill himself, probably when the Chancellery falls, or sooner. He actually believes that his death will somehow cause the Reich to rise from the ashes, and that he will rise also, 'like Jesus Christ,' he says, to lead again. He has gone completely insane, son, and it's frightening to be near him.

"I know how you feel about him. It appears that I can't change that—I simply want you to be prepared for what is about to happen."

Erich turned pale. Wolff's words had stopped him as sure as a Russian shell in the center of his chest. As shock set in, screaming broke the silence once more as the screen door from the kitchen to the garden slapped open against the brick and Fräulein Mueller clomped down the wooden steps and stalked toward the gate. Otto's eyes turned to see Klara framed triumphant in the doorway, arms akimbo.

"There's one last thing you should know," Wolff said, his gaze still trained absently on the kitchen. "Your grandfather Wolff will probably go to prison for a very long time, and he may not survive. You know how frail he's become. Von Koch will certainly join him; they're equally culpable, I should think." He did not mention that Kurt Wolff and the Baron both could share the gallows with Goering, Himmler and the rest, choosing to spare the boy any further trauma. Not that his son held any affection for either man.

"I expect to be sent away, too, but only for a few years, if I'm lucky. You and your mother should be safe, though. Please don't worry—you'll be taken care of while I'm gone."

When Wolff looked again at his son, he saw that tears had streaked the cheeks of the naïve youth who would stand defenseless against the Great Russian Bear. Without a word, the boy turned away and half-walked, half-ran toward the woman in the door.

CHAPTER ELEVEN

Otto Wolff was surprised to find himself among the High Command on such an occasion. It was 20 April, 1945, and Goering had summoned him to the Fuehrerbunker beneath the Chancellery for the celebration of the Supreme Commander's fifty-sixth birthday. Hitler had asked for him personally, which at this point in the war—and given the Fuehrer's present state of mind—Wolff considered a debatable honor at best.

It had been eight months since he was in Bremen, and his chances for returning home now were slim to none. The British were poised outside both Bremen and Hamburg. Escape from Berlin in most any direction had been cut off. For Wolff, travel to the west would be met with one of two outcomes—surrender, or suicide by enemy fire.

Neither seemed attractive at the moment, so he chose to sip his Dom Pérignon and not think about it. Rather he forced himself to view history in the making, rising above it all in a kind of out-of-body experience and, like a battlefield photographer, taking pains to record the event meticulously in his mind's eye.

He found himself upstage in a drama so taut it could be plucked like the strings of a mandolin. Amidst the false good cheer and empty tributes, giants maneuvered, quietly clustering and re-clustering, pairing off and then changing partners. Hitler seemed not to notice, or care, that no one chose him in this hushed dance macabre.

The pig-eyed Goering, grunting unintelligibly, crammed his puffy face with the Viennese pastries that were Hitler's favorite. The commander in chief of the Luftwaffe, which had been all but destroyed, still flaunted the Grand Cross on his chest as a message to the others that he, like the flaky delicacies he consumed, was also the Fuehrer's favorite.

Himmler hovered ominously. Completely in character in black dress attire, the devious SS chief sent chills through Wolff as he squinted through his pince-nez eyeglasses, ever plotting the Reich's next atrocity. His broad, guileless smile masked a soul as dark as the sleeve of his Gestapo uniform. Wolff wondered how one of God's own could become a Heinrich Himmler, a monster's monster with not a single redeeming virtue. A sip of champagne purged the thought.

The oily Goebbels sidled up to the Fuehrer and whispered into his ear as if whatever he had to say still mattered, nodding occasionally toward various muffled couplings. The swaggering, dwarfish propagandist with the crippled foot was neurotic beyond saving; *he would be a scorpion to the end*, Wolff thought, *as it was his nature*.

Only Martin Bormann, Hitler's right arm, stood apart from the rest. Perhaps the most sinister and conniving of the unholy assembly, the Party Secretary seemed to hear the Russian artillery beyond earshot of the others. Wolff could see the wheels turning, the eyes darting as if searching frantically for the way out.

The rogue's gallery of the Reich was complete with the Fuehrer himself. Wolff would remember him as jovial that day, but physically shattered. His hands shook violently, he dragged his right leg behind him, and his eyes appeared haunted by defeat. Like Bormann, he could hear the cannons.

The rest in this diabolical tableau would be remembered by history as somewhat more life-sized: Ribbentrop, Keitel, Doenitz, Krebs, last of the military chiefs of staff, and Jodl, who would sign the surrender papers in a little red schoolhouse in Reims two weeks hence, although they would later share the dock at Nuremberg with the big fellows. All, of course, would be reunited in hell.

Despite their differences, on one point they all agreed. The Fuehrer could no longer stay in Berlin. Singly and in groups they tried to persuade him to flee south where a narrow escape path remained clear to Berchtesgaden. They failed. The delusional Supreme Commander would make his last stand twenty meters beneath the Chancellery. The rest could go. Only Goebbels, Bormann and the air force chief, Karl Kollar, chose to stay behind; the others slipped into the night, Otto Wolff being one, and none would see the Fuehrer again.

For no reason, Wolff was the last to leave. As he turned toward the door, Hitler called out. "Wolff, I have something for you," he said.

Otto Wolff turned toward the Fuehrer who held out to him what appeared to be a child's toy pistol, and then he recognized it. "I want you to take this to young Erich. I'll always remember the look on his face when I let him hold it in his hands a number of years ago. Do you remember, Wolff—down at the Berghof, on the terrace?" *No, Otto Wolff would never forget.* "He couldn't have been more than nine or ten. Take it to him. I will have no more use of it, and I have no son to give it to."

In his trembling hand Adolph Hitler gripped his tiny Smith & Wesson revolver, the legendary pistol which all knew had been his companion since the early days of his rise to power. The weapon he had fired into the ceiling of the beer-hall during the famous Putsch of 1923, the firearm he would often place on the conference table as a not-so-subtle reminder of who was in charge. The Fuehrer slid the revolver into its worn, oil-stained leather holster, snapped the flap closed over the grip and handed it to Wolff.

For a moment Otto Wolff could not speak, in spite of his contempt for the giver. This was the magical effect the man could have on a person, even one who knew his every perversion. Then Wolff dutifully responded, "Mein Fuehrer, I am deeply honored. Erich will be overjoyed. Thank you, mein Fuehrer." He nearly choked on the words, which only served to increase his own self-loathing.

"Auf Wiedersehen, Wolff."

"Auf Wiedersehen, mein Fuehrer," Wolff said. He clicked his heels, turned and left Hitler's bunker for the last time. The revolver felt like ice in his hand, even through the leather of its holster. It was a sensation he could not explain.

Against all odds, Wolff snaked his way through the rubble and around the roadblocks to Bremen. He really had nowhere else to go; his chances of being obliterated in Berlin by a Russian shell were no less than being captured or gunned down by the Americans on the road north, but at least he would be doing something, not cowering underground like an animal.

Once outside the city he purchased a full ensemble of threadbare civilian clothes from an opportunistic Berliner for three packs of cigarettes, the last of Wolff's tobacco; he would just have to tough it out until he made it home, was shot, or died of nicotine withdrawal. The clothes were large enough to fit over his uniform, a layering which gave him much-needed warmth at night for the few hours he slept, mostly in ravines and barns or under bridges. During the day he hitched rides on civilian trucks with those Germans lucky or crafty enough to come upon the necessary fuel, or he boarded stray German troop carriers loaded with sick and injured comrades struggling to make it home from the Russian front. Once he stole a motorcycle from a barn and bucked it nearly a hundred miles before the tank ran dry.

In darkness he crept past Brit sentries at the Bremen city gate, slipping through the narrow passageways of childhood to his house. Erich answered his father's soft knock which he heard only because of his insomnia, a regular night visitor since Otto's jolting revelation months ago. The two talked until sunrise as Klara slept.

Wolff noted that his son had softened toward him. Klara's delusions had finally peaked, and, as the boy was bright enough, harsh reality had ultimately won out over her fantasies. He had accepted the coming defeat, the likely fate of his grandfather and stepgrandfather, and Otto's own probable incarceration. Erich had also come to terms with his own absence from the front: if the Fuehrer wanted it that way, who was he to question it. And as he thought about it, he concluded that returning from the front in small pieces was not his glass of pils. He would just as soon be alive as dead. Alive to fight another day.

To Otto's pleasure, Erich seemed no longer offended by Wolff's own passive role in the war—maybe it wasn't so bad to be tangential to the High Command. None of them drove the Panzers or flew the Messerschmitts either. They sent boys like him to do the dying. In the months since Otto's last visit, Erich had become pragmatic and hard. It wasn't normal in a fifteen-year-old boy, Wolff thought, but it was better than before. At least now he could be reasoned with.

What had not changed was his son's flinty devotion to the Fuehrer. If anything, it had stiffened. This disturbed him, yet he was certain that Erich's fixation would fade as childhood fascinations do. On the whole, he believed there remained a chance for the two of them. There would have to be if Das Rheingold were to endure.

Near the end of this most intimate exchange they had had since the war began, certainly their first as "man to man," Wolff reached into his valise and withdrew the saddle-leather holster and the pocket pistol given to him by Adolph Hitler in the bunker less than a week before. He laid the encased revolver on the kitchen table between them.

"Before I left, the Fuehrer gave this to me for you. He remembered how taken you were with it years ago at the Berghof. He said that as he had no son to pass it on to, he wanted you to have it."

The gangly man-child stared at the holster in disbelief. "My God, Father, that's the Fuehrer's revolver!" he said. "He wore it everywhere. It's the most famous pistol in the world. He wanted *me* to have it?"

"Yes, it's yours," Wolff said.

Erich reached out and touched the worn leather of the holster. He took it in his hand and ran his fingers over it like it was a living thing. Then he unsnapped the holster, slid the revolver out of its sheath and gripped it lightly, almost tenderly. "My God," he murmured.

My God, Wolff thought. He knew it had been a terrible mistake the instant he laid the precious artifact on the table between them. Unlike some Roman Catholics he had known who were convinced of the divine power of their icons, he had never believed that an inanimate object could embody either good or evil. Yet if it were possible, this pistol was most certainly the essence of the latter; the fire in his son's eyes was living proof. His expression was otherworldly, and it sent a shiver through Otto Wolff's body.

Klara broke the spell as she strode into the kitchen at first light. "You are here," she said in half-surprise, half-resentment, her face cast in stone.

"I am here," Wolff responded coolly.

Without the slightest gesture of affection, she said, "It's not good in Berlin."

"No, not good. We celebrated the Fuehrer's birthday in the bunker five days ago, and then everyone bailed out except for Bormann and Goebbels. Oh, and Kollar, too. Jodl may also be there still, but I'm not really sure. The Reichsmarschall had no further need for me and told me to go home if I could. He went to Berchtesgaden with a truck full of paintings and tapestries from Carinhall. The road south was still open, but it's probably in Russian hands by now.

"The Fuehrer refused to leave. He plans to stick it out in the bunker. Eva's there with him, of course. The Goebbels and their children will stay, according to Magda. 'What would life be in the Fatherland without the Fuehrer anyway,' she said."

"And how is it with you? Did you have a good trip?" Klara said with a twinge of sarcasm.

Wolff had to laugh. "If you call hiding in ditches, sleeping in barns and hitching rides on trucks filled with dying Wehrmacht soldiers a good trip, yes, I suppose it was good. I'm here, alive, which is a feat in itself."

Erich was impressed with what he saw as his father's first genuine act of bravery, and to a lesser extent that he risked his life to come home to him. He knew that it wasn't for Klara.

"What are you going to do now?" she said.

"Wait."

"Wait for what?"

"Wait for the surrender and hope that the British don't find me before I find them."

"Will they come for you?"

"Of course they will come for me. I was close to Goering. Other than Hitler, he's the biggest prize. They'll want to know what I know, and I know a great deal. I know too much."

"You will turn yourself in?"

"It's my only chance. I must control *something*. I think they may go easier on me if I cooperate. I don't expect that it will be as easy for my father. Or yours." Wolff had little patience left for sensitivity, least of all to spare Klara's feelings.

"My father?"

"Of course, your father. What do you think your father is cooking in those plants of his?"

"He's cooking, as you say, *chemicals*—chemicals for fumigating buildings and for killing lice. That's what he's cooking. How is that a crime? It's not like making guns and tanks and hand grenades."

Wolff laughed, nearly to tears, and then he turned brutal. "Your father's making chemicals to kill Jews. Beautiful blue cyanide crystals that make the gas to kill hundreds of thousands of Jews at Buchenwald and Auchwitz. Men. Women. Old people. Small children. Babies. That's what your father's making. I believe that will be seen as a crime most heinous, Klara, don't you think?"

Fire rose in Klara's face and her eyes became knives. She ran him through with her glare, turned sharply and stomped out of the kitchen, slamming the door behind her.

Minutes later she opened the door, still in a rage, and said, "Bormann called, and he sounded angry. He wanted you to call as soon as you got here."

"Bormann? What else did he say?"

"That's all he said."

"When did he call?"

"Two days ago," Klara barked, and exited the kitchen once more.

Otto Wolff had no idea what he might have done to prompt the Fuehrer's secretary to call him, particularly in anger. When he left the Chancellery it was at Hitler's urging, and Goering had released him without malice to return home. The end was near, and it was every man for himself.

Still, he reached for the telephone and, through a single line which had miraculously remained open, was put through to Berlin.

"Herr Reichsminister, this is Wolff," he said in his most servile tone. He had no intention of provoking Bormann in spite of the hopelessness of the situation and his disdain for the man.

"Wolff, the Fuehrer needs you here immediately."

"Why would the Fuehrer need *me*, Herr Bormann? I'm not important to him. He told me to go home only a few days ago, and the Reichsmarschall agreed."

"Your cherished Reichsmarschall is in custody, Wolff."

"The Americans have captured him, Herr Bormann? Are they in Berchtesgaden?"

"Nein. Not the Americans. Herr Goering is being detained by the SS for high treason. He attempted to take over the Reich three days ago. I'm sure you knew this. You are close to him, ja?"

"I knew *nothing* about this, Herr Reichsminister! I arrived in Bremen only a few hours ago. I'm astounded that the Allies did not capture me on the way. I don't see how I can help you."

"If you are not in Berlin in two days, Wolff, we will send someone for you. Two days! If you were not involved, you have nothing to fear."

"I'm *not* involved, Herr Reichsminister, I can assure you. Herr Goering will tell you that. I'll try to come, but I must tell you that all the roads between here and Berlin are in Allied hands, and no trains have run for weeks," Wolff said.

"Two days." The line went dead.

Wolff would later discover that Goering had wired the Fuehrer from Berchtesgaden on 23 April with an ultimatum: Should the Supreme Commander not acknowledge his demand to assume leadership of the Reich according to an earlier decree from Hitler himself, he, Goering, would take command all the same. He gave as his reason the inability of the Fuehrer to direct the defense of the Fatherland, isolated as he was beneath the Chancellery and without his High Command in tow. When Hitler failed to charge Goering, Bormann, on his own, ordered the Reichsmarschall arrested and held, the Fuehrer no longer of a mind to order, or veto, much of anything.

Otto Wolff had no intention of trying to return to the Chancellery. Even if by some miracle he could make it back, there was no reason to expose himself to Bormann's witch-hunt, should there even be a Chancellery, or a Bormann, left standing by then. He would stick with his plan; he would better cast his lot with the British than with that viper in Berlin.

He doubted whether Bormann would be able to arrest him anyway. No SS entourage could possibly make it this far from Berchtesgaden without being captured or killed, and there was no one left in Bremen to do the job; they had all fled at the first clap of Allied cannons from the west.

Still he knew that timing was important. He would wait out the two days Bormann had given him and stay close to Hamburg radio, which was now his only source of information on the war. Bremen had already been occupied by British troops, but none had come near his house. Apparently his and his father's efforts at anonymity over the years had paid off. Or they simply had bigger fish to fry. Yet it was only a matter of time.

Otto Wolff waited the two days and then two days more. There were no more calls from Berlin. Radio reports grew increasingly bleak with repeated accounts of ground given on both fronts, and city after city, town after town falling to one army or another. The announcers had by now abandoned any semblance of deceit; the Reich was being squeezed like a painful abscess by the British and the Americans from the west and the Russians from the east. Soon it would burst, making an end to it. He lost all sense of time as he stared at the Grundig, straining to hear any scrap of news through the heavy static. Then on the evening of 1 May, as he half-dozed to the depressing strains of a Bruckner symphony, the news came.

"Our Fuehrer, the brave and beloved Adolph Hitler, fighting to the last breath against Bolshevism, fell for Germany this afternoon in his operational headquarters in the Reich Chancellery. On 30 April the Fuehrer appointed Grand Admiral Doenitz his successor. The Grand Admiral now speaks to the German people."

So. Doenitz, Wolff thought. *Was there no longer a navy to command? What did it matter? It was over.* He listened as the Grand Admiral droned praise for the deceased, spewed empty words about "saving Germany from destruction by the advancing Bolshevik enemy," and ended with consolation no doubt conveyed from the Almighty's mouth to the Admiral's ear: "God will not forsake us after so much suffering and sacrifice."

It was almost a year later that he became privy to the bizarre chronicle of those last days and nights in the bunker. He was not surprised by the first-hand account of violent wrangling, accusations and toothless edicts interspersed with stretches of heavy gloom and drunken stupor; of eleventh-hour palace intrigue among the remaining few; of the odd union of Eva and the Fuehrer in the early morning hours of 29 April; of the cultlike murders of the six beautiful Goebbels children by lethal injection, ordered by their fanatical father with the cold sanction of Magda, the mother; the self-ordained deaths of the two of them from bullets to the back of the head, and the botched burning of their bodies.

It was Franz Haber, Wolff's cellmate, who regaled him with the details. Haber relished the telling and retelling of the events to all who would listen, and it was a story which always drew an audience. A junior aide to Goebbels, the young SS officer shared a cell with Wolff for complicity in some of the Reichsminister's more rapacious escapades and was an eye-witness to the final hours, or so he said.

Haber claimed to have observed the suicides of Joseph and Magda Goebbels in the Chancellery garden and to have helped douse them in gasoline before the Reichsminister's adjutant touched a match to their bodies. He held that the Russian bombardment was so intense that the faithful few were forced to scurry back to the bunker like alley rats shortly after the fire was set. As the Russians reported finding the partly charred remains the next day, Haber could only conclude that an exploding bomb had extinguished the blaze. "I can assure you that the fire was roaring when we left," he said defensively, lest anyone take the torchers to task for dereliction of duty. Later it was revealed that a shortage of fuel was to blame for the partial cremations.

But as much as this hellish tale seemed to excite Haber, he reserved his greatest narrative gifts for the grand denouement of one of history's grisliest dramas—the fiery end of the Fuehrer and his docile wife of barely thirty-six hours. In the hushed tones of one telling ghost stories round a campfire, he continued.

"The Fuehrer and Frau Hitler took each of our hands outside the Fuehrer's chambers," Haber said. "They smiled and seemed calm. Then they went into his quarters, and he closed the door behind them. I waited with Dr. Goebbels and Reichsminister Bormann and some others in the passageway. A few minutes later we heard a single gunshot. We expected a second, so we held back. None came, so several of us went into the Fuehrer's rooms and we found them."

It was obvious to Wolff that Haber had rehearsed carefully, knowing that he would have many opportunities to dazzle listeners with "the telling" for years to come. He wanted to get it exactly right for posterity, not to mention wring out every delicious drop from the bloody event. Although he, like Wolff, was an educated man, he was not above lavishing over a tale as historically monumental as this; in fairness, Wolff was not sure that he might not have lavished the telling also, had he been there himself.

"The room smelled of gunpowder and bitter almonds," Haber continued. "They were both on the sofa, dead as doornails. The Fuehrer had shot himself in the mouth—the bullet took out a piece of his skull and there were blood and brains spattered on the ceiling. The sofa was soaked, too.

"Frau Hitler had taken poison. I think Hitler did, too, the way his body was twisted in agony. That's something, isn't it—a gun *and* poison? He wasn't taking any chances," Haber laughed. "It was cyanide they took; I know that because I smelled it many times on my trips to the camps with the Reichsminister. Besides, they all carried their little blue capsules. 'Not as bad as torture,' they said. Anyhow, both their pistols lay on the floor at their feet—his gold-plated Walther that you probably remember, Herr Wolff, and a revolver—but Frau Hitler had not used hers; I could tell because there was no blood on her, other than what there was from the Fuehrer.

"The Fuehrer played music before they died. His gramophone was still spinning, but the record had come to the end and the needle arm was clicking. It was a recording of *Götterdämmerung*. Wagner. Have you heard it? It's about . . ."

"Yes, I've heard it," Wolff said. "And I know what it's about."

"Well, anyway, the bunker was deathly still." He whispered *deathly still* for theatrical effect. "All we could hear were the sounds of Russian artillery and shells falling in the gardens up above. Each time one exploded the walls would shake, the hanging lights would swing side to side, and dust and pieces of plaster would come down. We simply stared at the sofa. No one spoke, as if anyone could speak at a time like that. Finally Bormann raised his arm toward the bodies and we joined in a salute. *Heil Hitler!* we said, in unison, and that was that." Haber paused.

"That was that? What do you mean, 'That was that'? You didn't just walk away," Wolff said.

Haber was far from done. He was merely taking a brief intermission before the final scene and giving Wolff a moment to catch his bated breath. "There's more," he continued.

"I and some others wrapped the two of them in gray Wehrmacht blankets and carried them up the four flights to the gardens. They weren't very heavy. You've been up and down those steps a few times, Herr Wolff, ja?"

Wolff nodded.

"When we opened the door to the outside, the smoke and dust from the bombardment were so thick we could barely see the rubble a few feet away. We placed the bodies in a shallow crater and soaked them in gasoline from maybe a dozen cans which we carried up from below. The blankets were soaked through, and the gasoline pooled all around them.

"Although shells were still screaming into the Chancellery grounds at about three or four a minute, we barely heard them or the roar of the artillery just a few streets away. Goebbels himself struck the match and flipped it directly on the Fuehrer's body. The flame whooshed up, and almost set us all afire, too." Haber made a sweeping gesture and his pupils enlarged—out of genuine arousal, Wolff was convinced. "We stood back and watched as the flames began to consume the two of them. We raised our arms one last time as the flames shot high into the sky and black smoke billowed out of the pit. Then we walked slowly to the entrance to the bunker, oblivious to the incoming fire."

Haber fell silent, obviously shaken by his own narrative which was part show, part catharsis. Wolff's darker side urged applause, but mockery did not suit the moment. Only images of the Fuehrer emerged from the flames in his mind's eye. In spite of the unimaginable horror the Supreme Warlord had visited on Europe and the world, and his own indifference to all that Adolph Hitler and the Nazi party espoused, Wolff found it impossible to stifle a brief pang of empathy; Hitler could do that to a man, even in death.

Haber was good, Wolff gave him that: the terrifying Wagnerian motif had been seared into his memory—Siegfried and Brünhilde joined in death and transfiguration on the blazing pyre; Valhalla gone up in smoke; the world released from the curse of the Golden Ring.

Being there could not have been more real.

CHAPTER TWELVE

Rain beating on the skylight breached the silence of the lab as Pieter and Angela reeled from their discovery. After a disoriented few seconds, the stunned conservator managed to push open the darkroom door and switch off the Vidicom. The phantom swastika vanished from the screen.

"I'm assuming that the other three have the same mark on the back," he said, "and that there's no reason to haul them down here. Frankly, I'd rather not raise any more dust, with Nichter watching us like we were a couple of taggers with spray cans."

"Suits me," she said. "With Wolff back any day and Bergdorf on the prowl, there's no need to paint targets on our backs.

"So now what?"

"Well, first, I'm going to get this picture back upstairs and then stay the hell out of that room for a while. It's as hot as a cannister of plutonium. So unless you want to read in bed by your own glow, you should stay out of it, too."

"I have no reason to be up there. I'm on the Matisse installation night and day for the next two weeks. But then what?"

"You mean, do we drop it, or keep at it?"

"Precisely."

"I'm surprised you even asked that. How could we possibly walk away now?" Pieter said.

"I could walk away in a heartbeat."

Angela and Pieter both stared at the picture in silence. Only the rain on the windows interrupted the quietude. Finally, she said with a shrug, "Oh, what the hell, we've come this far."

The rain had frozen over by morning. Half the staff was icebound, and with kiddie tours cancelled and casual visitors countable on the fingers of one hand, one could have shot a cannon down the first floor nave and not hit a solitary soul. The tomblike atmosphere suited Pieter fine as he stared blankly at a tasty Corot in midcleaning and pondered the night before.

He knew funny business like this happened in places like New York and Paris and London every so often. It just seemed improbable that it could happen at the Mendelssohn. Still, he had no intention of blundering blindly into the wood chipper. Until he knew more, bearding Wolff was out. God knows what he might do if he caught them nosing around.

Pieter's mind raced. *For thirty years Wolff's been here, and he's still an enigma. All we know about him is Harvard and the Fogg, and that was a long time ago. Before that, who knows? And since Harvard, there's only been the Mendelssohn. That's it.*

His thoughts gathered momentum. *The painting was a gimme. Whose it had been, where it came from, how it got here shouldn't be so tough, now that they were pretty sure it was a Hals. With the other three pieces, Wolff could be implicated in some serious* merda, *as Angela would say. A little discreet digging might unearth a few bones, and he thought he knew where to turn over the dirt. But where Wolff goes when he goes is anybody's guess.*

The digging part wasn't much of a plan, but it would do for now. That alone could take some time, working on the sneak. The hard part would come after the excavation, but they'd just have to deal with that if and when.

"I'm cooking tonight. Can you manage that?" Pieter said into the phone.

"You expect me to change all my plans just because you're cooking tonight?" Angela said.

"What plans?"

"Never mind what plans. Are we going to talk about last night?"

"Tonight. We'll talk tonight. Not over the phone, okay?"

"What's the problem?"

"I just don't think we should talk over the phone, that's all."

"Whoa, you are spooked, aren't you?"

"Spooked works for me. Tonight, okay?"

"What's for dinner, if you don't mind my asking? You can at least tell me *that* over the phone."

"Does it make a difference?"

"It might."

"Seven okay? I have to pick up a few things."

"Seven, sure."

Angela heard the click. No goodbye, no nothing. She continued to hold the phone to her ear, absentmindedly, until the handset began to beep, and then she replaced it on the cradle.

He had no idea how much she resented this whole business. She had become so wired over the Nazi thing she could barely think about her day job. It was tough enough pulling the Matisse together with almost no help, and dealing with this hare-brained expansion plan—not that expansion was necessarily a bad idea, it wasn't—but the *people*. Lord God, the people. They couldn't agree on the time of day, let alone how to leverage sixty mil into a real, honest-to-God museum expansion. She could do it by her Own Self—her first words as a toddler—if the rest of them would just butt out, but that wasn't going to happen. C'est comme ça.

And then there was Pieter. She had begun to have night-mares about that big oaf. Damn him! He doesn't say much, just goes around sticking his nose under other people's tents like a meddlesome camel. And now he's dragged her into this. But he was one helluva cook, she gave him that. And really nice to be with, when he wasn't so insufferable.

So she would go to Pieter's, put Matisse, the expansion, and the Nazis on hold, and spend the next couple of hours in gourmet heaven. *How good will that be?*

CHAPTER THIRTEEN

When Angela looked at her watch it was seven-twenty. She was due at Pieter's twenty minutes ago. *Well, that's just too bad,* she thought as she left the mess on her desk, blueprints and schematics scattered about the floor, color chips fanned out on her small conference table. She switched off the light and stepped out into the empty, darkened Great Hall.

As she walked to the side entrance which opened onto the staff parking lot, she detected in her periphery a smallish figure shuffling toward her, silhouetted by a lone, amber night-light that lent the aura of a dimly torchlit burial chamber to the cavernous atrium. She was only mildly startled, knowing that the security people patrolled the galleries routinely through the night. Yet, the pace of the furtive shape was hardly the determined gait of a nightwatchman. As the figure drew closer, she recognized him and cursed her lousy timing.

It was Bergdorf. *Now what the hell was he doing, skulking around in the dark at this hour?* Angie thought. *Was he waiting for her, timing his own departure to coincide with hers, or was he simply retiring for the evening to one of the mummy cases, the little one next to Pieter's, maybe?*

"Good evening, Miss Desjardin," he said. "Working late, I see."

"Good evening, Herr Bergdorf." *And it's Doctor Desjardin, you little weasel.* "Yes, the Matisse is a bear, but it's getting there. We'll open on time, but it'll be a three-ring circus till then, I'm afraid.

"You're burning the midnight oil, too," she said.

"I'm a night person."

That I believe, Angie thought.

"When the director's away, there's much more to do, you know," he continued.

When isn't the director away? And where might he be now? she thought. *And what's he doing, by the way? I never see any results from his little junkets. No new pieces, no decent exhibits. He may be out there dancing for dollars, but he sure as hell never sends any of them my way.*

"Will Herr Wolff be returning soon?" she asked. "I'm anxious to bring him up to speed on the installation." *Whoops. You idiot,* she chided herself. She knew what was coming next.

"You know you could review it with me, Miss Desjardin. The director has given me that responsibility in his absence, didn't he tell you that?"

"I know that, Herr Bergdorf. I believe I'm keeping you informed of the important things. It's just that the director has been gone so long that I was eager to show him how terrific it's going to be," she tap-danced, but no cigar.

"Why don't I drop in tomorrow and have you 'bring *me* up to speed,' as you say. Say, ten o'clock?"

"Yes, of course, Herr Bergdorf. That will be fine," she lied.

"Oh, and by the way, I understand that you and Dr. Maxfield have taken a special interest in the Dutch gallery. Is there something about which I should be concerned?"

Angela's heart pounded, and she hoped that Bergdorf didn't notice her deer-in-the-headlights reaction. It wasn't fear so much as surprise. She didn't like surprises, especially now, and especially from him. "The Dutch gallery, Herr Bergdorf?" she stalled, giving herself a few milliseconds to concoct a response that he might conceivably buy.

"Yes, the Dutch gallery. Certain pieces in particular, I believe. Is there anything I should know, Miss Desjardin?"

"Oh, no!" she laughed. "On the contrary, Herr Bergdorf! You know, every so often you have to take time to smell the roses, that's all. Even when you're busy, or maybe *particularly* when you're busy. Pieter—Dr. Maxfield—suddenly took notice of how remarkable the pieces are that Herr Wolff loaned to the museum many years ago, and he wanted me to look at them again. He said I needed a break from a horrible meeting I was in and insisted that I come up to the gallery with him. 'To remind us of why we went into this business in the first place,' was the way he put it. He was right. It did me good. They really are beautiful paintings." *God, how lame was that? I'm dead meat.*

Still, she plowed ahead. *In for a penny, in for a pound,* she thought. "Oh, by the way, Dr. Maxfield told me that a small piece had been broken off the frame of one of them. It was the Leyster, I think." She went on to explain what had happened, and that the frame had already been fixed and returned to the gallery.

Bergdorf looked at her for what seemed like two lifetimes, although only a few seconds had passed before he said, "I see. Well, thank you, Miss Desjardin. I'll be down in the morning. Good evening." Then he stepped around her, continued on through the Great Hall and vanished into the darkness. She heard no flapping of wings, thus eliminating one of her theories about his ancestry.

Angela paused long enough for her heart to restart, and then continued on to the parking lot. Although she'd hoped that Bergdorf bought her fiction about smelling the roses, she really didn't care. If it was no sale, so be it; she'd handle him when the time came. But she would prefer not having him on her case just now. Things were weird enough as it was.

For most sane drivers, it would have taken five or six minutes. But it was more like three minutes-thirty to Pieter's place with Angela at the stick of her hot little Audi TT. Red. Loud. Fast. Varoom! Like its driver.

She liked his condo. Small, but with a killer view of the city from his balcony. It was like looking down from the Goodyear blimp. Breathtaking. He had redone the kitchen with an island gas range that would turn Martha Stewart Kermit-green, a huge copper hood to catch the smoke and soaring flames from his dramatic culinary exploits, a pair of monster ovens, a commercial-grade stainless fridge, and a horde of French copper pots suspended from the beamed ceiling. *Serious cook space,* she thought. The rest of his place she didn't care about.

"Sorry I'm late," she said as Pieter opened the door. She gave him a peck on the cheek and stepped inside, stripped off her navy pea-jacket and hung it on the newel post of the steps leading up to the single loft-bedroom. "I really am sorry. Bergdorf nailed me just as I was leaving, and it was disconcerting, to say the least. I'll tell you all about it over dinner. So what cooks, Julia?" she said as she followed him into the kitchen.

"Nothing fancy," Pieter said. "Just a simple farfalle tossed with smoked salmon, sun-dried tomatoes, onions and a few ribbons of radicchio in a white wine and cream sauce. You'll like it."

"Ummmm, sounds good."

"It is good, if I do say so myself. And the salad's even better. Romaine and red lettuce with a sweet balsamic dressing which I make with maple syrup, incidentally, tossed with gorgonzola and sugared pecans. And . . ."

"Stop! No more! Just feed me," she said in a husky voice.

". . . and a modest pinot grigio to wash it all down, if I may finish."

"You're going to make some lucky girl a wonderful wife one day, Pieter."

"I'll take that as a compliment," he said as he tossed the hot pasta with freshly grated parmesan, poured the wine and held her chair.

"Bon appétit!

"Mes compliments au chef!"

"Merci," Pieter responded.

For a few untroubled moments, the savoring of still another gustatory triumph from Pieter Maxfield's magic kitchen had managed to push her encounter with Friedrich Bergdorf to the back burner. And when the event inevitably pushed back she took evasive action, fearful that it would upset the chef and ruin the evening. But by her third glass of pinot she felt sufficiently girded for whenever her host chose to broach the subject.

Pieter took a sip of his wine. "You like?" he said, nodding to the large pasta serving bowl between them, still partly filled with his tasty salmon and cream concoction.

"What's not to like? Please, sir, may I have some more?" Angela said, holding up her bowl.

"Yes, you may. Now tell me about Bergdorf," he said, shifting gears as smoothly as her hot little toy at the curb while he spooned up a generous second helping of pasta.

The time was now.

"I was trying to forget. I was afraid it would spoil this lovely meal," Angela said.

"Nothing spoils a meal for me. Can't you tell?" Pieter said as he patted his modestly-bulging belly.

"I don't know if I'm screwed, or what," she began. "He just came right out with it on why we had taken such an interest in the Dutch gallery. I thought I'd be sick right there. It had to have been that bastard, Nichter, who blabbed to him," Angela said. "I thought you said he was a very sweet guy. Those were your words, remember?"

She told Pieter about the conversation, almost word for word, or as much as she could remember up to the part about the frame. "That's when I said what maybe I shouldn't have. I guessed that your very sweet guy, Nichter, must have told him about the frame, and that if I didn't bring it up it could only make him more suspicious. So I told him how you found the piece, about Nichter spotting where it came from, and you gluing it back in the lab. It was a gamble, I know."

"What did he say?" Pieter said, unruffled.

"All he said was, 'I see. Well thank you, Miss Desjardin. I'll be down in the morning,' and then he walked off, just like that. I have no clue what he thought. His face was a blank."

"I see," Pieter said.

"Pieter! This is not funny!"

"Do you like the wine?" he asked.

"Yes, it's very good wine! Why are you being so casual about this?"

"You did the smart thing. I would have done the same. At least it tells me we can't trust Nichter. My first take was right—he is a mole for Hans and Fritz. I should have trusted my instincts.

"Hans and Fritz?"

"Bergdorf and Wolff? The Katzenjammer Kids? The old cartoon strip? Two little German kids always up to something? Forget it.

"Now, let's finish this toothsome cuisine, and the wine. *And* my devastating dessert, which will remain a surprise until served. We shall enjoy each other's company—that's what I intend to do—and then we'll talk about what we shall do next. Okay?"

Angela felt huge relief that Pieter wasn't angry with her. Although the whole thing was still plenty off-putting, she was astounded that he was so calm. Of course he was calm. Nobody does calm better than Pieter. But it also seemed like he had a plan. This was something new, Pieter with a plan.

Suddenly, she was depending on Pieter. This was new to her, also—depending on *anyone*, let alone Pieter. She found herself relaxing and actually looking forward to what he thought they should do next. And the dessert.

"Okay," she answered. "Now please tell me what's for dessert!"

"Now this dessert *did* take some time, and I hope you appreciate it. I stole the recipe from a friend who owns the gourmet pizza place up on the hill. Butterscotch creme pie with a bittersweet chocolate crust and mocha whipped cream with shaved chocolate on top. Best in the world, hands-down. He actually made me sign an agreement that I would never make it to sell, and that I must always disclose the source," Pieter laughed. "On the back of a napkin."

When they had finished, Angela was on such a butterscotch high and so mellowed out by most of a bottle of Pieter's "modest pinot grigio" that she had to force herself to focus.

"Remind me why we're doing this, Pieter," Angela said, hoping beyond hope that they could just call the whole thing off.

"We're doing this because we cannot *not* do it. We took a vote, remember? It was unanimous as I recall."

"You're right, Pieter. It must have been the pie talking. So what now?"

"First, we need to find out more about Wolff. We know zip, when you think about it. All we have is his time at Harvard, but none of the real skinny on that—plus what he's done here, of course, which is damned little for as long as he's hung around. How he keeps his job is part of the question, don'tcha think?"

"No quarrel there, but even if we had the time—which we don't—it would be impossible to do any serious snooping without getting caught. We're not exactly invisible, you know."

Pieter paused, and then he said, "Okay, let's start with Harvard. I know a guy up there who can do some digging for me, and he'll keep his mouth shut. Old employee records, hearsay, that sort of thing. I'll have him turn over a few rocks and see what crawls out."

"Okay, that's the first thing. What's number two?" Angela said.

"We need to know where he goes and what he does there. He sure hasn't worked any magic for the Mendelssohn when he's been gone, or none I can see, but my gut tells me stuff happens the minute he walks on a plane."

"Maybe we could hack his computer, or get our hands on his datebook. Maybe he keeps his itineraries or his appointments somewhere in his office, or maybe Bergdorf does," Angela said.

"You don't know any nice young hackers, do you?"

"And just where do you think I'd meet a nice young hacker?" she said, "As much as my body aches for a nerdy geek to keep my feet warm at night."

"Don't knock us until you've tried us."

Angela ignored him. "Maybe there's something in his e-mail. Maybe he books online. Maybe I can get in somehow."

"Maybe you can. But in the meantime . . ."

". . . we chase down the paintings," Angela finished his sentence, a practice which had become increasingly frequent between them. "They've got to be on somebody's list. Frankly, I'm amazed that they've hung up there so long and not been spotted."

"Do you want to take a shot at it?" Pieter said.

"And just when would I do that?"

"Can you start on it, at least? If we don't move fast, this could all blow up in our faces before we have Answer One. Bergdorf already smells a rat, right?"

"It's safe to say he's caught a whiff of something," Angela said.

Bergdorf. Rats. She had forgotten all about Bergdorf. *I have to meet with that nasty little troll in the morning,* she remembered. Maybe she'd go to him and not wait for him to come around. Maybe she'd catch a peek at something useful, like Wolff's appointment book or an airline schedule.

"Sure, I'll give it a go," she said. If anything, the only daughter of world-class archaeologists knew how to dig. Knowing the real painters' names would speed things up; how many missing collections could there be holding the likes of Hals, van Eyck, Steen and Rubens—if they were all from the same collection, of course. If they weren't, it could take longer.

"It's late, Pieter. I think that's about as much as I can handle for tonight. Okay?"

"Okay."

"Your dinner, your pie, and the wine were exquisite! It was a lovely evening—most of it, that is. I'm not thrilled with what we're into. But this is what 'living on the edge' is all about, right? If you can't stand the heat . . ."

". . . get out of the kitchen. Now get out of *my* kitchen and go home. We have a big day tomorrow. And don't worry. Everything will be fine."

"I'll remember that when we're staring at the business end of a German Luger."

"You've been reading too much Alistair MacLean," Pieter

needled, although the thought had crossed his mind as well.

He gave Angela a brief hug and a kiss on the top of her shiny black mane. Pieter glanced back at the empty wine bottles on the table as she made her way to her car, and in an exercise in futility he shouted after her, "Watch your speed!"

CHAPTER FOURTEEN

Erich Wolff slept fitfully as the 747 slipped west over the Atlantic. The heavy Bavarian cuisine and the wine would normally have rendered him comatose, but thoughts of Berchtesgaden and his peevish encounter with Arthur Mendelssohn conspired against him.

A demon mix of childhood images jarred him out of the twilight. The spontaneous eruption of *Gaudeamus Igitur* and the loud cheering of gray-uniformed Nazi officers in the ancient Ratskeller beneath the Bremen Marktplatz shook him awake, and the headiness of the occasion swept over him once more. He remembered standing in a forest of empty brown wine bottles atop the long wooden table in this most famous of weinstubes, a stick figure of nine in his crisp new uniform of the Hitler Youth. His father's comrades toasted his initiation with chilled glasses of the Ratskeller's finest as a conflicted and inebriated Otto Wolff stood close by, his own glass extended also toward the astonished child. This, plus the surreal advances of the Fuehrer that cold afternoon at the Berghof, and the moment Otto gifted him with the Fuehrer's treasured side arm, he continued to regard as the pinnacles of his seventy years on this mortal coil.

Accompanied by the soft whine of the turbines, Erich Wolff's stream of consciousness flowed to the morning his father returned from Berlin. The bittersweet events of that day more than half a century ago were as vivid as the sunrise nosing under the pulled shade next to him as the aircraft vectored north toward Newfoundland.

The sweet was feeling in his adolescent hand the soft

leather holster and heaviness of his idol's trademark revolver, inhaling its exhilarating essence of gun oil, and knowing that he would hold the sacred weapon till his dying breath.

The bitter was the violent reaction of Klara to his father's rapier accusations of crimes inflicted by the Baron Friedrich von Koch, Klara's father, and his likely punishment at war's end. This was the flashpoint of their total estrangement; his father and stepmother barely spoke after that.

The bitter was also his father's candid prediction of total German surrender and of his imprisonment by the British. Erich's hatred of his father had turned not yet to love, a feeling he had never truly known in his three-score-plus-ten other than his passion for the Fuehrer. Still, his bias had at least modulated to understanding. His father had been merely the messenger and, to Erich's chagrin, he had been right about everything. Erich no longer faulted the man for his benign role in the war, or for his lack of fervor for the Reich. He was what he was.

"I don't know how long I'll be away," Otto Wolff spoke to his son as they sat at the small table in the kitchen of the family townhouse on the morning he was taken. "I don't expect that the Allies will take our money or our house, although I think they will not offer the same courtesy to your grandfather.

"You and Klara will be safe here. You will finish your schooling in Bremen, and then you will go to university in America."

"America! How could I go to America, father? They are our enemy. They are the enemy of the Reich!" Erich said. "I hate America!"

"America *was* our enemy. They are no longer. And the Reich is no more. The war is done. The Americans are an odd lot. As fierce as the fighting has been, I suspect they will embrace Germany and the German people again. They are quick to forgive—much too quick, I think—but that is their business. And good for us, ja?

"The High Command, that's a different story. There will be no forgiveness for them. Most will be hanged, I suspect. But I will do everything I can to separate myself from them. They will go lightly on me, I hope, as I was not involved in the killing or the camps. And I have a few bargaining chips which should help.

"But you, Erich, have done nothing. You will be safe and free in America," Otto concluded.

"But why America, father? I hate America!" Erich lashed out again. "Why not Germany?"

"Because America will offer the best chance for you. Germany is nothing now but rubble, and it will be many years before we will be the same as we were. By then it will be too late for you."

"But why would they accept me? What about the Hitler Youth? I took a pledge to the Fuehrer, and I will keep it!" Erich said defiantly.

"They will accept your money, Erich, which means that they will accept you. Not warmly, perhaps, but warmly enough. Fortunately, I have enough to send you there. The Hitler Youth will mean nothing to them. 'Little boys playing soldier,' they will say, 'being groomed as cannon fodder.' If anything, it will make you more intriguing to them, if not sympathetic. Americans are drawn to persons whom they think have led wicked lives. Look at the criminals and the cinema stars they worship," Otto said with a cynical smile.

"And you will keep your mouth closed—enough about the Nazis. They have heard enough about Nazis, and they don't like them very much. Pledges are made to be broken," he said. "The Fuehrer broke them left and right."

"But, I . . ."

"But, nothing. You will work hard in school, study your English. My wish is that you attend Harvard University near Boston. This is where the American elite are educated, and the best students from other countries attend there also. Do well, and you will have a future in America, or maybe later in Germany. When we've cleaned up this horrible mess we've made."

"But father, I . . ."

"It will be my way, Erich. There *is* no other way."

In the afternoon they came. Two British officers and half a dozen soldiers knocked at the door of 21 Böttcherstrasse and requested the company of one Otto Wolff, lieutenant of the Third Reich and aide to Reichsmarschall Hermann Goering.

Klara answered the knock with her patented sneer, which had in recent months become as permanent on her face as her pig's eyes and broad nose. She made no effort to hide her contempt.

"Ja?" she said. Frau Wolff blocked the opening, hands on hips, in the arrogant pose of a haystack-proportioned Wagnerian diva about to condemn them to eternal fire. Her graying Aryan blonde hair, braided, then twisted in a bun, added to her stature as she stared down from the raised threshold on the inferior Brits who dared intrude on her home, her country and her life. She had been expecting them.

"*Haben Sie Lieutenant Otto Wolff, bitte?*" one of the officers said in halting German.

"Ja," Klara answered.

"*Kann ich den Lieutenant sehen, Bitte?*" he asked, this time with a hint of annoyance tempered by typical British propriety, clearly put off by her open hostility.

"Let them in, Klara," Otto said sharply.

Only the officers ventured past the intimidating hausfrau as Otto Wolff greeted the two in the lavish parlor of the historic townhouse. He had dressed himself in gray tweed with a crisp, white shirt and a blue patterned tie, abandoning his military trappings in a calculated move to soften impressions of him as a loyal instrument of the evil Fuehrer.

"You are Otto Wolff, lieutenant in the German Wehrmacht and aide to Hermann Goering?" the ranking officer said, this time in English, having quickly noted Wolff's earlier command to Klara.

"I am that man," he answered in English with only the merest trace of an accent, his mastery of the language acquired at Cambridge prior to his art schooling in Munich.

"Come with us, Herr Wolff."

"Am I being arrested?"

"We have some questions, Herr Wolff. Please come."

"Of course I will come. I am ready, as you can see." Wolff extended a hand toward a packed valise resting against a blue velvet sofa centered beneath a dazzling French crystal chandelier, a gift from Goering. One of the soldiers knelt over the rich leather carry–all, zipped it open, and ran his hand through its contents. Satisfied, he re-zipped the satchel and stood.

"I was planning to come to your headquarters today, but the time slipped away from me. I apologize for inconveniencing you. So, shall we go, then," Otto said. He reached for Erich, who stood stunned in the doorway to the foyer, and he hugged his son, whispering something in his ear as they embraced. He nodded to Klara, lifted his valise, and led the two Brits to the door.

Only hours before, another team of American and British officers of higher rank and with a larger military entourage paid visits to a modest apartment next to the sprawling Wolff armored vehicle works, and to the walled estate of the one known to the Allies as "the Gas Man." Both Kurt Wolff and Baron Friedrich von Koch, co-fathers-in-law and co-captains of the Reich's massive industrial complex and its deadly output, went quietly. Neither was cognizant of why they could possibly be implicated in the whole affair.

Both would be outraged that they should be charged simply for producing a few Panzers and guns and grenades, or for cooking up a canister or two of pesticide. They were businessmen, not criminals; the war was none of their doing.

As Lufthansa LH430 began its decent, images of that day and the days that followed reeled in Erich Wolff's head. He was barely conscious of having eaten his breakfast and had no sensation of the super-heated black coffee that burnt his throat as his mind locked on the events surrounding his father's incarceration and the fate of his grandfather and the Baron von Koch.

CHAPTER FIFTEEN

It had been nearly four years from the time Otto Wolff left the parlor of the Bremen townhouse with the British officers to his unceremonious return on 3 June, 1949. On that day, he just showed up, and that was that.

The ten-year sentence which he drew for his role in "the shameless pillaging of priceless works of art from the defenseless victims of Nazi intimidation, to satisfy the unquenchable lust of Adolph Hitler and Hermann Goering for the possessions of others," as the military tribunal opined in its scorching verdict, had been reduced by more than six years, in exchange for Wolff's "full cooperation." To the serendipitous delight of his captors, he proved to be "totally reliable" in identifying, in elaborate detail, the thousands of paintings, drawings, antiques and pieces of jewelry which he and Goering had personally seized. His revelation which clinched the deal was the precise location of each tainted lot, information which left the Allies beside themselves with glee.

Among his other gifts, Otto Wolff had become a skillful negotiator. He had assessed correctly that, to the Americans and the French in particular, the value of these irreplaceable works far exceeded the importance of justice done, and that a few years off the sentence of a single inconsequential minion was little enough to pay for such priceless disclosures. His talent for negotiation was rooted in pure will. From his conniving industrialist father he had learned the first requisite of the bargaining art: *have the balls to walk away*. In this biggest deal of his life, Otto Wolff had been set to take his knowledge to the grave, a certainty that he ably communicated to his accusers.

Wolff's pinpoint accuracy was due to the meticulous records he had kept from the first day of his service to the Reich. The swath he and Goering had hacked through the Jewish-owned galleries, chateaus and gilded townhouses of France was thoroughly documented in his well-worn, and later, wildly famous journals.

The ones he handed over to the Americans were not these.

Before he was arrested, he had painstakingly entered each "transaction" into bogus copies. These intricately coded records were incomplete only for his having omitted those dealings with the choice few he had enlisted in his new enterprise, Das Rheingold—plus countless others he knew about only indirectly. He did include, brilliantly, the magnificent forty-seven works of the Gruenwald collection which he himself had stolen a second time; their last known address was a locked railcar destined for Alt Aussee, Austria. Otto Wolff had created true masterpieces of deception, works of art so convincing that their veracity in the minds of his captors exceeded only that of the Holy Word of God.

The original journals and codebook he had hidden behind a large foundation stone in the cellar of his home in Bremen; he shared magnanimously, sans codes, the doctored archives with the Allied art chasers who had descended with a vengeance on Paris and other major art centers of Europe. The brilliant capstone to Wolff's complex caper was that he had made himself indispensable as the one person on the planet able to translate each cryptic mark into real-life works, their legitimate owners, and their current resting places. Wolff had convinced them that no record of his system of intricate strokes and symbols existed outside his head. The famed "Wolff Journals" would later be placed under glass in one of the world's most prestigious museums, a modern-day Rosetta stone which drew long lines months after its debut.

The irony was that every larcenous event copied into the

Wolff Journals was absolutely, positively the truth. The ecstasy of the Americans over the voluminous details therein was more than enough to erase any thought of what might have been left out, or why; it simply never occurred to anyone that the documents were anything but a full accounting. Besides, what was there would keep them busy for decades.

Thus, Otto Wolff's "Ring of Gold" remained unbroken and undisclosed while its participants, as he had instructed, sat uneasily on their ill-gotten treasures and waited impatiently for his release. *Blackmail is one of the more effective business tools,* Otto Wolff mused as he bided his time behind bars. In fact, he would rank blackmail even higher on his list of Strategies That Work than *Have the Balls to Walk Away.* If pressed, the Harvard School of Business would likely have privately concurred.

Erich visited his father only three times during his four years away; Wolff was confined near Munich, some five hundred kilometers from Bremen, and travel was not easy in the years after the surrender. Otto mentioned nothing of his grand plan in his letters to Erich, certain that every word would be scrutinized by Klara. His epistles were carefully crafted to strengthen his bond with the boy while not widening the breach between himself and the spiteful Frau Wolff. He knew he was powerless against her until he was freed, and he would give her no reason to further poison his son against him, other than the ones that came to her unaided.

As he considered Erich still ill-prepared for Das Rheingold, their visits were innocuous, yet reasonably warm. Otto's agenda for these few hours together consisted mostly of nagging the boy about his education, gently steering him toward the study of art, and building bridges between them.

During each of those sojourns Otto would talk about painting and about the masterworks he had seen and handled as part of his service to Goering and to the Fuehrer. Like a child, the rangy teenager would insist each time on the recounting of Hitler's collection at the Berghof and the Fuehrer's special madness for Vermeer. Wolff would more than once describe to him every subtle hue and fragile brushstroke of *The Art of Painting,* the work he had stopped to admire one last time before his shocking encounter with the Fuehrer in Berchtesgaden during the imminent fall of Paris. Erich's obsession with the Supreme Warlord had not waned, and he savored every morsel of his father's recollections of the Berghof and its contents, though the boy already knew most of the Inner Sanctum, parts Otto himself had never seen.

Kurt Wolff was a frightening man, although he was decidedly less so through the bars of a prison cell. Prison had not been kind to Kurt Wolff, as Otto had predicted. His health had declined sharply since Otto's mother died, and by the time he slept a full night through, he was a threat only to himself. Had he had the foresight to smuggle into his cell the Nazi's own Final Solution, he would gladly have crunched down on the blessed capsule before the second day and welcomed the quick, albeit ugly, release that only cyanide can bring. He cursed himself for his uncharacteristic lack of planning.

"I am astonished that I am here," Kurt Wolff said to his grandson during the boy's only visit before the trial. Erich barely recognized the face he had seen fewer than a dozen times before, though they had lived in the same city. "They took everything— my factories, my accounts, even my Mercedes car," he complained. "How can they do that? *Why* would they do that? I have nothing, nothing to leave you."

Erich found this both amusing and hugely disingenuous, as his grandfather had never in his entire self-absorbed life shown any concern for his grandson's welfare. He had never given him a

, even at Christmas.

"What did I do? You tell me! I am a businessman. I did nothing wrong. I was doing my duty. I made Panzers, Ja? They were magnificent machines, and *I* was responsible—I alone, your grandfather. I'm proud of my tanks. You should be proud. The Americans should have such tanks!"

Erich sat quietly, allowing his grandfather to rant. It was probably all a mistake, and he would be set free once the *dummkopfs* figured it all out, Ja?

Although Erich as a child had been terrified of Kurt Wolff on those few times he was obliged to see him, he felt sympathy for him now. The old man had lost so much muscle and flesh from his towering frame that he resembled what a farmer might have put out to frighten the crows. His milky eyes peered from beneath snowy eyebrows; they were no longer the glowing coals of the man he once feared. Erich wondered, if Otto's prediction turned out to be so, whether his wasted grandfather bore enough heft to snap his own neck when his turn came at the gallows.

"Von Koch is here. And your father. If we two were so evil, why aren't we up in Nuremberg with Goering and Hess and Ribbentrop and Keitel? And that sniveling Doenitz, in his fancy uniform? Have you ever seen his uniform? We *deserve* to be there! Aren't we important enough?" Kurt Wolff said in a crazed contradiction of his earlier declaration of innocence. Erich listened, offering an attentive audience of one, the act of a dutiful grandson.

Kurt Wolff would find out soon enough why the Allies thought him to be a bad person. It had not so much to do with his beloved Panzers or the guns or the grenades, but with the tens of thousands of slave laborers he starved and abused and drove to their deaths in his factories and in the camps surrounding them. Once again, he appeared dumbfounded to hear the charges; of all the offenses he had considered during his rare lucid moments, this was the one which had seemingly never occurred to him.

Otto Wolff's assessment of the old man's chances had been correct. Kurt Wolff hanged with the rest, and his indignation at being excluded from the select company of the Nazi High Command at Nuremberg was salved at the end; his ashes were tossed, appropriately, with Goering's and Ribbentrop's and Keitel's in the one remaining furnace at Dachau. He would have taken satisfaction in knowing that his charred bits would be mingled with theirs for eternity.

Baron Friedrich von Koch's path took a different turn. Blowhard to the end, he railed at his accusers, denying bitterly that his chemical creations were meant for anything but good. He launched a litany of his company's various admixtures, only to be cut off by the chairman in mid-formula as he was extolling one of his personal favorites. The Gas Man then proceeded to lecture the tribunal on the harmful effects of body lice and the relief the "detainees" must have felt to be free of these nasty parasites. "You should thank me, not condemn me!"

Not only did the boisterous Baron disavow the slightest awareness that his wondrous compounds had been intended for anything but an humanitarian end, he exploded in righteous indignation at the idea that two-and-one-half million Jews might have met their end at the Auschwitz camp by inhaling the emissions from his colorful crystals. As a parting shot, he upbraided the despicable Nazis for their horrific misuse of his products, "if indeed such had even been the case." Von Koch punctuated his diatribe with one last outburst: "It was for *lice*! Why can't you understand? I knew of no other use. I condemn these terrible people if they murdered innocent Jews with my chemicals! They will burn in hell—but I am not guilty of any crime!"

The tribunal's reaction to von Koch's theatrics alternated between cynical amusement and open disgust. Following the briefest of deliberations, Colonel Clayton Alexander, chairman of the judges' panel, read the military tribunal's carefully worded response: "Baron Friedrich von Koch, this tribunal finds your treatise on the virtues of your compounds enlightening. We have no doubt that the particular formulation in question is indeed effective in the treatment of body lice, were the welfare of the host not an issue. We do have more than reasonable doubt, however, that you were unaware of its unspeakable application."

Von Koch stared in disbelief as the American officer continued, "In fact, based on the irreproachable testimony of innocent Jews about whom you spoke with such compassion who, by the grace of God, escaped your ghastly cloud of death, we are convinced that you were a full and willing partner in what your Nazi colleagues have chillingly described the 'Final Solution.'

"Dozens have attested to your presence in the camps during the activation of the gas chambers, and that you personally supervised the release of your deadly crystals through the vents above these so-called bathhouses into which your victims were led with the promise of a cleansing shower. Words cannot describe our utter contempt for you and your chemicals. You sicken us."

The Baron had fallen into a near-coma as the colonel came to the point. "Friedrich von Koch, this tribunal finds you guilty of the most abhorrent of crimes against humankind." The officer paused, looked harshly into the glazed eyes of the Baron, and continued. "True justice would have you sentenced to death by cyanide gas, which would be an appropriate alternative to the rope in your special case. In the scriptural credo of an eye for an eye, your beloved Omega Z, the compound of your own formulation which you found so effective at the camps of Auschwitz, Dachau and other equally notorious sites, might explicably be specified as the agent for your execution. But in the spirit of mercy, a quality which I and my colleagues find conspicuously lacking in your long list of self-proclaimed attributes, this tribunal has determined that you be hanged with the others until dead, three days hence. May God have mercy on your soul."

One British correspondent, who claimed to have witnessed the execution, told a quite different story:

"We watched through glass portholes as the Baron Friedrich von Koch clutched the dirty gray towel, like a drowning sailor grasps at a scrap of jetsam, and held it tightly against his terror-stricken face; it was one of the thousands which had been issued to unsuspecting Jews awaiting their 'showers.' The towel was an inspired touch offered by the colonel's aide who had been among the liberators, and who had seen similar pieces of tattered terrycloth still clenched in the hands of the Gas Man's victims.

"Von Koch held his breath in futile determination, as all do, I was told. Lethal mist filled the enclosure as the Baron's ruddy face turned darker and his eyes grew wider in half-surprise, half-horror. Then he pulled towel away in violent defiance, and with his last gasp he shouted, 'It was for the lice! The. . .' Then his body convulsed, his knees buckled, and he dropped in a lifeless heap to the floor. Although his heart had stopped, dark spots of urine and liquefied feces spread through his pale gray prison trousers like fresh-spilled coffee. As in life, the Baron had the last word: his gaping mouth, frozen in death, had yet to empty out his final epithet.

"'. . .lice!'"

The correspondent's account was never corroborated, and he was subsequently terminated under protest; no other observers could be produced. General records show that Baron Friedrich von Koch was hanged with the others, but the paperwork on his specific execution had somehow become lost. The manner of his death remains a grisly contradiction.

When the jumbo jet's tires screeched on the tarmac at O'Hare where he would make his last connection, Erich Wolff was limp. The rest he had coveted on the long flight from Frankfurt never came. So intense were his fragmented thoughts that they scuttled any attempt at a decent few hours sleep. What had started as a harmless indulgence, simple thoughts of the glory of the Reich and his beloved Fuehrer, had cracked the window just enough to allow the bad spirits to creep over the sill.

Their presence swelled into a trans-Atlantic nightmare. Images of the fragile Kurt Wolff in his tiny cell at Dachau and the faint sound of a bird's bone snapping as the old man dropped through the gallows trap like a half-filled duffel bag; the hideous end of the bully von Koch as, according to the British correspondent, he gasped his last in the paralyzing cloud; the sight of his father's tall, trim figure as he left with the British to fulfill his due; and worse than any of these, Klara's hateful countenance flickering like the frames of a silent film, the hostile face of a woman abandoned by her father, her husband, her stepson and, above all, her Fuehrer.

United Airlines willing, he would be home and asleep in a few hours, not that the city where he had spent the last thirty years of his life he would ever consider home. Berchtesgaden, he knew, was his spiritual home, though the breathtaking Berghof and all its surrounds had been leveled by unctuous hypocrites who stumbled over one another to obliterate the Fuehrer's sacred memory. Erich Wolff made a mental note that his own ashes should be scattered where the Berghof had stood. He would mention this to Herr Bergdorf in the morning.

The director was puzzled that he had not thought of this sooner.

CHAPTER SIXTEEN

Kate Raeburn was waiting at the barrier as he passed through customs. He spotted the slender, dark-haired woman at the railing in a small cluster of expectant locals and nodded. She smiled, waved discreetly, and moved toward the place outside the restricted area where she would meet him. He hugged her briefly with his free arm and they walked without speaking to the ground transportation exits.

A just-washed S600 Mercedes-Benz sedan, water still beaded on its black mirror finish, sat at the curb, emergency lights flashing. Friedrich Bergdorf sat stiffly behind the wheel. When he saw them come through the terminal doors he popped the trunklid, vacated the driver's seat, opened the rear door for the two of them, and proceeded to load the director's luggage into the massive trunk. Only after they had settled into the black leather rear seat and Bergdorf had pulled away did they speak.

"I've missed you," Kate said softly beneath the hearing of Bergdorf, she hoped, although she knew that Bergdorf missed nothing.

"It's good to be back," Wolff said dispassionately, the tiredness showing in his voice.

She had grown accustomed to his cold responses. It was his way, although his occasional flashes of charm were enough to reward her for the times in between. Undaunted, she gripped his arm and said, "Did everything go well? Did you find everything for Arthur?"

Erich Wolff and Kate Raeburn had never slept in the same bed. Yet the director confided in her the most intimate details of his elusive comings and goings. Over several years they had developed a curious attachment, she as his confessor, companion, and trusted mole among the local gentry, and he providing the power of position and persona she lusted for. Just to be seen with him was, for her, a rush beyond belief.

Wolff used her. She knew this, and she was okay with it. She knew also that he needed her; other than herself, there was only Bergdorf, her natural enemy in a bizarre triangle. Bergdorf, the steely automaton who, she had convinced herself, was hardly of the heart and mind to understand this complex, tormented man. She often told herself that she would die for him, although she was hard put to imagine a circumstance which might call for such a draconian test of her devotion.

She was also drawn to him because of his passionate anti-Semitism, which he held in check for the most part, but shared openly with her. His hatred of Jews, she reasoned, was rooted in his childhood closeness and lifelong obsession with the arch Jew-baiter of all time. It was a persuasion which would offend most everyone but her. For Katherine Raeburn, born Deborah Jayne Steiner to Misha and Rachel Steiner of the New York City Steiners, nothing could have bonded them more.

"I got him everything he wanted, but it's going to cost him," Wolff said. "The Zurich Matisse was still available, and the Chagall from Berlin, and the Kirchner. He backed off the Picasso, you know, which was too bad. It was the best piece. But I charged him an extra million on the three. The Yiddish pig persisted in calling me a Nazi again, in a most offensive tone, and mocked my quaint Teutonic articulation, so I raised the price to eight-point-three. He whined like a sick dog, but he agreed. He was too hooked to wiggle off."

"Maybe next time he'll be sweeter," she said.

"I doubt it," Wolff answered. "He can't help himself."

Yiddish pig. *That was her father, a Yiddish pig,* she thought. One coarse phrase brought it all back—the verbal abuse, the impossible laws and traditions, the constant pressure to accept the idea that women were inferior and meant by God to be slaves to men, the swinishness of her two brothers who were just like him. Erich was right: Arthur Mendelssohn was no different than the bullies in the unhappy house of her childhood, and she was thrilled to see the director screw him blind.

Misha Steiner had been a successful New York schlepper of Kosher foods and wines. The shelves of half the Kosher delis in Manhattan were stocked weekly with bright red boxes of Manichewitz matzos, quart jars of death-gray gefilte fish, and deep facings of Mogen David Concord delivered religiously—how else?—from the cavernous Steiner & Sons warehouse on the East River. Deli cases from the Battery to Central Park were stuffed with moist pink lox, crocks of bulk cream cheese, fat-streaked corned beef and greasy sash-weights of salami expressed by the family's ubiquitous fleet of "orthodox black" Steiner & Sons reefer trucks.

Misha Steiner terrorized Rachel and Deborah Jayne and levied on them all the canons and constraints of a textbook kosher household. If it had only been the rules, she could have managed; but Misha Steiner—and as they grew, her brothers Sasha and Jacob—were the most mean-spirited specimens of humankind she had ever known. They were ruthless in their business, and drew no line between the loading dock and the hearth. Try as she might, she could not recall a single gentle word or loving gesture directed her way, or her mother's, by any of the three in her eighteen years under the Steiner roof.

What finally case-hardened her toward the doctrines of her ancestors and severed her lifeline to the Almighty was their presumption that their so-called "faith" not merely justified, but demanded cruelty, although they never used that word. "Sternness" was the operative term, she recalled. She had read the Torah time and again, and the rest of the Book as well, from *In the beginning* to *And he shall turn the heart of the fathers to the children, and the heart of the children to their fathers, lest I come and smite the earth with a curse,* searching for any validation of their distorted interpretation, but she could find none. There was clearly no "turning of hearts" in her dysfunctional nest, and precious little "smiting" from on high. She could accept the ancient writings as bloody and uncompromising, the chronicle of a vengeful God. Yet she ascertained that apart from Jehovah's harsh dealings with Eve, Lot's wife and a few other recalcitrant members of her sex, women were regarded with great love, respect, and even reverence: Naomi, Ruth, and Esther, to name a few.

Her mother, Rachel, invariably sidestepped her theological questioning, not surprising for the woman who not once took her side or defended her against her father and brothers. Nor was the rabbi any help, dismissing her appeals for edification as the whining of an ungrateful child. *She would come around.*

But she did not come around. On the eve of her eighteenth birthday she moved out of the house and never looked back.

Then as her parting shot, she left Deborah Jayne Steiner behind as well; she enrolled at NYU as Katherine Raeburn, although she chose to be addressed as Kate. A voracious reader as a child, her only shield against the assaults of her father and brothers, she identified completely with the futile struggle between the willful Katherine of Aragon and the overpowering Henry and was smitten by the defiant queen's exotic Spanish lineage. Deborah Jayne could also relate to the Bard's cantankerous Kate and ached to be tamed by her own personal Petruchio. It was conceivable that she should select *Katherine* as her *nom pour la vie*.

Raeburn she appropriated from the so-called "Scottish Joshua Reynolds," Sir Henry Raeburn, Scotland's most distinguished portrait painter. Deborah Jayne was moved by the apple-cheeked innocence of the children who glowed from his canvasses, the essence of the pampered childhood she never had. In particular, she loved the artist's *The Drummond Children* at the Met and would sit for long periods before the work, insinuating herself into the gentility of their lives.

The newly-minted Kate Raeburn worked nights at Giancolo's Green Grocers beneath her third-floor walk-up where she gained a practical command of street Italian, at least some of the earthier parlance, and enough day-old fruit and veggies to tide her over between paychecks. Weekends she pulled desk duty at the university library, where she could study, have her books close at hand, and pick up some pocket change in the bargain. Her mother died in Kate's third term. She didn't attend the funeral; her family had made no attempt to contact her, and she read about it by chance in the *Post* four days after the burial.

Kate Raeburn took her degree in art history with honors and accepted an instructor's position at a small Jesuit college near the Mendelssohn, adjusting reasonably well to the cultural transformation from high-voltage urbania to the D-battery midwest. Other than a consuming appetite for art, she brought with her a hard-tempered hostility toward the faith of her fathers and an ironclad resolve to distance herself from the House of Steiner and her dark Jewish roots. Only Erich Wolff was privy to her secret.

Kate learned early in their relationship that Wolff was a private man, in spite of the shocking intimacies he had shared with her over the years, and that there were times for silence. He was not at all like Joe Richards, her dead husband, who left to Kate his place at the Mendelssohn board table—plus the eminently livable sum of one-hundred-fifteen million dollars—when he was felled by a massive coronary on the thirteenth hole at the Willow Knoll Country Club.

The high-profile heart surgeon and celebrated party animal was center stage during every waking moment, particularly when he loomed over the table in the operating room; cracking jokes or cracking chests, it was all the same to him. Dr. Joe was the only one on the Mendelssohn board with the effrontery to scuff up Arthur Mendelssohn and get away with it, mostly because Joe was an open book. He had nothing to hide and nothing to lose. There was the possibility, too, that Arthur might one day find himself under Joe's knife, and Kate mused that the chairman wasn't about to get on his bad side. With the good doctor's penchant for being first in everything, it was no surprise that he beat the blustering board chairman to the graveyard.

Kate broke Wolff's meditation as they made their way up the steep knoll toward his blue limestone mansion perched high above the brown, serpentine river below. A chain of barges heaped with coal moved slowly eastward against the current, pushed by a mighty diesel tug straining under full power. The mansion's single, castellated tower rewarded anyone with the stamina to climb to the top with a spectacular 360-degree panorama of the entire city and the lush, rolling hills to the south.

The house was a fusion of English and Northern European medieval, with a decidedly French twist. Although local critics ridiculed the structure as a "dog's breakfast," it had a pleasing uniqueness about it—clearly so to its original owner, one of the city's legendary beer barons from a century-and-a-half ago, and to its architect whose signature adorned many of the city's landmarks of the period.

As the iron gates creaked open in obedience to Bergdorf's hand-held remote, she said, "I think I should not come in. You look very tired. Maybe you could have Herr Bergdorf run me back down to the gallery," referring to her thriving art dealership in the heart of the city.

"No, I'd like you to come inside if you can spare the time, Katherine," the director said. "There's something I would like to show you." Unlike everyone else who knew her, he never called her Kate—always Katherine; nearly fifty years in America hadn't softened his Old World rubric. It was one of his quirks that she found oddly attractive. She didn't mind that he called her Katherine.

"Yes, I have the time, Erich," she said.

"Herr Bergdorf, you may drop us off and return to customs to claim the chairman's precious cargo," Wolff said. "I don't want to leave those paintings alone any longer than necessary. You can take care of the luggage later."

"As you wish, Herr Wolff," Bergdorf said. *Birds of a feather*, Kate thought, unless they were like school teachers who never refer to each other by their given names in front of the children.

Bergdorf eased the Mercedes to a stop in front of the massive oak double doors of the mansion. On cue he hopped from the driver's seat, or as near to hopping that a seventy-something aide-de-camp could hop, and opened Kate's door. She couldn't avoid his deprecating stare, harsher than usual. Perhaps it had to do with the "something" Wolff intended to show her, as if he knew already what it might be and didn't like it one damn bit.

Wolff left the car, gently took Kate's arm, and they followed Bergdorf up the worn marble steps to the entrance. The visibly distressed retainer entered the security code, and Kate heard the soft click of the lock. Bergdorf pushed open the door for them and, without a word, retreated to the car. Kate watched as the Mercedes retraced the winding drive which crested on slopes once thick with Catawba vines.

Kate walked to the edge of the long flagstone overlook which Wolff had added to the front of the house years ago; she remembered him once saying that the terrace greatly resembled Hitler's veranda at the Berghof which faced the breathtaking panorama of the Untersberg Alps.

"Standing out here on a clear, winter day with the snow on the hills, I can almost feel his breath," he said a few paces behind her, seeming to read her thoughts. His words sent a shiver through her, and she fought the images they conjured up. But the spectacle of the twisting river stretching for miles in either direction between the verdant slopes restored her calm.

"This is such an amazing view," she said. "Would you ever grow the grapes again?"

"No, I think not. It's too much fuss for too little reward, and I have neither the patience nor the time," Wolff said as they stepped into the foyer. "Although it would be good to see the grapes down there. It would complete the setting, wouldn't it?

"Maybe someday."

Wolff closed the door and reset the alarm. Kate glanced up at the sturdy Gothic arches which supported the foyer's steep, gabled ceiling, and her eyes traced the railing which surrounded the cantilevered gallery. She lowered them to the richly carved mantelpiece and the flickering Victorian gaslights on either side which cast an eerie amber glow over the entire space.

She had stood in this soaring vestibule many times, yet this time there was an aura about it that set her on edge. Out of nowhere she had the vague feeling that something bad was about to happen, yet something perversely exhilarating all the same.

Kate Raeburn was almost as drawn to this house as to Erich Wolff himself. He and his *Schloss auf der Rhein*, as he often referred to the iconic mansion, had a Svengali-like grip on her that, even if she wanted to, she doubted she could break. Like the British and Europeans who've grown attached to their homesteads, he had given his "castle on the Rhine" a name: he called it *Walhall*, which he pronounced *Val-hall*.

"It's Old High German for an ancient Norse word, *Valhalla*, from Scandinavian mythology," he had explained during one of her early visits. "It means 'the hall of those slain in battle.' Valhalla is where the souls of those who died feast with Odin for eternity. Odin was the early Scandinavian god of victory and god of the dead. Our German 'Odin' is Wotan who, as you know, pops up time and time again in Richard Wagner's operas.

"Is this more than you wanted to know?"

"No, tell me more," she had said, truly absorbed. They settled into his study off the foyer, and he lit a fire. The flames cast spectral shadows on the walls, a perfect backdrop for the rendering of *Der Ring des Nibelungen*. Aroused by her wide-eyed curiosity, Wolff careened through chapter and verse on Wagner's operatic mini-series about the cursed Rhine gold and the struggles among the gods, the giants, the dwarfs and the mortals for the magical golden ring. He saved his dramatic best for the grand finale in which Brünhilde throws herself on Siegfried's funeral pyre as Wotan's beloved Valhalla goes up in smoke.

Wolff spiked his fiery account with excerpts from the operas themselves, ranks of French horns, trombones and bronze-breasted divas roaring from his mega sound system with amps enough to rattle the tower windows. His eyes blazed as now, transported, he led her through the complex libretto. Kate had never seen him so worked up in the time she had known him.

"It was the Fuehrer's favorite music. He was inspired by Wagner from the time he was a small boy. He told me this often when I would stay with him at the Berghof," he said.

Kate Raeburn would remember that night always, Wolff looming over her like Wotan himself as his shadow stretched across the oak-beamed ceiling in the animated retelling of Richard Wagner's terrifying tale. His larger-than-life persona flooded her senses. It was then that she gave herself to him fully, no matter who he really was or where it all might lead.

CHAPTER SEVENTEEN

He reached for her hand in the gas-lit foyer and said, "Come, Katherine, it's time that I showed you this." Wolff guided her down the long, center hall to the staircase which led to the wine cellar, and they descended to the mansion's chilly undercroft.

She had seen his cellar once before. He had taken her there to select a bottle or two for the evening, and then he had given her a tour of his prized collection. There was nothing unusual in the cellar then that she could recall, other than the extraordinary wines themselves which numbered more than 600 German varieties alone, he said. So why now?

When they came to the bottom of the old wooden steps, he led her through the semi-darkness to a tall stand of racks against the cellar's furthermost wall. Kate stood perplexed as Wolff released her hand, removed a single bottle, free of dust unlike the rest, and reached into the opening. Then he stepped aside as one section swung slowly outward to a faint hum coming from somewhere inside the wall.

Concealed behind the dusty brown bottles was what appeared to be the door to a vault, much like she'd seen in the posh jewelry stores along Lexington and Park, and, to its left, a rectangular keypad with a glowing red light. Wolff entered several numbers into the keypad and the red light went out. She heard a short beep followed by the whirring sound of a lock sliding open. Kate shivered as he twisted down on the handle and pulled the thick, stainless steel door ajar.

"Come," he said.

An incandescent glow from the opening washed over the sleeping bottles behind her and cast odd shapes on the walls. Her eyes strained to adjust to the light as Wolff led her across the threshold. It took her synapses a moment longer to process the unfamiliar signals her optic nerves had relayed. When her scrambled brain cells finally regrouped in some semblance of order, Kate Raeburn, the case-hardened gallery owner and social sophisticate for whom there was nothing left to startle, was astonished.

"My God," Kate whispered as her eyes swept the rarefied space. The room took her breath away. What Wolff had revealed to her was a radiant study in chiaroscuro, a stunning tribute to the wonders of Baroque, art imitating theater as halos of golden light illumined each separate and unique player on a darkened stage.

"My God," she repeated. "It's so incredi . . ." Kate's voice trailed off as her gaze, out of control, raced from one treasure to another like that of a thief come unexpectedly upon Tiffany's window. But once she truly realized what she was seeing, her eyes became more those of the unsuspecting doe caught in the company of wolves.

"I'm not sure that was a good 'My God' or a bad 'My God,'" he said. "But whichever it may be, we are here, and we cannot go back, can we? So let's have a look round, ya?"

Wolff spoke the truth, the bastard, Kate thought. *There was nothing about this cryptic spectacle that did not reek of bad. It was immediately obvious that she had become entangled in something very nasty, and there was no escape. He was dead right: she could not go back.*

No, Erich, it was not a good 'My God.'

"Please," he said, motioning her to follow. He ushered her unhurriedly along the perimeter of the small gallery, halting every few feet on the black-and-white-squared Italian marble floor reminiscent of that in Vermeer's masterpiece, *The Art of Painting.*

Much as one of the faithful might in a great cathedral pause at each Station of the Cross and manipulate his beads, Wolff meditated aloud at each stopping point on the object hanging there.

One hour and thirty-five minutes later Kate Raeburn was still without words. What had rendered her dumbstruck were forty-three of the most unimaginably beautiful masterworks she had ever seen all together in a single small space. The paintings were hung salon-style on walls of rich mocha, end-to-end, floor-to-ceiling, yet each perfectly lit canvas sparkled individually in its muted setting like a priceless gemstone on velvet.

Wolff had lavished on her, in perhaps the most thrilling yet unnerving ninety-or-so minutes of her already art-sumptuous life, some 300 years of iconic British and European masters. The two of them had lingered, one by one, before the stately works of Joshua Reynolds and Thomas Gainsborough, the eighteenth-century arch-rivals of British portraiture; brooding canvases by the Venetian master Tintoretto and the violent Caravaggio; the joyous outpourings of Franz Hals and Rembrandt van Rijn and the incomparable flesh and sinew of Peter Paul Rubens, grand master of the Flemish Baroque. There were also the creations of Anthony van Dyck, the Spaniards Velasquez and El Greco, an elegant traveling altarpiece by Hans Memling, and several magnificent Dürer woodcuts. Erich Wolff effused vast knowledge of the works and their painters, drawing from the deep reservoir which had produced his seven scholarly tomes on art history, a few of which had become classics in their genre.

"Erich, where did these come from?" she stammered; from her NYU indoctrination, years as a dealer in old masterworks, and a decade on the Mendelssohn board as chair of the acquisition committee, she knew without hesitation how incredibly important these works were, and that she could never even guess at their worth.

"And why, for God's sake, do you hide them all down here behind your wine cellar?" she added as her voice regained a modicum of steadiness, although she already knew why.

"I will tell you all of this in good time, *mein liebchen,*" Wolff said in an affectionate display far out of character for the usually punctilious director. But first there is one more place you must see. Then perhaps you will understand."

Wolff took her gently by the arm and turned her to face a pair of large, solid mahogany doors centered in the gallery's back wall. The imposing entry would have been obvious at first sight had it not been for the total dominance of the paintings themselves, although it, too, was lighted to dramatic effect. Carved into the lintel over the opening was a deeply incised swastika in a wreath of intricately carved oak leaves. Looming above was the insomnolent eagle of the Third Reich, head peering left and gigantic wings stretched to the extremities of the supporting beam. Centered on the doors themselves and raised in high relief were two ringed swastikas the size of manhole covers.

Erich Wolff opened the doors as if entering the cage of a dozing lion. His tentativeness was justified, as he slowly turned the rheostat directly inside the opening, bathing the starkly contrasting space in an unearthly light. If Kate Raeburn was dazed by what she had just seen in the antechamber of Wolff's dark cellar, this place, most surely contrived by Satan himself, would have buckled her knees had Wolff not been at her elbow. A charging lion might have been a welcome alternative.

Wolff felt her tremble, and he said, "I'm sorry if this frightens you. But at least let me explain." Had she been able to find the words, she would have told him that it was less fear than excitement that sent electricity through her body. Suddenly Kate felt not the slightest twinge of fear, either of Erich Wolff or from the astounding revelations he was peeling away like the leaves of an artichoke; she was only experiencing an enormous jolt of adrenalin and the unbearable expectation of what was yet to come.

Wolff said nothing, giving her time to absorb the macabre setting. What first struck her was the ghostly, half-length portrait of Adolph Hitler which hung at the far end of the room. Coldly lit by a bluish white spot, the painting was flanked by two tall, blood red banners with harsh black swastikas in circles of white. They were suspended from the ceiling, the kind which had always bracketed the Fuehrer when he would whip the *Deutschvolk* by the tens of thousands into a mindless frenzy during rallies of the Reich. The sitter was rendered in his trademark gray-green military jacket with the silver buttons, and a wide, red armband with the ubiquitous swastika which gripped his sleeve; his eyes skewered her as if judging the worthiness of this presumptuous Jewess to stand in his presence, and the former Deborah Jayne Steiner sensed that she had not passed muster.

Kate managed to break free of the Supreme Warlord's stare and look about the room. Off-white stucco walls rose to meet a barrel-vaulted ceiling of red brick that reminded her of the subterranean beer halls of old Heidelberg where she had quaffed many liters of Pils during a liberating back-pack summer years ago. Stretched beneath the ghastly shrine was a rough-hewn table with benches on either side, its surface marred by deeply carved initials, slogans, and swastikas. Most of one wall was given over to dozens of faded photographs in plain black frames, a small glass case containing several vintage handguns, and an amateurish watercolor of snow-covered mountains grossly out of place in proximity to the paintings in the adjoining gallery.

Two remaining objects begged explanation: first, a low

scaffold, flanked by an amorphous gray sofa and two matching chairs, which showcased a meticulously crafted model of a city she did not recognize; and lastly, a life-size mannequin in full Nazi regalia, from the officer's visor cap with a silver eagle-and-swastika insignia and silver braid to mirror-polished riding boots. A handful of service medals decorated the breast pocket of the pewter gray tunic.

In less than two hours, Kate Raeburn's rock-like sensibilities had been ground to a fine powder like medicines in a pharmacist's mortar. Still she knew that this was not the end of it. Elucidation would follow, and her instinct told her that there would be terrible consequences in knowing. But she had no choice; Erich Wolff was going to tell her, and she would listen.

CHAPTER EIGHTEEN

W olff gestured for her to sit with him on the couch beside the strange toy city. In spite of the horrific anticipation, she was engrossed by the model's swooping suspension bridges, miniature monuments, glistening white skyscrapers, and elaborate formal gardens with their tiny bronze fountains. Seeing her strain to read the German text on a small brass plate in the lower right corner, Wolff read it for her. "It says, *'The majestic metropolis of Linz, noble heart of the Thousand Year Reich.'* It was the Fuehrer's dream to move the capital of the Third Reich from Berlin to his boyhood home. This is how he wanted it to look. He designed it himself."

"Somewhere I've seen a photograph of Hitler sitting over this model, studying it," Kate said. "This is not . . ."

"Oh, no," Wolff said. "This is not his original. I had this one made from Albert Speer's drawings which I tracked down after Speer died. The Fuehrer's model was destroyed when the Russians burned the Chancellery," he said with sadness in his voice. Then as a postscript he said, "The photograph you've seen is up there, next to the large one of the Fuehrer and me on the veranda at the Berghof." He pointed to the center point of the long photo wall.

Kate spotted the image she remembered of Adolph Hitler in his bunker, eyes cast down on his miniature city of dreams, lost in fantasy during the final days. But what struck her more was the large sepia print to its right of the Fuehrer kneeling to the eye level of a small boy in uniform, speaking in his ear as the child listened with rapt attention.

Wolff waited patiently as she focused for a time on the

photographs, and then he said, "Let me tell you why I've brought you here, Katherine."

She fixed her eyes once again on Wolff and braced herself. Wolff paused, running over in his mind one last time the words he had so carefully rehearsed, and then he said, "Katherine, what I'm going to tell you will shock you, and it would destroy me if it were ever made public. So I beg you never to utter . . ."

"Don't say any more, Erich! I don't need to know any of this. I don't care!"

"You *must* know, Katherine. You must know because until you came into my life I had never been truly close to anyone but the Fuehrer. I know that you and I have not been, as you say, 'intimate.' But that, for me, would have been unforgivable. I have never been unfaithful to him."

Wolff stopped, allowing what he had just said to sink in. And then he strayed from the script, uncontrollably: "What we had was . . . what happened . . . it was . . . it was so long ago!" he blurted out, unable to finish his wretched admission. "I was a boy—he was the Fuehrer!"

"The picture! There!" Wolff nodded to the enlarged photograph of himself and Hitler. "He knelt down beside me that afternoon, and at that very moment he whispered in my ear, '*Du bist mein Liebling.*' You are my *favorite. Mein Liebling! Ich bin sein Liebling!* I was his *favorite*, his *love!* Can you understand?"

Kate's eyes never left his. She was transfixed by Wolff's pathetic monologue, yet she felt the pain and resentment of being thrust forcibly into someone else's bad dream.

Yes, she understood. She understood perfectly. Kate felt sick, and her head began to spin.

"I feel this same closeness with you, Katherine," he continued. "But we can never be—I won't *let* us be—until you know everything that I've kept from you. And so much of it is in this cellar.

"Do you know now why I've brought you here? I want you to be with me forever."

Kate was close to losing consciousness. She had ached for this moment, but now she was paralyzed by equal measures of fear and euphoria. When she did not answer, he said, "Perhaps I've made a terrible mistake, Katherine." His words were clipped. "If you prefer I not continue, I will have Bergdorf take you home. Nothing between us will change, and all this will never have happened."

A deafening stillness settled over the director's sanctum, with only the faint *wooosh* of the wine cellar's environmental control system audible but unheard by either of them. Her heart thumping wildly, Kate's eyes finally cleared. Her panic passed, and she said softly, "Yes, I feel what you feel, Erich. I have for a very long time.

"I want to know everything."

CHAPTER NINETEEN

"My father stole the paintings during the war. He killed a man in cold blood to have them all to himself."

Before the hour had passed, Wolff had disclosed without emotion the heinous saga of the paintings which had just taken her breath away: that they were from the legendary Gruenwald cache, gone missing from the others after Paris fell and presumed lost forever; how his father and Goering had ripped them from the walls of the old patriarch's Paris townhouse and his cousin's wine caves south of the city just before the evacuation; how Goering's thugs had snatched the fleeing old couple at the Hague as they were about to sail to freedom; how Otto Wolff had lagged behind after the Wehrmacht had cut and run, culled the cream of the collection from the lot, substituted an equal number of worthless pieces from his accomplice, Maurice Gernand's storeroom, and slipped them aboard the Austrian-bound railcar under the nose of the Nazi officer in charge.

He told her about how Otto and Gernand had then hustled the choice Gruenwald paintings out of France to Geneva in the dead of night, and about Otto's ruthless killing of Gernand in broad daylight on their return. He then explained how he, Erich Wolff, with help from a handful of tainted U.S. Customs agents, had bootlegged them out of Switzerland and into the United States after his father died. "I simply appealed to their patriotic partiality toward your Benjamin Franklin, or let's say toward his *engraved likeness*," Wolff smirked, referring to the fat packet of crisp one-hundred dollar bills which changed hands upon the arrival of the paintings from Geneva.

Kate sat quietly through Erich Wolff's entire monologue. While the tale seemed beyond belief, she had no doubt that it was gospel; it was far too bizarre not to be the absolute God's truth. But when it seemed that he was at the end, she said: "Do you know what happened to the old Gruenwald couple?"

"I do not know," he said brusquely. *Case closed.* She wasn't sure why she had even asked the question. She knew the answer.

In the awkward moment which followed, Kate sensed someone watching them. She turned toward the open double doors just as Friedrich Bergdorf stepped inside the room. She could almost feel his heat-seeking stare and his feverish resentment.

Wolff glanced up and said, "Ah, Herr Bergdorf. You're back. Did all go well?"

"I have the packages, Herr Wolff," Bergdorf said curtly. "Would you like me to bring them in?"

"Yes, please, Herr Bergdorf. Just the chairman's paintings, for now. You know which ones they are. We should look at them them as soon as possible."

Although the wrapped paintings were not large, they were a struggle for the small man as he carried them one at a time into the room and placed them carefully against the wall. One of the two square packages would be the Matisse collage; the other a signature Chagall floating blue man. The last bundle, larger, but tall and narrow, would have been the Kirchner standing nude.

"The rest are in the foyer, Herr Wolff. I will store them after your dinner."

Kate wondered how he had managed to lift them from the trunk of the Mercedes, up the steps into the mansion and then back down the steep stairway into the wine cellar, and in spite of Bergdorf's antagonism, she felt sympathy for him. As if reading her mind, Wolff whispered, "Don't feel sorry for him. He would not let me help even if I offered. He's an intractable old woman. Ignore his icy stares—he can be a bit proprietary."

"May I get anything for you, Herr Wolff? Would you like me to open the packages?" Bergdorf said.

"No, I think that will be all, Herr Bergdorf."

"Will Miss Raeburn be staying for dinner?"

"Yes, but we will be here for awhile. Set a place for her."

Bergdorf nodded coldly and left. "He's upset," Wolff said. "You are the first person, other than the two of us, to ever have seen these rooms. But Herr Bergdorf is harmless, I can assure you."

"That may be—still, he makes me uncomfortable. Perhaps when I know him better . . ."

"I'm afraid that won't happen, Katherine. Nobody really knows Bergdorf. We've been together a long time, yet even I feel uneasy around him. He is loyal and competent, and I would trust him with my life. He was with my father, you know. I inherited him along with the paintings—and Das Rheingold."

"I guess that will have to be good enough for me then," Kate said with a forced smile, although she couldn't quite grasp the bond between Bergdorf and Wolff. She had always seen Erich Wolff as the quintessential bachelor, distant and controlling, but with enough old-world charm to captivate most women if he chose. It once frustrated her that he had never shown the slightest carnal interest in her, as she was not an unattractive woman; this had caused her on more than one occasion to question his "preferences." But as sex dropped down, and ultimately off, her Top Ten list, she no longer cared—he was here, and he was sharing, *with her*, the most private parts of his life. Nothing else mattered.

"May I ask one more question about the paintings?" she

continued, mentally bumping Friedrich Bergdorf from "cultivate" to "forget about it" among her Life Goals.

"What is that?"

"Are there any Gruenwalds left who might come looking for them? Has anyone tried to find them?"

"I would assume that any family remaining gave up long ago. There is, of course, more interest today in works gone missing during the war. Most museums share the grapevine and investigate suspicious provenance gaps in their own collections. We do that, and we've had no trouble so far," he said. "But because I keep these paintings here and have never shown them to anyone, other than you this afternoon, this is of no concern to me. It is enough that they give me pleasure.

"Oh, one other thing," he continued. "My father stole forty-seven paintings in all. Forty three are hanging in the next room." Wolff waited for Katherine to work the math.

"Forty-three? That leaves four, by my calculation," Katherine responded. "Where are they?"

Wolff flashed a trace of a smile. "You would never guess, so I'll tell you. They are on the walls of the Mendelssohn."

Katherine's eyes widened. "The *Mendelssohn?* Someone could *see* them there!"

"*Thousands* of people have already seen them there," he teased. "They've been hanging in the Dutch gallery for years."

"But wouldn't someone recognize them? Why would you *do* that? Aren't you taking a risk? And which ones are they? I've never seen them," Kate said, her questions tumbling out like those of a child.

Another smirk crossed his face. "Oh, you've seen them. Nothing is keeping *anyone* from recognizing them. I suppose that some historian one day might walk through and think he knows them. But who would that be, and who would put his good name on the line to challenge me? Yes, I am taking a small risk, a *very* small risk, but all of life is a risk, ja?

"Oh, I took precautions. First, since they're on loan from *me*, I have entered no provenance on them in the museum records, other than the titles and painters' names which I provided—and my own name as the lender, of course. Nothing else is required. Second, none of them is signed. Third, and most important, I've attributed them all to lesser artists of their periods, but not so 'lesser' as to be unbelievable to anyone but a true expert. Any decent painter can get lucky now and then, don't you agree?

"Finally," he said, "what sane person would downgrade his own paintings on purpose for public display—particularly someone with my credentials?

"They're safe enough."

"But why?" Kate said.

"You mean, why did I do it?" Wolff laughed. "Conceit, I guess. And for my father, who took the larger risk. And because of my anger over the unfortunate outcome of the war. And for the tragic loss of the Fuehrer. I would no doubt have become *Reichsminister* for *Künstmuseums*. Can you imagine being czar of the art world from London to Leningrad? The Fuehrer would have given me anything. Who would not be bitter?

"I chose four paintings, you may be interested to know, to honor the Fuehrer. One for each work in Wagner's *Ring – Das Rheingold, Die Walküre, Siegfried* and *Götterdämmerung*. They were his favorites. He would have been pleased.

"One of them is a small but very elegant van Eyck of a man in a blue smock. And there's a deliciously smutty Jan Steen, and a wonderful Rubens modello, and perhaps the most magnificent Franz Hals I have ever seen—a haunting portrait of a mother and a small child. They are alive, I swear to you! They are truly alive.

"The Fuehrer loved children," he said.

CHAPTER TWENTY

Wolff rose from the sofa and said, "There's more, Katherine. Come." She stood and followed him to the chilling likeness at the far end of the chamber. The sitter continued to examine her, stripping her of any residual defense from their earlier encounter, leaving her weak-kneed and helpless.

Wolff looked up at the portrait with glazed eyes. "Here, Katherine, is the greatest prophet the world has ever known. He was no less a martyr than Jesus Christ or any of the saints, destroyed by madmen who never really knew him, who had no idea of his noble view of the world and his monumental plans for mankind. I *knew* him. I *stood* next to him. He talked to me, *to me,* and I would sit for hours listening to him share his vision. I was only a small boy, but he spoke in a way that even a child like me could grasp. This was why he could inspire millions in the Fatherland to great acts of courage and sacrifice. But it was not enough.

"Except for the heroic German people, the world was quick to condemn him," he said, the gall rising in his throat. "But the truth is that the Jews were destroying our world, as they still do. Martin Luther knew this. The Pope knew this. And *you* know because you were once a Jew in an unbearable life. Only because you have an Aryan heart, Katherine, were you able to tear yourself away. The Fuehrer's grand plan would have saved us all. His Final Solution was inspired by God.

"This room and my life are a tribute to him. Does this shock you, Katherine?"

Eventually she found her voice, her eyes fixed in space, as she spat the words out slowly and bitterly. "My life was a bloody hell. I have spent most of it driving out the demons and stitching up the wounds inflicted on me by that evil father of mine and his wretched offspring and that sanctimonious rabbi and my jellyfish of a mother who *not once* stood between me and any of them. The scars will never go away. Screw them all!" she exploded as the tears which she had held in check for twenty-five years streamed down her flushed cheeks.

Wolff uncharacteristically put his arms around her and held her, like the father she wished she'd had, until, many minutes later, the tears stopped, and she continued.

"No, I am not shocked, Erich. I am overwhelmed. Show me more."

One glance into her reddened eyes told him that he had won her soul. She would be his Eva.

Wolff's hand swept upward, calling Kate's attention to the room in which they were standing. "This wonderful old ceiling was here when I bought the mansion. When I first saw it, it reminded me of the Ratskeller under the Rathaus in Bremen, right on the Marketplatz. But you have probably been there."

"No, I've never been to Bremen, only to Munich and to Heidelberg. And Berlin."

"That's unfortunate, Katherine. The Ratskeller is the most famous wine cellar in the world. They can offer wines from hundreds of German vineyards—and they serve only wine, as it has been since 1408, by irrevocable decree of the city fathers. The Ratskeller is where I honed my taste for the great German vintages, and some of the finer French wines which Goering liked so much, on those occasions when I returned to Bremen to see my father.

"The Ratskeller is where sixty years ago my father took me one evening in my new uniform of the Hitler Youth which had just been issued to me that morning. I am still not sure why we went there. He was never passionate about the Reich and often warned me about my own attraction to the Fuehrer. In fact, my father was such a reluctant Nazi that more than once, in my adolescent zeal, I nearly reported him to Uncle Adolph.

"Why we went to the Ratskeller that night? Perhaps he was simply moved by the phenomenon of fatherhood and wanted to show me off to his cronies. Or maybe he wished to lay to rest any suspicion about his own patriotism by putting me on display, his biological contribution to the Nazification of the Fatherland, ja?

"But anyway, there we were," Wolff continued. "Tobacco smoke hung so thick that you could barely see from one end of the room to the other, and it stank of six centuries of spilled wine and the unwashed bodies of several hundred Wehrmacht on leave, but it was an exotic fragrance to me. A dozen or so Nazi SS sat at this very table," Wolff said, slapping the scarred planks with the flat of his hand, "and my father lifted me right up on it amongst the wine glasses and tall brown bottles for all to see me in my crisp new khaki uniform.

"'This is my son!' he announced in a slurred voice, 'the future of the Third Reich. *Heil Hitler!*' Only I, knowing my father and his views on Nazi politics, could have detected the mockery in his tone, which teetered dangerously near the edge of discovery. *In vino veritas,* Ja? Nevertheless, all the soldiers, drunk if not more so than he, cheered and raised their glasses to me, and when I offered the salute in return and echoed *Heil Hitler!*—and threw in a hearty *Sieg heil* for good measure—they cheered louder. Even the waiters and the barmaids joined in. Then they began to sing, and the Ratskeller rang with the glorious sound of men's voices, my father's the loudest and most bitter among them, booming out *Gaudeamus Igitur, juvenes dum sumus."* Wolff sang the phrase in a quavery baritone. *"Then let us be merry while we are still young!* My God, it was overwhelming! And when they finished, my father gave me a sip from his glass. My First Communion, you might say."

Kate listened spellbound as vivid pictures of the event formed in her mind.

"When I was in Bremen years ago," Wolff said, "I happened to have taken supper one evening at the Ratskeller amongst the tourists, for old time's sake, as you say in America. I was seated at this very table, right in front of my own initials that I'd carved into it with my father's knife on that night. See? EW! And here are his—*OW*—next to mine."

Kate stared at the deeply gouged letters, bold if not artistic, although the director's steady hand even as a boy was a marked improvement over that of his father, clearly impaired by the effects of the wine. She ran her fingers over them and shivered as she imagined Otto Wolff's razor-sharp knife scraping into the dense oak slab.

"With little negotiation required, I purchased the table and the benches from the owner for a few thousand marks. The table meant nothing to him. You would have thought I had offered him the moon, yet I would have easily given him a *hundred* thousand.

"Did you notice the watercolor?" he asked. Wolff moved from the table and returned to the insipid landscape on the long photo wall.

"Paintings I understand," Kate said. "But this one puzzles me. Not the painting so much as why it's here at all. You'd have to agree that it would hardly draw a crowd at Christie's," she added with a hint of sarcasm.

The angry red of the Nazi banner on the adjacent wall

all but obliterated any artistry which might have inhabited the dreary work, although its total lack of inspiration could hardly be blamed on its juxtaposition with the screaming scarlet pennant. The composition lacked even rudimentary harmony, either in hue or contrast or architecture. *It was a terrible painting by someone who obviously had never seen the inside of an art school or had the benefit of intelligent critique,* Kate thought.

"Oh, I wouldn't agree," Wolff said in an amused tone. "I believe that Christie's would be most interested to offer it for sale. It's one of my most cherished possessions, and I would expect it to command a hefty price on the auction block. I doubt that five million would touch it, if I were ever to part with it—which I would not, of course. Can you see the signature?"

Kate's eyes dropped to the right corner of the picture and focused on the faint inscription which, on inspection, shouted louder than the sanguine stripe to its right.

AHitler, it read, the last three letters trailing off the lower edge of the paper.

Kate's recognition prompted a soft gasp. "It was a gift to my father. The Fuehrer presented it to him after he reported securing the last of the Gruenwald paintings on the train to Alt Aussee," he said with a sly smile. "Uncle Adolph was fond of exchanging small gifts with his inner circle, and he gave away many of his drawings and watercolors to Goering, Himmler, Hoffman and some of the others, although he would never have wanted them publicly displayed. He knew that they were not good, and he was embarrassed and frustrated by his own lack of talent. Still, he painted, ever hopeful. This was his last."

Wolff remembered how his father had ridiculed the work privately after Hitler, with much fanfare, presented it to him at the Berghof. He had only finished it the day before, and the paper was still damp from the preparation and from the paint, Otto Wolff had told his son. The elder Wolff had never framed it; in fact, Erich himself had resurrected it from the dustbin after his father returned from Berchtesgaden and shortly before he was arrested. He had carried it rolled in a tube as he crept through Allied lines to Bremen in the final days, only to show Erich what a miserable talent the Fuehrer truly was with the brush—still another attempt to lessen his son's attraction to the dangerous Supreme Commander—and then he consigned it to the trash pile.

But the boy thought the painting was beautiful.

"Tell me about the uniform, Erich," Kate said as she stepped away from the pallid watercolor and toward the dashing mannequin bedecked in the benign warm gray of an officer of the Third Reich. Silver braided shoulder boards and gleaming silver buttons drew a striking contrast with the soft black leather of the Sam Browne belt and black riding boots polished to a mirror finish. The black collar trimmed in silver piping was embroidered with facing wreathes of silver oak leaves, and the patent leather visor of the upswept Nazi officer's peak cap set squarely on the mannequin's head reflected a powerful pinpoint spot directed from the ceiling.

"It was my father's," he said. "As much as I hated him when I was a boy, I loved that uniform, and I longed to grow into manhood to wear one of my own. One of the great regrets of my life was that I never served the Fuehrer as an officer of the Reich. I would have worn the uniform with honor."

"You would have been very handsome in it, Erich."

"I've never told this to anyone, Katherine, and I know it sounds childish, but I put it on now and then, and always on the Fuehrer's birthday; my father and I were nearly identical in height, and the uniform fits me perfectly, even now. When I put it on, I open a fine Mosel, I sit down here and I play Wagner, and I imagine myself with the Fuehrer by the fire in his study at the Berghof, just the two of us, and I'm telling him about my plans for the great Fuehrermuseum and he is nodding his approval.

"Does this make me insane, Katherine?"

"Erich, we all have fantasies. No, you're not insane. Maybe you could put the uniform on for me some day? Would you do that for me?"

"In time, Katherine. When the time is right."

"This is my father," Wolff said to her, pointing to one of several dozen framed photographs on the long wall to the left of the portrait. His long, aristocratic index finger went to the image of a tall, very good-looking young officer of the Third Reich, probably in the same uniform that adorned the mannequin. He bore a dead-on resemblance to Erich Wolff as she imagined he might have looked thirty-five years ago. "And the Fuehrer, next to him—and I am standing between them in my Hitler Youth uniform. Goering is here to the left of Uncle Adolph, and Himmler beside him.

"And this is *The Astronomer* in the background, in the Great Room of the Berghof. The famous Vermeer," he said, almost breathlessly.

Kate stared at the photo. She had seen the painting in the Louvre and could recall the sitter's rich blue robe, and on his face and the ancient celestial globe that held his attention the play of soft light filtering through the leaded glass window. The entire art world knew of *The Astronomer's* honored place in the legendary Rothschild family collection, and that he had been snatched by the Nazis during the Occupation. And now here he was, proof positive, held captive in the nest of history's most ignoble bird of prey. Still oblivious and unmoved by his plight, focused in perpetuity on his solemn search of the heavens, *The Astronomer* was rescued in the nick of time at war's end, just before the Allies leveled the Berghof, and promptly returned to the reigning Rothchild, Edouard.

Kate Raeburn tingled as if an electric shock had surged through her. What else could this man possibly show her, or say to her, that could shake her more?

Wolff led her down the photo wall, identifying a bona fide who's who of the Nazi chieftains, formal portraits and casual groupings, many of which included Hitler and Otto Wolf and sometimes the boy, Erich. A number of the prints were inscribed by their subjects: *To Erich, with fondest regards, Hermann Goering . . . To Erich, Heil Hitler, Martin Bormann . . . Dearest Erich, God bless you, Albert Speer.* Each sentiment he read aloud with reverence and awe.

"And here's the most wonderful of them all," he said as he gestured toward one of himself and Hitler side by side in a routine photo-op pose. Instead of smiles, however, both wore somber, almost conspiratorial expressions, as if they had just surreptitiously agreed to invade still another European neighbor suffering under the delusion of one of the Fuehrer's predictable non-aggression treaties born to be broken. Across the bottom of the photograph was scrawled in a shaky hand a virtually indecipherable message, even to one learned in Teutonic linguistics. Wolff was only too happy to translate. "He has written," Wolff said in a near whisper, his finger tracing the words across the glass, "'*My dear Erich, If ever I were to have a son, I would wish him to be just like you. With my deepest love and affection, Adolph Hitler.*'"

Wolff beamed as he passed to the next photo. But suddenly he fell silent as he was describing an aerial scene of what seemed to be the whole of the German population drawn to the massive, multi-pillared Reich Chancellery. Abruptly he seemed to be consumed by the roaring hoards surrounding the great temple of the Fuehrer; he was goose-stepping with the endless ranks of Waffen SS parading like shiny black carpenter ants in tight formation; he joined in the swelling *Sieg heils* which repeated and repeated as if they had been captured on a continuous loop which blared from ten thousand speakers; he was transported by the screeching of his Divine Leader soaring above it all.

"Erich . . . Erich!" Kate shook his arm.

"Oh! *Es tut mir sehr leid.* I'm very sorry. I drifted a bit. I attended a rally like this with my stepmother in Berlin, and it all just came back to me. The whole experience was . . ." He searched for the word. ". . . Pentecostal. That's it, *Pentecostal!* I would liken it to the huge assemblies of your Billy Graham and the thousands of hysterical believers rushing to the altar to be 'saved,' as you say. Would that be a fair analogy?"

"From what I've read and seen in documentaries, you're pretty close. Although he's not *my* Billy Graham. You forget my illustrious roots, I think, Erich."

"Yes, your roots. *And* mine," he said. Wolff's comment confused her. Kate wanted to ask him what he had meant by "and mine," but she remained silent. He moved past his rogues' gallery of the Third Reich and approached the cryptic display cabinet which hung alone among the photographs.

The walnut-framed case showcased a small cache of firearms and a single apothecary bottle on a low shelf which held several large, jade green capsules. Kate Raeburn's spiraling descent into Erich Wolff's dark past, or, perhaps, into her own apocalyptic future, continued as he opened the hinged glass-front door and reached for one of the pistols which hung against the red velvet back of the case. "These are very special, Katherine," he said as he gently lifted from its mounting a gleaming, long-barreled Luger with a yellowed ivory grip.

"I was with my father when the Fuehrer presented this to him on the terrace of the Berghof. It was a reward, ironically, for his efforts in securing the magnificent Gruenwald pieces for Linz and for the Fuehrer's personal collection. Look at the grip! See the swastika carved into it? And read the inscription on the barrel! Let me translate it for you: *To Otto Wolff, loyal servant of the Third Reich, with my deepest gratitude, Adolph Hitler,*" he recited, having committed it long ago to memory.

"Here, you can hold it."

Kate took the heavy weapon gingerly in her slender white hand and tentatively slipped her finger under the trigger guard. "Is this the gun that your father used to . . ."

". . .to kill Gernand? Yes, this is the one. It was the only time he ever fired it."

She quickly returned the pistol to Wolff, who replaced it against the red velvet. He then took down a smaller, leather-holstered handgun from the case. His hand shook slightly as slipped the gun from its holster. It was a strange weapon, a tiny revolver that to Kate looked like a toy. Instinctively he lifted it to his nostrils and drew in the heavy aroma of gun oil as he had done so many times since his father had given it to him as a teenage boy.

"This was the Fuehrer's. He called it his protector—'the only protector he could fully trust,' he said. He carried it from the time he was a young firebrand in the Party."

"It's very small," Kate said.

"But no less deadly," Wolff responded. "The baby rattlesnake is the most lethal, ja? A 22-caliber bullet in the brain will do the job as well as a 45-caliber round, and with much less mess."

"How did you come upon this? It must be extremely valuable," she said.

"It is priceless. Historians believe that it was lost in the fire. No one knows that it still exists. But I would never sell it. The Fuehrer gave it to my father for *me* on his fifty-sixth birthday, after his party in the bunker under the Chancellery. The entire High Command was there. It was 20 April, 1945, just ten days before he took his own life. A sad day. He let me hold it once at the Berghof when I was a child and he must have remembered how excited I had been to feel it in my hand.

"It is the most wonderful gift I have ever received. Nothing I have is worth more to me than this," Wolff said as he lifted it again to his face to inhale its exotic aroma and rub the cold barrel against his cheek. Had he been alone, he would certainly have kissed it. "Take it," he said as he offered the diminutive weapon to Kate.

As she reached for the pistol, a slight chill gripped the room, or so it seemed to her, and on impulse she looked up at the glaring portrait; Kate was not surprised that the Supreme Commander's icy stare had not thawed, but appeared to have slipped a degree or two.

In spite of the Fuehrer's frosty castigation, she clutched the cold steel firmly in her hand and was strangely overcome by an almost irrepressible urge to squeeze the trigger over and over again, avenging every indignity and cruel act ever visited on her during her unhappy life. *I have a gun, and I'm not afraid to use it,* she thought. But Kate Raeburn *was* afraid—afraid of herself. Quickly she returned Adolph Hitler's beloved revolver to the protective custody of Erich Wolff, convinced that it was possessed by the evil man himself.

As Wolff lovingly replaced the weapon on its pegs and was about to close the case, Kate reached for his hand, preventing him from snapping it shut. "Erich, what's in the little glass jar?

My curiosity is killing me."

"An interesting choice of words," he said, without emotion.

"It's cyanide."

It should have been clear to the director that his guided tour was growing progressively upsetting to Kate, and that the cyanide capsules might have pushed her to the brink. Still he continued. "Kate, I must talk to you," he said. "Sit, please." Absently he pushed the power button of the room's elaborate sound system, and the rich unison cello line of *Götterdämmerung* insinuated itself quietly into the space.

In a day of startling "firsts," Erich Wolff's use of the more intimate "Kate" after so many years was among the most unexpected. For her, all of the other revelations which he had laid on her paled in comparison to this simple invocation; the igneous shell that had kept her from him had finally cracked.

"I like it that you called me 'Kate.' Will you keep calling me that?" she said softly.

"If that's what you would like . . . Kate," he said as they sat once again on the sofa facing the intricate model of Hitler's Linz. Wolff took her hand.

"Kate, I am an old man," he began.

"An old man?" she laughed nervously. "You're not . . ."

"*Look* at me, Kate. I'm an *old man*. I have no wife, I have no children. Only Bergdorf, and he is merely a servant.

"In my entire life I have loved only the Fuehrer." Wolff saw the hurt in her eyes, and quickly added, "And then my Kate came to me. My Eva."

It took only an instant to sink in, but then Kate's senses screamed for release. First, there was Wolff's profession of love for Adolph Hitler, then "my Kate," and now *My Eva? When will it stop? Please, God, make it stop!* she prayed frantically to the Yahweh she had rejected years ago.

"My greatest failing is never having served the Reich. I pledged myself to him, and I never fulfilled my promise. There was no chance for me. So I decided long ago that the best I could do was to die as he died and hope to join him in the flames. The cyanide is for this. And the revolver."

Kate grew woozy as his words were swept away in a swelling horn motif which materialized like spring wheat from the dark, fertile tillage of lower strings. *If this is a dream, please, God, let me wake up. Let me wake up now!*

"When he died, Eva was with him. I want you to be with me . . . Kate."

Please, God . . .

CHAPTER TWENTY-ONE

Suddenly transported as if someone had flipped a switch in his head, and totally oblivious to Kate's fragile state, Wolff persisted. "No one saw very much of her. Most of the time he kept her tucked away in Munich or Berchtesgaden and it was only in the last days that he brought her to Berlin. I was with Eva many times at the Berghof," Wolff said almost boastfully, his eyes glazed. "She was a beautiful woman. Intelligent. Passionate. Captivating." He chose his descriptors carefully, savoring each one like measured sips of very old port. The words blew in his mind across the dying embers of the Fuehrer's mountaintop retreat and rekindled the fire in his belly. Although he glowed hot with reminiscence, his recollection of Eva Braun could not have been more wrong.

History remembers her as a woman tepid as bathwater left standing, and no less shallow. The trivial Fräulein Braun was known to have spent most of her time swimming and dancing alone and watching trashy movies in the Berghof. Her bedroom was strewn with pocket novels which Hitler abhorred. Though she was not unattractive, photographs fail to support Wolff's claim of great beauty. The woman who twice tried to take her own life would primp endlessly, but for no one in particular as Hitler was seldom by her side, being either in Berlin or off to one of his command bunkers scattered about Europe. Erich Wolff's recall was that of an infatuated teen, the self-deception perfectly intact after nearly sixty years.

"During the times my father was with the Fuehrer and the others," he continued, "she and I would sit alone on the veranda drinking lemonade, looking out on the Obersalzberg, and though I was only twelve or thirteen she would talk to me as an adult. Many times I wished she had been my mother, and as I grew older I imagined her as my lover. This caused me great guilt even to have thought about her in that way."

Wolff stood and went to one of the shelves holding photographs and returned with a silver-framed picture. "Here we are together. She inscribed it, *'To my darling Erich, the Fuehrer's favorite. Love always, Eva.'*" The sepia photo showed a gangly adolescent in light-colored shorts and heavy, knee-length stockings, and beside him a plain, slender woman in a dark, polka-dotted dress. Eva Braun hardly showed the results of her preening.

Wolff's soliloquy gave Kate a few moments to pull herself together. Feeling more assertive because of his willingness to unearth so many skeletons, Kate risked a bombshell: "Erich, what exactly *was* your relationship with Hitler?"

After a long silence, he said, testily, "I thought that I had explained it to you. What more do you need to know? It was nothing. And it had no lasting effect on me," he protested. "My love for the Fuehrer has nothing to do with . . ."

"That's enough, Erich. That's all. I had no right. You were very young, and I can only imagine . . ."

"The power he would have had over a child?"

"Not only *children*, Erich—an entire *country*, for God's sake. Millions of adult human beings. It was very long ago."

"Yes, it was."

"But as long as I seem to be in full confessional mode, I will share with you one last and most painful detail of my life," he said.

CHAPTER TWENTY-TWO

Wolff stood a second time, went over to a small writing desk against the wall opposite the photos, lifted a tattered, leather-bound book from its center drawer, and returned with it to the sofa.

Kate recognized it immediately. "Is that the Torah, Erich?" she said, confused.

"Yes, it is the Torah," he confirmed in bitter resignation. "I can hardly bear to touch it. Still I can't make myself dispose of it. It was my mother's."

"Your mother's? You mean Klara's? Klara von Koch was a Jew?" Kate remembered Wolff's painful accounts of Klara and her violent, anti-Semitic core.

"No, Klara was my stepmother. This is the book of my natural mother.

"Her name was Hilde Meyer."

"Hilde Meyer? Your mother was Jewish?"

Wolff opened the worn Pentateuch, the five books of Moses, and removed a small brown photograph. "This is she."

He handed her the dulled print, somehow grown elegant with age under a spider-web of patina. It showed a lovely young girl with soft, full brows, ebony eyes, and hair the apparent color and sheen of fresh-picked blackberries. She was the exact opposite of her fair, Aryan son.

"She's beautiful, Erich."

"I despise her."

"Erich, she's your mother! She did nothing to you."

"She made me Jewish, like her."

197

"And like me," Kate responded.

Wolff continued without acknowledgment, "How could my father have done this? He *knew* what this would mean for a child that would come. My grandfather did the right thing, sending her away."

"The right thing? Even if she went to the ovens?"

"That is not my concern. It was the only way."

Kate stared at him in disbelief. *How could she ever have been drawn to a man so completely without a soul?* she asked herself. *How could she have been so blinded?*

"How long have you known about her?" Kate said after an awkward silence.

"I knew when I was a child that Klara was not my real mother, but I knew nothing about Hilde until father died in 1970. I found the book and the picture in his personal things. And also my original birth document and a note in with the papers . . ."

He would not forget that day. During such life-changing episodes, for those left behind memories often gush uncontrolled, sometimes flood the breast with sorrow, sometimes with bitterness, sometimes with supernal understanding and even forgiveness, albeit too late to comfort the forgiven; this they did for Erich Wolff, except for the forgiveness. As the old man lay on his deathbed, the signature events of their time together popped up in the younger Wolff's mind like brightly painted ducks in an arcade shooting gallery.

To him, Otto Wolff had been a study in contradiction for the four decades of their relationship. His long absences during the war Erich could resolve, yet the boy's toxic exposure to the hateful Klara had scarred his spirit like dripping battery acid, and he had never forgiven his father for leaving him alone with her. Still there were moments when his father was tender and wise, though Erich, like most adolescents, was loath to acknowledge Otto's gentler qualities during his rebel years.

He considered his father a coward for not having served on the Front, but at some point the boy came round to the idea that Otto Wolff, as did all others in the Third Reich, served at the pleasure of the Fuehrer; he had no choice. The murder of Maurice Gernand and the pilfering of the Fuehrer's paintings, brilliant as the caper might have been, remained an enigma to him—the acts were so unlike his father. Yet war has a way of making both saints and sinners of otherwise ordinary men, this he knew, and there was no reason to believe that Otto Wolff had been miraculously exempt from this uniquely human phenomenon. Besides, it was a long time ago.

Klara sat knitting in a stiff, ladder-back chair against the wall of Otto's bedroom where he had slept alone since returning from prison, seemingly oblivious to the fact that her husband of forty years was dying. Erich stood by Otto's bed, holding his hand in a gesture which would have been out of bounds before his father's stroke; physical displays had never been a dominant trait in the House of Wolff, and Klara would rather have consumed shards of glass than dispense so much as a simple hug. "Please Do Not Touch" could have been the family motto.

Erich had passed the time at bedside relating to his father various matters of Das Rheingold, that being the closest of all subjects to his father's heart, and the only one they still held in common. It was a report made unnecessary, however, by the fact that the son had years ago assumed full control and direction of the family business, and the father's involvement had become for the most part moot. Yet he would murmur a slurred response here and there, and offer an occasional slight nod of approval. As Otto Wolff grew weaker and closed his eyes, both fell silent, retreating into their own private worlds of remembrance. The only sounds came from the faint death rattle in Otto's throat and the rhythmic clicking of Klara's needles.

His lasting image of his father would always be of him in the striking uniform of the Third Reich. Pride had enveloped him as Otto, in full Nazi regalia and surrounded by his fellow officers, toasted him in the Rathskeller under the Marketplatz. The same gratification consumed him as he pictured Otto, in dress grays, standing alongside the Fuehrer by the fire in the Great Room of the Berghof, hands clasped confidently behind his back, the two of them in deep discussion over appropriate works for the Fuehrermuseum of Hitler's dreams.

Conversely, it was the same uniform he wore on the day Erich hated him the most. The day his father told him the truth he refused to believe—about the futility of the war, the Fuehrer's impending demise, his own likely imprisonment, and Erich's exile to America which would separate him from his beloved Fatherland and the Reich which would cease to be.

Yet he would never be free of his disgrace that Otto's glorious uniform had never displayed ribbons of the battlefield, or the humiliation of his father being led away by the Allied lackeys in that common tweed suit rather the immaculately tailored gray tunic and black-striped trousers of the Reich which hung unceremoniously in his armoire until the day he died.

He felt his father's grip grow suddenly less strong, and watched as his eyes flickered and began to fade. With a last, defiant effort he raised his free hand, which was now clenched into a fist, and reached for Erich, his dry lips moving. The son lowered his head to his father's voice, straining to hear.

"In my desk . . .in the study. . .are things for you only. Here is the . . . key," he whispered as he opened his hand and released a small brass key which dropped noiselessly on the soft goosedown comforter covering his long, nearly lifeless body. How he came to hold the key after weeks of confinement remained a mystery never solved.

After a long silence, Otto opened his parched lips once more, and Erich drew close. "Berchtesgaden," his whispered.

"What was that, father?"

"Berchtesgaden," he repeated, as a tear slipped from the corner of one closed eye and inched down his gray cheek. "I'm sorry for Berchtesgaden."

He knew. Of course he knew. How could he not, Erich thought, as the image of the back of Otto's black leather long-coat through the French doors of the Berghof flashed once again before his eyes.

"Don't be sorry, father," he said softly as he squeezed Otto's hand more tightly. "There was nothing you could do." This was as close as he could come to forgiveness.

"I love you, son . . ." were his last words, the first and only time he would utter what Erich Wolff had long conceded would never be spoken aloud, and then with his free hand he pulled Erich's face to his own and he kissed his grown son on the cheek. Otto's haunted eyes opened wide as if some stunning revelation had just been made known to him. Then they slowly closed, and his buzzing trachea grew silent. Klara looked up, like an animal detecting something amiss in the woods, knowing, then coldly finished her row of knitting. She stood from the chair, placed her needles, ball of yarn and half-finished woolen scarf on the cane seat, and came to the side of the bed; without ceremony or a tear, she pulled the quilted cover up over Otto Wolff's still, stone-hued face.

CHAPTER TWENTY-THREE

"I am not only Jewish, Kate, but I'm a bastard as well. What do you think of that?" he said, not really seeking an answer. He received none.

"I do think about her, what happened to her. There was a note . . . You may read it if you wish," he said as he opened the leather-bound book once more and removed a yellowed square of paper, folded twice and on the verge of crumbling.

Kate took it from him, held it unfolded for a moment, and then opened it slowly and carefully so that it would not fall to pieces in her hands. She struggled at first with the German, summoning her college Deutsch which she thought had long ago taken flight through disuse, but found to her surprise that she could decipher most of the elegantly penned script. The writer had the strong hand of an artist and an honest simplicity in his stroke; he might have become a decent painter, or a fine sculptor. *But for a single insane miscreant,* she thought, reflecting on the evil warmonger who stole lives and souls by the millions, among them Otto Wolff and his tormented offspring who sat beside her.

She translated slowly, aloud, so that Wolff could correct her if she missed something consequential.

> *My dear son Erich,*
> *I am ashamed that I have never told you about your mother and that I never had the courage to tell you face to face. Please forgive me. Her name was Hilde. She was a lovely young woman. She was kind and loving and we cared for each other very much. My Hilde*

was only sixteen and I was twenty-five when we were drawn to each other. She was a servant in your grandfather's house.

No one knew of our feelings until it became obvious that she was to have you. We wanted to marry, but your grandfather was outraged because she was servant, and worse than that, she was a Jew. A public betrothal would have ruined him in the Party. Her family name was Meyer.

Father refused to allow us to marry, and after you were born he took you and drove Hilde from the house. This has been my greatest shame, not standing up and claiming her. I do not know what happened to her after she left. I never saw her again. I ache over her fate. I think that because she was not Aryan, she went to the camps.

After that, father insisted that I marry Klara, which I did. It was a terrible mistake, but I was young and weak.

Please do not be angry with me. If I could change it now, I would. Do not be ashamed of your mother because she was a Jew. She was a kind and gentle soul, and you would have loved each other deeply. I know how you feel about Jews because of your attraction to the Fuehrer and his ideas. He was wrong, and I tried to tell you that in small ways as you were growing up, but I was afraid to say too much, fearing they would have hurt you.

The picture is of her. Wasn't she beautiful? This is her Torah also. She asked me to keep it for you. There are good words in it, and she lived by them. I urge you to keep the picture and the book always.

I have also given you your original birth document with my name and hers. No one has seen this but me, and now you. Again I beg your forgiveness.

Your loving father, Otto.

Wolff stared into space as she read, his face a portrait of tortured ambivalence. His expression did not change when Kate became silent. *Götterdammerung* had come to a merciful end, and each of them was alone with their thoughts.

Wolff rose slowly, replaced the Torah and the note in the desk and returned with several other small journals bound in leather. "These are my father's diaries. To be more exact, they are the true records of his and Goering's *transactions*, you might say. They are in code, of course, but whoever could decipher them would know precisely what pieces they claimed for the Fuehrer's museum, from whom they came, and where they might have gone for 'safekeeping.' He continued keeping these records through Das Rheingold, as have I; they're all in the desk. Here, Kate, let me show you . . ."

Erich Wolff proceeded to flip through them, a page at a time, patiently explaining to her how the ledgers had been kept for more than sixty years in fragments of thinly scratched German, cryptic symbols and numerals, the discovery and decoding of which would set the art world spinning off its axis.

"This one is the key," he said as he came to a tiny, worn ledger tucked between the others about the size of a deck of cards, only thinner. "My Little Black Book," he laughed. "These are the decoded symbols, letters and abbreviations for the dealers and the private collectors who received each of the pieces the journals refer to, plus what was sent off to the Fuehrer, to the mines, and to the High Command. In these little books are the complete records of Das Rheingold.

"Many of the pieces which were not pleasing to the Fuehrer—the ones he called *degenerate* by painters such as Picasso, Matisse, Chagall, Braque—were sold secretly through dealers or traded ten-for-one for second-rate masters on the Fuehrer's so-called 'approved list,'" he said.

"But I thought that your father turned these diaries over to the British when he was captured," Kate said. "To get a lighter sentence, wasn't it? In fact, I saw these diaries once in an exhibit somewhere years ago, along with fifty or sixty pieces that were recovered because of them. How could you possibly have them?"

Wolff laughed again. "Yes, those were his diaries you saw, Kate, but they were not these," he said, gesturing to the journals on his lap. "My father trained early on as an artist. He had a steady hand and an even better eye. The ones you saw were forgeries. Only he left out a few salient details—such as the Gruenwald paintings in my little gallery and hundreds of other works that he knew he could find later and sell for a huge profit."

Almost as an afterthought, he continued, "Oh, and of course he deleted all references to the dealers whom he would invite into Das Rheingold, as you would expect. How grateful they were to be spared the embarrassment of exposure! Not to mention the prison time. They were ecstatic about participating in my father's business, or so they said, and happy to sell him pieces he wanted for very low prices—ironically, as they did for the Fuehrer. I continue to enjoy the same courtesy," he said with a self-satisfied smile. "Not one of them complained, ever. They made too much money." He laughed a third time.

Wolff handed her the small black book to hold. She turned the stubby pages slowly, automatically, but they offered nothing to the casual reader. A more assiduous analysis of the German code names for the members of Wolff's exclusive little club would have revealed a true who's who of international art houses who were, and continued to be, covert players in his obscenely profitable scheme. And the entertaining pseudonyms for his private clients read like characters from a Jimmy Breslin novel, disguising a comparable "A" list of oil tycoons, financial fat cats, computer billionaires, media moguls, tabloid gangsters, Hollywood legends, and purple-robed royalty.

She handed the tiny ledger back to him, stunned by its all-star cast. Like the weapons she held earlier, she was glad to be rid of it.

"Now, Kate, you know it all," he said in a sigh of finality, the timbre of his voice suggesting that he expected some response.

Another wave of panic crashed over her as she concluded beyond any doubt that Erich Wolff was certifiably psychopathic. His obsession with the most diabolical despot of all time was ironclad proof of this. His vile fantasy of her, Kate, as *his Eva* was the repugnant idea of a maniac. And his belief that she would actually sacrifice herself, *with him,* to fulfill his gross delusion was horrifying.

Kate's own preoccupation with Wolff had morphed from obsession to fear, then terror, then pity, then terror once again in the span of a few hours. Her controlling sensation now was flight; she was suffocating in this cellar and in Erich Wolff's sulfurous aura. And now, for the first time, she too could truly feel the presence of the Fuehrer himself. Kate Raeburn desperately needed fresh air and blue sky and warm sun and the solitary sound of birds, and blessed release from swastikas and cyanide and piercing horns and blaring trombones.

Wolff took her cold hand and looked pleadingly into her

eyes. Her body stiffened, but she feared pulling away. "Erich, I must go. Frankly, this has all been. . .overwhelming. You must give me time to absorb it all, alone," she said, mustering every ounce of courage in her shaken body. "Will you have Bergdorf take me home, please?"

"Kate, I . . ."

"*Please*, Erich."

On cue, the big double doors swung outward and Friedrich Bergdorf appeared in the opening. She had come too unhinged to notice his uncanny timing, or care. Kate stood as Wolff released her, and without a word she turned and walked toward the gnomish aide, her lungs gasping for oxygen.

CHAPTER TWENTY-FOUR

Erich Wolff had been awake for more than twenty-four hours. The lack of sleep was beginning to drag him under as he sat with Bergdorf at the long mahogany table in the dining room. Kate Raeburn's untouched china and silver lay where Bergdorf had set it; he and Wolff had finished their own late suppers and emptied a bottle of Baden Riesling when the director broached the subject of Angela and Pieter's interest in the Hals.

"I am sorry if I alarmed you, Herr Wolff," Bergdorf said. "I certainly did not want you to shorten your stay, knowing how you treasure your times with Don Vittoria," he added with the slightest trace of a smirk.

"You were right to call, Friedrich. But it may have been just as Miss Desjardin told you, that they were simply admiring the paintings. God knows there's plenty there to admire. And there may have been repairs needed to one of the frames."

"I trust Nichter's instincts, Herr Wolff, but I don't trust either of them. We should do something," Bergdorf said.

"And just what would you do, Friedrich?" Wolff said, his eyes fighting the effects of the wine, lack of sleep, and lack of interest, and his mind still reeling from his disastrous attempt to woo *his Eva.*

"I think that we should take the paintings down and have them brought here." Bergdorf answered decisively.

"Well, do it then. You handle it. I don't care," Wolff said. "But what will you tell Miss Desjardin?"

"I'll tell her nothing. They're your paintings, and you can do with them what you please. But a little intimidation might stifle any interest she might have in poking around any further."

"You may be right, but how do we deal with her when she sees them gone? And with what shall we replace them?"

"I will tell her after they've come down and instruct her to replace them with other suitable works. I will tell her that you've found buyers for them and that the pictures must be sent for appraisal."

"Don't underestimate her, Friedrich."

"Miss Desjardin will not be a problem."

"If you say so, Friedrich," Wolff said, his will to debate fading fast, and his mind still focused on the disappointing business with Kate Raeburn a few hours earlier. "You make the arrangements, and I'll speak with Miss Desjardin afterward, if I must."

"Your afternoon with Miss Raeburn did not go well?" Bergdorf segued, considering the matter of the purloined paintings and Angela Desjardin closed.

"You don't like her, do you?"

"Who I like or do not like is of no consequence, Herr Wolff."

"I wish you would like her, my friend. I have special plans for her, you know."

"Plans, Herr Wolff?"

"Later, Friedrich. It's been a very long day," Wolff said as he rose slowly from the long table, showing every year of his three-score-and-ten.

Plans, Bergdorf thought as he cleared the table. He knew what Erich Wolff's *plans* were, and she would never agree. This he knew from watching them through the afternoon, and from her eyes in the rear view mirror.

Plans. The man was a lunatic.

CHAPTER TWENTY-FIVE

"Mike Murray."

"Mike? It's Peetie."

For Mike Murray, there was only one "Peetie," and still after ten years he didn't have to ask, "Peetie who?"

"Peetie! Jeez, Peetie, how long's it been? Where are you? You don't call, you don't write," he exclaimed, invoking the punch line to an old chestnut which had driven them both into hysterics after tossing back a few at the Bear Brew Pub—the U of M's watering hole of choice for the campus's nocturnal types.

Pieter laughed. "I'm calling now, and I'm still at the Mendelssohn. It's great to hear your voice!"

Mike Murray was Pieter Maxfield's closest friend and drinking buddy at the University of Maine until they went their separate ways for grad school. Murray was sufficiently brilliant to have landed a coveted instructor's position in art history at Harvard while pursuing his Ph.D. there. But well into the program he suddenly soured on the task. His change of heart was prompted by a rancorous brouhaha between his advisor, whom he worshipped, and a resentful assistant dean; the advisor, a promising star in the Crimson firmament, was sacrificed at the altar of *academicus civilitatis*, with no chance for advancement within the professorial ranks at America's most prestigious university. The advisor left shortly thereafter, leaving Mike Murray the innocent victim, his dissertation in shambles and himself an "untouchable" for his callow support of the losing side, a fatal miscue in the hostile halls of higher learning.

This first bitter exposure to the dark side of his chosen

profession was also his last, having turned his burning desire for the scholarly life to acid indigestion. In a sudden burst of self-realization, Pieter Maxfield's friend intuited that he had no stomach for academic acrimony. Addicted, however, to the exquisite learning environment of Harvard and to the agreeableness of Cambridge, he stayed on, outlasting his detractors and ultimately ascending to a top administrative position, the role which now made him potentially useful to Pieter.

"It's great to hear your voice as well, Peetie," Murray answered. "And to what do I owe this unfathomable honor?"

"I need a little dirt, Mikey."

"I'm knee-deep in it up here, my brother. Your wish is my command. What is it you need?"

"You had a graduate up there probably sometime in the early fifties . . ."

"The early fifties! Good Lord! *Monks* were keeping our records back then, and *illuminating* them, no less. I'll have to go to the caves for that stuff. Pray tell me who it is."

"His name is Erich Wolff, our director here."

"Wolff!" Murray snorted. "The Nazi!"

"The Nazi?"

"Ja, the Nazi. He's a legend here among the old boys, although I don't think he's known much beyond the inner circle any more. I knew he was down there with you, but I always thought you had the book on him. See, it pays to keep in touch, Peetie," Murray said.

"Well, as you no doubt remember, I was always a day late and a buck short. Why don't you enlighten me and save the humiliation for later," Pieter said.

"Okay. Here's what I know: Wolff was just a kid when he came here. Eighteen, nineteen maybe. A couple or three years after the 'Big War,' our geezers still call it. Did his undergrad work and just stayed on, right on through heading up the museum. He was hot stuff the whole time he was here. Wolff was a charmer, or so they said."

"Yeah, I know about his academic stuff, and the museum. The 'charmer' part is new, but what's with the Nazi thing?"

Murray paused for thirty seconds or so, thinking.

"Mike, you still there?"

"I'm thinking." More silence. And then he said, "Okay. The father. You knew his father was a big-time Nazi?"

"No, I did not know that."

"Actually, Papa was very tight with Goering. Hitler, too, so they tell me. He was mostly a high-class gofer for *der Reichsmarschall*, but between them they swiped half the art in Europe during the war, so say the old guys. You never see anything about him because he stayed pretty much in the tall grass, according to some of the ones who were around at the time—like an ancient historian who said he catalogued stolen paintings for old Wolff himself. Schmidt, his name was. Ernst Schmidt. I talked with him once. Told one helluva yarn. But he's long gone."

Pieter whistled quietly into the receiver. "So tell me more."

"Got himself sent away by one of those military tribunals after the war. They let him off easy because he told where all the art was . . .or most of it, at least."

"Most of it?"

"Well, seems there were some pieces he admitted having his hands on that never turned up where they should've. Really choice paintings—Schmidt remembered them. But Wolff said he had no idea what happened to them. Apparently his records were so meticulous that the Allies either swallowed his story or just didn't care. They were all in a ledger he supposedly kept for Goering which he turned over to the interrogators."

"How do you know all this?"

"Well, besides Schmidt, I was on a special team for the school to check out any quirky provenances in our collection, just to make sure we weren't sitting on any hot pieces. I learned a lot. That's how I know.

"Just a few more things," Murray continued. "The father, Otto, his name was, started a little art house in Bremen after he got out, and he did very well on his own. Well enough to send his kid here, at least. Don't ask me how. Must've made friends in all the right places during the war, ja?"

"What do you mean, 'on his own?'"

"On his own? Well, his old man, your guy's grandfather, was a mega-industrialist. You've heard of Kurt Wolff? The famous Wolff Works? Made most of the tanks and guns for Hitler? The old devil was monster rich, but the military court took it all away, right down to his shoelaces. Especially his shoelaces, right?" he laughed.

"And then they hanged him. The old guy had it coming, not so much for the guns and ammo—that's war, right?—but for the slaves he used to make the guns and ammo. A few million Poles, Slavs, Italians, French POWs from the early days before Pétain. Even French volunteers, so-called, who actually thought they were going to get good jobs in the German factories and had no clue. Granddaddy worked them to death, beat them to death, or starved them to death."

Murray was on a roll, as if he'd waited twenty years to tell the story. "So poor Otto, the son, wound up with zip," he continued, "except for a few years in the slammer and what ever he was able to squirrel away in Switzerland. Good stuff, huh?"

"Good stuff, yeh."

"That's about all I know, Peetie. Will that do?" Murray concluded.

"That's pretty good, Mike. Thanks!" Pieter said.

"Why do you want this, by the way?"

"I can't tell you, Mike, because there isn't much to tell, yet." Pieter hated to lie to a friend, especially after he'd been so helpful. But he couldn't chance a leak, though he was sure he could trust Mike Murray. "When I know more, I'll fill you in on the whole thing, okay?

"Meanwhile, keep all of this under your hat, alright? If you ever get out this way, stop by, and I'll give you chapter and verse, plus I'll fix you the best damn hasenpfeffer this side of Munich—in honor of the old Kraut, Wolff. It's one of my specialties."

"Hasenpfeffer?"

"Rabbit. It was my grandmother's recipe. She was from Bavaria. I serve it with a little spaetzle and a good Chianti—just kidding about the Chianti."

"Rabbit? Damn, Peetie. Is that what you eat out there? Rabbits? Do you shoot them yourself, like Elmer Fudd? 'You miswabble wabbit, Blam!' I thought possum was your big thing in the great American heartland—with squirrel on Sundays."

"Trust me, you'd like it. Tastes like chicken."

"Possum?"

"No, rabbit. Possum tastes like groundhog. Goodbye, Michael."

"Go Black Bears," Murray retorted, invoking the immortal spirit of U of M's venerable mascot.

"Bears," Pieter echoed.

"Wabbit. You miswabble wabbit," Pieter heard him mutter as the phone went dead.

Pieter processed Mike Murray's input in the same manner that he would reveal the secrets of a dust-shrouded masterpiece, one tiny area at a time, not to go too far too soon or assume too much. He sat quietly for a long time, playing back the key points of their conversation word for word, phrase by phrase, listening like a safecracker for each faint click of the dial.

Suddenly the vault swung open, and he knew.

CHAPTER TWENTY-SIX

Pieter's ebullience was short lived, his epiphany rudely interrupted by the ringing phone and the harsh reality that his
astute inductions were, for the most part, wild fantasy. It was a
helluva plot, but fiction nonetheless. He had only hearsay, a prick-
ly old director with a mean streak, and a few paintings with swastikas on the backs. But it was a start.

He picked up on the sixth ring, just before his voice mail
clicked in. "This is Pieter."

It was Murray.

"Something I just remembered, Peetie. Those missing
paintings I told you about? The ones Wolff said he had once but
that never turned up?"

"Okay? What?" Pieter said.

"They would have been from the Gruenwald collection.
I flat out forgot to mention it and thought it might be important.
Sorry."

"The Gruenwald collection?"

"Right. Paris. Seems Wolff fessed up to taking over five
hundred pieces of a dynamite private stash owned by a Gruenwald family right before Paris fell to the Allies. Said he had it all
packed up nice and neat, padlocked and shipped by train to Alt
Aussee. He even handed over the paperwork to the interrogators,
including the original bill of lading signed and stamped by the
Nazi in charge of the train who, he said, had checked every crate.
Wolff's signature was on it, too.

"But, get this—the train was captured even before it made
it out of the yard. The upshot was that forty or fifty of the best of

the lot had somehow vanished into thin air by the time the French had broken open the car and inventoried the contents. How the foxy Kraut pulled it off is the mystery of the century.

"I don't know what you're looking for, but does any of this help?"

"Lord, yes, it helps. Anything else?"

"Only that when they leaned on him about the missing paintings, he said, in perfect English, 'I may be a lot of things, but I'm not stupid enough to screw the Fuehrer.' Guess they felt he had a point. All this stuff is in the interrogation transcripts, if you know where to look.

"Incidentally, not one of these prime Gruenwald pieces has ever floated to the top, although some of the lesser ones have come on the market over the years. Odd, don't you think?"

"Odd, yeh," Pieter agreed.

"Mike, when we talked before, you called *Erich* Wolff 'The Nazi.' Why was that? Just because his father was a Nazi doesn't mean that he's one, too. Maybe he's ashamed. I would be."

"Does he *act* ashamed?"

"No. Actually, he's an arrogant bastard. I stay out of his way, but I don't think he's interested in what I do. He's mostly on the curators' backs. When he's in town, that is."

"He acts like a Nazi, then."

Pieter laughed. "I've never actually known a Nazi, but he acts like the ones on TV."

"Well, he acted like a TV Nazi when he was here, too, at least among his colleagues. He babbled endlessly about the Third Reich and about Hitler till you wanted to puke, so they said. The faculty was overjoyed when you took him.

"Oh, and by the way, Wolff was Hitler Youth. Proud of it."

Pieter sat with the dead phone still in his hand, not even hearing Murray's cheerful "Gotta go, Peetie." He couldn't believe his luck. Less than an hour ago he had nothing. Now he had a name which could be the key to everything—and enough dirt, maybe, to tie Erich Wolff to one of the most flagrant art heists of the twentieth century.

The recording spieled from the receiver: *If you'd like to make a call, please hang up and try again.* Pieter depressed the cradle and made another call.

CHAPTER TWENTY-SEVEN

*T*his *is Pieter, it's about ten. Buzz me. Nothing important.* On the contrary, it was seriously important, but for any resident reptile who might slither into Angela's voice-mail, *nothing important* was all they'd get.

Although she had said she would do some digging on Wolff's paintings, he gave a fleeting thought to poking around himself now that he had a name to work with. Two things stopped him: his self-admitted ineptitude when it came to the vagaries of the internet and, more important, the fear that his maladroit meandering might in some way turn up on the screen of someone who would then kill him.

He would wait for Angela, who at that moment sat across from the hairless Prussian gnome known as Herr Bergdorf, the mass of his outsized desk a fortress between them. Wolff's dwarfish assistant peered over the work surface like a tense watchman in the night. She had surprised him at his post just outside the director's office ten minutes before his scheduled appearance at her own disheveled digs currently stacked high with gallery floor plans, wall schematics, paint swatches, photos and other essentials of the looming Matisse exhibition.

Bergdorf's request to see her, albeit in her own office, had been a blessing in disguise. By going to him, she could sneak a peek at his space and maybe spot something useful without raising more suspicion: Angela felt she was already in Bergdorf's sights because of the Dutch gallery incident and his creepy probing the previous night.

She was prepared. Her arms were full of final drawings,

color samples for the walls to be painted over the weekend, press-down label copy, and an official exhibition catalog, twenty-five thousand copies of which had just been delivered the day before.

"I came to you, Herr Bergdorf, because my office is a wreck. There's hardly a place for me to sit, let alone you. I hope you don't mind," Angela had said as she stood in the open doorway. "Is there a place where I can set these things down?"

The look on his face told her he had forgotten about their meeting and that his intention to "drop in" was probably an impulsive stab at rattling her cage. Still, she forged ahead.

"You said last night you wanted to see me this morning, Herr Bergdorf?" she reminded him.

"Yes, I know. The director . . .he returned day before yesterday, and I'm expecting him any time now. I'm . . ."

"Would you like for me to come back later, Herr Bergdorf?" she said.

"No, no, come in," the gnome muttered impatiently. "Just put your things on the corner of the desk. I have just a few minutes, however. Show me what you have, Miss Desjardin."

Angela unburdened her arms on the corner of Fort Bergdorf, the surface bare except for a small, white notepad and a black marble slab with a single, gold Cross pen projecting from it like Excalibur waiting to be liberated. She lifted a few schematics off the pile and recited brief descriptions of what was there, which works went where, and why, explanations of the wall colors she had picked so not to distract from the fearless Fauve palette.

After the first few boards, it was clear that he couldn't have been less interested, and that he was simply hassling her for reasons unknown. Not that she cared; her real disappointment was that as he went through the motions of studying the drawings and swatches, her roving eye locked on nothing at all that would have advanced her, and Pieter's, excellent adventure.

And then she caught a break.

"I'm not so sure about white for the collages, Miss Desjardin. Give some thought to something in the 'putty' range," he said imperiously in a transparent attempt to justify his nosing into her business. "Or maybe even a charcoal. It could perhaps draw out the colors of the collages, don't you think?"

Putty! What a stupid idea! she stewed. Charcoal? Good grief! When Henri Matisse needs some putz like Bergdorf to "draw out his colors" is the day I go back to Vittoria and stomp the grapes.

"I'd like to make a note of that, Herr Bergdorf. Do you mind if I use your pad?" she said, nearly choking on her words. Angela Desjardin was gastronomically ill-suited to the fine art of kissing behinds, even as a strategy of deception. *Screw his putty. Not in his lifetime.* The gnome slid his blank white notepad across to Angela. "May I use your pen, Herr Bergdorf? I'm afraid that with everything else I carried over here, pen and paper were the last things on my mind," which was not entirely untrue.

He nodded coldly in the affirmative, inferring with the slightest raising of an almost nonexistent eyebrow that she should have been better prepared to gather the pearls which tumbled from his tight, Teutonic lips.

Angela effortlessly withdrew Excaliber from the stone and lightly wrote *putty* and *charcoal,* carefully tore the sheet from the small pad, folded it once and tucked it in the pocket of her navy blazer. Desperate for the tiniest clue, she had noticed earlier as she stood over Bergdorf the faint indentations on the blank top sheet of his pad of what seemed to be a sequence of fourteen or fifteen digits, possibly a phone number, left there from an earlier notation. Important or not, the numbers were now hers.

In the middle of his pretending, and her pretending that he was not, Erich Wolff suddenly appeared, and the gnome's focus shifted with an almost audible click.

"Thank you, *Miss* Desjardin," Bergdorf said dismissively, bringing closure to the bogus meeting and relief to the uneasy Angela. She gathered her stack of exhibits from Bergdorf's desk and vacated the premises with lightning speed lest she be sandbagged with a Colomboesque, "Oh, just one more thing, Miss Desjardin."

Sensing her arrival, Jerry Mason, her unsettlingly prescient intern, opened the door to her office without a word. She rushed past him and dumped her armload onto a chair already heaped with files. As she backed away, the entire pile slid off the chair and onto the floor.

"Leave it," she said, as he squatted down to pick up the mess. He rose and left quickly, eyes rolling, having seen more than enough times her not-so-subtle "Do Not Disturb" sign not to honor it unconditionally, no questions asked.

Alone, Angela fumbled inside her jacket pocket and fished out the scrap of paper from Herr Bergdorf's notepad. She unfolded the small, white square and strained to see the faint impressions.

With some effort she could trace most of the numbers, but the last few were illegible, even after she had rubbed a soft pencil over them as she'd seen them do a few times on the TV cop shows, on those precious few occasions when she'd succumbed to the mindless offerings of the tube. Nevertheless, the clean indentations and their sequence were quite enough to set her heart pounding: 00-39-0932-872 . . . She recognized instantly the double-oh international calling code. And the access code for Italy—39. What shook her was the area code for Vittoria—0932—and the first three digits of the telephone number of one Don Carlo Vittoria, her *dolce nonno.* Her sweet grandfather.

CHAPTER TWENTY-EIGHT

When her head stopped spinning, Angela saw the blinking red message light on her phone. She scanned through the first seven, all Matisse, all urgent, and then came Pieter's innocuous summons. *Nothing important. Right,* she intuited. She returned his call first.

"I just talked to Mike Murray up east," he said with an uncharacteristic edge to his voice that left no doubt as to just how important the call was. "Got a minute?"

"I'll come down," she said. Angela mentioned nothing about Bergdorf's notepad, and she wasn't sure if she would *ever* tell him, or anyone, about it, depending. If it were her grandfather's number on the paper, which she couldn't say with certainty because it was only partial, there would be some explaining to do. And it could be awkward for both her and the old man. She decided to keep it to herself, at least until she'd talked to Don Carlo. She slipped the scrap back in her pocket.

"I've been with Bergdorf. Let me return a few calls and I'll be there, okay?"

"I'll be counting the minutes until . . ."

"Yeh, yeh, yeh. Bye," she said as she cut him off and returned Charlie Murphy's call in Maintenance.

An hour later she walked into the conservation lab. She hiked up on her usual tall stool and waited. Pieter stood behind the big worktable in the center of the room, casually eyeing several small pieces which lay scattered about in various states of cleaning and restoration.

Then he looked up and said, "Have you done anything

about the paintings?" knowing that she hadn't, as totally im-
mersed as she had been in the Matisse. Angela knew that he had
something, or he wouldn't be baiting her with that sarcastic little
half smile on his face. *Sometimes she could just punch his lights out.*

"For God's sake, Pieter, you know what I've been do-
ing. And it has not been chasing down paintings," she shot back.
"And on top of everything else, I've got to deal with that creepy
Bergdorf hassling me.

"He didn't care about the Matisse. He just wanted to
tweak my beak over that thing with the paintings. But he didn't
get far. Just as he was about to start on me, Wolff blew in, and he
dropped me like a hot rock."

"Did you get anything? You *were* in his office?"

"Yes, I was in his office, no, I did not get anything," she
lied. "So why am I here?" She'd had enough of the games.

"Well, I've got something. And it could be big."

Angela knew that, if anything, Pieter did not blow smoke.
If Pieter says, "big," it's most likely bigger than that.

He had her attention.

Pieter relayed almost word-for-word his two phone conversations with Mike Murray, wisely omitting their sophomoric
exchange on the culinary delights of opossum versus hare. No
reason to give her any more grist for ridicule—she was resource-
ful enough without help from him. He told her about the father,
Otto, and his link to Goering and Hitler; the thousands of works
they looted, often brutally, from the Jews of Paris and elsewhere;
granddaddy Kurt, the big-time Nazi weapons builder cum slavemaster, and the horrific crimes which pushed him way up the
guest list for one of the more conspicuous of the postwar necktie
parties; and the probability of Otto's naughty little art ring, now
run, he assumed, by good son Erich.

He saved the best for last. There was Murray's revelation of the name, *Gruenwald* as the all-but-certain connection between Wolff and the mysterious Mendelssohn masterpieces. And finally, the yet unsolved disappearance of the cream of the stolen Gruenwald collection from a locked railcar on a night train out of Paris. With each new disclosure Angela's mind further distanced itself from the urgency of Henri Matisse and glommed instead on the implications of what she was hearing. When he finished, she sat motionless, her face suddenly flushed with private embarrassment for not remembering this spectacular heist; the Gruenwald caper was a classic case study in one of her undergraduate art history courses a decade ago.

Of course she knew the name, *Gruenwald,* and the Gruenwald collection, and all the notoriety surrounding it. But she couldn't bring herself to confess to Pieter, and barely to herself, that she missed such an obvious connection to the Wolff pieces.

Pieter's tie with Murray was a lucky stroke, Angela conceded. And Murray's exposure to the old German cataloguer was a happy coincidence beyond belief. *Given a choice, I'd rather be lucky than smart,* she concluded, thus dismissing her oversight without regret.

Pieter looked at her, waiting. Finally, she issued her tepid response: "Well, at least I know where to start looking."

Several times that afternoon Angela's fingers edged toward the keyboard on her desk, eager agents of a mind newly obsessed with the single name, *Gruenwald.* Each time, they withdrew, as common sense and paranoia reasserted themselves; things were getting sticky, and it was no time to get careless.

The scholarly path would have led her to *The AAM Guide to Provenance Research* and the *Répertoire des bien spoliés en France durant la guerre,* the most complete listing of art gone missing from

France during the war. She'd worked with both in the past and knew them like the path to her refrigerator, and they were a mere hundred steps away in the Mendelssohn library.

But for her to be spotted now at a library table with the *AAM Guide* in front of her, she decided, could raise some tricky questions and be extremely hazardous to her job security, if not her health. Nor could she send Jerry Mason, not that he wasn't equipped to do the digging. He was. But in her paranoid state, she would involve no one but herself and Pieter. She had no right to draw Jerry into to a risky escapade not of his own making. For now, she'd take her chances in cyberspace.

She would wait until she was safely ensconced in her tiny apartment, doors locked, shades drawn, where her laptop would be perfectly adequate for what her gut told her may not be the piece of cake Pieter's old drinking partner had implied.

Besides, if she didn't bear down on Matisse today, she'd be screwed. Gruenwald could wait. The jolly Fauve would prevail, or Wolff would have her for dinner, with not enough left over for a bedtime snack.

Speaking of which, her preoccupation with Pieter's bizarre discovery had whisked her well past the museum cafe's closing time, and she was suddenly ravenous. While the restaurant would be dark, she knew that there was always a stray dessert or the makings of a sandwich in the café kitchen after hours, and that Lucille would still be readying tables for tomorrow.

Angela rode the elevator to the ground floor and walked past the *Closed* sign into the cafe. After a quiet word with the snowy-haired, Lilliputian drill sergeant who had recently celebrated her fortieth year at the restaurant's helm, she poured herself a cup of hours-old coffee from the nearest carafe and took a table by the door while the diminutive manager left for the kitchen to scavenge for an orphan wedge of Death by Chocolate. It wasn't until she had settled in that she saw another person in the otherwise empty room watching her from the shadows in the far corner. She had never seen him eat.

Angela nodded and flashed her most ingratiating Colgate smile. He returned the nod, but not the smile; Bergdorf never smiled. But then she froze as he took a last sip from his cup, rose and began to walk toward her.

Oh shit, here he comes. He knows. I know he knows. How could he know? What will he say? What will I say? Why do I care?

What Friedrich Bergdorf did was walk past her table and through the door without so much as a howdy-do; he had already exchanged what passed for pleasantries with him, and once was enough.

Still, he knew. She knew he knew.

Yes! Fate had interceded, as Lucille pushed through the swinging door from the kitchen with cake in hand. "It was the last piece. You're living right, Angie," she said as she placed the plate and its ethereal contents before her. Lucille could call her anything, Angie included.

Bergdorf could go to hell. Life was good.

She hadn't slept. It was seven a.m. and she stared at the phone, frozen, unable to focus. Coffee hadn't helped. Calling her grandfather had always been such a nice thing, and she looked forward to their chats. Not only had she always cared deeply about his well-being and recently more so about his failing health, she welcomed the chance to use her rusty Sicilian dialect, a rich mix of Italian, Arabic and Greek. But this call would be different; while she couldn't be sure that the piece of a phone number she had lifted from Bergdorf's pad was that of Don Carlo Vittoria, she had a very dark feeling about it.

She had never questioned her grandfather's cachet. Her blind devotion to the old man had usually enabled her to gloss over his huge wealth and local clout as the product of hard work, shrewd dealings and "mostly luck," he used to say. *But how lucky must you be to control most of the oil and wine business in half of Sicily? Dolce nonno must be the luckiest one olive squeezer on the island. Or the smartest. Or . . .* Angela revived thoughts that rarely crossed her filtered mind where Don Carlo Vittoria was concerned, and she liked them no better now than before. Worse, she didn't like herself very much for thinking them.

But the business with Wolff and Bergdorf had hardened her. Or simply exposed a hardness which had always been just under the skin. Long-repressed details of her grandfather's *dolce vita* gurgled to the surface like the bubbles in a flute of Prosecco: bits and pieces of muffled conversations; the ant trails of desperate-looking characters winding to and from the main house; the perpetual homage paid by the villagers, as if a fluttering papal flag signaled the Holy Father in residence—which it actually had on many occasions, several while she was there; her grandfather's retainers, Paolo Ricci and Vincenzo Buscetta, family to her but unnerving to anyone who wouldn't know them. What did all this have to do with oil and wine? She persisted in asking this of herself, although she knew exactly what it had to do with oil and wine.

There was the villa also, a classic Sicilian monument to old wealth, surrounded by high, stucco walls and protected with floodlights, a White House-grade security system and a small brigade of bodyguards and round-the-clock patrols. *Why is that?* Angela knew that she insulted her own considerable intelligence simply by asking the question.

She knew why. She had always known why.

But most of all, there were the paintings. She, of all people, should have sniffed something the moment she became learned in the vagaries of the art world. The fact that they were priceless was not the issue; a wealthy oil merchant might marshal the resources over time to build such a collection, and a powerful Don could probably swing it, by hook or by crook.

But in the end, it wasn't a money issue; it was getting one's hands on such pieces at all, let alone so many of them. It would have been nearly impossible, particularly under the radar of the high-profile exchange of masterpieces through normal channels. This was serious work: the legitimate transfer of even one of them would have been a lead story for the trade media, and justify a mention in the *Times* as well.

This, *plus* the partial phone number, *plus* Pieter's hot flash on Wolff by way of Cambridge, added up to a big, fat *aha. How could she* not *call him?* Angela thought as she lifted the handset and punched his number into the keypad.

CHAPTER TWENTY-NINE

"*Buon giorno, sono Paolo,*" the familiar voice answered.

"*Zio Pauly, sono Angela!*" she said in as chirpy a voice as she could muster, given the minefield she was about to tiptoe into.

"*Gattina!*" Paolo Ricci responded in a jubilant roar. The aging bear still thought of Angela as the baby, and he had called her Pussy Cat from the time he would rock her to sleep on the veranda of the villa. Her grandfather's faithful praetorian and all-round "go-to" guy for what Don Carlo Vittoria called "untidy work" had been Angela's protector since she was a babe in his strong arms. If there was ever a person with whom she felt totally safe, it was her Pauly. Her Zio Pauly.

The ceremonial title of *Zio*, "Uncle," had been bestowed on both Paolo Ricci and Vincenzo Buscetta by Don Carlo on the occasion of Angela's baptism in the Church of Santa Maria delle Grazie. They stood awkwardly at the baptismal font with the rest of the family as the young priest, Father Ottaviani, placed his soft, wet hand on her tiny head and blessed her *in the name of the Father, the Son and the Holy Ghost*. Maria Vittoria and Guy-Alain Desjardin being only children, there were no "blood" uncles and aunts to help nurture her, a deplorable deficiency from her grandfather's point of view which, as was his way, he took upon himself to rectify. It was a mantle which Don Carlo's two henchmen took with consummate seriousness and wore with enormous pride, even as they fidgeted self-consciously at the altar in the threatening presence of clergy.

For an instant, Angela forgot her primary mission. Paolo's rich voice had acquired a gravely edge as he grew older, which only rendered him more dear to her; his familiar resonance took her back to carefree days when the two of them would roam the magical expanse outside the villa walls, he lifting her up on the ancient, fluted drums of long-toppled Greek columns to better see Don Carlo's endless olive groves and row after row of ripening Frappato grapes. Each adventure would end with the obligatory visit to nonno's garden of yellow roses, where Paolo had been solemnly instructed to cut for her the largest and sweetest-smelling bloom for the little table beside her bed.

The lore of Don Carlo's yellow roses had always amused her. She particularly loved Zio Vincenzo's menacing version of the legend which he shared with her one starlit evening on the veranda as the fragrance of the garden itself wafted over them. "The people in village believe Don Vittoria's roses are *condanna di morte*," Vincenzo whispered to the impressionable nine-year-old. "That the yellow rose, *Condanna D'oro*, from garden of Don Carlo, tell the man who receive it he will die with pain and by surprise. *Condanna D'oro* mean *a sentence of death*. There are stories. . ." her uncle trailed off in a quavering whisper custom-crafted to entertain her, which it did to the point of uncontrollable giggling.

The fact was that the stories were not entirely untrue; the unwelcome rose, the fragrant *golden sentence,* from Don Carlo's deadly garden did indeed invoke terror in many an enemy of the Vittoria clan, with swift and certain justice to follow. Still, the mythos reeked of pulp fiction to her, and she never completely bought the idea.

"*Come sta, Pauly?* Last time I called, your arthritis had flared up again. Are you feeling any better?"

"*Non mi sento buono, Gattina,* not so good. I take L'*aspirina*, but it not help. Old Paolo is not like when you were little. It is good there is not much to do now but care for him. It is quiet up here on the hill."

"Can you tell me about my grandfather before I talk with him, Pauly? Has he gotten any better?"

"No, Angelina, he get worse. He has the old person's disease, you know."

"Yes, I know. Does he remember anything? Anybody?"

"He remember things. He know some people. He know me, Blessed Mother of God . . ."

Angela could envision her uncle crossing himself, a reflex embedded from childhood. Like many Sicilian men, Paolo Ricci had been absent from the Church and the confessional for most of his adult life, convinced that, in spite of his mother's urging, *may she rest in peace,* and the tireless admonitions of Father Francesco, Father Ottavani's predecessor, the sins of his youth and the more egregious offenses committed in the service of Don Carlo Vittoria had consigned him irredeemably to eternal fire, *although he would have plenty of company.* Aside from weddings, funerals and the occasional baptism, Angela's beloved Pauly seldom darkened the massive carved doors of Santa Maria delle Grazie. *The hard benches are better suited to the women and the children,* he conceded.

". . . and he know you. He ask for you, Angelina."

She felt pain at his words. She could see her grandfather sitting motionless in his chair, looking out over his fields in the warm sun.

"Can he talk to me?"

"Sì, Gattina! If anybody raise his spirits, it will be you. Can I stay on the telephone with you? I do not interfere, but maybe I help. It get hard for him to understand."

Angela hesitated, thinking about the sensitive nature of her call. But then she reasoned that a difficult exchange could only be made worse without Paolo Ricci's help, given Don Carlo's fragile state of mind.

"Yes, I wish you would, Pauly. Thanks for suggesting it. Let me talk with him now."

Angela guessed that it would take Paolo some time to orient her grandfather to her call. She guessed correctly, as she listened to several minutes of muffled voices and other sickbed noises before she heard the click of a second phone and Pauly's soft breathing in the receiver.

"Angelina! It is you!"

"It's me, Nonno!" she said. "I just had a nice chat with Uncle Pauly, and he says you're doing well," she lied.

"Yes, I am well," he lied in return, in a voice weaker than when she had talked to him last, yet a voice still with the soft, re-assuring timbre she knew so well. It was a voice always filled with joy in spite of his apparent familiarity with the darker side. *How could you not love a voice like that,* Angela thought.

"Paolo keeps after me, though. He makes me do things I do not want to do. Won't you come here and rescue me from this evil man?" She could hear Pauly's soft chuckle on the extension.

"You do what Pauly tells you, Nonno. He may be stiff with his arthritis, but he's a whole lot bigger than you, remember. And meaner," she added, with a good natured snicker.

She and Don Carlo shared simple conversation, more or less, for the next few minutes, during which the old man displayed wide gaps of concentration and on several occasions clearly feigned recognition of things which normally would have been familiar to him. She hurt for him and prayed that the dreaded "old person's disease," as his faithful caregiver called it, would never strike her or any other living soul she loved. Paolo Ricci remained silent through it all, except for the gentle breathing which signaled his presence.

Angela had run out of time and the conversation was winding down awkwardly. *Il momento di verita* was at hand. *The moment of truth,* she thought. The final thrust of the sword. She startled herself with her unintentional choice of bullring jargon; she meant no harm to the tired old Sicilian bull, already so near death. All she sought from *el toro* was the truth, and she hoped to extract it without bloodshed.

"Nonno, I need some questions answered," she said.

"I will tell you what I can, mia bambina," Don Carlo said. "What is it you need to know?"

"There is a man I know who may have contacted you recently, nonno. His name is Erich Wolff, and he's the boss of the museum where I work. I've discovered several paintings owned by him that I believe were stolen by the Nazis during the war, and I think this man may be involved in some way. Not stealing the pictures, of course—he would have been too young—but hiding them for many years. If this is so, and if he knows that I know, it could be very bad for me."

She paused, hoping for some response. Receiving none, she continued.

"Do you know Erich Wolff? And do you know what he's up to?" she asked bluntly. There was no other way with her grandfather. They had always spoken openly, which was a defining mark of their unconditional love for each other.

Suddenly Paolo's soft breathing ceased, and there was deathly silence broken only by the faint trill of Diva, her grandfather's capricious canary, who sang only when it pleased her, and it pleased her less as she grew older.

Diva's warbling was at last interrupted by Paolo, who spoke for the first time since Don Carlo came on the line.

"Why do you call us about this, Angelina? Why do you

think your grandfather know this man?" he said cautiously, but without hostility.

"I found a telephone number, Pauly, quite by accident, which was written on some paper in the office of Herr Bergdorf, Erich Wolff's man. I could read most of it, and the numbers that I could make out were the same as yours.

"Director Wolff travels to Europe often, and he says that he goes for the museum—to buy new works, I had assumed—but he brings back very few things for so much coming and going. Because of these pictures I found, I think that he may actually be trading in art that has been stolen. When I saw the telephone number and thought that it might be yours, and because I knew that you had such a wonderful collection of paintings, it occurred to me that maybe he had tried to sell to you. Or that you may even have bought pictures from Erich Wolff—not knowing that they might have been stolen, of course," she added, trying to avoid any suggestion that she was accusing her grandfather of wrongdoing.

"Paolo, is this not the man who was with us just yesterday?" Don Carlo said.

Paolo Ricci knew that the old man had not remembered quite correctly, but that he had remembered enough. And that he wanted straight answers for Angela—this he knew instinctively from being at the Don's elbow for four decades. It was what he, Paolo, would have chosen to do also, because he himself would never deceive his Gattina or hold anything back.

"Yes, we know this man, Don Carlo, but he come many days ago," Paulo said, "not yesterday. Signor Wolff stay with us only two nights, Angelina—he often stay three or four days. He enjoy his visits, although he not like the rose garden, I think," Paolo chuckled, remembering the furtive conversation he'd observed between Wolff and Vincenzo Buscetta one cool evening on the veranda years ago during which the junior retainer's ritual indoctrination in the legend of the *Condanna D'oro* was lavished on the attentive director. It was a practice which Don Carlo did little to discourage, although one he felt best exercised by someone other than himself. Pauly's subtlety was not wasted on Angela. She knew that Wolff had gotten the message: *Do not ever mess with Don Carlo Vittoria.*

"Nonno," can you tell me why he comes to stay with you?" Angela said.

"Bambina, I have Paolo tell you. I get confused sometimes. Paolo, tell her what she want to know," Don Carlo said abruptly.

The truth was, Erich Wolff, and Otto Wolff before him, had been coming to Vittoria for nearly fifty years, at least once each year and sometimes more often. They would come like second-century merchants on camelback, bearing exotic goods from mysterious lands. Their treasures were not the cargo of swaying dromedaries—silks and spices and lacquer spread on Persian rugs for choices to be made; theirs were priceless paintings and sculpture and objets d'art, displayed in mounted color photographs which they carried in portfolios of rich Moroccan leather. These they would withdraw, with suitable fanfare, one at a time from their oversized cases, each more stunning than the last and accompanied by a learned discourse on the artist, the artistry, the provenance, the artistic or historical significance of the piece— and a pinch of hype for sweetening. Showtime at the villa was a sight to behold, an event Don Carlo looked forward to, before his illness, with heart-thumping anticipation.

"Signor Wolff come to see us this time each year, Gattina, like his father before him," Paolo Ricci said. "We entertain them with as much *ardore* as the Holy Father.

"Every time, they sell to your nonno pictures and statues. Many you know from when you were bambina.

"This time was not best for coming. Don Carlo was not feeling good. He buy nothing from what Signore Wolff show him, and he leave quick after the telephone call from Bergdorf."

"Is there more I can tell you, Gattina?" Paolo asked.

"Yes, just one or two more questions, Pauly, if I'm not disturbing you," she said.

"No, no, non c'è un problema! Per favore!" he said. *Non c'è un problema, Don Carlo?"* he repeated, deferring to the listener on the extension phone.

"Non è un problema," the old man said cheerfully, not a problem, but with a trace of caution which could simply have been read as a symptom of his creeping dementia.

"Did Erich Wolff ever talk about where he'd been before coming to see you, or where he might be going afterward?" she asked.

"He go many places," Paolo said. "He talk about them—London, Paris, Brussels, Berlin, Munich, Geneva, Zurich. So many I not remember them all."

"Barcelona, and Rome," Don Carlo added in a sudden burst of lucidity.

"These places he has dealers," he said. "Where he find the pictures he sell to Don Carlo," Paolo elaborated.

Angela scrawled down the cities as Paolo ticked them off. *Some operation,* she thought. *It's no wonder he's not around most of the time.*

"Can you tell me how Wolff was paid for the pieces he sold to Nonno, Pauly?" Angela said, sensing that it was time she wound it down. Her grandfather seemed to be fading fast.

"We send money to bank in Geneva—Bank of Zurich, I

remember. Always Swiss francs, no lire. There is no paper, no record, no *conto*—never bill—only what they say about pictures. But Don Carlo trust them. They not cheat your nonno. No one cheat Don Carlo.

"But I tell you, Angelina, we know nothing about anything he steal," Paolo said, a bit too quickly. "Never did Signor Wolff say anything about stealing. I am there every time. I know."

Paolo Ricci was lying. Angela knew that.

And the old fox knew also. You didn't get to be Don, and *stay* Don, by being *stupido*. She could forgive Paolo for the lie; he was only trying to protect her from the fact that her beloved grandfather was, besides being beloved, as ruthless and corrupt a specimen as the Good Lord had fashioned out of Etna's volcanic ash. She could forgive her nonno, too, for not denying Paulo Ricci's falsehood, whether because of his crumbling mental state or the reluctance of a doting grandfather to confess his sins to the granddaughter he cherished. Whichever it was, it didn't matter.

But something else bothered her more.

"One last question, Pauly. I know it's time for *pranzo,* and you and nonno must be getting very hungry. But can you tell me, does Erich Wolff know who I am? I mean, does he know that I am Don Carlo's granddaughter? Have I ever come up in any conversation as working at the Mendelssohn Museum? Has my name, Angela *Desjardin,* ever been mentioned? You would know this if you've always been with my grandfather during his meetings with Wolff, isn't that so?"

"Gattina, Don Carlo is private person. He never say your name to anyone. And he never talk about your mother or your father, or anyone who could be hurt because of Don Carlo."

"Hurt?" she said.

"Don Carlo has very bad enemies. I tell you many times,

very dangerous enemies." Paolo Ricci's voice became stern, admonishing, the voice she remembered when she had done something bad. "When you are *capo*, you have enemies. I tell you some would hurt you to hurt him. He afraid of this all the time. This is why one of us always with you when you come, wherever you go." His voice softened.

"The people in village know you. We cannot help that. But they love you like their child, and they love Don Carlo. He is one of them. He help them. Except for them and people here in the house, Gattina is only pussy cat who come to the kitchen for bones of the fish.

"No, Don Carlo never tell Signore Wolff about you," he said.

There was silence once more, broken only by the occasional twitter of Diva, testing again the dulcet tones which in earlier times had made her the toast of the villa. *She still had it,* the uppity songbird was convinced. Then Angela heard a new resonance purring softly through the receiver, and she recognized her grandfather's soft snoring. The old man had fallen asleep.

Paolo heard him, too, and said, "He is asleep. He sleep a lot."

"Don't wake him, Pauly. Just tell him that I love him. And I love you, too. And Uncle Vinny. Thank you for telling me all of this. It was very helpful to me."

"We miss you, Gattina. Please come see us. Your nonno need you," Paolo said. "He may not be with us many more days." And then he added, "And be careful with this Wolff. He has the right name—*wolf. Un lupo!* A dangerous one."

"I miss you, too, Pauly. And I will be careful. *Ciao.*"

Angela returned the phone to the cradle and sat very still, her coffee cold. She couldn't bring herself to uncurl from the security of her warm sofa and move on. *So that's what it is. He's deal-ing stolen art, the bastard, all over Europe and God knows where. And he—and Otto Wolff before him—had been passing it off to her nonno for fifty years. Fifty years, for God's sake.*

As she tried to take in the enormity of it all, and her own grandfather's complicity as a willing receiver of stolen goods, her thoughts turned to the old man himself. *What will happen when he goes? What will happen to Pauly, and Uncle Vinny? The villa? The businesses? The paintings, the incredible paintings?* She could see Don Carlo's enemies sniffing about even now, slinking out of the dark, tearing his flesh and carrying away the pieces before the body was stiff.

Even at death's door, Don Carlo had the juice to keep them at bay; a well-placed word was still enough to give even the most suicidal of the bandits cause to pause, Angela suspected. She also assumed that the punishment for coveting the old man's stuff, if the word got out, let alone making a grab for it, could be strikingly imaginative and unimaginably ugly. For those who as-pired, their passing would not be a peaceful, painless one.

Death does have a funny way of diminishing one's in-fluence, however. This thought had not escaped Don Carlo. His most agonizing concern during his waning years, far exceeding the prospect of his own demise, which meant nothing to him, was what would happen to his stuff and how he could preserve it for his family. He also struggled with how the people of the village— his people—would be protected from the jackals who would bleed them and tyrannize them.

The businesses he had written off in his mind long ago; no one loyal to him and his offspring had the stones to control them after he was gone. Paolo was brutal enough, and savvy, and feared. And he could be trusted. But Paolo was old and growing weak, like himself. And without Don Carlo's clout behind him, patient adversaries would make lunch of him in time; anointing Paolo would only prolong the inevitable.

Vincenzo was no better. He was younger than Paolo by ten years, stronger, and even more ruthless, but careless. Volatile, a bit of a *buffone*, and not the brightest flame in the candelabra. He would never learn that justice needed to be dispensed in surgical fashion. Violently, of course, for effect, but still "managed," as they say. The years would improve him, Don Carlo reasoned. He would either improve or be killed in the trying. But he was not a man for the here and now, maybe not ever.

The old man would settle for just knowing that Angela and Maria would have the villa and be able to live in peace, but that would hardly be possible without the oil and the wine, let alone the other enterprises that weren't quite so virginal as his delectable nectar of the gods. A simple bequest was out of the question: Sicilian law was an illusion. In his world, wills and codicils meant nothing without fear to enforce them; in his realm the only substitute for power was *more* power.

His fantasy had always been that Angela would follow him. While the idea of a *femmine* Don took some getting used to, it was not absurd. He could remember her as a child, skinny as a twig, sitting in his huge chair in the study with her tiny limbs, burnished golden brown by the Sicilian sun, extended to either armrest, the queen holding court. Bold, fearless, with an "off with their heads" smirk on her gorgeous face that could curl your hair and melt your heart at the same time.

He could imagine her in his chair now, young, unflinching, tough, a bit of a smart-ass, but wise—all that it took to take care of business, all except the venality. Did he mention deceptive? *Who could take a woman seriously*, they would think. And then,

Boom! He loved the *Boom* part. *Surprise,* the critical component of victory. *Boom!* It made him laugh.

She'd honestly never thought about it before. What will happen to it all? How could it possibly go on the same?

Her mother had no taste for power, and even less so the price of maintaining it. Maria Vittoria Desjardin belonged to the Ancient World, not to a sprawling Sicilian dynasty that now survived strictly on the illusion of sovereignty emanating from a dying man like the light from a burnt-out star. But even if she were so inclined, she would be incapable of swinging the big stick.

Pauly and Vincenzo knew where the bodies were buried, quite literally she assumed, but they weren't family. Whatever power they had was strictly by association; when Don Carlo goes to his rose garden in the sky, or where nothing grows, they will have only their own bare hands—hardly enough to sustain a stranglehold on a vast and complex enterprise.

Unless she didn't mind her dolce nonno's bones picked clean by hyenas, his legacy dragged off into the scrub bit by bit, she alone was left to defend his remains. The problem was, she *did* mind. She minded very much.

I am Donna Angela Vittoria. Kiss my ring. You say you need a favor? she thought, invoking the classic cinematic image imbedded in the culture for all time. It made her laugh.

And then she cried.

CHAPTER THIRTY

Angela decided not to tell Pieter about her call. She saw no need to expose "family business" until or unless it was absolutely necessary. She had to remind herself that their objective was simply to chase down a few lost paintings, not make the six o'clock news.

She was running way behind. Most mornings Angela Desjardin would have been at her post by now, bright-eyed and bushy-tailed, three double lattes to the good. But here she sat in her PJs, laptop on knees, and one last item to cross off her list.

Gruenwald.

She had hoped to do a little sleuthing the night before, but had stayed late at the museum. The detail in pulling together a major show like the Matisse was phenomenal, and, with no one but Jerry, nearly every item on the checklist had her initials beside it. One by one they would get done, but all in real time. No shortcuts.

The great thing about working at the Mendelssohn, Angela allowed, was that she was hands-on at almost every level. This gave her total overview and much more sway than someone with her same experience at the Met or the Boston or the Institute in Chicago, a huge plus for a self-confessed control junkie like herself. Having to report every minor detail to the director had gone by the wayside a year ago for the convenience of both parties, reflecting his grudging confidence in her to make the right decisions. Most of what she did run by him was largely for show.

The bad news was that experienced help was almost non-existent. And though hungry young interns overran the place,

Angela, unlike Pieter, had neither the patience nor the hours to train them. Her self-destructive temperament—*it takes longer to explain it than to do it yourself*—contributed mightily to her heavy consumption of midnight oil and her chronic exhaustion.

The short of it was that she had fallen into bed, comatose. No time for Gruenwald. But this was a new day, and she itched to give the Web a shot before her shower and the short sprint to work.

There was any number of scholarly ways to back up Mike Murray's input, all of them time-eaters. But Angela Desjardin, having long ascribed to the "I'd rather be lucky than good" mentality, opted once again for luck, an attribute which she was convinced was the extra gene in the Vittoria strain. Abandoning the tested but tedious, she pecked *Gruenwald collection stolen art* into her monster new laptop, barely out of the carton. It had power enough to lift the roof off her building, and sufficient memory for her to haul the Library of Congress around under her arm—juice she'd never need in a lifetime, but for an extra two hundred, why the hell not.

The heft of her new MacBook surfaced in a nanosecond as the first screen popped into view. It was the only one she'd ever need.

> *Missing Paris Masterpieces Object of Gruenwald Search. Jonathan Gruenwald, grandson of the original owners murdered by the Nazis in the Holocaust, has initiated. . . http//:www.gruenwaldart.com.*

Angela groped for a pen and something to write on, her eyes fixed on the screen as if the words might vanish into the cyber mist if she looked away. Her fingers found the *Times* crossword she'd worked several nights ago and the stubby No. 2 pencil with the worn-down eraser she'd used. She scratched down the

Web address in the margin of the paper and clicked on the site.

The preceding screen did vanish as she had feared, only to be replaced by another that gave Angela's heart a jolt. In the blink of an eye, a color image the size and proportion of a credit card emerged. It was a painting of a robust young woman with creamy skin and cheeks the color of roses. She wore a white cap made of what appeared to be lace, and her neck was graced with the delicate ruff collar typical of seventeenth century Dutch fancy dress—what a proper woman of means would have worn back then to have her portrait done. On her lap sat a child with golden hair, dressed in an elegant brownish orange dress. She wore a cap similar to that of the woman. Both had smiles that could have lit a room. The caption underneath read, *Frans Hals, Mother and Daughter, 1635, oil on canvas, 112 cm. x 90 cm.*

Angela stared incredulously at the display as her pulse shot up like a bottle rocket. Her heart began to thump wildly, and for an instant she thought she might black out, but she quickly regained her cool enough to scroll on down.

Beneath the Hals was another rectangle, but smaller. It was the picture of an old man in a stunning blue cloak. He sat at a table and pored over a very large book. Light shone through a narrow stained glass window, splashed color across the table's surface and warmed the elder's sallow skin. His hair was long and silver, his hands slender, and he was turning a page with tapered fingers. The caption said, *Jan van Eyck, The Scholar, 1447, oil on panel, 26 cm. x 19.1 cm.* The painting was clearly *Man in a Blue Smock.*

Next appeared a stately Gainsborough portrait of a well-heeled matron in a flowing blue satin gown, probably from the summer crowd at Bath. And finally, an immensely powerful Caravaggio surfaced, with figures which would have put a buff Arnold Schwarzenegger to shame. Wrapped around the four images was Jonathan Gruenwald's story. He was clearly dead serious about getting his pictures back, though the art world had long ago kissed them goodbye. *Au revoir et bonne chance.* Goodbye and good luck.

At this point all thoughts of Henri Matisse had vanished from her head like so much blue smoke, and Jonathan Gruenwald rushed in to fill the vacuum. Slowly and deliberately she poured over the long text which accompanied the photos, reading some passages several times before moving on. Her feelings wavered between outrage and euphoria.

> *Missing Masterpieces Object of Gruenwald Search*
>
> I am Jonathan Gruenwald, grandson of David and Anna Gruenwald who were murdered by the Nazis in the Holocaust. I have initiated a global search for forty-seven paintings which were taken from the chateau of my mother's cousin, Paul Gruenwald, on 9 June, 1944 where they had been hidden by my grandparents, the owners, to protect them from Nazi thugs. These priceless works had previously hung in their Paris townhouse at 51 rue de La Boétie. They were included in more than five hundred paintings, sculptures and pieces of heirloom jewelry looted by the brutish Nazi Luftwaffe Reichmarschall Hermann Goering and his aide, Lieutenant Otto Wolff, son of the German arms maker Kurt Wolff who was hanged for war crimes in 1946.

Gruenwald's account reflected almost exactly what Mike Murray had told Pieter the day before. Angela read on:

Sadly, the greatest loss was not the paintings but the loss of David and Anna Gruenwald, my beloved grandparents. These dear and gentle souls were arrested by Goering's goons and transported in freight cars, with many thousands of "offending Jews" like themselves, to the concentration camp at Auschwitz where they both met horrible deaths by poisoned gas at the hands of their Nazi captors.

Suddenly her excellent adventure had turned very personal and very sour. What had begun as one helluva buzz was now a deafening roar and had become much more than finding a few paintings. The image of David and Anna Gruenwald struggling for breath took Angela's own breath away. She had never been a vengeful person, or so she thought, but the mental pictures of the atrocity enflamed her already hot Sicilian blood, and her face flushed. Angela had seen Don Carlo this way, never quite grasping what could have been so terrible as to cause such rage in him. Now she knew; she was her nonno's own. His blood was her blood.

The forty-seven paintings in question disappeared from a train which had been loaded with the entire collection of Gruenwald works, and which had been dispatched to the salt mines at Alt Ausse, Adolph Hitler's Austrian storage facility for his ill-gotten art. The remaining pieces were recovered from sealed rail cars by the French army on 25 August, 1944 during the liberation of Paris, as the train had not yet left the Aubervilliers rail yard, and were eventually returned to the Gruenwald family.

What is exceptional about these forty-seven paintings is that they were the most beautiful of the entire collection. They include the works pictured here, plus those by Rubens, Van Dyke, Velasquez, Dürer, Rembrandt, Memling and Tintoretto.

Angela knew that if the four pieces hanging in the Dutch gallery were any reflection of the other forty-three, this would be one of the most remarkable private compilations of masterworks in the world today were it to exist intact. And the evidence was piling up that it did at least exist, maybe right under her nose.

A complete list follows. Someone, or ones, with knowledge of art and free access to the stolen works would have separated them from the others at some early point, a person with plans for them other than passing them on to the monster, Adolph Hitler.

Otto Wolff had the knowledge and the opportunity and the plan, of this she was certain—and the brazenness to pull it off. There he was, all that time, just lying in the weeds waiting for the right moment to steal them, right at the end of the great humiliation of France.

Not one piece from this group has been recovered in more than fifty-five years. This suggests that the corpus of paintings remains together, and may be in a single private collection.

Now just whose collection might that *be*? Angela at this point had moved far beyond the obvious, already scanning any number of strategies for smoking out the lot and hanging Erich Wolff out to dry.

> *I, Jonathan Gruenwald, grandson of the deceased owners and owner of Gruenwald Galleries of Paris, 31 rue de la Boétie, welcome any information leading to the recovery of these paintings and will pay a reward of 50,000 euros to those who step forward. You may contact me at this Website or by telephone at 33-612-421-005.*

The text concluded with a complete list of the forty-seven missing Gruenwald paintings. The list was alphabetized by artist and included the title of each piece, the year in which it was painted, and its size in centimeters, followed by a brief description of the subject and any other identifying characteristics.

Angela ran her finger down the list, stopping briefly at Jan van Eyck and Frans Hals, and then lingering over Peter Paul Rubens and Jan Steen. *All present and accounted for,* she thought. At least the four which presently graced the walls of the Mendelssohn.

She re-read Gruenwald's speculation about the whereabouts of the missing paintings. If the Wolf Man had four, he probably had the rest. In some musty old warehouse down by the river, or maybe in a big vault somewhere built expressly for stolen paintings, or in Wolff's old stonepile up on the hill where he could look at them every day. *That's what I'd do.*

Hands trembling, Angela captured the page in her C-drive. Pieter's words came drifting back. *Well, I've got something. And it could be very big.* And now *she* had something. She suddenly realized that they had information that could vaporize the honorable Dr. Erich Wolff and blow the lid off the Mendelssohn, not to mention shake up the art world pretty good. But what would be the point? Her first instinct was to find the paintings and settle everything quietly and quickly—if that were even possible. Only Wolff needed to go down. The unpleasant fact remained that now the whole mess rested totally in her hands, and Pieter's. *Lord knows she didn't ask for this, and she damned sure didn't need this in her life right now, particularly given her own grandfather's complicity.*

But one conflict had resolved itself: rage had trampled euphoria in the emotion sweepstakes. The vision of the frail couple, David and Anna Gruenwald, snatched only minutes from freedom, shoved onto a jammed rail car, and led like trusting lambs to slaughter had been etched painfully in her mind. As the vile accessory after the fact, Erich Wolff would pay, and the Gruenwald's paintings would be found and returned whatever the cost—still a pitiably small tribute to the innocent pair who had never hurt anyone.

She hardly felt the sting of the shower, hot enough to take the skin off lesser mortals. Most often it was the scalding water that brought her awake, but today she was well past awake and her mind was racing at warp speed. Matisse elbowed his way back into her consciousness. The wizard of Nice would not go away, no matter what else was ruining her life—no matter that her Nancy Drew fantasy of chasing down a handful of pilfered paintings had exploded into a full-blown crisis. She still loved the old Fauve, and she'd do right by him when push came to shove.

Angela dressed too quickly, abandoning her slavish European homage to fashion which, despite her shoot-from-the-hip style, she had always considered crucial to her professional persona. She would suffer the price later in the day with the appalling discovery that she had worn navy shoes with her black suit.

Angela tucked her new laptop under her arm and bolted for the door.

CHAPTER THIRTY-ONE

God, she needed him. Overnight her world had turned grim, and she craved his rowdy colors, his gorgeous lines, his fluid forms, his raucous good humor. Angela hurried to the museum, not only because she was very late on a very important day, but to be embraced by genius, to wander among the masterworks of the fabulous Fauve, now each in its honored place, and to put the finishing touches on this most remarkable exhibit. This was to be her day alone with immortality, before the rush of the media, the members, and the thousands of visitors about to descend on them; she had no intention of letting anybody or anything screw it up.

Jerry was standing in her office, hands on his hips like a nagging wife, glaring at her as she came through the door.

"Well, it's about time!" he barked, completely out of character for the mild-mannered intern. "All hell's breaking loose, and I was just about to call you!"

"Hell's always breaking loose. Why's today any different?" she said, unfazed, as she opened her lower desk drawer, slid her laptop inside, closed the drawer and locked it. Usually Angela kept nothing in her desk worth stealing except for her coveted stash of Snickers bars which seem to have acquired the inexplicable aptitude to grow legs. Jerry Mason was her prime suspect, but he was a crafty bandit who somehow had managed to escape detection with not a trace of chocolate on his lips or a crumpled wrapper in his wastebasket.

"Don't even sit down. We've got a water leak, for one," he said. "Ice must be melting on the roof from the other night, and it's dripping down the walls in 221 where the decoupages are. Pieter's up there now, taking stuff down. The night crew stayed over to mop up."

"That all?" she asked. "And do you mind if I take my coat off?"

"That all? No, actually, there's more. The water knocked out a thermostat and the whole second floor's hotter than bloody hell, not to mention the humidity. Sounds impossible, but it's true. The whole system's screwed. Ray Jackson's working that one, and three or four of the maintenance guys are up on the roof looking for the leak. How we got them in on a Saturday morning I have no clue."

"Welcome to the museum business, little man. If you can't take the heat, get out of the gallery," Angela said. "Don't sweat it, we'll get through it. We always do."

"And if you can keep your head when all about you are losing theirs and blaming it on you, you just don't understand the problem," Jerry fired back with a crooked smile, easing off a bit in the reassuring presence of his mentor.

"So, is that all?"

Jerry hesitated.

"What?" she said.

"The Wolfster was here."

"Wolff? Here?"

"Right where you stand. I don't think he even knew me. He scared the crap out of me."

"He's never here on Saturdays. What did he want?"

"He wanted *you*. Said he wanted to see you, pronto."

"He said, 'Pronto?'"

"No, *I* said 'Pronto.'"

"That's all he said? Nothing else?"

"That's it. Except he seemed a little edgy, even for him."

"Terrific. Okay, let's roll. You go and see how you can help Pieter. Number One is to keep those decoupages dry. God, if any of those get wet, we'll be in deep merde. When I'm done with Wolfie, I'll be up. Keep cool, little man. I've seen worse."

"Will you *please* stop calling me 'little man'?"

"Sorry. What would you prefer?"

"Jerry works for me."

"How about *uomo piccolo?*"

"That means 'little man,' doesn't it?"

"So? What name did your mother give you?"

"Jerome. Like in St. Jerome."

"I like Jerome. You will be Jerome."

"I'm already Jerome."

"So?"

Jerome shrugged.

Why she was so cocky was anybody's guess: the wheels were coming off upstairs, she'd been rocked an hour before by Jonathan Gruenwald's little bombshell, and Big Bad had just stopped by for Little Red, licking his chops, but she couldn't have cared less. Maybe it was because she had just gone one up on her nemesis. She had the goods.

"I'd better hustle on over there," she said. "No idea what he wants?"

"No idea."

"Ciao, little man. Oops. Sorry."

Angela wasted no time getting to Erich Wolff's office. She knew enough not to intentionally piss him off, or at least not yet. He probably wants to beat her up about the water or the heat or where she's been all morning. If that's what it's about, she'll just have to tap-dance. She'd gotten away with it before, mostly because the old Nazi's mind had been elsewhere. If he really cared, he'd be upstairs directing the traffic himself.

She entered Wolff's outer office, which was a good five degrees colder than the rest of the building from Bergdorf's stare alone. "Is Herr Wolff . . . "

"Yes, he's in there," he interrupted. "He wants to see you right away. Knock first." No "good morning," no "go to hell," just that frosty stare. She was growing weary of all of this man crap, it was as simple as that.

Two can play this game. She walked past him, tapped on the director's door, twisted the ornate brass knob and entered his barren world. *What a dingy space for someone in the art business,* she observed the few times she was asked inside. Two forboding Munich canvases, a no-name Düsseldorf landscape, and a decent, but sooty, Corot, all in need of a good hosing down, added nothing but drear to the walnut-paneled walls—not to mention the musty tapestry. He could have had just about anything in the museum except for the few icons everybody comes to see—the Monets, the Van Goghs, the solitary Caravaggio. If he favored works from home, he might have picked some of the more exciting ones—Kandinsky, maybe, or Franz Marc, or Kirchner—something with a little flash. Most of the good ones, of course, were on Hitler's no-no list, which is probably why they weren't there. *If it were her office, she'd fix that, tout de suite.*

"Herr Wolff?"

"Come in, Miss Desjardin," he answered with a chill in his voice as cold as Bergdorf's stare. *You could hang meat in here,* she thought. *What's with these two?* Without inviting her to sit, he said, "Are you aware of what's happening upstairs?"

The curtain had risen. She stood behind one of the clumsy oak and leather chairs, as if its bulk would somehow shield her, and said, "Do you mean the water leakage and the thermostat problem in the decoupages room?"

"That is precisely what I mean," he said.

"Yes, I'm aware of it, Herr Wolff. Pieter Maxfield is there removing anything that's even remotely in danger. My intern, Jerry Mason, is helping where he's needed, and I'm sure Pieter has his people there, as well." She skipped over the fact that it was Saturday, and Pieter's People had probably scattered to the winds. "The electricians are dealing with the temperature control, and maintenance is on the roof scouting out the leak. I expect that we'll be back to normal shortly." *Thank you, Jerome,* she whispered prayerfully to herself.

"We all hope so, don't we, Miss Desjardin?"

"Not to worry, Herr Wolff. I'm on top of it," she tapped.

He chose not to call her bluff and moved on.

"And just where were you this morning when all of this was happening, may I ask?" He usually didn't ask, and seemed not to care where she was most of the time. *What was special about today? Why was he jerking her around? And why was he in here at all? On a Saturday. He's never here on Saturday.*

"I spent a few hours at home on some last-minute details, Herr Wolff. It's quieter there, and I can get more work done—some kinds of work, that is. I'll be here the rest of the day and most of the night, no doubt, and tomorrow, too.

"We'll be ready."

"Yes, I'm sure we will," he said in a tone that sharply signaled his Prussian, zero tolerance mentality, and woe to those who failed to recognize it.

"Is that all, Herr Wolff? I'd like to get upstairs," she said. "I want everything back before I leave tonight."

"I would like that as well. That's all, Miss Desjardin.

Please keep me informed, as usual."

"Yes, I will. As usual," she answered. "Thank you, Herr Wolff."

Angela turned to leave, but before she reached the door, Wolff called to her. "Oh, one other thing, Miss Desjardin?"

She turned and took a few steps back toward his desk.

"You are familiar with the paintings I loaned to the museum? The ones in the Dutch gallery?" he said, his eyes narrowing.

Ha! This is why I'm here. The rest was smoke. His gaze was so acute that Angela reacted involuntarily, clamping down tight on any reflex that might set his bell ringing. She looked perplexed, pretending to fan through her mental rolodex of gallery occupants while she cobbled together some kind of credible response. She knew she would fail, and probably already had, but she felt she ought to at least give it a shot.

"Do you mean the Leyster, and the Christus, and . . ." She stopped, struggling, for his benefit, to come up with the others.

"Yes, and there's an Adam Pynacker—a particularly good one, I think, that could easily pass for a Steen—and a nice piece from the Flemish School. I'm surprised that you . . ."

"Oh, I know the pieces. Pieter and I were looking at them just a few days ago. What a beautiful gesture to hang them there," she gushed, as it suddenly clicked that the guard, Nichter, had ratted them out anyway and here she was, twisting on the spit, the flames licking at her tender Sicilian backside.

"As a matter of fact, Pieter fixed the *frame* on the Leyster yesterday, or the day before. Did Herr Bergdorf tell you? I think I said something to him about it."

"Yes, I know. What I wanted to tell you, Miss Desjardin, is that I may have found a buyer for all four of them, and that I'll be removing them for an appraisal. You will need to choose replacements." Wolff no longer watched her intently. He already knew what he needed to know.

"Do you know when you'd like them taken down, Herr Wolff?"

"Soon. Just be ready, if you will.

"Thank you, Miss Desjardin."

She left his office quickly, uttering a clipped "goodbye" as she passed Bergdorf, and burst out into the atrium. *He knows.*

"She knows?" Bergdorf asked when Angela was safely out of earshot.

"Of course she knows. Frankly, I don't know what took her so long."

"Why do you think that? Did she panic when you mentioned the paintings?"

"No, she was quite collected. Too collected. She manages her adrenalin remarkably well, a rare talent for someone so young. She's very good.

"It was the eyes. Did you know, Friedrich, that the irises expand when one is threatened? It's a predictable response triggered deep inside the brain. In the thalamus, I believe."

"I did not know that you were a student of neurology, Herr Wolff."

"I learned this from Reichsführer Himmler when I was only thirteen. 'You're in love with the Fuehrer's Eva, boy?' he said once. 'Ah, there they go! Your eyes. See? Don't be afraid, your secret's safe with me,' and then he would laugh. Herr Himmler talked to me a lot in Berchtesgaden. I think he had plans for me, even then. Perhaps heading the SS one day. He would have known these techniques. As chief of the Gestapo, who better to know who was lying and who was not, ja?"

"Ja, Herr Wolff. But what should we do about Miss Desjardin?"

"I think nothing, Friedrich. If we remove the paintings on Monday, there will be nothing to expose. And who is she but a nosy, annoying girl, no more, no less. There is nothing to fear from her."

"But what about the dummkopf, Maxfield?"

"Do not underestimate Dr. Maxfield, my friend. He may be many things, but he is no dummkopf. Fortunately for us, he cares about nothing but his solvents and his fancy instruments, Friedrich. That's why he hibernates in that beloved laboratory of his most of the time. No need to worry about him. Just get the pictures down and out of here first thing Monday and we can forget about him and Miss Desjardin and the entire matter. I would suggest also that you remove the files from Registration as well. That way, there will be no record that the paintings were ever here.

"I must admit, though, I will miss our little joke," Wolff said with a trace of a snicker. "We had a good run."

"Maybe I should encourage Miss Desjardin to focus her attention elsewhere," Bergdorf said, still dogged by the prospect of the meddling young curator making more mischief at their expense. "If she does know, she could cause trouble even after the pictures are gone. She is not just any nosy, annoying girl, as you say."

"Then what would you suggest?"

"Just an innocent chat . . . about how some things are best left alone?"

"You would threaten her?"

"No, I would simply advise her that the paintings are a private matter, and that the director prefers that she not trouble herself with them other than to find suitable replacements."

"As you wish. But speak softly, as they say, and show just enough 'stick' to convey the message, ja?" Beating her with it could produce the same result as striking a hornet's nest. Although I do not fear her, I would not want to feel her sting."

CHAPTER THIRTY-TWO

Angela hurried up the steps and rushed through the several Matisse galleries dedicated to the Early and the Peak Years, ditching her plan to savor the candy-colored goodies alone and in her own good time. She had disliked the designation, the "Peak Years," which was set by the exhibit's original curators. It was not the timeline she had a problem with, but rather the nomenclature: Angela viewed Henri Matisse's gifts far from having peaked years before his death. Some of his freshest ideas had sprung from crippled hands forced to abandon the brush for scissors, colored paper and paste. His infirmity had limited his tools to those of a schoolchild, a serendipity which may have driven his childlike imagination toward the wildly inventive *gouaches découpées* that became his signature works. And when he became bedfast, he instructed his assistants to tack paper to his bedroom ceiling and walls, on which he created remarkable drawings with sticks of charcoal affixed to a wand. Unfortunately, the exhibit catalog and marketing materials had been printed long before she was able to raise the issue, and there would be no change.

Through the opening to the disaster area she could see Pieter and Jerry, heads together, plotting their next move, and she was instantly aware of the temperature and the humidity. It was not so unpleasant that the typical museum visitor would even notice, but a decade of dealing with these things had rendered her skin a weather instrument of its own. Her skin told her that things were not good. And as she had no taste for returning soggy decoupages to their trusting lenders, things had better get a whole lot better soon.

Pieter saw her and began talking even before she was halfway across the gallery. "It's better than it was. It was ten degrees hotter an hour ago. By noon we'll have it where it needs to be," he said. "It's the dampness that's the problem. Until we get this wall dried out, our hands are tied."

"So what happened," she said.

"The water shorted out the thermostat, and after that everything just went haywire. The guys on the roof found the leak early and slapped a patch down, but they won't be able to do much more till it warms up outside. At least they stopped the water.

"Ray dried out the controls with his wife's hair blower, would you believe, and everything's back to normal on the electrical side," he said, nodding toward Ray Jackson, the resident technical savant, who stood next to the thermostat, grinning like a weekend hunter who had just brought down a mile-high goose with his trusty over-and-under. "God knows when we'll be able to get these decoupages back up though," Pieter continued, waving his hand at a dozen or so wild and wonderful images stacked against the far wall.

"We still have a few days before the press thing on Wednesday, but we'll have to repaint, of course," Angela said. "The hitch is that I just promised Wolffie this mess would be back like it was by tonight. Any chance of that? My butt is really on the line here."

"Sure, if we can dry out this wall, like in the next fifteen minutes," Jerry volunteered. "Ideas, anyone?"

"That's why Charlie Murphy gets the big bucks. Where is he, by the way?" Angie said, her head swiveling to locate her treasured Mr. Fixit, who had saved her skin so many times she finally had to open a line item in her budget for Murphy's "thank you" cigars. "Why isn't he up here?"

"It's Saturday, Angela. Charlie's at home. Nobody's here except the guys on the roof and Ray and the two of us," Pieter said, nodding to Jerry.

"So call him at *home, Jerome*. Get it done, okay?"

Jerry Mason fumbled for his cell. Within seconds he was talking with the Mendelssohn's chief of maintenance who was none too thrilled, having just settled in with a six-pack and a super-sized bag of kettle chips for a blissful afternoon of The Irish and USC on his brand new flat screen. Jerry winced, listened long and patiently until Charlie Murphy ran out of choice sentiments, then he gave Angela the thumbs-up. The wall would be dry and painted by nine that night, hell *or* high water; Murphy had no idea how, but he'd get it done. There'd be hell to pay on Monday, of course, if God's Team managed to knock off the heavily favored Trojans and he had missed it.

"I've got to talk to you," she said quietly to Pieter as Jerry and Ray moved on out of the room. "Can we go to the lab? It's more private there."

"That's fine. Let's go," Pieter said. They wove their way back against the rising tide of families with strollers, art schoolers in tattered jeans, spiky hairdos and sketch pads at the ready, and a small battalion of seniors, just off the retirement home bus and heavily armed with their menacing aluminum walkers.

They stopped for her laptop and finally closeted themselves in Pieter's sanctum, door secure. Angela wriggled up on "her stool" by a very large Thomas Cole seascape in early restoration, plunked her computer down on the long worktable, took a deep breath and began.

She told him everything, or almost everything. Absent from her animated monologue was her call to Vittoria. Maybe someday she would tell him about Don Carlo, the villa, the paintings, her grandfather's shady dealings with Wolff & Son, and of her fabled extended family in the backhills of Sicily. But not today.

Pieter listened, unblinking, as she shared at length the events of her morning. But near the end, he began to show signs of vexation. Finally he interrupted. "I presume you brought your laptop to show me Gruenwald's site? Wouldn't now be a wonderful time to do that?" he said testily.

"I was getting to that," she said. "Here, take a look."

Angela flipped opened her laptop and punched up Jonathan Gruenwald's site. Pieter placed his bear-sized paw on the touchpad and scrolled down the screen, studying the Parisian gallery owner's poignant appeal with no less scrutiny than he might have vested in any one of the new restoration projects scattered round his worktable. When his eyes came upon the small reproductions of Gruenwald's pictures gone missing, he stopped.

After a long, agonizing pause, Pieter said, "What in the holy hell are we *into* here? This is unbelievable. This is *totally unbelievable.*"

He continued to stare at the display, and then he said, "Do you have any more surprises for me?"

Angela hesitated, struggling over whether to expose her Vittoria connection, and then she said, "Pieter, I can tell you this much. Don't ask me how I know—you'll just have to trust me, okay? You're right about the syndicate, and Wolff is pulling all the strings. My source tells me he's doing business all over Europe, probably in New York, maybe in the Far East, and even right here. It goes back to 1946, back to Otto and the war, like you said. I know this for absolute certain. Take my word for it."

"You trust this source?"

"One hundred percent. And everything I know now screams that it could get very nasty, Pieter. We've gone too far and we can't go back. Wolff knows we know, and he's a very bad dude. This all comes from someone who's actually bought work from him—a lot of it over a lot of years. We've got to do something fast, or we're going to get hung out to dry."

"For God's sake, Angela! What can . . ."

"What can we do?" she interrupted. "First, we can get Gruenwald over here to see the pictures, to make absolutely sure they're his." Angela pointed to the open laptop. "Look at the photos! Do you have any doubt that the two we have upstairs are the same?"

"No, they're the same."

"The bind we're in is that even if Gruenwald says they're his, he could go through years of legal BS and international hassling to prove it before he can take just the *four* of them back. Wolff will fabricate a lot of shit, and he could be dead before it's all settled, if ever. And we'd be long gone from here.

"And as long as we're in this muck up to our knees, we might as well go all the way. Somehow we've got to smoke out the rest while we're at it, not just these four," she continued. "Wolff's got them, if none of the others have popped up in all these years. Not one. If they'd gotten spread about after the war, you would have seen at least a few since 1945."

"Keep talking," he said.

"What to do? For one, you need to run upstairs and get some shots with that dandy new Nikon of yours on the chance that Wolff could take them down before Gruenwald gets here. We'd be screwed then. Can you do that without being seen?"

"I'll handle it."

"Good. And I'll try to reach Gruenwald early tomorrow and get him over here fast, maybe Monday or Tuesday.

"Oh, and I said it could get nasty? Bergdorf has already

fired across our bow, and we could get hurt if we're not paying attention. So watch your back." She didn't elaborate about Bergdorf, and Pieter didn't ask.

"Hurt? What do you mean, 'hurt?'" You mean fired?"

"*Fired?*" she laughed. "I mean hurt. Like in *hurt* hurt," she said, thinking of Paolo Ricci's warning about Wolff—Paolo, who had seen enough mayhem in his life to smell it a mile off. "We're as good as *fired now*. It's only a matter of time."

"Are you serious?"

She shrugged her shoulders and arched her brow in a way that said, Hey, don't think it couldn't happen.

"Use your head, Pieter," Angela persisted. "Goering, Himmler, Bormann, and Hitler himself. Wolff probably *knew* Hitler and all the rest of those evil bastards. He may have been only nine or ten when it all went down, but his father and grandfather were major players. He had to be influenced. Then there's that Nazi business at Harvard. And look how he pushes people around here like that 'movie Nazi' you talked about. My God, the man's not like you or me. He's nuts."

"His father was just an aide, according to Gruenwald's site. I'd hardly call him a major player."

"An aide to *Hermann Goering*, for God's sake."

"Point taken," Pieter said.

"So, what happens after Gruenwald?" he continued. "Running to the locals or the FBI makes no sense. By the time any of them come around, there won't be a whiff of those paintings within a thousand miles, and we'd be toast."

"So, it's like I said. We attack."

"I'm sorry, Angela. It sounded like you said, 'We attack.'"

"You heard right. We attack."

"We? You mean you and me? You want us to attack *Wolff?*"

"We have no choice. It's him or us. Which would you prefer?" she said with a grim smile, eager to get on with it, knowing now that she had the juice to pull it off, and she would use it.

Every sweet drop.

.

CHAPTER THIRTY-THREE

"Well, the element of surprise should be in our favor. It's been sixty years since we attacked the Nazis, so I'm sure they won't be expecting it," Pieter wisecracked.

Ah, surprise, the great equalizer! Angela thought as she remembered as a child creeping up on the long-suffering Pauly, her unlikely playmate at the villa, and he never suspected. She always won their games, and it wasn't because he allowed her to win. She always won because she was ruthless, she was shrewd, and she was focused to a fault. She always won because he always underestimated her. She always won because she was genetically wired to act fast and unexpectedly, and had the stomach to pull the trigger.

She always won because it was her nature.

"Pieter, you could have been a great general! *The element of surprise!* History is replete with underdogs who won impossible victories through the element of surprise. Hannibal and his elephants crossed the Alps to surprise the Romans. Washington and his troops crossed the Delaware on Christmas Eve to surprise the British. David nailed Goliath between the eyes with a rock, no less! No sword, no spear, no armor. Imagine the first forward pass in football. It was Princeton versus Yale, 1879, and . . ."

"Okay, you made your point. There's only one thing we're a little short of."

"And what's that?"

"That's what the hell we're supposed to surprise him *with*. I'm fresh out of rocks. Got any ideas?"

"As a matter of fact, I do," Angela said.

In the time it would take to clean a small varnish brush, Angela disclosed her plan. Following Pieter's solemn pledge of secrecy under threat of a long and painful Sicilian demise, she reluctantly revealed as "need to know" her unconventional family ties and the unseemly relationship between her grandfather and the Wolff cartel. Pieter responded with stunned silence. When she had finished, his slight nod was enough to seal the deal. All that remained was execution—and one unanswered question: How did this remarkable woman know so much about Ivy League football in 1879?

"Now let's get Matisse tidied up. I'll call you when Murphy gets in and we'll put poor old Humpty back together again, okay? And don't forget those pictures. *Please* don't forget, Pieter."

"Good as done," he said, and nothing more. Angela slid off her perch next to the Cole. She glanced at the dean of the Hudson River School's unspoiled scene of surf, spray and foam-drenched rocks as she might draw refreshment from a frosty glass of mint tea, then closed her laptop and retreated with a perky, "Later." Her departure left Pieter unsettled, so he opened his desk drawer, fished out his "dandy new Nikon," exited the lab and headed up the marble staircase to the notorious Dutch gallery.

True to form, the invincible team of Murphy, Maxfield and Mason had returned the decoupages room to its former state, the defiled wall dry and painted closer to six than to the original nine o'clock deadline. Angela didn't ask how they did it; she didn't want to know. How Charlie Murphy worked his magic was part of his mystique.

But the short of it was that by eight-fifteen the decoupages had been re-hung and were looking good, Murphy was happily out the door with a fresh box of Cubans under his arm, and Angela's sweet Sicilian buns were saved for toasting another day.

Ah, the luck of the Irish, she thought as she, Pieter and Jerry each quaffed a Killian's in the back room at Limerick's.

Angela had not told Pieter about Bergdorf's little social call before she left the museum; there had been no time. And even if there had, she knew it would only have rattled him more. She correctly surmised that Pieter did not deal well with danger, and that bodily threats were as foreign to him as life forms from another universe. He simply could not relate to danger as a concept, other than the normal perils of everyday life—car accidents, house fires, muggings, hazards he could avoid, for the most part, simply by *taking care,* which he did to distraction.

She, on the other hand, had grown up with authentic danger at the knee of her grandfather and, oddly, welcomed it as a sign that she was truly alive; adrenalin was as vital to her functioning as her rich, Sicilian blood. The stupidest thing one could do was to underestimate one's enemy, and those who did were in for some rude surprises—thus saith the man in her life who was no stranger to menace. To Don Carlo Vittoria, no threat was ever idle, no affront went unpunished. Which is why she took Bergdorf seriously despite his awkwardness and his silly attempt at theatre.

"I feel that it is my duty to tell you, Miss Desjardin, that your interest in Herr Wolff's paintings has not gone unnoticed," he said as he looked ominously across her desk. "I don't know what has inspired this undue interest, but that's not important. Suffice to say that you would be better served by forgetting that you had ever seen those paintings. For your own good, you should know that Herr Wolff is a very powerful, and at times, very dangerous, man."

His rehearsed lines were accompanied by furrowed brow, piercing eyes, the thickest Teutonic accent he could muster, and a sinister sonority clumsily crafted. Herr Bergdorf clearly had little experience in the threats department; in the mountains of Sicily, harrowing threats were issued daily, like the weather report, and delivered with the chilling incisiveness of Anthony Hopkins on his best day. This is to say that Bergdorf's presentation skills had room for improvement.

"Undue interest?" Angela said, injecting a large measure of incredulity in her voice, with just a pinch of resentment *to taste*, in a theatrical parry of her own. "I don't understand, Herr Bergdorf. I've looked at them only once or twice in the two years I've been here. Is there something I don't know about those paintings?" she said, her eyes narrowing.

She couldn't imagine his bringing them up at all, let alone in such a ham-fisted manner. If they thought she knew about the paintings, nothing would have confirmed her suspicions more than this "undue" display. *Just take down the damn pictures, you idiot, and lie low. Don't come sidling in here and try to scare me.* "Are you threatening me, Herr Bergdorf?" She said this in a tone which, even to the terminally naïve, would have been taken as a counter-threat.

The gauntlet had been thrown.

"I have nothing more to say, Miss Desjardin," he said as he stood, turned and walked out of her tiny office, his pale face turned hot pink with fury.

Angela's first reaction was to laugh. *Never underestimate your enemy* quickly supplanted her amusement, followed promptly by anger. *Did they really think she was that stupid? Or that easily shoved around?*

She would deal with it.

Angela, Pieter and Jerry lifted their glasses in a modest toast to Matisse, whole once more. Tomorrow would be Sunday, still time for her long sought one-on-one with the Master.

CHAPTER THIRTY-FOUR

On most Sunday afternoons, his townhouse on the rue de la Boétie would have been dark. Even on cold winter weekends, there were far better adventures to be had in The City of Light than staring at the confines of one's own home, as opulent as it was. But Jonathan Gruenwald's *petite amie du jour* had suddenly taken ill, or so she said, and he was weighing whether to go alone to the soirée to which they had both been invited or ask another on such short notice. It was in this momentary state of indecision that the phone rang in his study.

"Âllo, Jonathan Gruenwald, ici,"

What incredible luck! Angela thought as she said, *"Âllo, Monsieur Gruenwald, je m'appelle Angela Desjardin.* I am calling from the United States. I found your website and may have information about your missing paintings."

"You saw my website?" he said. "I am amazed! You are the first to respond. I thought that no one would ever see it!"

"No, on the contrary, Monsieur Gruenwald, I found your site, and maybe I can help you."

"What is it that you know, Mademoiselle Desjardin?" he said. "Oh, please excuse my rudeness. Is it 'Mademoiselle,' or is it 'Madame' Desjardin?" he asked politely.

"It's 'Mademoiselle,' Monsieur Gruenwald. Thank you for asking."

"Well, Mademoiselle, I'm very excited! Please tell me what you know," he said somewhat breathlessly, stunned that he may have actually gotten some result from what seemed at the time like a castaway's note set to sea in a bottle.

"I'm the curator of European art at the Mendelssohn Museum in the United States," she said.

"I know of the Mendelssohn. I recall that you have an outstanding collection," he said, "although I've never been to your museum. Most of my visits to the States," he said with an easy familiarity, "are to New York where I deal, and sometimes to Boston or Philadelphia."

"We have hanging in our galleries what I believe are four of your missing paintings, Monsieur Gruenwald."

"Four! Can you tell me which they are?"

"First, let me provide you with some context, and then I'll tell you what I *think* the paintings are," she said.

"Yes, that will be good. Please give me the 'context,' as you say, Mademoiselle Desjardin."

"First, you should know that our director of many years is a man named Erich Wolff, who is the son of Otto Wolff—most likely the Nazi officer you mentioned on your website."

"Erich Wolff! The son! Yes, Erich Wolff!" he blurted into the receiver. "He is your *director*?"

"Yes, and he has been since he came here from Harvard University thirty years ago. I would guess him to be about seventy. He's very tall and slender, with white hair and ice-blue eyes."

"Like his father. His father was tall and had very cold, very blue eyes, I've been told by those who actually saw him during the war. Yes, please continue."

"The paintings have been hanging in one of our galleries for a long time and apparently have never aroused suspicion, I tell you with some embarrassment. For reasons I can't explain, they have been attributed on their labels to other painters who themselves would not have drawn a great deal of attention, although the pieces are magnificent. I'm ashamed that I had overlooked them myself until quite recently."

Jonathan Gruenwald listened patiently as Angela continued.

"According to the labels and to Herr Wolff—he insists that we address him as *Herr Wolff*, incidentally—he loaned them to the museum himself. If these are paintings taken from your family, particularly by his father and from such a famous collection, I'm mystified, Monsieur Gruenwald, as to why he would expose them so openly. But then, he's mystifying on many levels."

"Yes, that is very strange. But please go on."

"Our chief conservator, Pieter Maxfield, and I recently examined one of the paintings in our lab. We found traces of a small swastika which had apparently been stamped on the back of the canvas, like I know the Nazis used when they recorded the pieces they stole during the war."

"At the Jeu de Paume. This is where our entire collection was kept and catalogued for a few weeks before Wolff tried to ship it off to Alt Aussee. It never left Paris, as you know from reading my site," he said.

"Somehow," Angela continued, "Wolff discovered our interest in the paintings. He told me yesterday morning that he has found a possible buyer—which I don't believe—and would take them down soon to be appraised. Then his assistant, Friedrich Bergdorf, actually threatened me with non-specific pain and suffering if I didn't keep away from the paintings and butt out of Herr Wolff's business."

"*Bon Dieu!* Please be careful! Those paintings aren't worth it—they've caused enough grief already," Gruenwald blurted.

"I'm not afraid of Bergdorf. He's nearly eighty, for God's sake. I can handle him. Wolff, too, if it comes to that," Angela fired back in her trademark style. "Nevertheless, time is critical, I think you'd agree." Angela was taken with Jonathan Gruenwald's spontaneous concern for her, even though they had never met, and Gruenwald was instantly aroused by Angela's blistering retort. *This was a woman he had to know better.*

"Yes, obviously it is," he said once he had regained his composure. "Mademoiselle Desjardin, can you tell me which paintings you believe they might be?"

"I'm almost certain that the paintings are the Hals, the Rubens, the van Eyck, and the Steen, from the list you provided on your site. The Hals and the van Eyck are the same, as best we can tell, as the ones you pictured.

"Monsieur Gruenwald, I think you should come immediately to verify them before they're taken down. I'm afraid that, otherwise, we may never see them again," she said. "It may already be too late, I'm sorry to say."

Gruenwald remained silent for a long time.

"Monsieur Gruenwald, are you still there?"

"Yes, I am here. I will take the first available flight out of Paris, either tonight or in the morning, and I should be there sometime tomorrow. I'll call you when I get in." Angela gave him her home number, her cell number and her direct line at the Mendelssohn.

"Do you have any evidence that *Herr* Wolff has the rest of the paintings, Mademoiselle Desjardin?"

"No, I have nothing, Monsieur Gruenwald—only an educated guess," she answered, not wishing to speculate on the whereabouts of the remaining forty-three works. "But I think the circumstantial evidence is pretty strong."

Jonathan Gruenwald was clearly overwhelmed. The recovery of his family's paintings after more than sixty years gone missing had seemed an impossible dream for so long that the prospect of actually doing so had caught him unprepared.

"Mademoiselle Desjardin, I'm somewhat overcome at the moment, as perhaps you can tell. But I promise to be myself again when I see you tomorrow—and it *will* be tomorrow, if I have to fly the plane myself.

"Oh, and may I say that your French is exquisite. You speak like a native, Angela—may I call you Angela?"

"Yes, please do. And *merci* for the compliment. My father is French, and I took a degree at the Sorbonne. I spent many years in Paris, especially as a child, Monsieur Gruenwald. I also speak Italian, with a Sicilian twist. That would be from my mother, who was born in the small town of Vittoria. They are both archaeologists."

"Ah, *les Desjardin*! I've read about them! I'm most impressed, Angela. And please call me Jonathan. I'm not as formal with names as many of my countrymen. Which is not to criticize us, it is just our way, as you would know. I will look forward to seeing you tomorrow! And I will call you from the airport when I arrive."

"*Avec un peu de chance.*"

"Yes, with luck. *À demain*, Angela."

"*À demain*, Jonathan."

With luck, the paintings will still be on the walls when he shows tomorrow, Angela thought. *With luck, Friedrich Bergdorf will not appear in the middle of the night and kill me in my sleep. That would be too bad, before I had a clean shot at him, and the other one.*

She would have liked to go to the museum for a walk-through of the finished exhibit; tomorrow was shaping up as "eventful," especially if Jonathan Gruenwald should appear early in the day. Still, she needed time to figure all of this out: how to lock down the four paintings long enough for Gruenwald to get a good look, which won't be doable if Wolff pulls them down before tomorrow; how to flush them out if he does; how to unearth the rest of the Gruenwald pieces; how to keep the dastardly duo from inflicting pain on this poor, defenseless *ragazza* and the *gentile gigante,* her gentle giant, Pieter.

Angela wasn't all that worried. She knew now that she had all the firepower she needed for a pain-free stalemate, at the very least, and that it wasn't impossible for her to break enough glass to do all of the above. But it would have to be one hell of a blast.

The one thing she was totally sure of, the merde was going to fly. And there wasn't a thing she could do about that unless she just walked away. And it was way too late for that—the die was cast with her call to Gruenwald.

She had just about decided to push all her chips on red, all or nothing, when her solitude was broken by the ringing phone.

"Angela," she said, with a tinge of irritation.

"Gattina, questo è Paolo."

"Pauly! What a nice surprise! Why are you calling me, Pauly? We talked only a few days ago. Is something wrong?"

"Your grandfather, he is not so good. He has not long, Gattina. He get much worse since we talked. The *dòttore* say his heart fail, and there is not much we can do to help him."

"Oh, Pauly! I am so sorry. Can I do anything for him? For you?"

"It is hard to hear his words, he is so weak. He calls for you, Gattina. He wants to see you. He must tell you things."

"Pauly, if it weren't for my new exhibit which opens this week, I would come tonight. The soonest I can be there is Friday. Can he hold on till then, do you think?"

"We try, Gattina. I tell him you are coming. It will give him strength. I call your mother, and she will be here. This make him happy. We fill his bedroom with the roses, which he call now *L'Angelo D'oro*, Golden Angel—for you, Angelina—because he know you love them. Today they are il Condanna D'oro; the roses say he is dying."

"I will come as soon as I can, Pauly. Please kiss him for me, and my mother, too."

"I will, Gattina. Please, I tell you one more thing?"

"Of course, Pauly, What is it?"

"This Erich Wolff. Be careful. He is very dangerous man. He could hurt you if he think you were a threat to him. I would come to protect you, but . . ."

"Pauly, thank you for warning me, but your place is with my grandfather, and I'm relieved that you are there. Yes, I'll be careful."

"I should have told you when . . ." His voice trailed off in regret. "But I could not shame Don Carlo . . ."

"I understand, Pauly. Not to *worry*—I'm a big girl. And I'm *Sicilian*, remember? We Sicilians know how to take care of ourselves, si, Pauly?"

"Si, Gattina. But be careful."

"Do not worry, Zio Pauly. Ciao."

Angela slowly replaced the handset on its base. So soon it had come. *One thing at a time, God, please. One I can handle. Now two? Maybe more? Is this why you made me Sicilian?*

Not expecting an answer, she decided to leave for the Mendelssohn. She had already resolved one huge dilemma—what to do about the Wolfster, and his *liberated* paintings. The other she would deal with among the vines and the olive groves and her nonno's perfumed yellow roses.

They would speak to her, and she would listen.

CHAPTER THIRTY-FIVE

Golden light streamed through the large, floor-to-ceiling window of the salon which fronted on once-fashionable Fourth Street. When the Indian summer sun was in just the right position in the very late afternoon, shortly before it dropped below the horizon, its rays would glance off the glass office tower across the street and turn the Raeburn Gallery radiant amber. While dazzling only for a short time, the intensity would annihilate any piece that was even remotely light-sensitive; fugitive colors would fade quickly under the solar assault.

The space was better suited for sculpture and large, splashy oils—impact pieces more likely to pique the interest of the passing elite who flitted from Brooks to Tiffany's to Saks like fat, furry honeybees, pollinating the local economy. Vulnerable works on paper such as watercolors, pastels, and prints, more intricate pieces which demanded up-close viewing, or pricey works too tempting for late-night exposure in the gallery's increasingly crime-prone locale, she displayed in the softly lit inner rooms where most of the real business was done.

Kate Raeburn sat at her eighteenth-century ebony and gold leaf desk near the rear of the salon, its rich matte surface void of the stacks of papers, magazines, catalogs and other tools of the trade which would normally occupy her. She had spent most of the afternoon straightening and clearing and filing in a futile attempt to keep from dwelling on the startling events of Friday, and she had finally achieved "desk nirvana," an elevated state to which she had rarely risen in her years as a successful gallery owner.

Kate could view her entire domain from where she sat and see easily anyone entering or leaving the gallery. Still she was well out of the blinding swath of sunlight which bathed the exotic Brazilian tigerwood floor and the spindly Alberto Giacometti statue, which cast a grotesque shadow across the wildly striped hardwood and halfway up the blanket-sized Jim Dine heart. The gallery's signature masterpiece embellished her letterhead and business card and positioned her among the cognoscenti as a dealer to be reckoned with.

Giacometti had become part of her animus since Joe's generous estate had permitted the indulgence. She had felt akin to the sculptor's tormented works since her days at NYU, never dreaming that she would ever be able to afford an original, particularly one so extraordinary as this. All that changed on the seventeenth green at Willow Knoll.

The gallery was closed, this being Sunday, offering her the solitude to ponder the events of the last forty-eight hours. She had shut herself up in her city-view apartment on the hill, shades drawn, since Friday evening in total withdrawal from a world which, for her, had turned terrifying and bizarre.

Her thoughts were as conflicted as the "civil unrest" which months before had shredded a predictable patch of the city's real estate only a few blocks from her gallery. On this quiet Sabbath, the downtown streets were empty; the hoodlums and their pursuers could have sprayed the asphalt with lead from curb to curb and not harmed a single, sorry soul. It was the time and place for reflection she could no longer avoid.

After a day-and-a-half of failed attempts to focus, Kate's brain had begun to reassemble itself as human tissue frequently does. She was now lucid enough to spool through the clips of Friday's trauma: Erich Wolff's surreal tour of the long-lost Gruenwald masterpieces; their deadly provenance, and the grisly account of his father's cold-blooded dispatch of the dealer Gernand; his ghastly shrine of Nazi memorabilia; the sickening tang of his childhood relationship with Adolph Hitler; and most horrific, his plan to shuffle off this mortal coil in the manner of his idol, via cyanide, a well-placed bullet from Hitler's tiny pistol, and fire, no doubt. Fire rekindled from the ashes of the Fuehrer and Eva Braun which still smoldered in his feverish mind.

The role he'd created for her in his morbid little scene was unspeakable. *His Eva! The very thought made her nauseous. The man was as completely demented as Hitler himself. To this extent, at least, he had attained his dream.*

She brooded over how he could have controlled her for so long. The obvious explanation would have been her father. Yet the abuse of Misha Steiner over her first eighteen years would not have rendered the former Deborah Jayne Steiner easy pickings for any Jew-hating firebrand who might have wandered down the path. But Erich Wolff was hardly one's garden-variety Nazi. He was a silver-tongued Satan with a continental flare and a stupefying past. *He knew Hitler, for God's sake. He was . . . he was . . .* she couldn't bring herself even to think the words which described their vile bond, though he was just a naïve boy who might have as quickly been absolved as the sinless child who succumbed to the wicked wiles of the parish priest.

Then there was her vulnerability as a lonely widow still very much in her prime; in the grips of an Erich Wolff, such a woman could easily turn to tapioca. She allowed herself to wallow in this lame rationale for less than an instant. *It was, of course, bullshit,* she thought. *Any woman with the street smarts and credibility of a Kate Raeburn would never give herself over to an operator like Erich Wolff—hateful father notwithstanding, widow or no widow—and she was no fool. She just did it, no excuses.*

Her ruminations were like live ammo, shells screaming from opposing sides of the hedgerow, bursting in her head as they found their mark. And then, in a sudden rush of Bodhisattva-like clarity, Kate's hatred of her father, her brothers, the rabbi, her ancestry, lifted like acrid smoke over a stilled battlefield. Suddenly she knew that it wasn't the theology at all. It wasn't Judiasm, which was, in spite of its laws and rites and solemnity which simply did not suit her, a path that, in retrospect, seemed to her inherently good and fair and generous—not unlike other faiths which centered on the idea of a benevolent God; it simply came down to her own father and his twisted interpretation of what it meant to be a good servant of Yahveh.

If this reconciliation seemed overly charitable, at this stage in her life, what did it matter? It's over. Let it go, she told herself.

At once she understood Erich Wolff—as much as one can understand a true psychopath. His history, his associations, and the times he lived through, were enough to turn any human being certifiably mad. This changed in no way her fear of him, but nonetheless broke his hold on her so palpably that she could hear the chains shattering and skittering across the hardwood floor.

As her eyes traced the tortured silhouette of the Giacometti sculpture against the sunlight, she knew what had attracted her to the contorted statue—and to the twisted rhetoric of Erich Wolff. Their mutual deformities, of body and mind, had somehow eased her pain and low esteem. Years of therapy had alluded to this. Now she faced it head-on and it came clear to her. She would have peace once she rid herself of both, and as she cast out the spectre of one Misha Steiner now and ever.

It was so simple once you knew.

But it was not as simple as just walking away. Particularly from Erich Wolff. The fear she could handle; actually, it differed very little from the trepidation she had held of her father, although the prospect of a violent death had never been part of that equation—other than the few times as an early teen when, not unlike so many other desperate adolescents, she had contemplated *taking the gas pipe,* Willie Loman's quaint nomenclature for ending it all which she remembered from *Death of a Salesman.* Erich Wolff's compelling invitation to join him hand-in-hand in his grande finale would be spurned, of course, without regrets.

She would avoid Erich Wolff for the next several days. Some excuse would come to her—illness, the business, *time to think.* But she had to be seen at the Matisse opening. Her absence would be noticed. Between now and then, Kate would find a way to extricate herself from this strange bond turned suddenly scary.

But the double bind of what to do about the Gruenwald paintings and the incriminating diaries churned in her stomach like spoiled food. These were huge matters, and being privy to them was an honor she would have been just as happy to decline; knowing where the bodies were buried was a no-win position, and a dangerous one for the particular body who knew how they got there.

Until she figured it all out, she would make herself scarce, and watch her back.

The sun had dropped below the skyline, and the Raeburn Gallery fell into shadow. The overhead spots were off, and the glow of the Tiffany lamp on the corner of Kate's desk provided the only light in the nearly dark expanse. She had lost track of time and had violated her own rule never to be alone in the gallery after dark, especially on a weekend night when the streets in this part of town were largely deserted. Only an occasional car passed, and a homeless person peered through the window at her, his flammable breath steaming the glass, a startling reminder that she had stayed too long.

Kate made a note to call the real estate woman in the morning. Her lease was up soon, barely enough time to relocate to the tree-shaded square of Sycamore Village, the suburban bastion of old money where most of the other tony downtown merchants had, since the riots, scrambled like prescient rats from a burning building. A shopper's paradise for more than a century, the core had become a monument to bureaucratic bickering, misguided subsidies, and a crook-friendly lack of jail space. It was now a checkerboard of empty storefronts that were once a magnet for the city's rich and famous; only long-term, iron-clad leases had kept the two or three remaining retail anchors from bailing. It was time to hold the agent's feet to the fire to find her decent space elsewhere.

As she retrieved her purse from the desk drawer and reached to put out the light, she saw a shadow at the main door to the gallery, and then came a knock on the glass. She assumed that it was the scruffy specimen who only minutes before had disappeared from the side window, making a last desperate attempt at a handout.

"Go away! The gallery is closed. Please leave!" she shouted, to be sure that whoever stood at the door could hear her through the heavy glass.

"Kate, it's Erich! Please let me in."

Kate stiffened and, for a moment, couldn't speak.

"Erich! Just a minute," she said as she opened her purse, fished out the key, and walked to the door which she always kept locked from the inside when she was there alone, even during the day. As she approached the door, she could see his face through the glass. It was drawn and gray beneath his dated fedora. He had pulled the collar of his black overcoat up around his neck against the wind. *The Gestapo come calling* flitted across her mind.

She unlocked the door and he pushed inside, shivering slightly and murmuring an uncomplimentary comment, in German, on the inclemency of the weather. She looked past him to see parked at the curb the silhouette of the large Mercedes, engine running, and the stoic face of Bergdorf in the ghostly green glow of the dash.

"Kate, I've tried to reach you. Many times, at your place and here. I've left messages. Are you alright?"

Kate had listened to his messages, each growing more edgy, the latest nearly out of control, but she was determined not to pick up until she knew exactly what she was going to say. Still she didn't know, but she had no choice but to let him come inside. It would have been worse to send him away.

"Answer me! Are you alright?"

"Yes, I'm fine. You have to understand how overwhelming everything was to me on Friday, Erich. The things you showed me, the things you told me. I just needed some time to absorb it all. *Please* give me time."

"That is the point, Katherine," he said. "Time may be running out for us." She took note of his lapse into "Katherine," and she was alarmed by it, even more so because she had no idea what it signaled.

"What do you mean, 'time may be running out?'" Her voice had begun to betray her fear. She declined to ask what he meant by *for us,* because she didn't want to know.

"I think that maybe there are people who either know or suspect what we've been doing—with the paintings, maybe with Das Rheingold, with all of it."

What we've *been doing?* she thought. *When did he become* we? Although she'd known about Das Rheingold and his business with Arthur Mendelssohn and a few others, the Gruenwald paintings were new to her. And whether she knew these things or not, she had had nothing to do with any of it.

"*Who* knows, Erich?" she said.

"It could be Angela Desjardin and Pieter Maxfield. Bergdorf told me they've been snooping around the Dutch gallery this week, and that Maxfield took down the Hals to repair the frame, or so he said. Just in case, I'm having the paintings removed in the morning and taken back to the house. I'll put them in the cellar with the others."

"So then why are you worried? There'll be nothing to see by the end of tomorrow," she said casually, struggling to control her panic. But she was not ready for his sudden non sequitur.

"Kate, have you thought about what I said?"

After an awkward pause, during which she was, for the most part, able to regain her composure, she said slowly but firmly, "Erich, you know how we feel about each other. There's just so much. Please give me just a few days more. Can we talk on Wednesday evening, at the party? We can sneak downstairs—I want to see the paintings again, they're so beautiful."

"But Kate . . ."

"Wednesday?" she pleaded.

"Wednesday will be fine," he said. "I'm happy that you're alright. I was worried."

"Thank you, Erich."

"May we take you up to your place? You shouldn't be here alone at night, you know."

"I have my car."

"Let me at least walk with you. Then I won't worry."

Kate turned out the antique Tiffany, pitching the gallery

into darkness except for the glow of the halogen street lamps which shone through the long window. She locked the main door from the outside, glanced through the windshield at Bergdorf, cadaverous in the greenish cast from the instrument panel, turned and started toward her car.

Wolff grasped her hand. His icy fingers made her shiver, and she murmured something about the cold to cover for her spasmodic chill. The long, black Mercedes followed them slowly like a big cat stalking its quarry until they reached her silver Jaguar.

The homeless man was nowhere in sight. At that moment she would have welcomed him with open arms.

CHAPTER THIRTY-SIX

Henri Matisse commanded the entire southwest wing of the second floor. Beyond the sprawling special exhibition area where they romped in total abandonment, his "children" spilled out onto the colonnade and surrounded the atrium in a thunderous stampede of color, linear wizardry and rampant good cheer.

Angela looked up at the massive signature work which dominated the entrance. It was an exuberant decoupage of brilliant blue, green, red, orange and purple leaves on a snowy white ground, jewels of pure color cut from painted paper by the old man's arthritic hand during his last days. They were arranged as if a dust devil had swirled them up into the air like dry leaves on a brisk October day. On a tall gray panel near the decoupage, the exhibit's theme, lettered in a spare Century Gothic type, read:

Color Unbound: Le Bonheur de Matisse

It was Angela who conceived the few words which, in her mind, said all that needed saying. Color Unbound, she reasoned, was the upshot of the artist's headlong plunge into the wilderness of hues where he hacked merrily through the spectrum, liberating color like a genie from a bottle.

No longer would a tree be green if its creator saw it as blue. Or if the tree itself would rather be blue. It was an idea which would seldom surface past kindergarten—an abstraction unlikely to emerge as old age sets in, usually around eight or nine or at whatever age one becomes too insecure to ask why or too ossified to ask why not.

But not only would the tree be blue, it would be a satisfying, joyous blue, like an old pair of slippers or a good armchair, as the

Master himself once said.

As for *Le Bonheur de Matisse,* The Happiness of Matisse, could such works radiate from any but a man completely happy with his art? Joy intense enough to dull the pain of cancer, of divorce, of imagining those he loved in the callous hands of the *Geheime Staatspolizei.* To the end, the days for Henri Matisse were warm and sunny, full of promise, laden with surprises, brimming with expectation. Only the nights would be long.

Color Unbound: Le Bonheur de Matisse. Perfect.

Angela took a deep breath and entered through the eye of the maelstrom, allowing herself to be swept along by its unrelenting current of color. She was seeing it seemingly for the first time, although she had planned every detail herself and watched over every nuance of its birthing like a jealous midwife.

She lost track of the hour as, one by one, windows opened onto the soul of Henri Matisse. There were works from his early years which he spent copying the still lifes of Chardin and the Dutch painter de Heem, peaking with tributes to Corot, Pissarro and Monet; then came the fruits of his foray into *plein air*—lush landscapes painted out-of-doors in Brittany, on Belle-Ile and Corsica, where for him *everything shone, all was color, all was light,* in his words; finally, the exhibit exposed his reckless affair with color, a romance which only grew hotter till death did them part.

Angela chose to place his dozen or so sculptures randomly throughout the main gallery, rough-hewn bronzes of thick-bodied women and craggy male nudes; the more than fifty etchings, pencil drawings and pen and ink sketches she gave to the colonnade, allowing the master's gift for chaste, fluid line plenty of space to breathe—*the purest and most direct translation of my emotion,* he said.

But it was the "nuclear core," as Angela called it, that energized the entire exhibit, like the sun illuminates the planets and lets them each glow in its own mystical way. Here she hung the greatest of the works on canvas, masterpieces graciously loaned by the most important museums in the world: portraits of women in shocking clashes of red and orange and violet; dancing dervishes in neon pink on emerald grass against a cobalt sky; landscapes in colors that God Himself might have used had they occurred to Him; interiors and fabrics and floral bouquets infinitely more dazzling than their originals; huge, contorted nudes in rainbow hues, all given life by his exquisite, deceivingly simple lines.

Scattered among the oils were the decoupages, the great legacy of his last days and perhaps the most imaginative and forceful of all his works. These amorphous shapes he would cut laboriously from gouache-tinted paper as he lay in bed or sat propped up in his wheelchair, directing helpers where to paste them against large sheets tacked to the wall.

And finally there came a touch of pure inspiration: in a small, sunny alcove which divided the main exhibit area into two essentially equal spaces, Angela had recreated a slice of the artist's studio in his beloved Le Régina overlooking the Mediterranean in Nice. The universally revered canvas of his studio window open to the sea ruled the space and hung against a wall papered with decoupages-in-progress. The old man's wheelchair, which she had begged shamelessly from its reluctant owner, sat in one corner, his battered felt fedora tossed casually on the seat next to his violin in its open, blue velour-lined case, another treasure for which she had prostrated herself. The floor around his chair was strewn with varicolored scraps from his brilliant cutouts. And on the walls were sepias of himself with Monet, with Picasso, and alone in his wheelchair, feet bare and hands at work with scissors and paper.

In the opposite corner hung a gilded cage on a stand. Inside, a yellow canary flitted nervously from perch to swing and back, a living tribute to the master's aviary where he cared for more than three hundred parakeets, thrushes, pigeons and other rare species. Angela had named the canary *Diva*, and Diva sang relentlessly.

For any lover of great art, *Color Unbound: Le Bonheur de Matisse* would have been more a pilgrimage than a casual afternoon at the Mendelssohn; for Angela, as she finally retreated from the exhibit area, it was a dream come true, and for a time nothing else mattered.

But as if a light had been switched off and another flipped on, the ugly business of Gruenwald and Wolff and her *dolce nonno* rose up like a roomful of screaming monkeys. Diva's frenzied chirping faded as, in what could best be described as a reflex action, she made her way toward the Dutch gallery.

Half expecting to be confronted by four empty spaces, like the gap-toothed grin of the demented "cracker" from *Deliverance*, Angela gave a sigh of relief that the paintings were still hanging in their appointed spots, goading her to please lock them down before they vanished again. *Now if they'll just stay put until tomorrow . . .*

Thus assured, she wove through the handful of visitors straggling toward the exit in the final minutes before closing and headed for the lab on the chance that Pieter had forgotten that it was Sunday and had wandered in absent-mindedly.

Her knocks went unanswered. Sundays after closing always gave Angela the creeps, and now with all the goings-on, this Sunday would be worse. She left quickly. Jonathan Gruenwald would keep, and she had little doubt that Pieter would not have failed to photograph the paintings.

Domani. Tomorrow.

"Of course I shot the paintings. The camera's right here in my desk. I always do what you tell me, Lucy," Pieter said. The thought of the Peanuts poster on her bedroom door as a thirteen-year-old malcontent, Lucy bitching in French that *nobody understands us crabby people,* skipped across her synapses.

"Good," she said. "Now guess who's coming to dinner?"

"I'll bite. Who?"

"Try Jonathan Gruenwald."

"Gruenwald?"

"Gruenwald. I talked with him yesterday, and he's all aquiver. Said he'd hop the next plane, whenever that might be. In any case, he'll be here sometime today, or so he said."

"What are you going to do with him? How are you going to smuggle him in? It's Monday—we're closed. Nobody but staff is here."

"I know that."

"He'll stick out like a Harley in the Tour de France."

"Not necessarily. I'll just meet him at the staff entrance, and I'll introduce him as a friend from Paris to anybody who wants to know. I have friends in Paris, you know."

"So you tell me."

"He'll call me from the airport, and we'll take it from there," she said as she wiggled up on her familiar high stool. Angela filled Pieter in on her conversation with Gruenwald, but said nothing more about her plan. He didn't ask.

"I said 'dinner,' right? Thought we'd all have dinner together, you, me and Jonathan. . ."

"Jonathan? He's Jonathan now?"

". . .and figure out what to do next," she continued, ignoring the needle. "You available?"

"Shall I cook?"

"No, let's go to the hotel. We'll need your undivided attention and the full weight of your genius."

"I do a very nice *coq au vin* ..."

"Hotel."

"Hotel."

Angela slipped down from the stool. "Okay, that's it. I'm off to Marketing. Push, push, push. She drives me nuts, Robertson. Something about the press luncheon, she said.

"I'll let you know when Jonathan calls."

"I shall wait with bated breath and brush up on my *parlez-vous* till then."

On the way to the marketing conference room, a windowless broom closet on the second floor tucked behind a tiny floral still-life gallery and miles from the nearest staff office, Angela had to pass through the now infamous Dutch room. She looked straight ahead, her mind fixed on the expected call from Jonathan Gruenwald and hoping that it wouldn't come in the midst of her ordeal with Marilyn Robertson, whatever that turned out to be. An abrasive, untidy woman with hair by Hamilton Beach and the profile and temperment of a small Frigidaire, the Mendelssohn's marketing director greased the press like an auto mechanic, the sole reason for her tenure at the museum. She had *the gift*. Wolff tolerated Marilyn Robertson only so long as he didn't have to sit too close to her. The others had no choice, Angela included.

Angela had nearly crossed the gallery when her alarm went off. She froze, then turned to confront her worst fear. *They were gone! God, they were gone—all four of them—and in their spaces, nothing. Not even the cream-colored removal tags, absent under threat of death to the one, or ones, who would take down a work without due notice.*

Hals, Steen, Van Eyck and Rubens had left the building.

She wanted to shout out. Cry rape. Dial nine-one-one. Although it weren't as if Wolff hadn't warned her. Any reaction on her part, Angela knew, would escalate the deadly little game they'd been playing, and definitely not in her favor. She would do the escalating on her own terms, when and how. Until then, she would zip it and smile.

Angela willed her legs to move. As she covered the last few paces to the conference room-cum-broom closet, her mind raced ahead to Jonathan Gruenwald and what she would tell him when he arrived. *Just the truth,* she knew. *What else could she do?* Thank God they still had the photos, which might be enough for now. But first, get through this ridiculous meeting, whatever it was about, and then deal with Jonathan when the time came.

The room was barely large enough for a small table and six chairs. At one end sat The Fridge herself, already steamed by the curator's trademark tardiness and tapping her yellow No. 2 impatiently on the tabletop. Given a choice of the five remaining chairs, Angela chose the polar opposite, sitting at the far end of the table near the door. *The poor thing could benefit from the attentions of a gentleman caller,* she thought, charitably dismissing Marilyn Robertson's mean streak as privation of male companionship.

Still steadying herself from the shock of the downed and missing paintings, Angela broke the ice. "So what is this?" she said through her teeth.

"I'm moving the press luncheon up from Wednesday," The Fridge said bluntly. Gilding the lily was not in Marilyn Robertson's make-up, at least with staff.

"Moving it *up*? How can you move it *up*? It's already Monday!" Angela said. "To *when,* may I ask?"

"Tomorrow. Betsy's already contacted them all and re-scheduled the caterer," she said, referring to her assistant, Betsy Crowe, whose life as a single mother with two small children the marketing dominatrix had made a living hell since her first day in a job she couldn't afford to lose. "And I need you to tour the exhibit, like you were already going to do.

"I presume you have no problem with that?"

"No problem? Of course I have a problem! Do you have any idea what I still have to do to make this exhibit ready just for *Wednesday*? No, I can't do that," Angela said.

"But the show's already installed. It's done."

"That's what you see. And do you think I just pull a press presentation out of my bum? I *need* tomorrow—every damn minute of tomorrow!"

"That's why you get the big bucks, Angela," Marilyn Robertson said, cranking their already contentious relationship up another notch.

"So why is this? What's the rush?"

"It's simple. The *Journal* promised me front-page in color on Friday *and* a major feature inside if they could see it earlier and take pictures. Something they'd already planned hit the wall and they need us, now. Such is life in the world of spin, *capisce*?"

Capisce? Angela couldn't help but roll her eyes. "So just bring the *Journal* people over ahead—no dogs, no ponies, no lunch. Keep the rest of them till Wednesday," she said.

"Can't do. If the other papers and the TV vultures find out that we had the *Journal* first, and they will, they'll give us squat. *Nada.* The way it is."

Nada? Angela rolled her eyes again.

"Damn, Marilyn . . ." Her mouth open to continue, she was interrupted by a Vivaldi sonatina in squeaky mouse music emanating from her cell.

"Sorry," she said, poking at the keypad and raising the butter yellow Nokia to her ear.

"Angela."

"Angela, Jerry. Somebody on the phone for you. Do you know a *Gruenwald*, or *Gruenfeld*, or something like that? Funny accent. French, I think. Says it's urgent?"

Merda! "Hold him, Jerry. Tell him it may be a few minutes." She punched out.

"Gotta go."

"What do you mean, 'gotta go?' What about tomorrow?"

"Do I have a choice? Fine. But don't do this to me ever again, Marilyn. *Ever*," she said, with no doubt whatsoever that Marilyn Robertson *would* do it again, whenever it damn well pleased her. Whenever she got her ass in a sling, she'd do it. Always had, always will.

Angela rushed out of Marilyn Robertson's broom closet and in less than a minute she was sitting at her own desk, door closed, phone to her ear.

"Jonathan?"

"*Angela, je suis ici—à l'aéroport,* Jonathan Gruenwald said. His luscious French was like Debussy to her. *God, I miss Paris,* she thought. "Where should I go?"

"There's no need to come here, Jonathan, at least today. I'm afraid I have bad news."

"Bad news?"

"Jonathan, the paintings are gone. Erich Wolff must have taken them down early this morning. They're probably in his home by now, under lock and key."

There was dead silence from Gruenwald's end of the phone. And then he said in a voice midway between anger and despair, "Gone? How can they be gone? Why are they gone?"

"He told me on Saturday that he'd be taking them down for an appraisal. Said he had a buyer, which is preposterous. He had a *stroke*, most likely, when he figured we knew something. I had no idea he'd be removing them so soon—in the middle of the night, it seems like."

More silence from Gruenwald's end. Then, "Now what, Angela? Isn't there anything we can do? Confront him? Call the police? Call your FBI?"

"Jonathan, we do have the photographs. Pieter Maxfield took pictures yesterday. We have those, and maybe they'll be enough for openers."

"For openers?"

"It's poker talk, Jonathan. Have you ever played poker? It's a card game."

"Poker? Like in the westerns on TV?"

"Never mind poker, Jonathan. We have the . . . "

Once again Angela was interrupted, this time by the *call waiting* beep.

"Jonathan, hold just a minute.

"Angela," she said as she depressed the *call waiting* key.

"Angela, it's me, Pieter." His voice was agitated, almost panicky.

"Pieter, I have Gruenwald. He's at the airport. I'll get right back."

"Angela, wait . . ."

She cut him off and returned to Gruenwald.

"Jonathan, we have the photos," she said. "You need to see them, and then we must talk. Take a taxi to the Plaza hotel downtown. I'll call ahead and get a room for you. Pieter Maxfield, our chief conservator, and I will meet you there for dinner in the main dining room, say, around nine? It's called the Rosewood Room. Is that alright?"

"*C'est bon.*"

"Between now and then try to catch a few winks. I want you to be bright-eyed and bushy-tailed for tonight, okay?"

"Bushy-tailed?"

"*Éveillé.*"

"*Éveillé.* Awake.

"Yes, awake."

"Nine o'clock, then. *À ce soir,* Angela.*"

"*À ce soir,* Jonathan." Angela hung up the phone, and then remembered Pieter. Her head was spinning, and she hoped he wasn't going to slip another nasty surprise in her bag.

"Pieter? You still there?"

"Angela! Bad news."

"What now, for God's sake."

"The paintings are gone."

"I know the paintings are gone. I was just up there."

"And my camera's gone, too. The pictures were still in it."

"The pictures you took? Damn, Pieter, what happened?"

"How should I know? The camera was in my desk drawer when I left last night, and the lab was locked tight, like always. When I opened the drawer this morning, the camera was gone. I've looked everywhere. That's when I ran upstairs and found the paintings gone, too. Somebody was in here and swiped the camera overnight."

"Was anything else taken?"

"No, nothing. I've checked."

"Not that it matters, but who has a key, besides you?"

"Security, of course, and Bergdorf or Wolff, most likely.

"How would they know you shot the paintings?"

"You tell me. No one saw me. There was no one around. You can believe me on that."

"I believe you," she said. If Pieter was anything, he was careful—and on this one, he would have been careful to a fault.

"Well, so be it. But if we don't stir the pot soon we're going to be screwed.

"And now here's Gruenwald, expecting to see his paintings. I already told him about them being gone, but not the photos, too. I didn't know that when I talked to him. He's good for tonight, incidentally—nine o'clock at the Plaza. I'm putting him up there."

"What are you going to say to him?"

"Well, after he gets over his apoplexy that there's nothing here for him to see, we're going to talk about stirring the pot."

CHAPTER THIRTY-SEVEN

Angela and Pieter climbed the red-carpeted staircase to the Plaza's second floor lobby. She had chosen the Plaza for Gruenwald not only because it was the most elegant hostelry in the city, but because of its famous interior. Most people who knew about such things agreed that the Plaza was perhaps the best example of art deco hotel design in America; the hotel's dominant architectural motifs were copied from the 1925 Paris Exposition which gave the Art Deco style to the world. Angela knew that this would not be lost on Jonathan Gruenwald and that he would appreciate the gesture.

He was waiting for them at the top of the steps. And he was smiling, a trait uncommon in France on first meeting, although Angela knew that the French could be the most convivial people on earth. His apparent warmth signaled a man at ease with cultures not his own.

"Angela? Pieter?" he said as the two of them reached the top step of the grand staircase. Jonathan Gruenwald was taller than Angela had pictured him, not as tall as Pieter, or as "full-figured." His features were sharp, and his wheat-colored hair grayed slightly at the temples. It startled her for an instant that he bore such a striking resemblance to her own father. She figured him at no more than forty, but drop-dead good looks can deceive, she told herself.

"Jonathan!" Angela responded.

"*Bonsoir et bienvenue, Jonathan,*" Pieter said warmly and extended his hand. "*Je suis enchanté de faire votre connaissance.*" Pieter's French, Angela observed with surprise, was not as shabby as he had led her to believe; his command of the language, however, remained slightly tainted by a distinct *Québécois* inflection, the result of the Pine Tree state's sizable French-Canadian population and its influence on Pieter's acutely sensitive ear.

"Bonsoir et merci, Pieter," Jonathan responded in kind and gripped Pieter's hand with strength which surprised him and suggested some heavy lifting of his own.

"I came down from my room an hour ago simply to inhale the incredible beauty of this hotel. It's one of the most remarkable examples of French art deco I've ever seen! And when I read the words in the ceiling mural, *Bienvenue aux voyageurs,* I felt immediately at home. Thank you for putting me here!" Gruenwald said in impeccable English, to Pieter's great relief.

"I had hoped you'd like it, Jonathan. If the motifs look familiar, it's because the architect borrowed many of them from the Paris Exposition—with spectacular results, don't you think?"

"Spectacular indeed!" he agreed, his eyes sparkling with excitement.

"Shall we take a table? You must be exhausted from your flight, but we have a lot to talk about," Angela said, "and not much time."

"That will be fine, Angela, although I feel quite rested. But I hope we'll have time enough to get to know each other after all of this is settled," he said as he held eye contact a second too long.

Now I remember why I like French men, she thought. *They never confuse their priorities.*

Pieter ordered champagne—an inexpensive yet tasty brut "to celebrate their coming together and hope for a successful outcome," as he expressed in a gracious welcoming toast. His selection was shamelessly intended to impress his guest, and he was not disappointed; an approving nod and a slight tip of the glass was ample validation of his choice.

They exchanged the briefest of small talk before Angela said, "Jonathan, I'm sorry to tell you we have a new problem—but not a hopeless one."

Gruenwald's face dropped, but he listened patiently.

"I thought it would be best you knew exactly what we're up against before we talk about how to deal with it—which we will.

"Erich Wolff has your four paintings we talked about on the phone. We saw them. We've been studying them. They're no longer in the gallery, as I told you on the phone, but my guess is they're in his house up on the hill, at least for now." Angela took a sip of champagne to allow her words to sink in.

"My instinct tells me that the rest of them are here, too, somewhere. All forty-three of them. I have no proof, but they're here somewhere in the city, I know it."

"Well, that's all good," Gruenwald said. "But please tell me the problem."

"The problem," Pieter jumped in, "is that my camera was stolen from the lab last night—which I always keep locked, even during the day. The pictures I took of the four paintings were still in the camera, and I was planning to print them out this morning to show you. It had to have been someone with a passkey—a good guess would be Friedrich Bergdorf, Wolff's assistant, or even Wolff himself."

"So you have no proof then that they were even here? No paperwork? No nothing?" Gruenwald said.

"No nothing. Only the word of the other curators, maybe, that they were once hanging in the gallery. Or Nick Castle, the former European curator, might remember. He'd love to nail Wolff, but he's in Kansas City at the Nelson-Atkins, and we've had no time to call him.

"Sorry," she continued, "but by the time we got it together, those four pictures, and all the others, would be long gone," Angela said. "That's why ringing up any of the big agencies like the Holocaust Claims Office, Art Restitution, or even the FBI would be pointless. Even if they believed us, it could be weeks, maybe months before we got any action."

"What about your police?" Gruenwald said. "Can't they do something?"

Angela laughed. "You have your Inspector Clousseau, my dear Jonathan, we have ours."

The Frenchman laughed, too, in spite of his disappointment. The Pink Panther was one of his favorite films, and he had once sold a painting to Peter Sellers as a neophyte gallery owner, right before the great comedian died.

"And even if our locals were Hercule Poirot, Sherlock Holmes, and Charlie Chan all rolled into one, they'd still need a warrant to get inside the old mansion—and they'd need a better reason than we have right now to ask for one. The way Wolff is hooked up in this town, the chances of any judge serving one up are slim to none, regardless of the evidence," Angela said.

"Erich Wolff knows that you know about the paintings, and maybe even where they came from?" Gruenwald said.

"He knows, Jonathan," she said. "But he's still jerking us around. He's clearly not afraid of us, and for now, that's a good thing."

"So what do we do?"

"Remember the game, poker, we talked about on the phone?"

"Yes, I remember."

"I think it's time to deal the cards."

By the time Angela had walked them through her reckless scheme, Gruenwald was smiling once more. It was not the easy smile he had flashed when they first met, but the tight-lipped smirk of an angry victim plotting payback for a terrible wrong. The image of a trusting David and Anna Gruenwald walking hand in hand to their unsuspected death welled up inside him, and he could finally taste revenge. The boldness of Angela's plan had stirred him, and the revelations about her dark connections had only fanned his desire to get to know her better.

Pieter was not smiling. He sat mute, astonished a second time by Angela's murky disclosures. In the time he had known her, Angela had never shared any of this with him until the previous day. He knew about her Sicilian lineage, but she never talked much about it, at least to him—and now here's Jonathan, and it all spills out, albeit necessary, he conceded.

Pieter knew also that dire circumstances call for dire measures, usually taken by one or more gritty souls willing to risk all for what's right. He had to applaud Angela for putting it all on the line—her job, her good name, maybe even her life—to pull Wolff up short and avenge the old Gruenwald couple.

Finally, he was forced to admit to a touch of jealousy—for the first time he allowed that she meant something more to him than simply that of colleague and sidekick. His Yankee candidness told him, however, that *he*, unfortunately, was the sidekick. He was Tonto and Angela wore the mask, and that would likely never change—not exactly an ego booster to a natural-born backwoodsman from the rugged state of Maine.

But for right now, it was clear that Jonathan Gruenwald was *the man*; he, Pieter, would have to adapt. Someday he'd figure out just where she fit into his life, if at all. Until then, he'd best hop aboard or go on home. The train was leaving the station.

Only then did Pieter smile. If anything, he was adaptable.

The details of Angela's plan were few. It reminded Pieter of one of his favorite films, *Force 10 From Navarone,* where Harrison Ford and Robert Shaw set off a few well-placed wads of plastic explosive inside a dam wall to wash out a bridge downstream plus a few thousand Germans and the tanks they rode across on: you couldn't be sure if *anything* would happen, even after the fireworks, until a few cracks opened in the face of the dam. Then you'd best run like hell.

Like the movie, Angela's plan was long on the bang, but short on guarantees. It was a plan nonetheless, and frankly, more than Pieter and Jonathan had come up with. About all they could do was duck and then stick around to pick up the pieces. Hopefully there would be at least forty-seven of them, and they would look very much like old paintings. The three agreed that unless a better idea came along soon it was this or nothing, and Jonathan hadn't come all this way for nothing.

They talked into the night, consuming three more bottles of an excellent Beaujolais, Gruenwald's treat. He was riveted by Angela's and Pieter's blow-by-blow of the discovery of the four paintings; of their furtive examination of *Dutch Mother and Child, c. 1634* and the ghostly appearance of the coin-sized swastika on the back of the canvas; Angela's tense staredowns with Erich Wolff and Heinrich Bergdorf; and the myriad of delectable details that had made their exploits a story worth telling. When they had finished, he was more worked up than ever.

In turn, Gruenwald gave them the full account of how Hermann Goering and Otto Wolff stormed his grandparents' empty brownstone at 51 rue de La Boétie, and then, on a tip from a disloyal retainer, roared on in Goering's long, black touring car, Nazi flags fluttering, to his cousin Paul's chateau in the south where they struck the mother-lode: David and Anna Gruenwald's remarkable collection of paintings, sculpture and jewels tucked away throughout the manor and in the wine cellars.

He told them, from the recollections of his elderly cousin's remaining servants, how Otto Wolff had stripped the sprawling chateau of piece by priceless piece, loaded them onto Wehrmacht lorries, and stacked the spaces remaining with cases of cousin Paul's best vintages.

Gruenwald then chronicled the tragic end of David and Anna, from their brutal removal by the Gestapo from the ferry at Le Havre, to their near starvation at Buchenwald, to their stumbling trek to the place where they breathed their last, his grandfather's spindly arm around Anna's skeleton-like shoulders to the end. The details had been passed on by eyewitnesses to him and to his father over the years.

"There was a woman," he said. "A young German woman. A Jew. She watched over them in the camp, as she did many of the old people, I was told. When they took my grandmother and grandfather to the showers, she went with them. So they wouldn't be afraid. The three of them died together, holding each other." Jonathan Gruenwald poured the last of the wine.

"Her name was Hilde. Hilde Meyer. Bremen had been her home. I've tried to find her family for years, to thank them, but with no success." His voice trailed away.

On this wrenching note their evening ended to the accompaniment of clinking glasses, rattling plates and the muffled voices of staff already setting tables for breakfast. Angela and Pieter walked Jonathan Gruenwald to the elevators and then retraced their steps down the Plaza's marble staircase to the street.

Pieter took Angela's hand; she did not pull away, but welcomed the gesture as they made their way down the deserted sidewalk toward her car, lost in their own thoughts. The only other sign of life was a homeless man huddled in the doorway of the art gallery with the twisted bronze sculpture in the window, a block from the hotel.

CHAPTER THIRTY-EIGHT

Tuesday passed quietly. Only the growing tenseness in every fiber of Angela's normally bulletproof frame telegraphed that this was no regular day at the office. The impending showdown with Erich Wolff had tied her in knots, not because she was afraid to confront him, but out of angst that her gritty move would meet with disaster. It was a huge gamble, but one she was drawn to like Amarillo Slim to a green felt table.

Dutifully she filled the four empty spaces in the Dutch Gallery with other Netherlandish works from storage. She conducted The Fridge's dog and pony show that morning and made a few last minute label changes which, without her atypical fidgeting, could have been left well enough alone. And with the jocular assistance of Ray in maintenance and his bright yellow cherry picker, she adjusted several overhead spots which had slipped out of focus, leaving several of the most powerful pieces in shadow.

Angela spent most of the evening with Jonathan Gruenwald at *La Grenouille*. "The Frog" was a little piece of Paris whipped together by the onetime sous chef of its Left Bank namesake who had become smitten by a callow young tourist and had followed her home to America like a lost puppy. On reentry, she dumped him for more promising pickings, and the forsaken sous chef was left in a state of glorious French melancholy. Thus abandoned, he opted for the only viable antidote appropriate to a heartsick cuisinier: he opened a restaurant.

Angela and Jonathan's conversation over dinner was absent of any of the matters which had brought them together. For a few hours, Angela's appetite had returned to its usual carnivorous state, primed by the doleful chef's signature Tournedos Rossini, which she washed down with most of a bottle of the same extraordinary vintage Jonathan had selected the night before at the Plaza.

And for a few hours, her passion for the sun-baked Sicilian countryside was seriously challenged by the electric surge of The City of Light.

Wednesday for Angela was spent in curator's purgatory. Waiting. For the evening and the opening and the hoopla, and in particular, the gathering of royalty at the Castle. The Wolfster would be in his firmament, jerking the strings of his puppet board and lording it over the city's rich and famous who, for reasons still a mystery to her, jockeyed endlessly to bask in his radiance.

Further complicating her life that day was the call from Vittoria.

"É Paolo, Gattina."

"Pauly! Why are you calling me? Is it my grandfather?" she said as a sense of dread swept over her. The words slipped out, uncontrolled: "Is he dead?" She came around from behind her desk and closed the door.

"Yes, it is Don Carlo. No, he is not dead. But he will die soon. He want to see you. He *must* see you. It is *important, Gattina.*"

"I'm *coming*, Pauly. You *know* I'm coming. On Friday. Two days from now. My reservations are made. I can't come sooner."

"I tell him you are coming. He never remember when I tell him. But he know inside, and it keep him alive.

"*La Lucertola* is here."

"My mother?" Angela said, remembering her affectionate nickname, The Lizard, given to her as a little girl by her grandfather's protectors as they tried in vain to catch her in their endless games of hide-and-seek among the ruins.

"She is with him now, and that make him happy. But he want you."

"Pauly, *please* keep him alive. I'll be there. I will."

"Only God can do that, bambina. And I do not think that God owes him any favors. But I do what I can, with His grace," he said in rare obeisance to The Almighty. "We will be overcome to see you. Arrivederci, Gattina. Ti amo."

"Ti amo, anche, Pauly." I love you, too.

"And now it is my great pleasure to introduce to you Dr. Angela Desjardin, our lovely young curator of European art, whose imagination and hard work are principally responsible for the magnificent exhibition you see here tonight—with a little help from Monsieur Matisse, or course," He quipped in a rare descent into humor.

"For those of you who have not had the pleasure of knowing Dr. Desjardin . . ." Wolff went on to gush over Angela's pedigree, mentioning the Sorbonne, Cambridge, her doctoral work at Princeton, and even her time at the Vatican. This surprised her, as she was convinced that he remembered nothing about her beyond her initial interview. But then it made perfect sense if taken as a tribute to himself for having selected a person—make that a *woman*, a *young* woman, and not a bad-looking one at that, she had to admit—with such impressive credentials to hover over the museum's important European collection.

"Dr. Desjardin . . ."

Erich Wolff had welcomed in the Matisse exhibit's main gallery approximately one hundred guests comprised of Mendelssohn board members and spouses, senior staff, and a few handpicked high rollers who held serious promise for major gifts. The group applauded Angela enthusiastically, having just wandered through what was probably the most hyped special exhibit to be seen at the Mendelssohn in the past decade—give it up for The Fridge—or maybe since the museum was savvy enough to have attracted *Treasures of the Hermitage* back in the 70s, immediately after the Soviet détente. A very young Nick Castle pulled this one off. How soon we forget.

One would never have guessed that this was the same Erich Wolff who five days before had hammered his star curator with innuendo about the suspect Dutch gallery paintings, and had not long thereafter sent his grotesque minion, with little success, to put the fear of God in her. But on this night he was his typically unctuous public self as he lavished on Angela and roamed deftly among the guests, brown nosing those not yet on his "gotcha" list, and shamelessly imperious with the ones on whom he had the goods. Tonight was his night, and he would make the most of it.

Angela volleyed with a few disingenuous comments of her own—"It's a great privilege to be a colleague of such a distinguished and scholarly figure as Dr. Wolff, and of the remarkable staff he has assembled here at the Mendelssohn," *Two can play this little game,* she thought. She offered a few consummately sincere observations on the artist, the work, and the "Herculean efforts" of the exhibit's organizers in New York, who had flown in for the occasion and had been lionized by Wolff early on. She concluded with a modest "Thank you all for coming," and relinquished the floor to her learned and kindly mentor, the Right Reverend Dr. Wolff.

The plan was to regroup for champagne and a lavish buffet at Wolff's *Schloss auf der Rhein,* a consequential stone pile of architectural history which, to the city's cultural elite, bore an aura of almost unbearable panache. To be invited to the director's

Castle on the Rhine for cocktails would have been the highlight of the social season even for those who could have bought and sold Erich Wolff many times over or who twisted uncomfortably under his thumb.

They arrived in ones and twos, snaking up the torch lit drive to the mansion in their black or silver Mercedes sedans. Now and then a sleek Jag would sneak into the procession, and on occasion, a well-preserved Cadillac Fleetwood or Buick Park Avenue driven by one of the city's vanishing breed of old money conservatives—*although they really would rather have had a Beamer*. The women were draped with rare exception in basic black; the men were uniform in vintage tuxedos, many of them threadbare from years of command performances at the symphony, the opera, and other obligatory venues.

As quickly as the weather had turned icy only a week before, an unseasonable warming had whooshed up from the south. The resulting light rain and a rising mist cast an eerie web over the *Schloss auf der Rhein* made even more spectral by lightning on the horizon and the rumble of thunder far off. The guests hurried up the wide, limestone steps, the women fearing that the dampness would wilt their three-hundred dollar coiffures and render valueless their extravagant afternoon with Maurice, groomer of choice among the female guests.

Once snugly inside the gas-lit foyer, coats spirited away by dutiful museum interns shanghaied for the occasion, the entourage was set upon by white-coated servers bearing silver trays of Veuve Clicquot '89 in crystal flutes. Strains of *On the Beautiful Blue Danube* wafted over the genteel gathering as they clustered like magnetized metal shavings into their familiar cliques.

Angela and her escorts breezed in fashionably late, their arrival timed for maximum effect. All eyes turned as Pieter and

Jonathan, impeccably tuxed, flanked Angela like dancers in a Ginger Rogers movie as they stepped onto the crowded set. Only herald trumpets and a red carpet could have added to the scene.

Angela had undergone a breathtaking metamorphosis from the modest, painfully professional curator, hair in a twist, who had greeted the guests at the museum merely an hour before. Dazzling now in a Matisse-red, skintight cocktail dress, liquid Sicilian hair flowing over her bare shoulders like midnight over moonlit dunes, she triggered startled glances from the moment she burst into the room. Jonathan carried with him a long, narrow white box which he tucked discreetly behind a tall, leather-upholstered chair in the foyer.

Each of them took champagne and plunged into the buzzing crowd, most of whom had collected in the Versailles-like drawing room which occupied much of the right wing of the mansion's first floor. Decorated in the French Neoclassical style and painted in soft lime green and white, it was lighted by several crystal chandeliers and a dozen or so matching sconces around the perimeter. Suspended over the Carrara marble mantle was a huge Louis XVI mirror in an intricately tooled gold leaf frame which effectively doubled the light and set the room ablaze with the reflections of ten thousand prisms and a thousand bulbs.

Gold brocade drapes hung at each of the massive, floor-to-ceiling windows, and the freshly polished inlaid floors begged for dancers, although the room was far too crowded to boogie. The musicians, nested in a convenient niche by the fireplace, set the tempo with every waltz known to man, from the mighty *Emperor* to *Tales from the Vienna Woods*. *When the devil seduces, he does it to Strauss*, Angela thought.

Speaking of the devil, Arthur Mendelssohn, the chairman, was the first to approach them. He took no pains to disguise his attraction to Angela, in spite of his spindly, sun-dried wife who stood nearby in deep conversation with Franklin Applegate, the corpulent custodian of Asian art. *Unless the rotund curator had a secret life as a tennis pro, there would have been precious little for the two of them to talk about,* Pieter thought, himself having once been set upon at a museum luncheon by Gloria Mendelssohn with a friendly match in mind, on or off the court.

The chairman's gaze was hardly lost on Angela, as well as on several other board members who had strayed unintentionally into his predator zone. "I can see you have a fondness for red, Mr. Chairman," she said, not-so-subtly acknowledging his full-body stare. "You must have been ecstatic with the Matisse, am I correct?" she said.

"You are correct, Angie," he said, showing no embarrassment at having been caught in ogle mode. "I have two small ones of my own, which I treasure." *Now there's an opening,* Angela thought. *I'm sure you do.* "Maybe someday you could give me the private, curator's tour. I'd like that," he said. *When pigs make lazy circles in the sky,* she told herself.

"I would be honored, Arthur," she said, returning his impudence in kind. It would be a cold day in the Sahara before she gave Mendelssohn a private tour of anything. Not to get in any deeper, she moved on, her twin escorts trailing like attendants to Her Royal Majesty.

Angela saw Katherine Raeburn from the corner of her eye standing near the pass-through to the castle's original art gallery, once home to a bevy of Hudson River School masterpieces which now live in the National Gallery in D.C. She expected Wolff to be hovering somewhere nearby, but he was not, so she moved toward the Wealthy Widow Kate. Angela liked Kate's gallery a lot, even though her own tastes didn't run toward the gallery owner's edgier appetites. The two of them had developed a decent relationship, and she found Kate Raeburn to be a stimulating acquaintance, if not overly outgoing.

The gallery owner looked detached and appeared not to be having a good time. When she spotted Angela moving toward her, she brightened. "Angela! What a wonderful show! Congratulations on such a beautiful job!" Kate said.

"Thank you, Kate. Coming from you, that means a lot to me," Angela said sincerely.

As a milling crowd will do, the other guests shifted suddenly away from the two of them, leaving them briefly alone. Even Pieter and Jonathan had been distracted, which relieved Angela of the obligation to introduce her mystery guest to Kate, although an introduction by name only would have meant nothing to Kate Raeburn, she was sure. After an awkward silence, Kate moved closer and spoke in her ear.

"Angela, can I talk to you sometime soon? Alone, just the two of us?"

"Well of course, Kate. I'd like that," Angela said.

"It's about Erich. I'm worried about him. And about myself, frankly. I have no one to talk to, and I feel comfortable with you . . . if it wouldn't be an imposition, Angela." It was well known that Erich Wolff and Katherine Raeburn had been an item for several years, although there had never been any outward show of affection between them. So Angela was not totally blindsided by Kate's overture, yet she questioned why she'd been singled out.

"You can trust me, Kate," Angela said, not knowing whether Kate could trust her or not after all that had happened, and particularly with what was likely to go down yet this evening. But she could hardly say otherwise.

"I'll call you tomorrow," Kate said.

As quickly as the celebrants had parted, giving Kate and Angela a private moment, they closed ranks again, and the two of them were once again surrounded. Pieter and Jonathan were back by her side as, one by one, board members continued to congratulate her.

Kendall Frank, who had done three years for coming up a little light with the IRS—four hundred grand light, to be exact—was back bigger than ever, welcomed with open arms by the board that kept his chair warm while he worked on his backhand at Hillsdale Minimum Security Farm. Frank, now chair of the board's endowment committee, was effusive: "I read a great deal about Henri Matisse while I was away, and seeing your exhibit tonight was a dream come true, my dear!"

Kenny Frank became an instant legend as the result of his incarceration, and friends and unknowns alike would pepper him with questions about prison life—*did he know anyone there, did he meet anyone famous, what was the food like, did he have chores.* He returned a celebrity, with more currency than ever, less, of course, the four hundred thousand, plus interest and penalties, he had to cough up to the Feds for his indiscretion.

Go figure, Angela thought.

Right behind him came Lucille Frank, the "long-suffering spouse," who, rumor has it, had gone hot and heavy with Jack Schroeder, chairman of the personnel committee, the whole time Kenny was away. *A woman has needs,* she supposedly confided in her signature "drama queen" fashion to Mary Sinclair, her closest friend, who promptly spread the sticky tidbits like strawberry jam over hot croissants.

Mimi Redpath glided by, touched Angela's arm ever so lightly and, without a word, gave her the knowing nod of approval indigenous to the leisure class as she stalked a tray of Veuve

Clicquot like a schnauzer tracking a plate of Snausages. Mimi Redpath, by sheer weight of considerable wealth and generosity, had found herself suddenly thrust into the coveted position of vice-chair of the board, the slot which delivered the most cache for the least amount of work—and virtually no chance to move to the top thanks to Arthur Mendelssohn's self-appointed chairmanship for life. Hers was an appointment for which she gave thanks at least once each day, coincidental with her afternoon affair with the grape.

John and Cynthia Morgan, both board members emeriti and two of Angela's favorites, hugged her warmly and promised a considerable gift in her honor. John, a small, silver-haired and self-effacing connoisseur with a remarkable knowledge of European art, had been Angela's confidant during the early going, and Cynthia had been like a protective grandmother to her. She knew she could never repay either of them for helping her through her first weeks and months, other than be the very best at her job that she could possibly be. Which, for them, who expected nothing in return, would be payment enough.

And so it went, Angela accepting glad hands and praise from an endless stream of board members and benefactors, until she at last spotted the host working toward her through the clutter of live bodies.

"It's showtime," she muttered under her breath to Pieter, who had not left her side since her quiet exchange with Kate Raeburn. "Maybe you'd best retrieve our pretty white box."

"Here he comes, Jonathan. Look alive," she said, nodding in the direction of the advancing Erich Wolff. The director stopped briefly to share a shred of gossip with Arthur Mendelssohn, and then he was standing in front of the two of them, beaming like the master of the realm. The one thousand lights reflected in his steel-framed, designer glasses and his breath reeked of champagne.

"Everyone was overwhelmed with the exhibit, Angela. I hope they've been telling you so," he said.

"Yes, they've all been very kind," she said, thinking that this was the first time in her memory that Herr Wolff had ever addressed her by her given name.

"And just whom do we have here?" Wolff said, looking at Jonathan and smiling. "I thought that you and that great bear, Pieter Maxfield, were, how do you say, a 'hot ticket?'" Erich Wolff was in a very good mood; Angela had never seen him so ebullient, or ever attempting humor, for that matter. It was not one of his strengths.

"Herr Wolff, I've taken the liberty of inviting a friend. I hope you don't mind." She ignored his clumsy comment, charitably writing it off to the effects of the Veuve Clicquot. Besides, she had business to do—whatever he had to say was irrelevant.

"Of course I don't mind. *Me casa, su casa.* I'm delighted to have you," Wolff said, extending his hand to Jonathan, who took it firmly. "Angela, won't you introduce us?"

"Herr Wolff, this is Jonathan Gruenwald, from Paris. Jonathan, this is Herr Wolff, our director."

Her words seemed to cut through Erich Wolff like Solingen steel. Stunned, but quickly recovering, he said, "Well, Monsieur Gruenwald, welcome to my home and to the Mendelssohn. What brings you here?"

The moment of truth had arrived.

In the instant Jonathan Gruenwald failed to respond, Wolff turned to Angela. His ice-cold eyes pierced hers in an unmistakable sign that he had lost his good humor and that she was to blame.

On cue, she leaned forward, placed her lips to Erich

Wolff's ear, and whispered, "I think he's come for his paintings."

Boom. Boom, Boom. Don Carlo would have been beside himself.

Flushed from champagne, the excitement of the evening and the closeness of the room, Wolff's face drained of color as her words struck him like angry fists. The dazed director, effusive and unguarded only seconds before, had been bushwhacked by the most unlikely of assailants. His eyes turned from ice to mist; all was blurry as Angela flexed to deliver the final uppercut. *First, you've got to get their attention,* she thought as her latent instinct for cold dispatch, another of Don Carlo's legacies, rose in her gut.

She opened the long white box which Pieter had handed her and removed its contents.

"My grandfather wanted you to have these with his best wishes. He knew how important this night would be for you, Herr Wolff. They're from his garden. He said you'd know about them," she said, extending a tightly bound sheaf of long-stemmed yellow roses toward the confused director. "He calls them *Condanna D'oro.* They're lovely, don't you think?"

"Your grandfather?" he said, critically wounded.

"My grandfather, yes. Don Carlo Vittoria. I think you know him?"

"Your grandfather?" he repeated softly, almost to himself.

"I am Angela *Vittoria* Desjardin. I thought you knew, Herr Wolff," she said, glaring dispassionately into his eyes.

He made no effort to take the bouquet. The intense perfume of the roses suddenly sickened him. Pieter and Jonathan stared in silence, neither quite believing the bizarre theatre which had just played out before them.

"Please excuse me, Monsieur Gruenwald," Erich Wolff said. He turned, walked unsteadily through the opening to the adjoining gallery and was gone.

Friedrich Bergdorf had witnessed the entire performance from only a few feet away. His eyes never left Angela and her escorts from the moment they had passed through the large oak doors into the foyer more than an hour before. Seeing him standing there, Angela turned and held out the rejected bouquet to the glowering gnome.

"Herr Bergdorf, would you put these in some water, please. They might look nice on the mantel, don't you agree?" she said. And then, for reasons unknown even to herself, she drew one golden rose from the green tissue paper sheaf as Bergdorf snatched the remaining blooms and raged toward the kitchen.

Angela held the single rose to her nostrils and inhaled its familiar scent as she thought of her dolce nonno and his precious garden. He would be pleased.

CHAPTER THIRTY-NINE

Pieter watched Angela's steely performance in a state of near paralysis. Finally, he croaked, "My God, Angela, I can't believe you did that!"

"Well, believe it. The son of a bitch," she responded in a voice as hard as a hangman's heart. Her eyes burned into Friedrich Bergdorf's back like glowing orange pokers as he exited the room.

"Shouldn't we follow him?" Jonathan said, less perturbed than Pieter. He had just assumed that the encounter was *le comportement routinier* for this extraordinary new woman in his life, and he found it enormously provocative. "Follow Wolff, I mean."

"No, he's not going anywhere. We should wait now. For the dam to crack, right, Pieter?" Angela said, calmer now.

"But the paintings . . ." Jonathan said.

"If they're here, they won't be going anywhere, either," she said.

"But what if he . . ."

"He won't. He won't touch them, if that's what you're thinking.

"Wait," she said. "Just wait." Frankly, she had no idea *what* he would do, but her instincts said, "wait," and wait she would.

Apparently no one in the crowd had seen the exchange between Angela and Erich Wolff other than Bergdorf, who failed to return after stomping out with the bouquet, and the party ritual continued unabated. Lies and gossip, recycled from soirées of the previous weekend and predictably embellished, continued to swirl about the room to tinkling Waterford and the surreal accompaniment of *Blue Danube*, now in its fifth or sixth iteration.

The three huddled by the foyer archway, expecting any minute some explosive denouement, the fissure which would breach any time now from the back pressure of a clandestine life. *He would be back,* Angela thought. *He's the host—he has to return sooner or later, either his mind in shambles, or as if nothing at all had happened. If the former, he would lead them somehow to the pictures; if the latter, if he were really the Ice Man he liked to portray, they were roadkill.*

But as time passed, she began to stew over whether they should have followed him. She looked at her watch and decided they would give the shaken director a few more minutes, Pieter and Jonathan having long since consigned the last word to Angela. It was, as it had been from the first, her show; they would wait.

Katherine Raeburn had wandered off before the confrontation and had missed the meltdown. "Have you seen Erich?" she said as she approached Angela in the doorway.

"No, not recently, Kate," Angela said. "He left the room rather hurriedly some time ago. I have no idea where he might be."

And then, impulsively, she opted to probe gently to confirm what she would have bet her life on a few minutes before. "Kate, you know Pieter, I believe. And this is my friend, Jonathan Gruenwald. He owns a very important art house in Paris. Jonathan, this is Kate Raeburn. She has a marvelous gallery in town which you should see before you leave. You two should have lots in common."

Kate flinched visibly at the mention of his name, but extended her hand. "Jonathan, it's such a pleasure to meet you," she said. "I'd love to have you stop in. How long will you be staying?"

"I really can't be sure, Kate. It depends on how soon I can finish some business here which came up quite suddenly," he said, offering no more. His clipped reply, innocuous as it might have seemed to anyone else, was enough for Kate Raeburn. It would not have mattered if he had said nothing—the mention of his name was enough: He knew the paintings were here, and he had come for them. And Angela had told him.

Kate's flicker of recognition, however well concealed, was like a blaring news flash to Angela. In a single twitch, she knew beyond any doubt that Wolff had the paintings.

The guarded repartee between Kate Raeburn and Jonathan Gruenwald might have evolved into awkward but meaningless shop talk between two gallery owners had it not been for the remarkable thing which happened.

Angela stood with her back to the archway, as did Jonathan and Pieter. Kate Raeburn faced them, and may have been first to see him over their shoulders. Her eyes widened and shock stiffened her as she stared, mouth agape, into the gaslit foyer.

The other three turned to look. What they saw was Erich Wolff framed in the opening, ramrod straight, a soft, almost mystical smile at the corners of his mouth. He had changed from his Armani and now stood immaculate in the dress grays of a Nazi officer, in a prideful pose which might have been modeled by Joshua Reynolds, eighteenth-century painter of the aristocracy, or struck in the family living room by a costumed child about to embark on a wondrous night of trick or treat.

From the patent leather peak of his visor cap with its silver eagle and swastika emblem to the pressed tunic and knife-edge riding breeches, he was every inch a spectacle. He had pulled on black riding boots buffed to a high sheen, and high on his left arm he wore a blood red band emblazoned with history's most hated icon. Completing the ensemble was a hip-mounted Luger, the signature handgun of the Third Reich, protruding menacingly from its black leather holster.

The musicians, slightly elevated above the rest by a small platform, were among the first to see the director's entrance. As if caught from behind by a swift jerk of piano wire, they choked off the umteenth playing of Beautiful Blue Danube in mid-stream, thus signaling to the gathering that something was clearly amiss. Heads turned in unison toward the opening, and the celebrants stared in disbelief.

One could have heard the champagne bubble in the glasses as Erich Wolff strode confidently from one to another, gripped their hands, and spoke softly in German. *"Es ist Zeit zu gehen."* It is my time to go. *"Danke für deine Treue und Freundschaft. Auf Wiedersehen."* Thank you for your faithfulness and friendship. Goodbye.

And then he rocked each of those whose hand he shook with a firm *"Heil Hitler!"*

The room remained deathly silent as he made his rounds and eventually stood once again by the archway, stared brutally into the eyes of Angela and whispered bitterly, *"Sie Judas, brennen Sie Hölle!"*

As if on cue, stage right, lightning bolted only yards from the house, striking a centuries-old pin oak which shaded the stone veranda in summer and splitting the ancient specimen at the fork. The bifurcated trunk fell slowly toward the house with a long, loud crack. Its uppermost branches crashed through the large window to the left of the fireplace and settled across several feet of the drawing room's polished parquet floor, narrowly missing several guests. An enormous clap of thunder followed which rattled the remaining windows and shook the guests from their near-comatose state. The rain followed, pelting the windows like machine-gun fire in a relentless assault.

Wolff himself was dazed by the blast. In total panic he looked up at the swaying and still-jangling chandelier above his head, reached out for Katherine Raeburn and barked, *"Die Bomben! Die Russen kommen! Komm, Eva!"*

Stiffened with fear, Kate took his hand in meek compliance. He dragged her into the foyer and the two of them vanished down the long hallway.

Angela was the first to recover. "Pieter, he's going to kill himself. And Kate, too."

"Kill himself?"

"Don't you see? This is how Hitler said goodbye to his staff in the bunker before he and Eva Braun went into his private quarters and swallowed cyanide? I heard him say, *Es ist Zeit zu gehen*–It is my time to go," she said, exhibiting for the first time her grasp of German to add to her fluent Italian and French. "And he said to me, 'You Judas, you burn in Hell!'

"My God! He called Kate 'Eva.' Didn't you hear him? He thought the thunder was bombs–that the Russians had come for him. He's psychopathic, Pieter! He's totally nuts! The man actually thinks he's Adolph Hitler!

"We've got to find them. He's going to kill Kate, too!" Angela repeated as she rushed into the foyer and down the hallway to the staircase leading up to the maze of bedrooms on the second floor, Pieter and Jonathan close behind her.

"Angela, he's got a gun!" Pieter said.

"I saw it," she shouted back at him. "But what can we do? If he kills Kate, I'll be responsible. I caused all this to happen!"

They reached the top of the stairs and, remembering the Luger on his hip, began cautiously opening doors one by one into empty rooms. The master suite was at the far end of the long corridor; it, too, was empty.

"There's nobody up here. Where the hell are they?" she said.

"You mentioned Hitler's bunker. Is there a cellar?" Jonathan said.

"How do I know? This is my first time here. But there probably is. A wine cellar, I'd guess. There were vineyards up on this hill once. Let's find it," she said as she raced to the head of the stairs and started down. The hallway below was now jammed with party guests, stunned and confused, not knowing what to do or where to go. Back on the first level, the three forced their way through the crowded passageway, hurried back toward the kitchen and found a down staircase. "God, we've lost so much time! She could be dead already," Angela said, now on the verge of panic herself as she rushed down the steps.

At the foot of the stairs they found themselves in a stone cellar among row after row of racks constructed in hundreds of small cubicles. In each cubicle several dusty bottles lay peacefully on their sides, quietly aging in the darkness. A quick look around revealed no other signs of life.

Oddly, no one had followed them at first, either upstairs to the private areas or down to the cellar. Then, in twos and threes, they crept down the steps after Angela, Pieter and Jonathan.

As they looked helplessly around the undercroft for any clue to the whereabouts of Erich Wolff and Kate Raeburn, *and, for that matter, Bergdorf,* they heard the rich sonority of brass emanating from the furthermost corner. They glanced in the direction of the music and saw the soft glow of light on the ceiling near the source of the sound. Angela ran down the back row of racks, guided by a vertical shaft of light at the far end and a luminous golden wedge on the stone floor. She motioned for Pieter and Jonathan to follow her.

They came upon the partially open panel, camouflaged by a short rack section also filled with bottles, which they would never have found had it been closed. As Pieter drew the panel open further, the music grew louder and light cascaded out into the darkness. They stepped inside, and as their eyes adjusted to the glare, they froze.

Angela at that moment became startlingly aware of what Howard Carter must have felt as he first stepped into the musty inner tomb of Tutankhamun. Jonathan was overcome as his eyes swept over the treasures, the disappearance of which had tormented him since he was a boy and which he had vowed would hang once more in the family brownstone at 51, rue de la Boétie. Pieter was first to notice the four familiar paintings from the Mendelssohn stacked rudely against the far wall among the dazzling masterworks which once comprised the cream of the famous Gruenwald collection.

But still there was no one. The only suggestion of life came from the vibrant images on the walls and from the crescendo of French horns, timpani and soprano wailing from behind the two massive mahogany doors directly across from them.

They approached the elaborately carved portal with no thought of what might be on the other side. What Erich Wolff had in mind for himself was of little concern to them, now that they had found the paintings, but any plans he had for Katherine Raeburn were clearly not well-meant, or so it seemed from her panicked reaction as he dragged her from the drawing room upstairs.

Pieter, stopped momentarily in his tracks by the two intimidating swastikas centered in the door panels, reached for one of the polished brass handles. His huge hand had hardly touched the latch when, during a lull in the relentless pounding of unison trombones, a sharp crack penetrated the relative calm. He pressed down on the release and pushed the door open.

They were met face-on with an overpowering scent, unknown to any of them and pungent enough to cause a stinging sensation in their eyes. They would later be told that hydrogen cyanide releases an odor of bitter almonds, although bitter almond is seldom on anyone's list of familiar fragrances. Then their eyes focused on a tableau which would remain acid-etched in their minds like a Dürer image of hell burned into copper.

"Please come in," Friedrich Bergdorf said as he trained a menacing looking pistol on the three of them, a weapon which Pieter recognized immediately as a vintage German Luger, standard military issue for soldiers of the Third Reich. He had seen many like it in old films about the Great War, as his father had been fond of referring to World War II, always in the hand of some notorious Nazi officer who was ultimately outsmarted, disarmed, or blown away outright by one daring Allied protagonist or another.

"I'm sorry you had to witness this. It was to have been a private affair," Bergdorf shouted. He had to speak loudly over the bombastic finale of *Götterdammerung–Fliegt heim, ihr Raben!* Fly home, you ravens! which blared from the arsenal of speakers hidden about the room.

Erich Wolff was sprawled across a shapeless, gray upholstered sofa. His limbs were extended in an almost posed stiffness, and his face was twisted in agony. Blood still trickled from a fresh, black hole in his right temple, ran from the corner of his gaping mouth, and covered most of his gray tunic, his trousers and the back of the sofa cushion. His right hand hung limply over the edge, and on the stone floor immediately beneath his hand lay a tiny, toylike revolver. There appeared to be no exit wound, suggesting that the caliber and velocity of the missile provided insufficient force to penetrate his scull more than once. It would simply have ricocheted about, scrambling his brain matter like the yolk inside a punctured eggshell.

Kate Raeburn lay stretched across Wolff's lap. Unlike his contorted body, hers was relaxed, except for her fist which was clenched in a tight ball. Blood had spewed across her face and the décolletage of her expensive black sheath dress. Bergdorf remained motionless, his gun hand steady.

Faces began to appear in the doorway, but none of the guests were disposed to enter, seeing the pistol in Bergdorf's hand. Quickly they drew back and raced for the steps, cell phones in hand. Angela struggled to assimilate the roomful of priceless paintings, the bloody corpses on the couch, the bizarre setting riddled with reminders of Nazi terror, and the silent Bergdorf's detached gaze as he allowed the Luger to do his talking. He seemed as rigid as the two lifeless forms before him, letting the final strains of Richard Wagner's concluding theme wash over them. Glimpses of hellish red banners, grotesque black swastikas, and the Mephistophelian glare of the Fuehrer swirled around her in a blur as she battled to get a grip.

The smell of gasoline jolted her out of her trauma. The fumes rose from a thin pool which surrounded the sofa, ran beneath a large, low table on which was constructed the model of a city she did not recognize, and trailed off to a red plastic can at Friedrich Bergdorf's feet. It was then she knew that they had stumbled on a twisted tribute to Wagner's notorious immolation scene–Siegfried and Brünhilde on the pyre, Valhalla rising in flames, and the world released from the curse of *Das Rheingold*. Even for one not familiar with the music, the parallel reenactment of the suicides of Adolph Hitler and Eva Braun and the burning of their bodies in the bombed-out Berlin Chancellery garden would still have been evident.

Wagner's masterpiece ended in a bombardment of brass, like the deafening thunder which sent Erich Wolff running for cover not ten minutes before. The room fell silent, save for the sound of the hurried footsteps up the wooden stairs and the cries of the guests fleeing the cellar in chaos.

As the noise abated, Bergdorf spoke, softly.

"He was insane, you know. He was the Fuehrer's favorite. *Du sind mein Liebling,* the Fuehrer whispered once into his ear on the terrace at the Berghof when Herr Wolff was just a boy of nine. 'You are my favorite,' the Fuehrer said. 'My pet.' That is something you don't forget. It was the 'something' that turned a lonely and vulnerable child into a pathological adult."

Bergdorf's monologue sounded rehearsed, yet was so reasoned and calm and absent of rancor that one might have expected him to lower his weapon and set it aside, but he did not. "As you can see," he said, gesturing casually around the room with the pistol, "the Fuehrer was his life. His greatest regret was that he never served to the glory of the Reich.

"Miss Raeburn knows all of this. She will tell you."

Angela concluded that Friedrich Bergdorf was as deranged as Erich Wolff had been; it would be no easy task to coax the story out of a corpse, even if Bergdorf chose to spare their lives, which did not look promising at the moment.

"Herr Bergdorf, please put the gun down. There's no need for this," Angela said.

He ignored her and continued.

"What you smell, that would be cyanide. Herr Wolff took a capsule only a few minutes ago. And then he shot himself, just as the Fuehrer did, but not before he suffered terrible pain, as you can see. I would like to tell you that you drove him to it, with the sudden appearance of Mr. Gruenwald here," and then, glaring at Angela, "and with your yellow roses, which terrified him. I knew about the roses, of course, but not about your relationship to that gangster, Don Vittoria, Miss Desjardin. That was a surprise. I would like to tell you that you are to blame, but I would not give you the satisfaction. He had *always* planned to go this way, as his final salute to the Fuehrer. You simply hastened the event."

Angela winced at his vilification of her beloved dolce nonno, although it would have been difficult for her to refute the charge; Don Carlo Vittoria was a long shot for sainthood, to say the least. This she knew, in spite of his deep friendship with the Holy Father which she had witnessed on several occasions. She had to laugh at their puzzling bond. *The ultimate Odd Couple in the Garden of Good and Evil*, she thought.

"As you might have surmised," Bergdorf continued, "Herr Wolff ordered me to set fire to this place, just as the Fuehrer had ordered von Choltitz and Speidel to burn Paris. I was to burn everything. Himself, Miss Raeburn, his journals, your paintings, Mr. Gruenwald, this house. *Everything.* I spread the gasoline before he died to assure him that I would do so, but, like Speidel, I could not."

Pieter was growing increasingly anxious. "Please, Herr Bergdorf, give me the gun," he said. Unlike the usually cool conservator, Jonathan Gruenwald seemed the calm one and genuinely engrossed by Friedrich Bergdorf's serial bombshells.

"You shall have the gun in time, Dr. Maxfield. Please let me finish," Bergdorf said.

"It was the only order I ever disobeyed either from Erich Wolff or his father, Otto. In the end, it was I who was disloyal–to them and to the Fuehrer, and for this I am ashamed. But I could not destroy the art. It was I who loved the art, even more than Herr Wolff–I who loved it, who cared for it. You would have never thought that, would you, Miss *Vittoria* Desjardin?

"Your paintings are in the next room, Mr. Gruenwald. This is what you came for, isn't it? Take them. Put them on display. The world should see them. They have been hidden too long."

Friedrich Bergdorf raised the Luger, and Angela, Pieter and Jonathan tensed. "This was Otto Wolff's pistol. The Fuehrer gave it to him, for his *loyalty,*" he said with a dry laugh. "He had it inscribed."

Bergdorf squinted at the elegant calligraphy incised into the flat surface of the weapon and read, first in Deutsch with rich, mocking flourishes, and then in English, although Angela understood every word of the original German: *"To Otto Wolff, loyal servant of the Third Reich, with my deepest gratitude, Adolph Hitler."* Bergdorf emphasized the word *loyal.* "This, after he stole forty-seven magnificent paintings intended for the Fuehrer. The ones he took from your family's collection at the chateau, Mr. Gruenwald.

"You may wish to know also that he was directly involved in the capture of your grandparents, their whereabouts so gratuitously disclosed by one of the *loyal* servants in their own household. Ah, loyalty, a vanishing virtue, is it not, Monsieur Gruenwald?" It was Jonathan Gruenwald's turn to wince.

"He gave this lovely toy to me just before he died." He gestured with the Luger and pointed it in the general direction of the dead Erich Wolff. It was then that Angela noticed the holster on Wolff's hip, flap open and void of the sleek, blue-steel weapon he had worn earlier into the drawing room.

"I consider it an honor to use it now. It's the least I can do."

His aged hand shaking almost uncontrollably, Bergdorf lifted the deadly firearm which had once claimed the avaricious life of one Maurice Gernand, gallery owner, on a desolate precipice in France.

"To loyalty," he said.

"No! Bergdorf, *No!"* Angela shouted, expecting that he would shoot them all. The three of them stood horrified, unable to move as Bergdorf, devoted to the end, placed the weapon in his own mouth and squeezed the trigger.

In the barrel-vaulted cellar the explosion was deafening, and it would have been louder still had it not been muffled by the shooter's palate and absorbed by the tangential mass of brain tissue. A 9mm Parabellum Luger was never known for its surgical precision, as the back of Friedrich Bergdorf's skull confirmed: gray pudding, bits of pink skin and splinters of bone, spattered and streaked with cherry red, created a macabre, abstract fresco on the white stucco wall behind him as the bullet exited, ricocheted wildly off the plaster, and then randomly ripped through the canvas of the glowering Supreme Warlord of the Third Reich in the general vicinity of the heart, a mere sixty years too late.

Blood poured from Bergdorf's mouth as he slumped to the floor like a sack of dirty laundry, overturning the open, half-filled red gasoline can as he fell; the notorious Luger struck the floor, clattered across the gas-soaked flagstone and clicked presciently against Angela's silk scarlet shoe as if goading her to accept stewardship of its violent legacy, the torch of evil passed. Only God's grace prevented the searing heat of its still-smoking barrel from sparking the inferno Erich Wolff envisioned for his ceremonial passage.

As they stared at the fallen Bergdorf, a soft moan came from the direction of the sofa where the bloody Wolff and Katherine Raeburn lay. The three turned instantaneously to its source as Katherine's eyelids flickered and she moved to raise herself. She brought her hand to her face as blood stung her eyes, and then she screamed.

"What *is* this! What happened here!" she gasped as she stared at her own wet hand. Her eyes shifted to the contorted Erich Wolff and the blood which soaked his body and stippled the front of her. In shock, she then looked down at the small, blood-and-gasoline drenched heap which was once Friedrich Bergdorf. Finally she saw the three mute figures frozen in trauma by the horror they had just seen. For her, it was a scene which would play out hundreds of times in sweat-soaked nightmares yet to come.

It was Angela who finally blurted, "My God, Kate! We thought you were dead!" and hurried to her, oblivious to the blood and to the deadly fumes which rose up from beneath the sofa.

"He wanted me to *die*," Kate said. "He wanted me to swallow *cyanide*. A capsule." And then she looked at her own blood-smeared fist and slowly opened it. "This one," she said. Angela stared down at the bottle green capsule which Katherine Raeburn had squeezed so tightly even as she was unconscious.

"He took one himself, he bit down on it and I heard it crack, like glass. I guess it was glass. I could smell it, it took my breath away. He began to scream and twist and gasp for breath. Then he raised this little gun to his head, it was Hitler's gun once, I think, and then I must have passed out.

"Is he dead?"

"Yes, he's dead. They're both dead," Pieter said, confirming the obvious.

The three were riveted by Kate's account, which had briefly masked the revulsion which had just ensued. She went on, trance-like. "Bergdorf poured gasoline all around and told Erich that he would set fire to it as soon as we were *dead*. I was paralyzed. I couldn't move. *I couldn't move!*" As her story unfolded, she fell further into shock and became silent.

Pieter was the first to regain his composure. He fished his cell phone from his tuxedo jacket and shakily dialed 911, even as sirens approached *Schloss auf der Rhein*.

Angela was the last to leave Erich Wolff's stinking little shrine. When the others had gone, she turned back, viewed his twisted corpse one last time, and then dropped the single yellow rose in the crimson pool at her feet.

"Brennen Sie Hölle," she whispered.

CHAPTER FORTY

The police questioned Angela, Pieter and Jonathan at the mansion till nearly sunup. They held Kate Raeburn not as long, but nevertheless downloaded all she could remember before she passed out on Wolff's blood-soaked sofa. The detectives unofficially declared the deaths a simple, if somewhat unconventional, double suicide, their supposition confirmed by the medical examiner at the scene, subject to routine autopsies. Painstaking hours of debriefing later would reveal the macabre prelude to the shootings. Angela's deadly sheaf of *Condanna D'oro* was never pursued, and the single yellow rose found at the scene was overlooked altogether in light of such obvious causes of death.

Had the police come upon two bloody bodies in any other house in town, their grisly demise so obviously self-administered, everyone except the cleanup crew could have gone home early. But this one was different. The high-octane guest list, the celebrity of the host, and the macabre setting in which the deeds were done demanded that all constabulary stops be pulled; the whole ugly business would be Page One coast to coast the next day, and the city's finest had no taste for national embarrassment. Thus another sleepless night for Angela, already bleary-eyed from weeks of sixteen-hour days.

She spent most of the next day in emergency session with the Mendelssohn board. Although many remained in varying degrees of shock, all having witnessed Erich Wolff's surreal behavior the night before if not the actual bloodletting, they managed to address their brief, but consequential, agenda. That would have included the museum's public response to the events of the past evening.

Marilyn Robertson was in her element, bluntly outlining her hastily concocted crisis management plan so incisively that the members simply stepped aside so as not to be flattened, as if she were a piano dropped from a third-story window. This done, they moved on to whether or not to postpone the members' opening for the Matisse. They would not. And, finally, who would assume the ball-busting role of Interim while they mounted the search for Erich Wolff's replacement.

The pragmatic Arthur Mendelssohn reminded the board that while they all felt "shocked and saddened by the tragic events of last evening," it was their solemn duty as board members to "pick up the flag and charge ahead." He could have left out the part that Erich Wolff would have wanted it that way. Erich Wolff wouldn't have given a flying pfennig one way or the other, and they all knew it, as evidenced by random smirks around the table. They also knew that Wolff's foot had now and forever been removed from their necks, one bright spot in the unfortunate occurrence, which accounted for their somewhat less than somber mood. The chairman's foot, however, remained firmly in place.

When they came to the last agenda item, Mendelssohn dismissed The Fridge to work her slimy magic on the media, leaving Angela at the table as sole representative of the staff. Seconds after the boardroom door closed behind the museum's marketing director, the chairman, not one to tap dance on the issues in spite of his oft-compromised integrity, looked directly at Angela at the far end of the long, mahogany table and posed the question.

None of the directors showed surprise.

Angela spent most of that evening with Kate Raeburn, neither of them wanting to be alone with their memories of the past twenty-four hours. They had left the board meeting together and had settled in the secluded back booth of Limerick's.

"Will you take it?" Kate said.

"I don't know. I have some unfinished personal business, Kate, which I have to work through before I decide anything. I told Arthur this, and he's okay with it.

"I'll have an answer for the board in a week. But I'm very flattered. I hope you know that."

Angela didn't elaborate on her "unfinished business," and Kate didn't ask. But as their "quick Killian's" stretched into dinner and cappuccinos, the full saga of Erich Wolff cascaded from her lips like the overflow from the previous night's downpour.

By evening's end, she had deluged Angela with every squalid detail of Erich Wolff's pathetic life, assembled from the bits and pieces he had shared with her: how the Gruenwald paintings had been heisted by his father, Otto; Otto's cold-blooded murder of Maurice Gernand; the boy Erich's dark relationship with Adolph Hitler; Erich's Jewish mother, Hilde Meyer and her callous rejection—which, when tied to Jonathan Gruenwald's account of the last hours of his martyred grandparents, made Angela sole possessor of Hilda's true identity and the heart-breaking circumstances of her final days.

Kate told her about the hideous deeds and grizly end of Wolff's grandfather, Kurt, the Nazi arms manufacturer, and his stepgrandfather, the Baron, maker of lethal gas. She revealed the details of Das Rheingold and Wolff's fastidious journals which listed in tiny, coded scripture each grimy transaction of both his father and himself for more than fifty years. Finally, she disclosed Wolff's insane obsession with the Fuehrer and the Third Reich, the surreal assembly of Nazi memorabilia in his self-styled bunker—and most startling, his bizarre proposal of marriage.

"And there you have it," Kate said in an emotionless monotone, her eyes fixed in a blank stare. Both of them sat in stony silence for several minutes, Kate fighting valiantly to regain her composure, Angela overwhelmed by Kate's stupefying tale.

When the color returned to her face, Kate reached slowly into a black canvas tote which she had carried from the museum. From the bag she withdrew four leatherbound logs plus a small appointment book, all scuffed with age and deeply oil-stained from years of handling, and placed them on the table between them.

"These are the original journals," she said. "The codes are in the little one. I took them from the cellar last night after I talked to the police. I have no idea why they didn't stop me, and I'm mystified that I had the presence to take them. I thought you would know what to do with them."

Angela could barely bring herself to touch them, knowing now of the heinous crimes chronicled between their covers, masquerading as innocuous "transfers" of paintings, sculpture, antiques and heirloom jewelry. She knew that if they were authentic, Wolff's diaries were as volatile as a gas leak; the inevitable spark would wreak havoc on the entire international art community and add a scurrilous new chapter to the history books sixty years or more after the fact.

Angela gathered the logs from the table, returned them to Kate's tote, and set the bag on the booth bench next to her. Tomorrow she would lock them away and figure out how to handle them after the dust had settled. Regardless of how or when she chose to expose the evidence, she knew that Das Rheingold would collapse like a house of cards the instant Erich Wolff's spectacular demise hit the six o'clock news. But thanks to Wolff and Son's meticulous accounting, its global conspirators would have nowhere to hide. Only the high-profile prosecutions and the just restitution of the pillaged art would keep Das Rheingold alive in the world's memory, at least until the next juicy scandal oozed up to take its place.

Angela badly needed rest and had hoped that it would come on the long flight to Rome. But her mind roiled from the trauma of the past few days as the Boeing 747 cruised at 45,000 feet toward daybreak, denying her the luxury of unconsciousness.

And now there was the business of Vittoria.

While she had not graced the inside of a church since the day of her grandmother's funeral, she nonetheless prayed that her dolce nonno would be alive and lucid when she arrived. As her mind called up images of better days in the villa and the years of unconditional love and hard wisdom shared, courtesy of the infamous Don Carlo Vittoria, she struggled to grasp how a person could be so deeply loved and, at the same time, so universally feared. To her, love and fear were irreconcilable; one was either loved or feared, but not both. Perhaps someday she would understand.

These were her thoughts as the tires of the cramped commuter aircraft screeched on the runway in Catania and the plane taxied to the gate. As her foot touched the apron at the bottom of the steps, her eye caught sight of a tall, slightly stooped figure in a dark suit and tie. He stood beside the familiar black Lincoln town car parked inside the fence of the new *Aeroporto di Catania-Fontanarosso*. The figure waved, and Angela felt totally secure for the first time in a long time.

She ran the fifty yards between them and threw herself into his still-strong arms.

"Pauly, is he . . ."

"He is alive, and he ask for you."

"Thank God."

"*Sí, grazie dio.*"

CHAPTER FORTY-ONE

As they snaked their way between the coast and tiny Vittoria, embraced by the ripening olives and vines heavy with the sweet-smelling Frappato grape, Angela thought that this would likely be as close as she would ever come to paradise, given the strained relationship she suffered with her Creator. But it wasn't He who was the problem; her long absence from the confessional, she told herself, merely reflected her long-standing aversion to dealing with middlemen, or middlewomen for that matter. This liberated attitude placed her in perpetual bad standing with the local *prete*, Father Valentino Ottaviani, and any number of hawk-eyed nuns—not to mention the Blessed Mother. *But if she opted for God Direct, what was so wrong with that?*

Wherever this thought was headed, Angela chose to cut it off at the pass; this was no time for another gut struggle over her beef with the Church. She focused instead on the pure refreshment of this hallowed ground and its seminal influence on her life, which at this moment needed a major housecleaning.

She kicked off her shoes and pushed her feet up on the dash, as she had done as a child rolling over the hills with Paolo Ricci at the wheel. She remembered how she would slide across the wide bench seat and scrunch up next to him and hug his arm, inhaling the familiar scent of olive oil and tobacco in his clothes, which was the best part of her day and which made her the happiest. Without thinking, she snuggled once again against his wiry frame and squeezed his arm as they motored toward the villa. She could tell that it made him happy, too.

Paolo gently explained her nonno's fragile condition and

his eagerness to see her. "Expecting you is keeping him alive, I am sure. The dottore think so, too," he said.

"What could be so important that he must see me, Pauly?"

"This I cannot tell you, Gattina. He must tell you himself. But he love you. That would be reason enough, do you not think?"

"Yes it would, Pauly. And I love him, too. I would have died not to have kissed him one last time," she said as tears came.

A long silence followed, and then Paolo Ricci said softly, "I have one other piece of bad news, Gattina."

"*No!* No more bad things!" Angela cried.

"I am sorry, but I must tell you. Vincenzo is dead."

"Uncle Vinny? No, Pauly, don't tell me this!"

"Yes, Uncle Vinny," he said.

"How?" she wailed.

"It was the spineless Mancuso *fratelli* that kill him. They always skulk behind Don Carlo like mangy dogs, snapping up the scraps he leave, just wait for him to die. But they never test him until now, and now he is too weak to put them down. Don Carlo should have taken care of them when he was strong. I could have done it easy. But your nonno say not to worry about them. 'They are nothing,' he tell me. 'I do not want the old mother to be alone.'"

"Yes, my grandfather has told me about the Mancuso brothers. But what about Uncle Vinny?"

"It was sure to happen. You know your Zio Vincenzo. He has the *caldo testa*. The hot head. They come across him drunk in the village a week ago. They insult Don Carlo, say that he is going to die and then they would take everything. It make Vincenzo angry, and with his temper, well. . ."

"How did they do it, Pauly?"

"With a knife. At a restaurant where Vincenzo was drinking. Vincenzo charge at Alberto Mancuso. Alberto hold him, and

Nicolo, the little *serpente*, stab him. From behind. From behind!"

"Did they arrest them?"

"No, no arrest. The polizia are too afraid. They say Vincenzo cause it. The people in the town are very angry, but they are afraid, too. They think that when Don Carlo is dead, that is the end of it. No more peace. Only fear."

"Is there nothing that can be done?"

"No, nothing. Don Carlo weep for Vincenzo, but he do nothing. He is too old and too weak."

Angela seethed. Neither of them said another word as the Lincoln climbed the narrow ribbon of road bisecting a large grove of ancient olive trees and a sea of lush vines nearly ripe for picking. When the walls of the villa appeared at the crest, sprawling above Don Carlo's massive estate like a lion dosing in the sun, she knew she was home.

Even from a distance, Angela recognized the lean, angular lines of the figure that stood on the veranda, her black hair, now mixed with pewter, blowing in the wind. The woman looked out through the open gate and she waved. Paolo Ricci eased the car into the courtyard and inched toward the house.

Angela leapt out as he pulled to a stop and ran toward the open arms of her mother.

"*Maria!*" she shouted. Her mother had always insisted that Angela call her by her given name; this was her acknowledgement of their equality and her respect for her daughter as a woman in full. It was the same objectivity which had helped to establish Maria Vittoria Desjardin as one of the world's preeminent archaeologists.

Her dispassion stopped where love began, however, as she wrapped her long, muscular arms around Angela, lifted the daughter who could do no wrong, and spun her around with as much ease as she had when she was a small child; years of digging in hard-scrabble earth and lifting chiseled stone had rendered her stronger than most men. "Angelina! Oh, how I have missed you!" she said as she kissed her warmly on the cheek.

Paolo Ricci stood back from this joyous reunion, observing that Angela would need all the strength and support she could muster from her tiny family—unless one counted the several hundreds of her extended kin in the town, and the dozen or so retainers of many years who would lovingly serve her every fancy.

"Your father is back in Amman, hopelessly entangled in Jordanian red tape over the new project. You know how they are about the French. He's at a crucial point in the haranguing and wasn't able to fly over. He told me to come alone, mostly because he thinks women antagonize them and that I'd be more of a hindrance than a help. Subtlety was never your father's finest point. He's probably right, though. 'Shut up and dig' should be my motto, I suppose. I should have it tattooed on my backside. Anyway, he sends his love." She gave Angela another kiss. "That's from him," she said.

"So how is it, my pet?"

"You would not believe what I've just been through, Maria. It'll take all night to tell you, and most of tomorrow. But how is nonno? Can he talk? Can he understand what you say?"

"He goes in and out, pet. But he keeps asking for you. It makes me jealous. I know he loves us both, but you're special."

"Why does he want to see me so badly, can you tell me that?"

"He wants to see you because he's dying. He wants to tell you he loves you, and he doesn't want to go before kissing you one last time. He and I have said our goodbyes. It was very sad. Now he must be with you, my darling."

"Oh, I know. And I want to be here, too."

"But it's more than that."

"More? Do you know what it is?"

"Yes, I know. But I think he should tell you."

Angela searched her mother's eyes for some clue to her grandfather's motives, but none came, and she knew that she would have to wait.

"Can we see him now?"

"Come, let's see if he's awake," Maria said as she took Angela's hand, squeezed it, and led her inside the villa.

Don Carlo Vittoria lay still on the narrow hospital bed which Paolo had had brought in to make it more comfortable for him. He was uncovered except for a loose, pale blue gown, as the weather was warm. A fresh breeze blew up from the sea and through the open window, rippled the filmy, white curtains and washed over his matchstick body, bearing away as much as possible the unmistakable smell of death. A loosely arranged vase of his beloved yellow roses did what it could to counter the deadly bouquet.

The old man's face was the color of parchment, tired and drawn, his eyes closed, his breathing labored. The only other sound came from the rococo gold wire cage suspended from its crook-shaped standard in the corner; Diva, Don Carlo's constant companion in these last days, sang tentatively and sporadically from her perch, sensing that something was not as it should be.

Angela took his skeletal hand and said, *"Nonno, sono Angelina."*

She turned her head toward Paolo. "I had no idea . . ." she said in a soft voice. Paolo smiled weakly and nodded.

"Nonno, sono Angelina," she repeated, this time louder and more sharply.

Don Carlo's eyes flickered, and then they opened. He

fixed them on Angela, and a small, peaceful smile crossed his translucent face.

"Angelina," he whispered.

Angela held his hand for several minutes. Neither spoke as a tear formed in the corner of his eye, broke free and slid down his weathered cheek. The others watched as grandfather and granddaughter communicated without words as they had done so often when she was a child and he was the strong, vital patriarch. He coughed several times, which seemed to tire him more, and his breathing became raspy.

His lips formed words, but none came. Then his eyes opened wider and caught sight of the small yellow rose above Angela's right breast, and a second smile relaxed his anxiety. Don Carlo Vittoria's Golden Angel, *Il Angelo D'oro,* had come to take him home. His frail grip on her hand grew stronger, and he willed himself to murmur in his Sicilian tongue.

"Angelina, I am dying. You will take my place. You . . ." His mouth quivered and became silent once more. Suddenly his phlegmatic breathing grew louder and more rapid, and just as abruptly it stopped altogether. His eyes remained open, frozen on Angela's anguished face for eternity.

Don Carlo Vittoria the loved, the feared, the worshipped, the despised, the benefactor, the bandit, the *sweet grandfather,* was dead.

Without warning, Diva burst into song as if celebrating his release from the conflict of his life.

Angela, tears streaking her cheeks, continued to warm his hand in denial as she looked helplessly up at Maria. Then she gently brushed her fingers over his eyes to close them. Her mother, tearless, having shed her own long ago, nodded that it was okay. It was good.

CHAPTER FORTY-TWO

"Shouldn't we call Father Ottaviani? And Pietro Palazzolo?" Angela said. She and Maria and Paolo sat at the large table in the villa's kitchen, talking softly and haltingly about the meaningless things which often precede the hard decisions attendant to death.

"No, not the priest. There will be time. And not the undertaker, Gattina. Not yet," Paolo said. "We must speak about certain things. And it would be best if no one know he is dead."

The cook, Theresa, had made coffee, the black, bitter brew of the mountains, and she poured it shakily for the three of them as her own time for tears had come. Maria sipped the syrupy liquid from the steaming cup and then said, "You heard what he said to you, pet?"

"Nonno? Yes, I heard. He was confused. He meant you. *You* will take his place."

"No, he was not confused. He meant what he said: *You* will take his place. He told this to me several days ago. Don Carlo Vittoria is dead. Long live Donna Angela Vittoria," Maria said. *"Donna che possiede l'autorià matriarchala,* to be more precise. You, my dear, are the matriarch of the Vittoria. You are in charge."

"But Maria, *you* . . ." Angela stammered.

"*Me?* No, not me," she laughed softly. "I have neither the cleverness nor the courage to do what Don Carlo did. He knew this. The real truth is that I am not ruthless enough. And ruthless rules here in the hills.

"Surely you must have suspected things about your grandfather? I can assure you they are all true, and more, which is why I felt it necessary to go from here years ago.

"I'm not judging him, not now. He was what he was. And I've always loved him and I always will. But I have my work, and I would be unhappy doing anything else. It can only be you."

"But I have *my* work!" Angela pleaded.

"Yes, you do," Maria said, without elaboration.

"Yes, I do," Angela repeated defiantly. "And what makes you think I'm any more ruthless, as you say, than you? Or ruthless at all?"

"I don't know that. The reality is that Don Carlo has left everything to you, pet. This house, the art, the groves, the grapes, all his businesses. Everything, except for a few sentimental things he passed on to me. Half the economy between here and Catania is in your hands. Now. Today. You are a very wealthy woman—if, of course, you can hold on to it," Maria said with a grim smile.

"But what will happen if I don't want to be 'the matriarch of the Vittoria,' as you call it? What if I want to stay where I am? I haven't told you, Mother, but I could soon be named director of the Mendelssohn, and I may want that!" This was the first time that Angela had called the tall, sinewy archaeologist *Mother* since she was a small child.

"That's wonderful, pet! I'm very proud of you, as I've always told you. But to answer your question, what will happen? The plain truth is that if you don't *take his place*, as your grandfather said, all of this that was his—and is now yours—will be taken. It's inevitable. The *avvoltoi* are circling. If this is not protected," Maria said, waving her hand generally about the kitchen, "it will be gone. That would make me very sad and very angry if that were to happen. Angry at them, not with you. But I cannot change, and I cannot expect *you* to do what you do not want to do. This must be your decision, and only yours.

"Now, Paolo needs to talk to you, and I would rather not be present. The less I know about some things, the better. When you're finished, then you can decide about the priest, and Pietro Palazzolo. And the other business." Maria's impassive tone was no surprise to Angela. It was her way, and was no measure of how deeply she loved her daughter, this Angela knew.

Maria stood, placed her strong hands gently on Angela's shoulders, and then she left. Theresa slipped out as well, as she had done so many times when the men had gathered around the table in her kitchen. There was no need to ask her to leave; she was glad not to know some things also. Her lips would be sealed, of course, against the questions which were certain to come from down the hill about the waning state of Don Carlo's health.

Angela had no need to ask Paolo Ricci what he would say to her. She already knew: If she did not act swiftly before it was known that Don Carlo was dead, it would all soon be gone. Paolo could not decide for her, although he would "take care of things" if that were her wish. That was his "humble role," he would tell her. Once for Don Carlo Vittoria, and now for her.

Pietro Palazzolo had his work cut out for him. There was Don Carlo Vittoria, the pinnacle of his life as the village *impresario di pompe funebri.*

It wasn't simply dressing the body, digging the hole and lowering him in it.

It was the church: The Madonna delle Grazia had to be made ready for the thousands who would file past the coffin, with the hundreds of floral arrangements from family, friends and enemies alike which would have to be placed with great artistry and political adeptness.

It was the procession to the cemetery, and the musicians:

Two cornets, a battered baritone horn and a bass drum were fine for most, but would not do for Don Carlo Vittoria.

It was the food: The *veglia funebre* would be held at the villa afterward, but hundreds of dishes, maybe more, still had to be assembled and laid out for the throngs who would come.

And the priest would have his say—about everything. Ottaviani's fingerprints were omnipresent in all sacraments having to do with prominent members of his flock, regardless of their attendance in mass or their familiarity with the confessional. Finally, the family must be consulted, although he did not expect Angela to be difficult.

This would be Pietro Palazzolo's shining hour, the capstone of his career. Yet one slip would be to his everlasting shame.

But if Don Carlo were not enough, he had Alberto and Nicolo Mancuso to prepare. Throats slit, both of them, as they came out of Arturo's Trattoria the night before. Bloodiest mess he'd seen since poor Vincenzo tangled with them less then two weeks ago, *may he rest in peace.* It was a wonder to Pietro and many others how old Paolo managed it with such alacrity, although no one would ever prove, or seek to prove, that he was even there. Paolo Ricci was too clever for anyone to prove anything. This, in spite of the telltale pair of fresh yellow roses innocently placed at the Mancuso's threshold only hours before the incident by an anonymous village boy who was carefully instructed to knock loudly and then scamper unnoticed into the darkness. He left no card. None was needed. *One could only imagine their terror,* Pietro thought, *exceeded only by their own stupidity for venturing out that night.*

The old woman wants them stitched up, displayed in open coffins. *She forgets that I am merely an undertaker, not an illusionista.* If he had his way, he'd stuff them in the same box and sit on the lid, or leave them for the dogs; they were two mean *stronzos,* and they got what they deserved. *No, the Mancusos could wait. They had only one other appointment after his. And the Devil was in no hurry.*

For the first time in three days Angela was alone. She sat in her nonno's chair on the veranda and looked out over the groves which were now hers, fighting her instinct to think. These had been hard days, and they had left her drained; any attempt at rational thought, she knew, would be fruitless, if not disastrous.

The last of the mourners had left the villa, and she could hear the faint rattle of dishes as Theresa and the others cleaned up. Only Father Ottaviani had stayed behind, at her request.

For the locals, Don Carlo's funeral and wake would become events second in memory only to the celebration of Angela's own birth, Maria had told her. Every Sicilian delicacy known to man, from a hundred kinds of antipasti to huge trays piled high with cannoli, and a king's feast of steaming pastas, meats, fish, salads and cheeses between these gustatory bookends, had covered an endless length of cloth-covered planks on sawhorses spread across the terrace. Pietro Palazzolo directed the buffet with great virtuosity, cementing his reputation as maestro of the funerary arts.

Don Carlo had instructed months before that his own cellars be opened for the occasion. His best vintages flowed like water, and under their heady influence somberness turned to celebration of the life of the deceased and of this, his final act of generosity. As the processional band's repertoire evolved from lugubrious to ebullient, mourners in long lines greeted Angela with kisses of sympathy and small gifts of remembrance borne of genuine compassion or intended to curry favor, or both. No one mentioned the "coincidental" passing of the Mancuso brothers; somehow, carried on the wind or communicated via some other uniquely Sicilian variation of jungle drums, the word had already reached the narrow, cobblestone streets. And the message of *il Condanna D'oro*.

Angela was in charge.

And if there were any doubt, one needed only to hear their repetitious salutations: *Donna Vittoria, accetti le mi condoglianze, per favore.* Donna Vittoria, please accept my condolences.

Their obeisance was not lost on her.

She could afford to lose Vittoria; like Maria, she would have all she needed without it. To stay would be grief from start to finish. Running the businesses would be brutal enough, and that would be just the lawful ones. Add a steady parade of Mancuso-types testing her, gunning for her like the trigger-happy bullies in an old Western ever provoking the world-weary marshal, and Vittoria would be no walk in the park.

But leave this place? Leave dear, sweet Pauly to the vultures? Leave this house, these paintings, this breeze from the sea? Leave these people who have loved her grandfather and Maria and her, *Donna Vittoria?* Leave it all to the next mangy Mancuso brothers?

"You wanted me to stay, Angelina?" Father Ottavani's voice startled her, as he had slipped silently from the house in his soft, gold-brocaded slippers and now stood directly behind her, out of her line of sight. He was still in his funeral vestments. And, in foresight, he had also draped over his shoulders the confessional stole which he always carried with him in anticipation of the occasional repentant parishioner whose sins were simply too heavy to bear to the church. Seldom did the opportunity arise, but should it happen, he would be ready. Today he considered a sure bet.

The priest continued to address her as he had when she

was a child. *Angelina.* Over the years he had seen her only on those several occasions when Don Carlo had been honored by His Emminence at the villa, and once or twice on the arm of her grandmother as they walked together down the aisle of the Madonna delle Grazia. That was a long time ago.

Angela recovered quickly from the start he had given her and said, "The Mass was perfect, Father. Although I doubt you saw very much of my grandfather when he was alive, I know he would have been pleased."

"*Al contrario,* I saw more of him that you might have expected, *mia bambina.* And he was always kind enough to invite me here when the Holy Father came to stay, which I hope you will continue to do," he added, not subtly. "I'm happy that you approved of the service."

After a very long and very awkward pause, he asked, "Is there anything else?"

Angela detected the obsequiousness in his voice. Although he still bristled over not having been called for the sacraments before Don Carlo's body had grown cold, he would not wish to be excluded on the occasion of the Pope's next visit, were that ever again to happen. Nor would he risk over such a minor matter the Vittoria household's generosity toward the parish, should Angela choose to extend it.

"Please sit for a minute, Father," she said.

The priest lowered himself into the empty chair facing Angela, adjusted his robes, folded his hands and waited for her to speak. He knew about her instructions to Paolo Ricci—the entire village knew—and he ached for the words from her which would reaffirm his divine sovereignty. *Father, forgive me for I have sinned.*

As they sat, the mute image of Don Carlo Vittoria suddenly appeared before her. His expression was kindly, and the soft, loving smile she knew so well crossed his face, signaling that he trusted her. And then he was gone.

Minutes passed before Angela looked into the priest's rheumy eyes, hesitated, and then said with weary finality, "Thank you, Father, for staying."

"Is that all, Angelina?" he asked with a hint of despair.

"That's all, Father."

"Donna Vittoria," the prete said coolly after a moment of silence. Then he nodded, stood slowly and returned to the house, his vestments rippling in the breeze.

When he had gone from her sight, Angela rose from her nonno's chair. She walked up the long, steep hill behind the house and into his garden, where she remained for a long time.

CHAPTER FORTY-THREE

It had been a frenzied few months for Donna Angela Vittoria. In less time than it took to consume one of Theresa's sumptuous Sicilian breakfasts, she considered her options and concluded that a life of crime did not suit her. This, in spite of the wicked tingle she felt from her cold dispatch of the Mancuso brothers—an act for which she felt no remorse, and certainly no need of the pious Ottaviani's forgiveness. Rather, she hoped that grace would be dealt from Above for what she allowed was really not a very nice thing to do.

But Angela was hardly naïve.

She would not forget how the polizia turned their backs on Vincenzo's murder, either out of fear as Paolo said, or collusion. It didn't matter why. Nonno would never have allowed this, nor would she, ever again. And no Mancuso wannabes would ever threaten her or her family, or the lovely, innocent people of Vittoria. She would protect them at any cost. This much she owed the old man who had been the love of her life.

This meant that she would have to be visible in Vittoria and try like hell to be as strong as Don Carlo, only on her terms, which did not preclude more bloodshed if necessary.

Thus in a sweeping act of triage, Angela immediately began to distance herself from the old man's shady shenanigans simply by walking away, a diversionary tactic akin to tossing spoiled meat to jackals; all his murky enterprises were instantly and voraciously gobbled up by the lowlife who had circled the villa in her grandfather's last days.

While they fought over the rancid pieces, she systematically began to retighten the stranglehold on the legitimate core of the Vittoria domain, Don Carlo's once great oil, wine and citrus empire which had slackened precipitously during his long illness. She would defend these businesses to the death.

Angela surrounded herself with a loyal entourage of enforcers, handpicked from a short list of devoted family friends proven capable of dispensing justice the old-fashioned way, when there was no other way. With Paolo's counsel, she was quick to grasp her beloved island's centuries-old principles of survival and prosperity: Intimidation would continue to be the weapon of choice, and no amount of diplomacy or legalese would ever replace a good punch in the mouth.

Not to be neglected, nonno's rose garden she continued to nurture meticulously, should one or two of his golden blooms be required now and then to drive home a point. And so, with the images of the messy demise of the Mancuso brothers fresh in the minds of those who would break her rules, Donna Angela Vittoria emerged as one to be feared.

With Pieter's help, she had begun to trace and repatriate those works from the villa which her dear Don Carlo, *may he rest in peace,* had so misguidedly acquired. The rest would remain enshrined in the villa which she placed in the loving care of Paolo Ricci and Theresa the cook, the village's hottest new ticket. There had been rumors that they would marry.

Kate Raeburn managed to remove all forty-seven Gruenwald pieces from the *Schloss auf der Rhein* to the interim custody of the museum. At Jonathan Gruenwald's suggestion, his stolen works would later be the centerpiece of a massive exhibition of purloined art which had been recovered since the war, and which Angela easily gathered from other museums and private collections around the world on the strength of her own sudden celebrity. It became the Mendelssohn's most breathtaking exhibition in its 125-year history and thrust her instantly into the global spotlight.

She rejected straight away Marilyn Robertson's tasteless plea to include Wolff's dark memorabilia in the show, refusing to compromise the art with tabloid hype or risk arousing anti-Semitic notions in the community or elsewhere. The museum's marketing maven had assured her that such a move would gain worldwide attention and draw long lines. "If anything, we should hold a bonfire benefit in the parking lot, burn the garbage, and give the money to the Holocaust Museum in D.C.," Angela blasted. "That would get us some precious ink, don't you think?" The Fridge promptly shot to the top of Angela's "to do" list and was crossed off by day's end.

All but the disturbing contents of Erich Wolff's bunker, his treasured German wines, quite comfortable where they were, and a few odd pieces of furniture had been taken out of the great stone mansion within weeks of "the incident," yet to be dealt with by the museum's lawyers.

As Angela settled her tiny, five-foot frame behind the massive, nineteenth-century Benn Pitman desk which she had had dragged up from storage—a sensation, she imagined, akin to being ensconced behind the wheel of a 20-ton semi—she struggled with her own identity.

Donna Angela Vittoria exhilarated her. It made her feel very close to her beloved Don Carlo and held the promise of extending the nobler parts of his legacy. And yet *Director Desjardin* had its appeal: Running this little jewel of a museum could also be enormously fulfilling, she thought.

Or even the long shot was worth speculation: *Madame Jonathan Gruenwald. It could happen.*

The possibilities were endless.

These things she considered as she shuffled through her latest stack of congratulatory notes from New York, from Paris, from Amman. From the Vatican.

For Angela Vittoria Desjardin, life was good.

Very good indeed.

EPILOGUE

Of all the sensational fallout—Arthur Mendelssohn's dishonorable discharge from the museum board and Kate Raeburn's consensus elevation to the head of the table, the international ruckus over Das Rheingold and the dozens of prominent art houses it had brought to their knees, and the shocking exposé of Erich Wolff in sordid detail on the front pages of every rag from London to Sydney—the fire was the least publicized, but the most bizarre.

Michael Cameron was the first to see the flames. He was driving home from Concert Hall past midnight after conducting a rousing performance of the city's all-time crowd-pleaser, Beethoven's Fifth. As he negotiated the narrow, twisting road toward the small estate which had only recently been leased for him by the orchestra's powers-that-be, his dash lights low to sharpen his night vision, a golden flicker in his periphery drew his attention to the massive limestone edifice up and to his right, which, in daylight, dominated the landscape for a quarter mile either way.

Normally the huge stone mansion would have been lit like the Magic Kingdom—to bolster the security of the house and its contents and to salve the ego of its former owner. But since Erich Wolff died, the Castle on the Rhine had remained virtually invisible after sunset, except in a full moon where its spectral façade stood out against a darkened sky like a set from a Bram Stoker film. On this night only stars provided the backdrop for the young maestro's unearthly experience as he screeched to a stop in the middle of the deserted road.

He saw the blaze through every window of the mansion's

ground floor. The first level appeared to be fully engulfed, and fire had also begun to penetrate the upper stories. Michael Cameron was mesmerized by the spectacle as sparks swirled from the castle's open bell tower, accompanied by billowing black smoke eerily aglow in the hellish orange light. There was no fire equipment on the scene and no sirens in the distance. It was then he realized that he might have been the first to see the blaze, and he fumbled in the dark for his cell phone.

Impulsively, he pulled off to wait for the trucks, remembering his fascination with fires as a young boy in South Bend and the raucous arrival of the shiny red engines with their elegant gold lettering and long aluminum ladders. The tall, rangy conductor unfolded from his Spitfire green XKE, spread his fingers over its black fabric top, and stared at the raging castle reflecting off the Jaguar's mirror-like bonnet. He was suddenly aware of how deathly quiet it had become, the road still absent of vehicles other than his own.

Then he heard the music.

It was faint, but unmistakably Wagner. To his unfailing ear, the first dire surge of unison brass was more than enough: *Götterdämmerung*, Twilight of the Gods. He had conducted the piece many times. *My God,* he thought, *the immolation scene. Valhalla up in flames, Siegfried and Brünnhilde toasted and transfigured in the blaze.* Then as abruptly as it had begun, the music faded into the crescendo of wailing sirens and the roaring of the glorious scarlet machines of his childhood.

He stood in the darkness for the next hour, watching the futile efforts of the city's bravest to douse the flames. Finally he left, pondering the demonic performance and the remarkable coincidence that he was called as an audience of one, one of a handful who would recognize with certainty the few, hushed measures of the fiery masterpiece. Then he chided himself for his overactive imagination and chalked off the entire episode to the hallucination of just another overworked musician badly in need of a holiday—a story best left untold.

But the fire was real, he reassured himself.

When the trucks pulled away close to dawn, only the superheated stones of the charred and gutted *Schloss auf der Rhein,* like the ruins of the Berlin Chancellery and its great marble halls, remained as a pathetic memorial to the Fuehrer and his *Liebling,* the darling of the Reich.

ACKNOWLEDGMENTS

I am indebted to the curatorial and conservation staff of The Cincinnati Art Museum for its invaluable input in the early going. To the members of my Monday Morning Writers Group for their encouragement, intelligent critique and ongoing support. To my other very talented writer friends who have helped me through the rough patches and made astute suggestions. To Dan Bittman, friend and world-class designer, who created the book's powerful cover design. To Mo Conlon, who edited portions of my manuscript and shared priceless experience from her distinguished editorial career. To my devoted family and friends who have so often asked, "How's the book coming?" and to whom I've so often replied, "It's getting there." And, most importantly, to my most passionate cheerleader, my lovely wife, Shirley, for patiently and painstakingly slogging through my final draft to make *Devil's Gold* as good as it could be, and for her ceaseless understanding during those long, solitary hours at this infernal machine.

ABOUT THE AUTHOR

*D*evil's *Gold* is Barry Raut's first novel-length work. He also writes short fiction, memoirs, travel pieces, and art commentary, and teaches creative writing in the Osher Lifelong Learning Institute at the University of Cincinnati. A career copywriter and advertising agency executive, his consuming interest in World War II and the plundering of art masterpieces in Western Europe, plus a decade of training in art history as a docent at The Cincinnati Art Museum, inspired the book. He is a graduate of Miami University, Oxford, OH and lives with his wife, Shirley in Milford, OH.

LaVergne, TN USA
05 January 2011
211163LV00005B/9/P